The
Potting
Shed
Murder

Also by Paula Sutton

Hill House Living:
The Art of Creating a Joyful Life

PAULA SUTTON

The Potting Shed Murder

RENE
GADE

RENEGADE BOOKS

First published in Great Britain in 2024 by Renegade Books

1 3 5 7 9 10 8 6 4 2

A CIP catalogue record for this book
is available from the British Library.

ISBN 978-0-349-70376-3

Typeset in Berling by M Rules
Printed and bound in Great Britain by
Clays Ltd, Elcograf S.p.A

Papers used by Renegade Books are from well-managed forests
and other responsible sources.

Renegade Books
An imprint of
Dialogue
Carmelite House
50 Victoria Embankment
London EC4Y 0DZ

www.dialoguebooks.co.uk

Dialogue, part of Little, Brown, Book Group Limited,
an Hachette UK company.

To my family – my life, my love and the reason behind my move to beautiful Norfolk.

To my Aunt Helen – who encouraged my love of big dreams and my wild imagination.

To Mary – who gave me my start into selling vintage; the beginning of everything.

Welcome to Pudding Corner...

Oh, the humble and peaceful English country village. This paragon of beauty, this model of excellent living. The eidolon of safety and calm that serves as the exemplar of all things wholesome and good.

Who can help but extol the virtues of the sleepy and quintessentially English wilderness that forms this clustered settlement of quaintness ... A veritable paragon of innocent and simple virtues that have lain unchanged – and unchallenged – for generations ...

A lovingly maintained village green, a centuries-old church steeple, a kindly family doctor and an ever-present vicar ... Who can resist the draw of this harmonious, cake-filled community spirit, full of friendly watchfulness, benevolent advice and sweet tea – and not forgetting the unrelenting kindness behind the quietly twitching curtain.

This gloriously unmodified, uninterrupted and unvaried way of life – this reflection of all that is great and – sometimes – good. This bucolic green and pleasant land where lies are unheard of, envy is absent, no one harbours a secret, and strangers – that know their place and stick to the rules – are always made welcome . . .

Welcome to a place where nothing bad could possibly ever happen. Welcome, my friends, to Pudding Corner.

Meeting the villagers...

Daphne Brewster: New to Pudding Corner, having relocated from urban South London to rural Norfolk. A kind and inquisitive do-gooder who takes the side of the underdog, the village's Vintage Lady and amateur sleuth.

James Brewster: Affable husband to Daphne, who is disapproving of her detective predilections.

Imani Antoinette Brewster: Daughter and eldest of the Brewster children.

Archie Brewster: Twin son to Daphne and James.

Fynn Brewster: Twin son to Daphne and James.

Byron: The Brewster family pet; a characterful miniature dachshund named after Lord Byron, the 1800s poet.

Aggie: Short for Agnes; Daphne's vintage beloved car, a 1969 Morris Traveller.

Marianne Forbes: A snobby and entitled ex-Sloane Ranger raging at the supposed injustice of her lack of financial clout and village social status.

Timothy Forbes: Long-suffering husband of Marianne, content with the simple life – unlike his other half.

Tarquin Forbes: Marianne and Timothy's son.

Charles Papplewick: Headmaster of the village school, Pepperbridge Primary School, allotment enthusiast – and murder victim.

Augusta Papplewick: Headmaster's wife, self-appointed guardian of parish social and moral standards – and soon-to-be widow on a mission for revenge.

Doctor Ptolemy Oates: Jolly neighbour to the Brewster family, expert in local history and McVitie's Fruit Shortcake lover.

Minerva Leek: Quiet and unassuming friend of Daphne, outcast from the village.

Silvanus Leek (known to his friends as Silver): Young son of Minerva, best friend to Imani Brewster.

Nancy Warburton: Formidable village gossip and proprietor of the Pepperbridge Convenience Store.

Patsy Warburton: Younger sister to Nancy and fellow gossiper.

Mrs Freestone: Official editor of the *Village Pump*, a monthly newsletter for the parish.

Reverend Gerald Duncan: Local vicar.

Mrs Musgrave: The headmaster's secretary.

Inspector Hargreaves: Local police inspector dreaming of exciting cases beyond bucolic village life.

PC Maxine Clarke: Ex-pupil of Pepperbridge Primary School, now a local PC.

Locations in the story . . .

Pudding Corner: A charming hamlet in West Norfolk. Home to Cranberry Farmhouse and the Brewster family.

Pepperbridge: A larger village next to Pudding Corner, and home to Pepperbridge Primary School.

Cringlewic Heath (commonly known as Cringlewic): A small domestic enclave situated in the middle of Cringlewic Woods and bordering Oxwold Overy Estate.

Oxwold Overy Estate: A large shooting estate owned by an unmentioned character.

Cranberry Farmhouse: The country home of the Brewster family; a late-eighteenth-century farmhouse, complete with an ancient Aga, large attic and cellar rooms.

Wellingborough House: A handsome Georgian house in Pepperbridge belonging to Charles and Augusta Papplewick, having been in the Papplewick family for several generations.

Prologue

The final straw was an argument over a parking space. It had been an otherwise normal and unassuming weekday morning in the life of a busy family of five, bar the fact that, on that particular day, both Daphne and James had been able to drop the children off at the smart south London prep school (which they could no longer afford to pay the fees for) and were now sat alone in their battered old Volvo estate.

Life with young children seemed to be comprised of a series of lists filled with ways in which to fritter away money they didn't have. The twins, Archie and Fynn, had reached the stage where everyone wanted to offer them ballet lessons, chess lessons, violin lessons and piano lessons – all at a price. The eldest child, Immy, seemed to have a museum excursion, a football tournament or a camping trip every other week – again, all at a price. What with that, the school fees, interest rates inflating the mortgage repayments, and scrambling to find the salary for a nanny who took great pleasure in reminding Daphne about the twins calling her 'Mummy' for months after Daphne returned to work, meant that negotiating the life of their apparent dreams based on two salaries stuck firmly in the ever-so-exciting-but-financially-unviable media industry was a near-impossible task.

The aim that morning had been to visit the bank on Streatham High Road together, to find out if there was any wiggle room on the mortgage repayments, in the hope of squeezing yet another unaffordable term or two of private schooling from their rapidly dwindling reserves. Once that box had been painfully ticked off – or not – Daphne and James would then go about their daily routines in offices situated at opposite sides of London, only to return when they were too exhausted and strung out to communicate with any semblance of civility or grace – except perhaps towards a bottle of cheap supermarket wine. In that respect, this unfamiliar coming together on a weekday morning felt like a snatched and illicit date.

Having chatted comfortably during the slow traffic along Thurlow Park Road, it had all seemed pretty straightforward until the inevitable circle round the back streets to find a parking space close enough to the main road to warrant not simply driving back home again and walking up to the bank on foot. With increasing impatience, they had driven up and down, across and back again, until the amiable chatter descended into tense silence.

James, the less aggressive driver of the two (in Daphne's humble opinion), had been moving at a slow and stealthy creep, hoping not to scare off any potential departures into stubbornly taking more time to leave. It was a regular sport in built-up areas such as these just off the South Circular. In an otherwise mundane life, you were forced to take your small wins where you could find them, and hogging a parking space for no other reason than bloody-mindedness seemed high up on the scale.

Daphne had seen the space first. The golden ticket, the pathway to parking nirvana. An empty space on a quiet and narrow back road situated perpendicular to the bank. It was as though the parking gods on Mount Olympus had blessed them – Caerus maybe – the god tasked at bringing about all that is convenient in the moment? *Ha*, Daphne acknowledged wryly – the exorbitant school fees had brought about that little nugget of information, if nothing else ... 'THERE!!!' she had screeched, shattering the silence, while she simultaneously jabbed and pointed her finger towards the space, her voice repeating the word with a guttural urgency normally reserved for situations of great emergency. Quick to spy the direction of Daphne's attention, James had slammed on the indicator and expertly turned the steering wheel, about to glide effortlessly into the awaiting sweet spot. The timing should have been perfect, the location was certainly ideal, and suddenly life – for a few minutes at least – seemed to be back on track.

In that short, sweet moment, all thoughts of overdue bills had left James's mind. For a brief second or two, his increasingly tired, defeated façade, sallow skin and dark circles – all results of editing news programmes throughout the night and minimal weekday hours spent in daylight – were momentarily aglow as he steered the car towards his first and possibly only small win for the day. His eyes were focused directly on the prize, and the prize was only two car lengths away with zero obstacles in its path. He could sense Daphne straining against her seatbelt, willing them towards the empty parking space. It was a done deal. He was her knight in shining armour, her Lancelot, hell – he was Lewis Hamil—

'NOOOOOoooooooo!!!!'

He heard the rage in Daphne's voice before he spotted the other car. It took a moment for him to comprehend the fact that his wife was practically hanging out of the Volvo, mouth furiously distorted and angrily agape, shouting a fury of expletives. It was then that he realised the object of her rage was a group of men in a battered white Vauxhall Astra GTE that had driven in from the high road and headed towards 'their' parking space without hesitation. The car bonnets were now seconds from touching, engines revving from opposite sides of the space.

James could tell that his wife – a born-and-bred south Londoner who had only recently begun taking self-defence lessons after a spate of local muggings – had designated herself to take charge of the situation, and before he could hold her back, she was out of the vehicle explaining, in no uncertain terms, why the group of youths needed to reverse their car out. It was a tense stand-off that probably only lasted a few seconds – but to James, at least, those seconds had felt like hours. Daphne's hands were resting on the bonnet of the other car as she leaned towards its windscreen, proving she meant business, and stared directly into the driver's eyes. She was an immaculately presented thirty-something Black woman with her hair in a low ponytail, a flick of jet-black eyeliner accentuating her deep brown eyes, crimson red lipstick, dressed in kitten heels that needed reheeling and a sample-sale Prada skirt. The type of woman who had been brought up to never complain about her lot and had been conditioned to be quietly polite at all times thanks to her education at an all-girls convent school. She was a woman for whom it came naturally to open doors for the elderly, to enquire about everyone else's wellbeing before looking after her own, and certainly never to show emotion – particularly anger – in public. Today, however, she was a woman who was at the end of her tether. A woman pulled in all directions: exhausted, beleaguered, working a full-time job that seeped its tendrils insidiously into her evenings, weekends and holidays, affording her limited time or concentration to extend to her three young children, let alone her husband or that elusive 'me time' that she saw plastered across the pages of the very magazine where she herself worked. As Daphne's hands curled into a furious grip on the car bonnet, her defiance was clearly now far more than a matter of a parking space. It was a matter of personal pride, honour and justice. She was the mouse that had decided to roar . . .

James sat immobilised and in awe, watching his unflinching wife in the midst of her standoff. Not for the first time, he admired her strength, her sass and her conviction. There were not many women in the world who would have been so unbending in the face of such a motley group of youths at 9 a.m. on a Tuesday morning just off the South Circular . . .

And then, all at once, it was over. The offending car reversed out of the space and, moving speedily and erratically, eventually double-parked on the other side of the road. Daphne turned triumphantly and, at her cue, James slipped quickly into the space – thanking God that he had managed to make it a smooth manoeuvre. What crushing indignity it would have been to have won the battle, only to mess it up with a forty-two-point turn ...

Daphne returned to the passenger seat, her eyes alert and her skin flushed. She needed a few minutes to collect herself; her breath was heavy, and her chest moved fast. They watched silently while three of the four youths exited the car opposite them and headed towards the high road. They were all big and burly, and each of them could have taken Daphne down with a quick flick of the hand.

After a few moments of loaded silence, Daphne and James finally turned to face each other. There was a second more of calm before they both burst out laughing.

'Well, Daphne Brewster,' said James, 'they really hadn't reckoned for butting heads with you this morning!'

Daphne smiled wryly. As she had slowly calmed down, she realised how often she was on edge these days. It hadn't taken much for her to launch headstrong into the confrontation; it had been instinctive. A rage-fuelled, fiery response burning within her. An automatic defence against the anger and frustration that she continually felt with her life. Last week she had told off, without hesitation, a group of foul-mouthed and raucous teenagers for not standing when an elderly lady had needed a seat on the bus. She had also recently chased down a neighbour's au pair for not collecting his dog's poop – the dog that he was so obviously begrudgingly forced to walk. The rage that she could not reveal at work was slowly bleeding into an uncontrollable urge to right the wrongdoings she witnessed on a daily basis. She despised bullies and was intuitively on the side of the underdog, but this increasingly reckless behaviour was getting too much. She was close to burnout, and she could feel it . . . In fact, they both were. Something had to give, and she feared, at that precise moment, that it might be her sanity.

They had been about to exit the car when the three lads returned – however, this time, they stampeded back around the corner with balaclavas over their heads. They crossed directly in front of the Volvo as Daphne and James sat watching open-mouthed. As if in slow motion, the last of the three turned to stare momentarily at Daphne. Their eyes locked for a split second – the split second immediately after she had registered the sawn-off shotgun gripped in his hand. It was the first time in her life she had seen a real gun. In that moment, as their eyes met, he communicated to Daphne that she'd had a lucky escape. That morning there had been far more important business at hand than the fight for a convenient parking spot – or perhaps her 'brave' little attempt at standing her ground might not have ended so well.

The car opposite, which they now realised had kept its motor running, sped off down the road with all four boys safely inside, just as a heavy-footed, out-of-breath security guard belatedly rounded the corner. His face was red from puffing, coughing and spluttering, his ill-fitting uniform strained against his stomach, and his arm was held aloft as if waving the robbers off. He stopped in front of the Volvo before violently expelling the contents of his stomach onto the pavement next to them. The sound of multiple sirens followed shortly afterwards.

They sat in shock for a few minutes before Daphne turned to James and muttered the fateful words that would set off a chain reaction of change in their lives.

'James, darling. I think it's time we left London.'

Chapter 1

Silence.

It was the thing that Daphne had claimed she'd wanted most, yet perhaps it was the one change that left her feeling the most unnerved and slightly ... discombobulated? Was that the word?

They say be careful what you wish for, she thought as she tucked a stray curl back into the silk scarf that kept her shoulder-length black hair from tangling during the night. Who 'they' were she hadn't a clue, but still – 'they' were infuriatingly right. Silence kept her up at night. Silence made her wake up early in the morning. The silence was unsettling – frustratingly so. The nights at their new home of Cranberry Farmhouse were proving to be too eerily quiet for a city girl, it seemed. A tad too still. A smidgen too calm. Where was the muffled sound of distant drunken chatter as the pubs closed?

Where were the sirens or the traffic noise that they'd complained about for so many years? The constant and familiar backdrop to city living that had contributed to their original desire to move to the country ...

Now that Daphne had the peace and quiet she'd thought she craved, she was left wide awake by the 'loudness' of it all as it dominated her mind during the nocturnal hours usually reserved for sleep. She'd read far too many novels, seen far too many bad movies (and a few rather good Netflix series) not to be occasionally compelled to strain to hear ... what? A scream? An unexplained scratching at the three-hundred-year-old bedroom door? She chuckled wryly to herself as she lay in bed – at least her sense of humour was still intact, even if it had taken a darker turn.

James lay deep in slumber, breathing quietly next to her and, for the first time ever, she wished that he was a snorer. She wished that he would make a substantial enough amount of noise to justify her wide-awake state and give her something to focus on. Pushing him onto his side with an angry and self-righteous 'harrumph' would be better than the limbo of listening to the nothingness and staring at the ceiling in the dark, as fathomless and stygian as the still night air around her. The house didn't even creak. Weren't old houses supposed to creak and groan when there was nothing else to cloak their movement? An ex-neighbour 'friend' of hers, having looked (uninvited) at the estate agent's write-up of Cranberry Farmhouse prior to the move, had asked Daphne whether the house was haunted ... But try as she might, Daphne had sensed nothing out of the ordinary during their three viewings. Just a quiet sense of calm, as though the house had felt satisfied and relieved to be filled with people, movement and voices once more.

Suddenly jolted out of her thoughts, Daphne's body stiffened. She perked up and strained her ears – was that a sound she had just heard? Perhaps a fox or a cat? (Although weren't foxes now the preserve of urban gardens? She had yet to see one beyond the occasional flattened roadkill since arriving in Norfolk – and even then it was more often deer than foxes that littered the long stretches of rural lanes.) Or perhaps the sound had been distant footsteps crunching along the gravel . . . ? Daphne instantly regretted her earlier cavalier attitude towards the nocturnal quiet. Silence was far preferable to the menacing sound of unknown footsteps . . .

Then more identifiable sounds came to shift the mood once more. Starting with a chirp here and a chirp there, followed by a steady build-up to a symphonic cacophony of birds. She could even hear the pigeons scratching on the roof or – heaven forbid – were they inside the roof? Regardless, the spell had been broken. Dawn had arrived; slivers of light had begun to slip through the solid Georgian shutters. Soon she would hear the occasional car in the distance, and perhaps the deep rumbling of a tractor motor.

Despite the jumpy start, these early morning sounds – and their timings – were slowly becoming familiar to her. Within a few moments, she knew that James would start to shift and then turn over, subconsciously hearing the same distant noises from deep within his slumber. It was often at that precise moment that she would start to feel the slow grasp of sleep drawing her in at last. Oh, the irony of falling asleep just as everyone else was wakin—

'Mummmmy!!!' She bolted upright with a start. The bed-clothes next to her were still warm and rumpled but empty, and she could hear the shower spluttering, pipes clanking and rumbling down the hall. She could tell from the exact pitch and volume of her daughter Immy's whine that this was at least the third or fourth attempt to caterwaul their mother out of bed. *What was that she'd been thinking about not wanting silence?* she mused as she climbed out of bed.

Their new morning routine was becoming familiar and even quite pleasurable in its predictability to the Brewster family. James would descend downstairs first to let Byron out. The poetically named Byron was the newest member of the family – a long-haired and characterful miniature dachshund presented as a moving school sweetener for the children, but now admittedly more Daphne's constant companion than the children's. James would then prepare the children's breakfast, while Daphne searched for various bits of forgotten sports kit, plaited one set of pigtails and reminded her twin sons to pull a comb through their tightly coiled hair. The children had taken to country life like ducks to water. Eight-year-old Immy, with her deep brown eyes that echoed her mother's, long and wavy golden-brown hair always plaited into two 'Pippi Longstocking'-style pigtails, and an insistence on wearing a neatly tied bow at each end, was thankfully as happy running through muddy fields and climbing trees in overgrown woodland as she had been rampaging in tarmacked urban playgrounds. Meanwhile, five-year-old identical twins Archie and Fynn, with their cherubic chocolate curls framing cheekily freckled noses and inquisitively fox-like hazel eyes that appeared to turn a dark shade of green depending on the level of mischief being concealed at any one time, were as happy as pigs in mud with the amount of space they now had to wreak good-natured havoc in. In fact, Daphne thought, they often came home looking far more unkempt than pigs in mud after their numerous excursions into the local fields with their older sister searching for interesting looking bugs and sticks to build dens with, but from the joy hidden beneath their mud-smeared faces, Daphne was happy to indulge the trio in their free-range adventures.

After breakfast and a few false starts to gather sports socks and homework, and indulge a treat-hunting Byron, the three Brewster children would follow their mother out towards Aggie, the light blue vintage Austin Morris Traveller parked next to the old cart shed that was supposed to store wood for the log burner but was invariably empty. There the gangly legged threesome – chattering excitedly while balancing various schoolbooks and projects – would stand impatiently kicking at the gravel, or each other, while Daphne opened the five-bar gate, shouting strict instructions to keep a tight hold on Byron's lead as she did so.

It was usually at this point that their closest neighbour, the elderly Doctor Ptolemy Oates, would, upon hearing the crunch of gravel, be exiting his own house and walking towards his own car in perfectly timed synchronicity with his neighbours. Today, true to form, she could just hear the click of his front door and the gravelly plod of his footsteps as he neared the gate.

The first time it happened, Daphne had felt that the seemingly coincidental timing of their meeting had been simply a polite excuse for their new neighbour to introduce himself.

The third time, she wondered whether he might be lonely, as it seemed that he had been waiting to pounce on their imminent departure. By their fourth week at Cranberry Farmhouse, Daphne fully expected to see the ruddy-veined but jolly face of the bumbling doctor as she hitched back the gate every morning. It was another ritual that she had become used to – even allowing a few extra minutes for their daily chats. Despite the potential for their new neighbour to become a nuisance, Daphne didn't mind their morning conversations. Doctor Oates was cheerful and easy-going, and often rather witty. He was also incredibly well informed about the local area, having lived there for most of his life. She enjoyed his stories about the historical significance of the village, Pudding Corner, and the nearby woodland of Cringlewic Heath, which were both mentioned in the Domesday Book in 1086, he had told her. The stories that really piqued her interest during these daily musings were those about the village's connections to witchcraft. The area had suffered greatly at the hands of the infamous Matthew Hopkins – the self-appointed Witchfinder General who had terrorised the whole of East Anglia in the seventeenth century. Hopkins had found rich pickings in the villages just south of King's Lynn, where Pudding Corner was located, and rumours of witches' covens, banes, curses and middle-of-the-night sabbat rituals had remained part of local folklore ever since.

Their burgeoning and unconventional friendship had initially surprised Daphne, to say the least. Back in London, she had hardly known the names of her neighbours, and they had lived right next to each other – sharing a party wall in their Victorian semi-detached house for over seven years. Life in London had been far too hectic for morning chats over the garden gate. The rush to catch the train, Tube or bus, or deliver one or all three children to various parts of south London while still managing to arrive at work on time and unflustered was precision timed to perfection, not leaving a moment for pause or friendly banter. Daphne had been determined that her family's new life in Pudding Corner would be different. A more immersive life, with a sense of belonging. A life where they truly knew their community and integrated fully into it. Of course, there was also the fact that Doctor Ptolemy Oates usually brought along a box of homegrown vegetables to proffer with his chat. That, she had to admit, helped a lot. This morning his hands were filled with a box loaded with frost-tolerant Swiss chard and purple sprouting broccoli.

'You have convinced me to get stuck into my own vegetable patch, Doctor Oates,' Daphne said as she eyed the doctor's proffering gratefully. 'But I'm absolutely clueless about how to start? The garden beds are already there – I think – but hidden somewhere underneath a mound of waist-height cow parsley and stinging nettles, unfortunately.' She chuckled wryly, imagining the back-breaking task she had ahead of her to make the beds suitable for planting in again.

'Well, young Daphne, I'm just your man. I know a thing or two about gardening, you know.' The Doctor tapped the side of his nose knowingly, as if allowing Daphne in on a little-known secret. 'My recommendation would be to embark on the 'no dig' method – far better than trying to clear the entire area, and far better for the soil in any case!'

'How fascinating – "no dig"? I like the sound of that. In

fact, anything that saves me time and still gives me perfect vegetables is a fabulous idea in my book. You are a fount of knowledge, Doctor Oates!'

'It's a pleasure my dear, but we must never be afraid of spending time on the things we love. Patience is a virtue – as is knowledge. "Our patience will achieve far more than our force", after all, and you wouldn't want to end up like those Oxytocin-injecting farmers!'

'Oxytocin-injecting farmers, Doctor Oates?' Daphne repeated, nonplussed.

'Yes – nasty chemicals, to make them grow faster and bigger. It's a terrible business. No patience for letting things grow at their own rate and in their own time. We must nurture and love from afar, and we will reap the benefits – wouldn't you agree, Daphne?

Speaking of knowledge and patience, did you know about the priest hole at Oxburgh Hall? No? Remind me to show it to you one day. Fascinating thing. The poor martyrs would spend days, even weeks on end, holed up in there until it was safe. I think the National Trust will be opening it up again soon. Now, that is a great example of the virtues of time and patience . . .'

'It's a date, Doctor Oates!'

Having filed away Doctor Oates's latest enthralling snippet of local history to be retold to James later, Daphne would then embark on the morning school run. The family had begun their new adventure at the start of the autumn term in September. Now, in the mild frost and low sun of early spring, having already spent their first admittedly rather haphazard but decidedly cosy Christmas in their new 'old' home, the drive to and from school, watching the seasons slowly evolve, was one of Daphne's favourite parts of the day. The children loved being clasped into their seatbelts on the long back bench seat of Aggie the Traveller, giggling as they slid against each other along the timeworn leather, with Byron curled up happily in a decidedly fancy wicker car seat, taking pride of place up front with his nose pointed towards the passenger seat window. Wanting to encourage the children to take notice of the seasonally changing landscape, Daphne would eagerly point out the daily changes in the deciduous trees as they drove past, rallying the children into watching the slow progress of each one 'reclothing' itself with its spring foliage. The immense pleasure that she received from having found herself transported from south London's bustling urban land- scape to one of a picturesque set of sleepy adjoining villages in the English countryside never failed to astound her. The large expanse of fields between the ridiculously quaintly named Pudding Corner and the larger but no less charmingly named village of Pepperbridge caused her to delightedly catch her breath whenever she turned the 'famous' corner that indi- cated the edge of her village.

The corner itself consisted of a crescent-shaped row of medieval thatched cottages dating from the fifteenth century, each with a prominent curved bay window featuring dia- mond panes and a pudding-bowl-shaped thatch top beneath multiple decorative chimneys and larger thatched toppings of varying tiered roof lines shaped like curved helmets. It was like an image from a fairy tale: exquisitely quaint and impossibly picturesque. The curved row ended abruptly after six pudding-shaped houses, but not before leading the eye to an unobstructed view of the vast Norfolk sky above a sea of golden fields of wheat and corn. To Daphne, it was perfection.

They may have only been living in the area for a few months, but already the local sights – and the residents – were becoming fascinatingly familiar. As Daphne drove along this morning, she recalled the first time that she had read up about the two villages, having just completed the first viewing of their soon-to-be home.

'The parish of Pepperbridge, which also covers the hamlet of Pudding Corner, is located in West Norfolk,' she had read aloud to James as he navigated the free-flowing A11 on their way back towards the traffic-jammed enclaves of London. 'Roughly equidistant between the better-known market towns of Oxwold Overy and Belchley ...' she continued.

'Oh, stop it!' James had spluttered out loud, half laughing, half choking in disbelief. He gave Daphne a quick glance. 'You've got to be joking. Belchley? As in belch? You can't have Pudding, Pepper and Belch all in one area, surely?'

'Well, Norfolk was once known as the "breadbasket of England",' Daphne had replied, 'and we might be going to live in a Cranberry, so obviously delicious-sounding place names are a thing in these parts!'

For most of the way home, they had laughed at how the word 'belch' fitted into that theory, both sensing in unspoken acknowledgement that, despite their mirth, their future most likely lay in a place called 'Pudding' and a home called 'Cranberry'.

A few months later, they had quickly settled into life in their late-eighteenth-century farmhouse at Pudding Corner with its pleasingly symmetrical Georgian façade, three sets of staircases, two concealed jib doors, large farmhouse kitchen complete with ancient Aga, larder and pantry, six generously sized bedrooms filled with squeaky, uneven floorboards and all surrounded by an acre of overgrown garden. There was also a large attic and a dark and ominous set of cellar rooms which Daphne had yet to properly investigate due to their lack of electricity beyond a certain point. In all it was an incredible change from their old London house and despite the ever-present threat of it turning into a bottomless money pit, they could still hardly believe their luck in managing to acquire it.

Meanwhile the children's school was located a mile or two away, in Pepperbridge. The school had been the final egg in the colloquial pudding of their grand decision to leave London. Having been reassured by the outstanding Ofsted report, they had been both pleasantly surprised and quietly nervous to find that the village school consisted of only 102 students, four classrooms and the grand total of four full-time teachers, plus an extremely dedicated headmaster, Mr Papplewick, and several support staff. It was a far cry from the large, multi-cultural West Dulwich prep school that the children had departed. The thought of dropping three children of proudly mixed heritage, all with beautifully brown skin, into an almost exclusively Caucasian environment had not been an easy decision. What if they were called names? What if they were made to feel 'othered'? Was her own need to escape the rat race more important than her children's need for visible representation? Would she be enough? How could she ensure that they didn't lose their pride and uncensored joy in who they were and how they presented? James, as a blond and blue-eyed white male, may have been sympathetic to her fears, but in the end, they both knew that it would fall to Daphne to take the lead when it came to the final decision. It had been a conundrum indeed, but one where Daphne's instinctive desire to see the best in people, combined with her appetite for adventure, had been the frontrunner in the decision-making process. Her children would be an asset to any school community, she thought indulgently, with a huge dose of maternal pride. For Daphne – wishful thinking or not – there was also a distinct charm attached to the idea of the children experiencing an 'old-fashioned' school environment where everybody knew each other by name and the community was small, safe and compact. In fact, the entire area felt rather like stepping into the mythical and mist-enclosed village of Brigadoon on the one day of its annual appearance.

The local newsletter, known as the *Village Pump*, described Pepperbridge as 'a bustling village boasting an array of interesting independent shops', which in reality numbered only four that were vaguely useful, if one included the post office. There was an old-fashioned butcher's; a hardware and ironmonger's that randomly sold floor tiles and swept chimneys; and a convenience store which could inconveniently be closed at any time of day depending on how 'fatigued' its owner, Nancy Warburton, and her sister, Patsy, felt at the time. A few doors up from the 'convenience' store was an attractive but empty double-fronted shop with bullseye windows and a sloping door – it was unclear what it had been before closing down, but Daphne had walked past it many times since her arrival, feeling from the first sighting that it would make the perfect premises for a creative little business of her own. There was also an artist who sold hand-painted pottery and local souvenirs on the corner of School Lane – one of at least two 'shops' which were operated out of 'converted' front sitting rooms. There were two pubs – the Bullseye Inn and the Harvest Moon – which sat at either end of the village; a local takeaway which comfortably straddled the cuisines of two continents – fish and chips and Chinese food – thanks to a rather fortuitous love match cemented at a catering college in Milton Keynes; a modern post office (the original post office was now a very attractive period home); a sports and social club that hosted Brownies and Cubs on a Thursday evening; and Egg & Cress, 'one of the finest tea rooms in the area' according to its owner and self-appointed village hairdresser, Cressida Lovell. There was also a lovely garden centre and farm shop just on the outskirts of Pudding Corner, and various villagers kept honesty boxes next to wooden carts and egg hutches, filled with allotment or garden produce to take as one wished. It was all very civilised.

What Pudding Corner lacked in amenities, it made up for in beautiful stone and flint cottages dating back hundreds of years, a plethora of stunning Georgian architecture and a smattering of tall Victorian Gothic houses that leaned imposingly and precariously over the narrow pavements of the high street. It was a charming village – in fact, Pudding Corner and Pepperbridge were both charming villages, with a mild and gentle rivalry between them which only really appeared during bowls tournaments.

Today, as Daphne drove her car slowly through the winding village streets towards School Lane, she spotted the

distinctively impatient trot of her new 'friend', Marianne
Forbes, a few hundred yards ahead of her on the pavement.
Daphne was still in two minds about Marianne. As a fellow
ex-Londoner, Marianne had latched on to Daphne immme-
diately upon their first meeting, which had been rather
reassuring and flattering initially, but had since increasingly
felt like a friendship of convenience – with almost all of the
convenience tilted heavily in Marianne's favour. The friendship was more of a 'Darling, I'm so sorry to ask, but would
you mind picking the children up from school for me and
dropping them home? No wait, I'll pick them up from yours,
darling.' Which inevitably meant that Daphne would end up
giving Marianne's children their supper along with hers, while
Marianne finished whatever hair appointment or afternoon
coffee date (that would inevitably turn into early-evening
wine) she had organised.

  In Marianne's defence, she had given Daphne the opportunity to try out a new and spontaneously born career. Thanks
to Marianne's initial encouragement, in three short months
of village life, Daphne had not only become known to the
parish as 'The Vintage Lady', but had also found the perfect
reason to take up residency in the little double fronted shop
that she had so admired . Becoming The Vintage Lady had
been unexpectedly swift and had taken a huge leap of faith. It
seemed that the people of Pepperbridge and Pudding Corner
liked to attribute 'labels' to everyone in the villages – especially when it came to newcomers, whose real names needed
to be seasoned for at least a year or two before being cemented
into the consciousness of locals.

Daphne had been standing in line at the Pepperbridge

post office when she'd an epiphany. Despite the small queue, the slow crawl to the front desk had her next to the village noticeboard, and it was while she was absent-mindedly reading some of the more interesting notices – lost cat with three legs, greenhouse for sale (collection only), that sort of thing – that she had decided to take the plunge and put up a notice of her own. Knowing from experience that hesitation brought with it self-doubt, and there was no time like the present, she had grabbed a pack of lined cards from a wire rack and fished a pen out from her handbag. In large, looped handwriting she scrawled: *Painted and vintage furniture for sale, decorative antiques and kitchenalia – design consultations and commissions available. Please call Daphne on Tel: 204 598.*

She had just pinned it up, and was having second thoughts, when a clipped voice bellowed behind her, 'You paint furniture? Like all of that shabby-chic yumminess? How fabulous! It's about time we escaped the tyranny of the Swedish flatpack in this area. I have six dining chairs that need a good going over. Inherited them from my mother-in-law and they're ghastly. Do you use Annie Sloan paint? I hear she's all the rage. Anyway, here's my address. I've seen you at the school gates, haven't I? If you can pop by after two p.m. on Saturday to give a quote, that would be marvellous.' And then Marianne was gone.

Marianne had moved to Pudding Corner with her husband and two children, going from a reasonably modest two-bedroom maisonette in Fulham, London to a tall and sprawling Georgian house that made up a large section along the village's main street. When asked why such an obviously sociable urbanite such as Marianne had found herself in such a rural part of Norfolk – and not the smarter, more 'sophisticated' shores of North Norfolk (aka Chelsea-on-Sea) – she adopted the typical estate agency speak of her husband, proclaiming that there was 'so much more bang for your buck on this side of the "Fork"!' In truth, faced with the reality that she could not keep up with her old school and university chums *and* afford to put their children through the private-school system in London or North Norfolk on their combined salaries, Marianne had done the next best thing: looked for the best-looking house in a cheaper area.

Marianne had been born into a life of upper middle-class privilege and had thoroughly expected to keep it up through either a large inheritance or a profitable marriage. Alas, for her, neither assumption had been forthcoming. Her husband had been born into privilege but had a rather more cavalier approach to where the money for such a privileged lifestyle came from. Timothy had spent most of his thirties feeling bewildered yet accepting and then, unlike his wife, he had finally come to terms with his displacement on the social ladder. One day he had been a confident twenty-something with wealthy parents to fall back on, swish holidays and a bright – if unambitious – future bankrolled by Mummy and Daddy ... The next, Mummy had tragically and unexpectedly died after a short illness, and a panicked Daddy had swiftly remarried, leaving Timothy to become a nonplussed man-boy reeling from the realisation that money didn't actually grow on trees. Even worse was the realisation that it certainly could no longer be harvested from the trees in the grounds of his father's Hampshire estate where his new wife – of similar age to Timothy, and now with two tiny Tims of her own – guarded the leaves fiercely.

For Timothy, meeting Marianne had been a lifesaver. She was posh, she was dynamic and, more importantly, she owned her own flat in west London's Fulham. What had started out as a perfect match was now a not-so-comfortable alliance of two posh people with little hard cash between them, living in a beautiful-but-crumbling old house in rural Norfolk. Both were determined to keep up the façade of a lifestyle that they could no longer afford, with the biggest bone of contention being their children's schooling. Marianne was prepared to accept temporary defeat during their primary school years. After all, a sweet little village school could be attributed to English eccentricity – didn't Sir Paul McCartney send his children to village schools? However, it was the next stage that scared her witless. She wanted – no, needed – her children to attend the famous private school in nearby Cambridgeshire. It was placed firmly in the centre of her vision board – and what Marianne wanted, Marianne was determined to get. For this particular manifestation, however, her children would need a scholarship in the place of ready money, and an excellent referral from their current headmaster, Mr Charles Papplewick. But there lay the rub . . .

Charles Papplewick was an amiable enough fellow who spent most of his spare time tending to his prized Red Acre cabbages at the local village allotment when he wasn't working; but he wasn't the real problem. The very real problem – or rather – everyone's problem, was Charles's tyrannical wife, Augusta.

Augusta Papplewick ruled the roost in Pudding Corner

and Pepperbridge. An athletic and intelligent woman in her late sixties, Augusta was the head of the PTA and the WI, on the board of school governors, on the parish council, Akela and Eagle Owl, and sometimes secretary (in name only, of course, to make sure that he was on the right track) to the local council representative. With her own private income thanks to her dear departed father's early property investments and subsequently dodgy reputation as an exploitative private landlord in 1970s Derbyshire, she'd had a lifetime's 'career' as the headmaster's wife and general patroness of Pepperbridge parish. Augusta had always been, and would always be, the sticking point for anyone's hope to progress through the school or social systems. Among her many roles, Augusta's favourite was unofficial gatekeeper to the integrity of the parish – which in broad terms meant that she saw herself as judge and jury. To everyone.

Marianne had complained to Daphne on several occasions that if only the ridiculously fair and morally unbending Mr Papplewick could escape the lure of his bloody red cabbages, or the shackles of his bitter wife, and succumb to the notso-subtle flirtations of Marianne, then all would be fine with this world. If she could circumvent the beady eyes of the wife and persuade the headmaster with her 'blatant and irresistible upper-class charm', then perhaps she could convince him to help her get them out of this dead-end village. Lord knew that her own husband wasn't doing anything significant to advance them . . .

However, Charles Papplewick, it seemed, was a man of unflappable integrity, and Augusta Papplewick didn't take kindly to anyone whom she felt was trying to get above their station – least of all newcomers who laughed too loudly in the company of her loyal husband. Marianne and her husband Timothy, for all their fake smiles, long vowels and faux joviality, would be classed as newcomers for at least another decade, and smug newcomers didn't get assistance – not if Augusta had anything to do with it.

Back on the school run, Daphne had found a place to park swiftly – with thankfully no backed-up London South Circular traffic or altercations with armed robbers necessary. She was now slowly – very slowly in fact – making her way towards the school gates having lingered for a while pretending to sort the children out as all three had taken turns to cuddle the dog before climbing out from the back seat of the car. Inwardly, Daphne was equally as relieved to see all three of them chomping at the bit to get to their friends in the playground as she was annoyed by their urgency to hurry along when she was attempting to avoid Marianne this morning; she really wasn't in the mood to hear another diatribe about the 'weak' headmaster and his wife's 'obvious lack of judgement'. It was bad enough listening to Marianne moan about her own apparently financially deficient husband, but most of her vitriol these days was towards their soon-to-be retiring headmaster. 'I could bloody well kill him!' she'd muttered dramatically under her breath on more than one occasion. 'It's just one measly letter of recommendation, simply marking up a grade or two. Would it hurt to write one good report?'

Daphne walked through the arched school gate, a small boy swinging and dragging her along on each arm, with Immy the eldest having run off towards her friends almost as soon as she had left the car. The picturesque little village primary school had been built in 1843 by the local land-owner or 'lord of the manor' for the children of his estate workers – although many at the time suspected it had been built specifically for the children of his many mistresses, since his attention to the architectural beauty of the build-ing and lifelong patronage of the school had gone over and beyond for the norms of the time. The schoolhouse itself and the quaint belltower that sat atop it were now Grade 2 listed, and Daphne secretly felt that the entire set of build-ings looked like a scene from a Hollywood adaptation of a Charles Dickens novel.

She headed straight through a closed off white-picket-fenced area to the reception class's garden and deposited her youngest two children there before turning around to quickly scan where Marianne was in order to make a swift escape. She contemplated leaving before the bell had been rung, or at least waiting to see the children disappear into their classrooms from the other side of the school fence, when Immy walked up to her with another child in tow. The little boy was of similar age to her daughter, and Daphne had seen them playing together before. His hair was long and tangled, his clothes looked too big – his jumper was most likely (and rather skilfully, Daphne noted) hand knitted, but was made for a much larger child, and through the endearing scruffiness she could see that his eyes were large, bright and sparkling with intelligence. He had the longest eyelashes and the narrowest face of any child she'd ever seen – in fact, he resembled a little elf.

'Mummy, this is Silver,' Immy introduced her new friend.

'Silver? Do you mean Sullivan?' she asked her daughter, then turned inquisitively to the friend.

'No,' the little boy said in a surprisingly serious and steady voice. 'My name is Silvanus. It means "god of the forest".'

'Well, it's very nice to meet you Silvanus, god of the forest,' she said with a smile.

The bell had rung, kisses had been blown and Daphne was making her way quickly to her car with great relief at not being spotted. She was intending to drive on to the large supermarket in Oxwold Overy to collect some paintbrushes for a recent sideboard commission.

'What on earth were you doing talking to that boy?' bellowed Marianne, seemingly out of nowhere, her perfectly coiffed blonde bob flowing away from her face, obviously having hightailed it straight after Daphne. Marianne had the look of the type of woman who took great pride in being compared to the late Princess Diana – even though the similarity was fleeting. Expensively highlighted hair, a shimmery pink lipstick that was best suited to the Sloaney heyday of the 1980s, with her upturned shirt collar, peg-legged chinos and single strand of pearls completing her unintentionally trending retro look.

'Goodness, Marianne, you startled me! What boy?' Daphne was playing for time while she fumbled in her handbag for her keys. She knew exactly which boy but could tell that the conversation was going to immediately turn into a rant.

'The boy that Immy was talking to, of course! Don't encourage them, and certainly don't let Immy play with him.' Marianne gesticulated animatedly, wagging her finger towards Daphne in a dictatorial way that made Daphne arch her eyebrow.

'Why ever not – he's just a little boy?' she murmured quietly, restraining herself from flicking Marianne's still wagging finger away as it grew closer to her face.

'Don't you know? It's a group of them. A commune or a cult or something. They're oddballs. They live in the woods just outside Pepperbridge – in caravans or huts, I think. No running water at all, except for the river. Apparently, they think they're witches. Nutters, the lot of them – I've seen the mother hovering around the gates. It's probably the one thing that Augusta Papplewick and I agree on – she can't bear them either – they're bad news for the community. Just think of the property prices if it looks as though we have travellers nearby!'

Daphne looked Marianne squarely in the face. For the first time, she acknowledged to herself that she didn't particularly like this woman.

'He's just a child, Marianne. I doubt that they think they're witches . . . and I need to go home to paint.'

Chapter 2

After a morning of rainclouds, the light streamed in through the meticulously clean bullseye glass of the front windows at Wellingborough House. It was teatime and Augusta Papplewick's small and neatly manicured hand gripped the delicate china cup and saucer as she swirled the liquid around with a much polished but battered silver spoon. To anyone watching closely, it would have been her white-knuckled grip that gave away her true mood, rather than the apparently absent-minded stirring, all the while watching intently from under her lashes as her husband of forty-three years slowly undid his shirt and tie, then folded them neatly on the bed. It was a ritual that he had performed every afternoon after school for the past thirty-six years. He would change into what he called his 'civilians', usually a Monty Don-style pastoral smock shirt from Old Town in Holt, a pair of old canvas chinos and a pair of scuffed and tired forty-year-old Dutch clogs (a honeymoon purchase). He called it his 'wind-down time'. Augusta thought that he looked like a Pilgrim Father and would have liked him to sex it up a bit more; perhaps undo a button or two. A bit more twenty-first-century Keith Richards – who at seventy-nine was at least a decade older than her husband – than seventeenth-century William Brewster. But her husband was a creature of habit, and his habits tended to be rather straitlaced – and borderline anally retentive if she were being truly honest. He'd been old before his time for as long as she'd known him, and little had changed. On the plus side, he was tidy around the house, loyal, easy to manage (i.e. manipulate) and quite clearly devoted to keeping her happy – which gave her little reason to quarrel.

As regular as clockwork, post-paperwork, post-school admin and after catching up with the day's events, admission queries, curriculum changes, local authority news and a final briefing with his secretary, Mrs Musgrove, Charles would walk through the door of Wellingborough House at precisely 5.30 p.m. Then he would wash his hands in the deep Belfast sink (original 1963 version – there was nothing intentionally trendy about the way they lived; everything was accidentally *au courant* in the Papplewick household) and give his wife a brief peck on the cheek, enquiring what she would like for supper as he walked upstairs to the bedroom to change. More often than not she would follow him up, always with dainty teacup and saucer in hand.

Having folded his clothes and taken note of her dinner preferences, Charles would descend the medieval staircase that went directly into the kitchen, grab a trug and a pair of secateurs from the bench under the utility window, peck his wife dutifully on the cheek once more and exit the house via the back door to make his way towards his allotment in the north-east corner of the village. A pipe, a box of matches and a tin of tobacco would be in the single pocket of his shirt. It was a daily ritual in a village filled with pleasant and uncomplicated daily rituals. The residents of Pepperbridge seemed to have settled into a steady set of polite – and rather old-fashioned, to the eyes of an outsider – routines that had been born out of years of unchanging village life.

Augusta could have prepared the evening meal herself, of course, and had it waiting for her husband's return from school. After all, it was he who had been through the trials and tribulations of running a school filled with whiny village children all day ... but there was an unspoken and rather chivalrous need that Charles felt to look after his wife, and Augusta in turn accepted his desire quite willingly. There was no submission involved; Augusta was not a timid or fragile woman. Quite the opposite, in fact. She was simply a woman who believed in her right to be held up on a pedestal by her husband (and any other individual within her scope). She also believed that coming home to cook and clean was Charles's way of letting the stresses of the day drain away. Yet she could think of several other more pleasurable ways of letting off steam ... She may have been an agile woman of sixty-five who practised yoga and played tennis, but she had long since resigned herself to the fact that grandiose displays of romance had been absent from her husband's mind for years. She had learned to respect the fact that whatever passions he'd once harboured for her had now been channelled into his love for the village, and his dutiful feelings towards the pupils and parents at the village school.

It was a shame, in Augusta's not-so-humble opinion, since Charles had seemed destined for greater things in his youth. The local council and then an MP, perhaps. The inheritance of her father's money could easily have subsidised any political ambitions of Charles, but her husband's own ambitions had always involved this community where he had been born and the helping of others – particularly those less fortunate than himself – rather than his own advancement. He was a local boy whose father had been headmaster at the same school when Charles himself was a boy, and despite the illustrious education that followed, including attending Cambridge, Charles had chosen to dedicate his life to keeping the school alive and thriving; stopping the little village from ageing too fast and dying too quickly.

Augusta sometimes felt that *they* were ageing too fast and dying too quickly. At one point in their early courtship, they had been physically demonstrative to the point of being a public nuisance, although Augusta had never been quite sure whether it was early passion or pent-up anger that had spurred him on. In fact, it was his one-time obvious desire for her that had led Augusta to sacrifice her need for a more exciting, more adventurous life in favour of her husband's love for this quaint village. She had forgone the things that might have been, the places she might have visited and the friends she might have kept – quite willingly at the start, she had to forcibly remind herself. The truth was that she still loved her husband dearly. He was a loyal and steady man. A man of principle and dignity – such good, solid traits. She had proudly stood by his side at prizegivings and country fetes throughout the years, lending her support to the well-respected headmaster who had returned to the village rather than fleeing to the city. Over time, her own role had grown beyond that of the headmaster's wife. The committee heads, the fundraising galas, the Women's Institute and charity runs. These increasing little snippets of power had somewhat filled the gap where her own ambitions had once lived, and she had learned to quell her frustrations by whipping the various committees into shape.

As the years passed by, long after they had regretfully accepted that they would not have children of their own, Augusta's impassioned love for her quiet husband took on a more complicated form. He had retreated into himself long ago and, in the growing absence of physical affection, Augusta had slowly adjusted her requirements for indicators of love from her husband. She imagined deep down that he still loved her – he'd just forgotten how to express it without assistance, that was all. She littered their life with enough small and discreet tests to prove that he did. She hadn't always sat waiting for him to finish work and return to organise supper. She had once been eager to please him and show off her own culinary skills, taking pleasure as he enjoyed her offerings. She was, in fact, a very good cook – but there was only so much lasting joy to be had from a man whose head was more often than not stuck in a textbook or an exam paper. At first, she allowed him to come home only occasionally to a quiet and empty kitchen – just to see if she could induce some sort of a reaction. Anything to acknowledge that he had a strong sense of feeling – or, failing that, an indicator that he felt a modicum of interest. However, the ever-patient, always polite Charles would merely observe the situation with stoic acceptance, and not a word of displeasure would be uttered. It didn't take him long to fall into line and ask whether she would like him to make something for supper. Time passed by – years even – and Charles simply adapted to this new change in his evening routine, using it as an excuse to grow more interesting produce on his allotment.

Where he would have once made a delicious yet straight-forward cottage pie, Charles now prepared a spiced North African-inspired Moroccan stew, complemented by mash made from minty potatoes that he had grown himself, or roasted kohlrabi with goat's cheese and tarragon or some other such herbs and vegetables grown in his meticulously cared-for allotment.

Augusta had rather begrudgingly enjoyed her husband's cooking, and so had added to her tests by gaining an increasingly childish pleasure in making Charles do other unnecessary things for her. The more unfair it appeared, the better it felt. The tests were never too unreasonable. Never too challenging. She didn't want him to become frustrated with her – but asking him to go downstairs and make her a cup of tea once he was settled in bed, only to appear to be asleep when he returned, couldn't hurt every once in a while. She wasn't angry with him, she assured herself – just a tad bored with his decades-long lack of interest in anything physical beyond those pecks on the cheek.

Today, she pursed her lips as Charles exited through the back door on his way to the allotment. Frustration turned to the familiar supressed anger, and supressed anger turned away from the direction of her husband, and towards uncharitable thoughts – any suitable target annoying her in the village. That simpering, anaemic-looking traveller woman was particularly irritating at the moment. She didn't understand why Charles gave her or her Victorian-waif-like child the time of day. He'd indulged that group of travellers for years. Accommodating their presence and practically bending over backwards to be civil towards them. People like that brought no added value to the village – it was clearly the opposite, whether they'd had a presence on the outskirts of the village before Augusta herself had arrived or not.

There were many residents who got on her nerves. Especially newcomers who appeared to get on with everyone far better than she had when she'd first arrived four decades ago. Surprisingly, the new Black woman seemed acceptable. She appeared to be well spoken, well educated, and the children were always smartly dressed despite being from crime-filled London. What was her name? Daphne, was it? Daphne Brewster? She could be a prime candidate for a useful new – and pliable – PTA member, and her presence would look good on the school brochure for Ofsted too ... She certainly seemed to be far less obnoxious than that other Londoner – the ridiculously entitled and social-climbing Marianne Forbes.

She had been so disappointed in Marianne. The inane woman thought it was wise to flirt with Charles in order to flatter him into writing a glowing recommendation for the St Jude's school scholarship. Well, that recommendation would be written over Augusta's dead body. Marianne had made her bed by overstepping the mark, and now she could jolly well lie in it.

Augusta stretched her face into a humourless smile as she poured another slug of vodka into her teacup, tipped it back in one gulp and stared stubbornly at the pile of potatoes on top of the Aga waiting to be peeled. The potatoes could bloody well stay there until Charles returned. 'Small battles ...' she sighed into her now-empty teacup; such a pretty and delicate pattern on their wedding china. She stretched to pour herself another generous glug and returned the bottle to its hiding place behind the Royal Dorchester soup tureen with its matching bone china ladle. 'Fortnum & Mason Earl Grey Infusion my arse,' she muttered under her breath, slurring slightly.

A mile or two away to the north, in the sister village of Pudding Corner, a rather less frustrated Daphne Brewster was busy cleaning paintbrushes in her own traditional country kitchen. The doors were flung wide open, and the milder spring weather was now well on its way. The chairs that she had painted for her new 'friend' Marianne had set off a rather swift, surprisingly intense chain reaction among the parents and local community surrounding the village school. Despite the area being prime antiques territory, it was as though every household for miles around had breathed a huge sigh of relief at the thought of being able to refresh their timeworn interiors without having to leave their front door. It wasn't just painting things, either; Daphne was being asked to source vintage items and style them in her own distinctive way in a few local homes too. She was more than happy with her sudden reputation as a budding interior stylist – a moniker that Marianne had first used – and vintage trader 'up from

London, you know'. Whether it was the novelty factor of getting to interrogate the new Londoner, or simply a sudden collective dislike for three-piece suites, Daphne did not know. What she did know, however, was that she had miraculously and quite unexpectedly been given a shove into a new potential career, and her ambitions had once again been stoked.

It had not been Daphne's intention to move to the countryside and never work again. Her ex-colleagues and London friends had looked at her pityingly on the occasions when they'd discuss what could possibly come next for her. It was true that she had isolated herself from the possibility of being able to travel to the city to continue working as a shoot producer for an interiors magazine, the *Stylish Home*. She had been determined to draw a line beneath her old life and this new one, and the idea of once again producing advertising shoots for demanding people made her shudder.

She had left the city for a reason, and that reason did not involve attempting to emulate her career in the reassuringly unflamboyant backdrop of deepest rural Norfolk. The thought of sullying these beautiful and tranquil surroundings with the same stresses and drama of London was quite frankly a wholly depressing idea. Not only would her nerves not be able to handle it, but her husband and children would have more than a few words to say on the matter themselves. The children, in particular, preferred this calmer and less absent version of their mother. The move had been all about being present for the family . . . but it hadn't tempered her ambition or her need for independence. Painting and sourcing vintage furniture was nothing like the responsibility of organising a four-day shoot for a high-end furniture brand, but at least it gave her a dedicated mission, and allowed her a certain amount of creative fulfilment. (She shuddered at the memory of one brand insisting on painting the walls of a location house a bright and garish pink to complement their new collection – then refusing to return it to its original colour when they decided not to use the wall as a backdrop after all, thus forcing an exhausted Daphne to repaint the entire wall herself with three coats.)

She was about to start work on an unusual request for one of the more unassuming mothers at the school gates. She was the mother of Silvanus, the child with the large eyes and baggy clothes whom Immy had first introduced her to several weeks back and who was now proudly described as her daughter's 'best "boy" friend'. To be honest, Daphne had been rather surprised by this particular commission. Silvanus's mother, Minerva Leek, had not seemed the type who would want to pay for a painted piece of furniture. It appeared, however, that her son felt otherwise, and had requested a sleigh-style bed painted in rainbow colours and stars for his sixth birthday, and who was she not to oblige? Daphne had not failed to notice the disapproving glances of a few other disgruntled mothers who had assumed they would take precedence over Silvanus and his mother. But Daphne was nothing if not fair. Minerva had asked her fair and square, ahead of the other commissions, and had been extremely polite about it – almost shy, even. Immy had been invited to her first pyjama party and, having a hunch that there would be few attendees at this particular birthday celebration, it was the least Daphne could do to help out someone who appeared to be a fellow outsider in the village. Besides, over the past two months,

Minerva and Silvanus had increasingly become the subject of Marianne's scorn and, for that reason alone, Daphne felt a desire to be on her side. It was always Daphne's first instinct to defend the excluded and overlooked, and if giving priority to painting a child's bed was what that took, then that was what she would do.

She had already sanded down the wood. Thankfully, it was a solidly made bed, structurally sound with no signs of woodworm, and painting it would be a straightforward job. An undercoat to stop the knots showing through, and then two coats of colour on top. The tricky bit was going to be the intricate design and lettering, but after that followed the simple task of varnishing it to seal her artwork. It was all new territory to Daphne, but it was a skill that she had been practising for months and she was determined to master it. Getting this one perfect was important for more than her own personal professional pride.

Daphne hated bullying of any kind, and school-gate bullying – involving parents ganging up on other parents – was a particularly unpleasant behaviour. It was often sly and insidious, featuring seemingly small slights and innocent topics. Not being invited to a coffee group may appear nothing to some, but to a young mother feeling misplaced and lost, hovering alone at the school gates, it was a potentially devastating blow to an already battered confidence. Daphne knew the feeling very well. She had always appeared confident at the school gates in London, but the manic dash though the gates to catch the train to work, while noting the mothers who were able to head straight out to coffee mornings and bonding yoga sessions, always left her feeling like an outsider. The irony was that in the months preceding the 'big move', when Daphne stood at the school gates with no job to dash off to, she had felt a similar pang of regret at seeing how confident and together the working mothers appeared as they multitasked, carrying school bags and talking into their smartphones while negotiating a child in each hand through the playground. That had been Daphne once. Had she too made it look so effortless while inside she was flapping? Had the coffee mothers back in London not seen her own constant panic hidden just beneath the surface of an artificially cool and controlled exterior?

She had noticed the familiar glimpse of controlled anxiety behind Minerva's eyes. She never actually allowed herself to appear in an outwardly panicked state but, like Daphne, Minerva often arrived in the playground at the very last minute and had usually disappeared by the time the crocodile lines of paired-up under tens began to snake their way into the classrooms once the bell had been rung.

What had been unexpected was Minerva's willingness to approach Daphne despite her unwillingness to interact with anyone else. Her smile had been warm and friendly. A little shy perhaps, but open and welcoming. Daphne wondered whether it was an acknowledgement of being an outsider in the area. Daphne was the only Black woman with children at the school, it seemed. In fact, apart from one of the GPs at the local surgery in Pepperbridge; Mrs Brinton, the British woman of Chinese heritage who co-owned the local chippie with her husband; and a lady who owned a florist in Burnham Market, Daphne had seen hardly any people of colour at all. She didn't doubt that there were more people of colour out there, but the thing that she had come to realise with village life was that people seemed to stick with their own community, and where you landed was what you got. It was a certainly a change in demographic, but as long as everyone remained as polite and open-minded as they had been so far, then she could cope. The main problem that locals seemed to have was with the people they called the 'Townies': second homeowners – particularly Londoners. The type of people who contributed nothing to the local economy and arrived with their pre-packed shopping for two weeks in the summer, but kept their price-inflated houses empty for most of the year.

Minerva may have been white in a very white demographic, but what set her apart was a distinct lack of convention. She wasn't a Boden wearer or covered in tweed and Dubarry boots like the other mothers. She wore all black, from head to toe. Often full-length skirts that dragged over her feet so you had no idea whether she was wearing shoes at all. The darkness of her clothes contrasted with the translucence of her skin, as though she had remained out of sunlight for her entire life. She was so pale that you could see thin blue veins though the skin on her cheeks, only partially hidden by her poker-straight hair, which hung down to her waist in two great swathes either side of a centre parting.

Marianne had immaturely joked that 'Manky Minerva' and her son lived in a commune near the woods on the outskirts of the village, with a bunch of other deluded women who believed themselves to be witches but were probably just hippies growing weed. Despite her relatively new village status, Daphne felt that both assumptions sounded ridiculous, and were obviously an incredibly unfair attempt to exclude a shy woman and her child simply for living in a different way. During Daphne's short time in the school community, she had even noticed the headmaster's wife giving Minerva several disdainful side glances.

Either way, Daphne would rather determine things for herself. She was due to deliver the bed's pieces to Minerva at some point on Friday; they would then build the bed together and dress Silvanus's room into a magical fairy-tale abode just before his birthday tea. Minerva had already given her a few complicated directions through the wooded area that led to the 'so-called' commune – a place that she had previously only heard described via Marianne's disparaging and spite-filled tongue, although when or why Marianne had had reason to visit the 'commune', Daphne did not know.

What she did know was that in the absence of the magazine shoots filled with high-maintenance editors, photographers and stylists to organise that had dominated her old life, Daphne welcomed this new challenge of defiantly breaking through village hierarchy. Perhaps, despite the sense of quiet, Pepperbridge wasn't so far removed from the politics of the city after all. It was bound to be an interesting afternoon.

Chapter 3

At first glance, one wouldn't have known that there was anyone else in the bedroom apart from the quietly sleeping child, whose floppy limbs lay half-under, half-uncovered by a crocheted blanket on the rickety makeshift camp bed. It would have taken a while for the eyes to adjust before noticing an almost imperceptible movement in the corner. A sliver of moonlight highlighting the subtle shift of a bent knee as it settled itself into the battered armchair – a discarded gem discovered atop a pile of renovation rubbish in a village skip and rescued from almost-certain destruction at the recycling centre. It had a slight hint of mustiness to it, of course, but living in a single-glazed, three-hundred-year-old gamekeeper's cottage, among dense woodland, brought a musty aroma to most things.

Sleep evaded Minerva. She was feeling nervous about many

things – not least the birthday tea that she had reluctantly promised and that was due to take place in about twelve hours' time. Minerva had often feared that Silvanus would fall victim to the cruelty of the village children, just as she had growing up. Minerva had never had a birthday party of her own as a child . . . and neither had she been invited to any.

Her childhood might have been described as idyllic to anyone stumbling across their little enclave of Cringlewic. It consisted of three ancient and small farmworker's cottages – including the gamekeeper's cottage where she and Silvanus lived – a derelict gatehouse, some ancient church ruins, four mobile homes and a Romany caravan nestled deep within the wood adjoining the Oxwold Overy estate. She had grown up with an immense amount of freedom. Climbing trees, bathing in the stream at Oxwold, campfires on most evenings, and a distinct lack of rules or restrictions – beyond attending the local school. The group of women who had made up the little community known as Daughters of Agnes were symbolically named after Agnes Waterhouse; the first woman to be executed for witchcraft in England in 1566. They may have believed in the Wiccan freedoms of an unstructured upbringing, but they were astute enough to understand that even the most intuitive and wise Wiccan needed the practical tools of at least a basic education – alongside the Magickal tools of Pagan teachings. Some of her contemporaries had been home-schooled, and a small minority of others had attended the village school on and off over the years. Minerva's mother, however, had insisted that she attend conventional school and receive a basic education alongside her Wiccan one – much to the disapproval of other community members at the time.

Minerva continued to watch Silvanus sleep – as she did most nights from the close and comfortable proximity of her salvaged armchair. He had arrived quite accidentally late in her life. Motherhood had never been a particular aim for her. But from the moment he had arrived, serious and watchful even as a new born, he had become the all-consuming purpose to her life. He was her light, her heart, her everything – and she was willing to sacrifice anything in order to protect him and give him the best possible start. Even if that meant sending him to the very same school that had caused her years of suffering at the hands of playground bullies, many of whom she pretended not to notice at the school gates now.

School was a necessary evil – at least, it would be until Silvanus turned thirteen. Then, like her, he could make up his own mind about whether to continue with a formal education or not, and they would battle it out with the council when the time came. She had considered home schooling from the start but, like her own mother, she feared the act of isolating him from other children of his own age, as well as depriving him of an education that was beyond her own capabilities to impart. And then there was the not-so-small fact that *he* was at the school.

It was a decidedly sticky situation, what with the secret that had the potential to derail a fair few lives in the village. She was surprised that no one had noticed the family resemblance as yet. The serious eyes, the narrow face. The fear that someone would put two and two together induced the metallic taste of fear in Minerva's mouth at every morning drop-off. Each morning she sat fussing in her old Ford Fiesta, pretending to check random things in the glove compartment or on the back seat so she could reach the playground just before the first ring of the final bell. She had become expert in the accuracy of her timing, arriving at the perfect moment to simply wave Silvanus off into class. Eyes downward at all times, she would give him a quick and self-conscious kiss as he joined the crocodile line winding its way into the reception class. Although her heart would be crying out to stay and protect him at all costs, she would force herself to do an immediate about turn and hurry back to her junk heap of a car without bumping into anyone.

Head down, hood up, eyes on Silvanus only. She was aware of how awkward she looked, but as defence mechanisms go, avoiding eye contact and being labelled as the village weirdo was a good one – a label that she had, after all, worn for most of her life. She was as rarely spoken to now in her forties as she had been in school. Just as she preferred it these days. She felt bad for Silvanus, of course. She didn't mean to intentionally scupper his chances of having a play before school each morning, but it felt safer that way. It was selfish, she knew, and she had to pretend not to notice the disapproving looks from other mothers, or the occasional glare of disdain from the self-appointed queen of Pepperbridge, Augusta Papplewick. She always avoided eye contact with the headmaster, too, although every once in a while she would catch his silently supportive glance and she felt compelled to look back shyly.

Now, she sat in her chair and shivered despite the mild evening air. He'd told her that tonight would be the night that he finally told Augusta the truth, and it made her feel sick to her stomach. She tasted that familiar sensation of metal in her mouth again. She felt the terror of having opened up a Pandora's box of secrets. She knew that even her fellow Daughters of Agnes would be shocked to know the whole truth. Perhaps she would become the social pariah of her own small community as well as the village. She hoped that they would be forgiving towards Silvanus, at least. After all, he was just a child and an innocent part of an otherwise complicated situation. Thank goodness Daphne Brewster and her friendly gaggle of confident children had showed up. For the first time in his life, Silvanus had a real friend whose mother didn't disapprove of him.

Daphne would be bringing the new bed along after school and had also volunteered to bake a cake for Silvanus's 'party', which meant that at least three children would show up for him. Daphne seemed lovely. Fearless and buoyant, despite also standing out from the other people in the village. Minerva was glad that Daphne would be with her when the truth came out. She needed that distraction, and who knew whether Daphne or anyone else from the village would speak to her after tomorrow?

Silvanus stirred and mumbled incoherently in his sleep. She could see from the violet and pink tones filtering through the cracks in the shutters that it was beginning to get light outside. It was what locals called a 'vanilla' sky and it was supposed to be a lucky omen. Yet she feared and longed for, in equal measure, what the day would bring.

A few miles away, the early light was beginning to seep through the pantry window and through the crack of the kitchen door where the silhouette of a man in pyjamas sat in semi-darkness, nursing a cup of hot water and honey. All sensible people would be tucked up in bed at such an ungodly hour, desperate to squeeze in a few more hours of slumber before the day truly began. But despite his lack of sleep, Charles Papplewick was feeling more alive and invigorated than he had in decades. He'd spent far too many years living a half-life and now, at last, he could see a clear way out – and that fact thrilled him to the point of ecstatic insomnia. He swirled the honey round the mug slowly – being careful not to make any sounds that would awaken his sleeping wife – and contemplated his years as headmaster in the village.

He had a few big regrets, but dedicating his life to the children of Pepperbridge Primary had not been one of them. Pouring all his feelings into a job that he did indeed enjoy had made good moral sense, but he had always known it hadn't truly necessitated the full extent of his time over the past forty years. Deep down, he knew that every opportunity to take a vacation – even during school holiday time – he had refused selfishly and unfairly. He had instead encouraged his wife to take holidays on her own, often letting her down at the last minute and citing Ofsted reports, staff shortages and school inspections as the excuse. At the age of sixty-five and with retirement looming at the end of the term, he was conscious that time was running away with itself and, finally, he'd grown tired.

Yet it had not been the endless commitment to work that had left him feeling weary and in need of a change … No, work had been a blessing. Work had been a distraction, and seeing children flourish and mature and leave the village school equipped to face young adulthood and beyond had been an absolute pleasure. Being faced with a marriage that left one feeling an empty sense of duty – rather than love – would drain the life force out of even the most resilient of spouses. To put it plainly, keeping up the charade of being devoted to Augusta had sucked him dry of feelings – and better late than never, he had decided that he so wanted to feel again.

Today, he already felt different. Today, Charles had woken up and felt a sense of release. Tonight, he would tell his wife that although he felt affection, he no longer loved her ... The truth was that he had never actually 'loved' her, but telling her that would be cruel and a truth too far. Tonight, he would pack up a bag and leave Wellingborough House, his neat and organised home of forty years. Tonight, on the last leg of his final months before retirement, he would finally be free to live his life properly. A little late in the day, perhaps, to become the man that he wanted to be, but it felt right to put plans in place before it was too late.

Would he have felt this way if it hadn't been for Minerva? No, probably not. She made him feel excited about the future. At last, something to feel truly passionate about and to really live for. Life, at last, had some meaning beyond simply a sense of duty. The future was calling, and once he had got through the potential ugliness of this evening, tomorrow would be the start of a brand-new life – come what may.

Marianne Forbes shoved her heel into Timothy's calf for the seventh time in a row and still he lay fast asleep, blissfully unaware that his wife was wide awake beside him, seething with pent-up anger. They weren't even facing each other in the bed. She couldn't actually see his face – but she could hear him breathing far too rhythmically and deeply, and simply the knowledge that his relaxed and recumbent form was enjoying any sort of respite from the current situation annoyed her.

Surely only an immature man who was obliviously secure in his position in life could be so complacent about their child's future? Marianne lay trembling with fury – or was it the cold? The house was so big and draughty (far too expensive to heat properly), she wasn't sure. No, it was most definitely a feeling closer to rage . . . She had shoved the prep school rejection letter under Timothy's nose when he eventually arrived home last night, but his only response had been to resignedly ask her whether their darling son was really cut out for St Jude's Prep in the first place. How dare he question his own son's suitability?

If her husband's lack of ambition infuriated her, then the village school's hold on the potential advancement of its 'more deserving' pupils drove her mad. She blamed the weak headmaster, Mr Papplewick. Between him and his ghastly snob of a wife, he had blocked the only inexpensive option they had to get her child into St Jude's Prep. Charles Papplewick had refused to play ball with the reference. He claimed that little Tarquin might struggle academically with the curriculum at St Jude's. Well, what the hell did he know? School wasn't about suiting the curriculum to the child – it was about choosing the best opportunity to elevate your child's future.

Today she was going to give him a piece of her mind. She would find him and tell him exactly what she thought of his small-minded attitude and his ridiculously small-fry school. She was fed up with playing nice and she was not beyond using a threat or two to aid her cause. She'd demand that he write that reference or she would threaten to make a formal complaint about the looks she'd seen passing between him and the traveller mother who tried to sneak in quietly every morning at the school gates. Marianne was no fool. She knew flirting when she saw it. She had seen how he watched Minerva as she attempted to make herself as invisible as possible in the playground. Why was that? An affair perhaps? She'd threaten to make trouble for Charles Papplewick all right – and for his dreadful wife.

Tonight, after school, and as soon as she'd dropped the children home to Pudding Corner – maybe she'd dump them at Daphne's – she would return to Pepperbridge where she would corner Charles Papplewick and blackmail him to write that recommendation if it was the last thing she did. She would make it happen by any means necessary – anything at all. This little backwater village would not get the better of her.

At precisely 8.30 p.m., Charles Papplewick walked determinedly out of Wellingborough House for what he knew would be one of the very last times.

It had been an eventful day of mixed emotions, and, despite his current distress, he was desperately trying to hold on to that fading feeling of optimism. A very eventful day indeed. The rain was driving down hard but he hardly noticed as he made his way towards the safe haven of his allotment. The allotment always made him feel calmer and more at ease. It had an almost meditative impact, which was one of the reasons he chose to flee there each afternoon after school.

He took his usual route, albeit several hours later than normal and through rising puddles in the semi-darkness, but it had been the first and only place that he wished to retreat to after the showdown with Augusta. He pulled up the collar of his thin jacket against the driving rain and avoided the brambles along Mrs Smythson's cottage front on the corner. She'd had many a warning from the local authority to cut her hedge back so that people could pass without having to walk in the road, but it seemed that she had either forgotten or ignored the notices. The route was reassuringly familiar and brought him much needed comfort as he passed the traditional cottages, and the occasional far grander Georgian frontage, despite the inclement conditions.

The conversation hadn't gone entirely as planned. In fact, no conversation today had gone as planned, and he'd had to rethink quite a few things. He feared that, whatever happened next, he was going to let down quite a number of people – at least for a while – and that made him feel miserable. He would sit in his potting shed for a few hours, smoke his pipe and gather himself together before making his next move. At least he had the whole weekend to compose himself and contemplate this new turn of events before returning to school on Monday and, very soon, at the end of term and the commencement of his retirement, he would have the rest of his life to make things right.

He didn't like to break promises. After a few false starts, he had made it his life's work to always do the honourable thing by people. But that had been compromised in recent years, culminating in today not feeling like an honourable day at all. He sighed deeply and continued his familiar walk up the lane, through the shortcut in the Bergenson's orchard, past the post office on Fleet Street, and towards the paddocks that made up Grimoire Equestrian Centre.

He heard a car pull up a tad too quickly before he saw it, the headlights startling him as he turned to see who on earth was screeching along the lane at this time of night . . .

It was yet another tick to add to his list of miserable encounters for the day. Moments later, as the car eventually screeched off, he continued to make his way even more slowly and miserably towards the allotment, wondering how he had been able to handle the chaos of other people's emotions around him. He recalled the many angry faces and threatening words of those who had seemed so disappointed in him in the past twenty-four hours. As if on cue, the rain poured down even harder in a particularly dramatic fashion, drenching him to the bone. No more than he deserved. He had a spare gardening tunic and dungarees hanging up in the shed, along with a pair of old wellington boots, so he knew that he could change into dry clothes in a minute or two.

It would be strange to return to school on Monday. No doubt the village would talk at first, but he'd given them forty years of service with not a hint of gossip thus far. A few wagging tongues wouldn't hurt him now. He continued up through the gap that led to the gate, signalling the start of the allotment. At last, he could rest his mind for a while. He'd reached it. His happy place. His space for quiet introspection and contemplation surrounded by all manner of flora and fauna and expertly cultivated vegetation. He would get out of his wet clothes and wait it out until the storm passed – the meteorological one at least.

He was intrinsically a good man, wasn't he? He'd never intentionally set out to hurt or deceive anyone, but his life had been a series of miscommunications and deceptions that had thrown things off course, and now it was time to make things right. The walk had cleared his head. He was beginning to feel a slow and subtle wave of optimism creep over him as he undid the padlock on his potting shed door and walked inside. It was larger than it would have seemed to the casual observer from outside. Basic and utilitarian, but functional and handsome with its silvered wood walls and hooks filled with small treasures and keepsakes. There were the usual tools for gardening hanging up of course, but alongside the spades and hoes and secateurs were pinned fading photographs and paraphernalia that reminded him of happier times. Tickets from a concert down in London. The key ring from his first ever car – a Mini – with a tiny, knitted penguin attached. There was a gardening almanac on the small desk, a transistor radio on a makeshift shelf and a camping stove (which wasn't strictly allowed) on a metal stand next to the desk. The small windows were slightly dirty, but clear enough to see out into the darkness. It was rustic, but with a cosiness to it that made it welcoming. A perfect retreat. He'd sat and contemplated life in here on many occasions.

Alone with his thoughts, he was remembering what real love felt like. That was what he had to focus on now. If he could remain focused on that, then everything would be OK. Outside, the rain had stopped for the moment. Perhaps the worst was over?

By sunrise, Charles Papplewick was dead.

Chapter 4

Nancy Warburton took her duties as the village oracle extremely seriously. There was little that she didn't know about the residents of Pepperbridge parish. Contrary to the lilac-rinsed victory rolls and bespectacled grandmother-like appearance that she purposefully cultivated with the presence of a permanent floral pinafore, she was an extremely sharp-eyed and observant woman.

For instance, she knew exactly who was responsible for the salacious letters that were sent – supposedly anonymously – to be published in the *Village Pump* once a month. She had once spied a particularly fruity one atop a pile in the office of Mrs Freestone, the esteemed editor of the eight-page parish newsletter. Of course, by spied, she meant read in full, examined the typed lettering, made a note of the paper, ink colour, idiosyncratic spelling and colourful language in order to assess that it was one of three people in the village. Seeing a smudge of typewriter ribbon ink on Reverend Gerald Duncan's thumb as he handed over payment for a loaf of McVitie's Jamaica Ginger Cake (in the absence of his poorly housekeeper who usually ran the errands) was the final nail in the coffin confirming his guilt.

Nancy kept her secrets close to her chest, of course. Possibly to be used at a later date of her own convenience. Possibly not. The beauty was in the knowing. The hinting and watching faces react in shock and surprise. That was the beauty of getting older and seemingly more invisible. People tended to say and do things in front of you without thinking of the consequences, and she played up to her matronly role with gusto. It suited her to be seen as a harmless hypochondriac who spent most of her time arguing with her sister – until suddenly, with the speed of a scorpion with a sting in her tail, she would turn on her unsuspecting victim and leave them reeling.

She was a distinctly different type of bully than Augusta – but cut from a similar weft of cloth in their mutual enjoyment gained from watching people squirm. Nancy's particular power, however, came from hidden truths and gathering knowledge brought about by quiet and stealthy observation, rather than Augusta's more obvious method of intimidation and snobbery.

She knew Augusta's secret. She knew that she and the headmaster were not in a happy marriage. In fact, she had predicted that forty years ago. She had seen the error of Augusta's pride and pomposity as a young bride entering the village on Charles's arm. She had noticed Augusta's early attempts to ensure that her new husband's attention stayed with her and could see the exact moment when Augusta had realised that she was fighting a losing battle. Four decades of observation later and she could tell from the way they sat silently together in church, heads turned away from each other and observing different areas of the congregation, that theirs was not a partnership built on romantic love. It wasn't the sort of comfortable silence that some long-term couples grew used to. There was a lack of intimacy and a palpable air of crackling tension there. Not noticeable to the average person, she was sure. What the average person saw was a dignified reverence. A poised and solid couple at the helm of a village filled with people who didn't expect public displays of affection from their headmaster.

But Nancy knew better. Living in the intense hothouse conditions of a small village for all of her sixty-five years, she had honed her observational skills to great effect. She had correctly (albeit privately) predicted eight divorces, six illnesses (two terminal), and more interestingly, at least a dozen affairs over the past half a century – often before the people involved or the partners affected had realised themselves. It was ironic that she hadn't predicted her own short and swift marital demise. In fact, it had been over and done with so quickly that most people in the village had no idea that she had ever been married at all, and assumed that she and her sister were simply eccentric spinsters – but that was, of course, another story, and one that she didn't often delve too far into.

Life had confirmed to her that most people ended up marrying the wrong people and lived to regret it. She certainly knew that the headmaster would have been far happier now with her younger sister Patsy had he succumbed to the will of the village matriarchs (including his own mother) over forty years ago. There were many things that she had enjoyed having a front-row view of over the past half a century or so, but seeing her younger sister fade into a lonely spinster alongside her – far before her time – had not been one of them, and for that she would never forgive Charles.

The truth was that she had allowed her own life to fester until the rank stench of disappointment had caused her to relish the power in poking away at the misery of others. In her mind, she had come to terms with her own failure to reach marital happiness a long time ago. Any feelings of resentment or anger towards Charles and his nasty wife, she blamed on the maternal love she had for her sister . . . her poor, cast-aside and rejected 'little' Patsy.

Nancy's 'little' sister Patsy had a voice that could at best be described as 'beefy' and at worst with menacing Kray-brother undertones. It made even the most innocuous comments sound terrifyingly confrontational, as though she were constantly poised on the cusp of an argument, a tightly coiled and rusty spring that could cause violent damage.

Yet despite her larger-than-life voice, at the age of sixty, she had resigned herself to the fate of always being known as the 'little' Warburton sister, and had taken to standing quietly behind Nancy when the shop was open. It wasn't that she was embarrassed about her vocal tones; she was naturally talkative and loved to laugh. But rather like her sister, she had come to realise that a quiet and watchful demeanour drew more information out of unsuspecting bystanders than engaging in arbitrary conversation – especially when one's voice had the gravelly texture of an overflowing ashtray and was sure to startle if not accidentally intimidate.

The sisters made for quite the eccentric pair, standing quietly sentinel-like behind the shop counter on the days that they deigned it necessary to stick to the advertised hours and remain open. For the local villagers it was a very convenient place for a quick pantry-cupboard shop – despite the inflated prices and the occasionally out-of-date tin.

There were times when the sisters could be heard squabbling behind the doors, yet if one were to peer through the letterbox, as customers inevitably did when faced with a 'closed' sign on the door yet booming voices from within, they would sometimes glimpse them standing at the top of the stairs in sudden silence, looking for all intents and purposes like the elderly version of the Grady twins in *The Shining*.

The sisters were fiercely protective of each other, and even more so of their right to be the purveyors of local gossip rather than the source of it.

Nancy may have been the watchful one, but Patsy was prepared to take things a step further. She had learned from the best in her sister, but where Nancy was discreet, Patsy was far more willing to take risks to find out what she wanted to know.

On the night of Charles Papplewick's death, Patsy had seen him pass the shop as he did every afternoon, but nearing 9 p.m. was much later than usual. She knew this because she had sneaked out for a quick cigarette just before *Prime Suspect* started, on the pretext of putting out the recycling bin. It was jet black outside on account of the rainclouds more than the time of night. The rain was coming down increasingly hard, but the temperature was actually quite balmy and mild – the sort of weather during which it would be hard to fall asleep, she imagined absent-mindedly. She was leaning against the side alley wall, sheltering under the corrugated iron lean-to, just about to enjoy a final deliciously deep draw of nicotine, when she jumped further back into the shadows, startled by the unmistakable sound of his heavily splashing footsteps rounding the corner through the deluge. His gait had seemed unusually purposeful and agitated, and she had felt it best to draw no attention to her presence. Not least because she probably smelled of cigarette smoke, but also because it was unusual to see him in any state other than calm acceptance. As he sped past, she could sense from the grim look on his face that he must have just left an argument.

Surely it was far too late for him to be heading to the allotment, she mused to herself, her interest piqued – and yet that was the direction that he was heading in. Despite the knowledge that her sister would soon be questioning her whereabouts – after all, *Prime Suspect* was about to start in a few minutes – she felt compelled to know where Charles could possibly be heading in such an agitated state, and why.

It took her only a few minutes to decide to follow him. Rain or not, this felt far too juicy an opportunity to ignore. Thankfully the rain muffled her own footsteps. Unlike Charles, who seemed in a world of his own, she was being careful to avoid the puddles, and had no desire to be seen.

Stealthily trailing behind him by a few hundred yards,

and slipping in between houses and hedges when necessary, she soon noticed a vaguely familiar green Volvo screech up to the kerb beside him, trailing along as the driver called out through an open window.

Due to the rain, she couldn't quite hear the words being spoken from the person in the driving seat, but she edged as close as she could before stopping and straining to listen – echoing Charles's own pause in the rain.

Whoever was in the car appeared to be raising their voice before the door was flung open and a lone figure walked determinedly towards Charles on the pavement. Patsy's heart was in her mouth. Should she intervene? Did Charles need help? Was he in danger? She watched him stand his ground as what was now obviously a woman continued to shriek at him threateningly. She edged closer, mindful to remain in the shadows, and was just able to make out the tail end of a sentence before the mysterious figure returned to the car, leaning at one point on the bonnet before getting in. Charles remained still and silent, looking at the figure who had just been berating him incoherently through the rain. Then the accelerator was pressed hard, and with a slight skid, the car took off. The words she had heard sounded like 'or else!' It was definitely a woman's voice – and an angry woman at that.

She stared as Charles stood in the rain and watched the car depart. She saw his shoulders drop and then droop as the car sped out of sight – as if the burden of what had just been said was just too much. All at once she felt an intense urge to go to him, to comfort him and say that it would all be OK – after all, they had developed some semblance of a mutually respectful friendship in the ridiculous kerfuffle of their youth. A crack of thunder brought her to her senses and the sky lit up for a split second as a bolt of lightning spread across the clouds. For a fraction of time, every roof in Pepperbridge could be seen in stark and intricate detail. Every ancient chimney and every broken tile. It reminded her of another night, a long time ago . . .

How could she possibly explain being out here in the rain and watching him? Within a few minutes, a rather less determined-seeming Charles continued his route towards the allotment. Patsy hesitated, trying to decide whether this could be the moment she had been waiting for. The moment where she could acknowledge his role in her past.

Thinking the better of it, she turned back and retraced her steps towards the shop. Her sister would be waiting and wondering where she had gone. Charles Papplewick and *that* conversation could wait for another time. She had already waited forty years – another few wouldn't hurt now.

A few hundred yards up the road, Nancy had watched the unusual events unfold from a distance. She had indeed wondered where her sister had disappeared to, although she was well aware that Patsy was still partial to a cigarette or two, despite her protestations. She'd assumed that Patsy would return reeking of Trebor mints and cheap cologne to mask the unmaskable. However, after a few minutes longer than normal, Nancy's radar was on high alert. Patsy didn't normally take this long to puff on her not-so-sneaky cigarette, and she would *never* intentionally miss the beginning of *Prime Suspect* . . .

Determined to creep up on her unawares, Nancy had grabbed her mackintosh and stepped out to spy on her sister, but she was nowhere to be found. Starting to get concerned, she was relieved to see Patsy scurrying into the distance in the wake of another shadowy figure further up the lane. She saw her sister dip and dive in between houses, attempting not to be seen by whoever was ahead of her. Well, two could play at that game, thought Nancy, as she pulled her collar up tightly around her ears and followed quietly. Patsy had learned from the best – and Nancy *was* the best, after all.

Nancy had seen the car pull up beside Charles, the muffled sound of shouting as Charles stood there, seemingly taking the abuse in the rain. She had then seen her sister's hesitation, sensing her desire to go to Charles, and finally witnessed her about turn and reluctant retreat.

So, Nancy deduced, Charles and Augusta had clearly finally had the long-overdue argument. But who was the mystery woman with the car? She had been too far away and it had been too dark to see, but she knew that Augusta didn't – or at least wouldn't – drive, so she doubted it had been her.

Speeding back into the house ahead of her sister, Nancy went straight to her bedroom, quicky grabbed her towel to dry herself off and turned off the light. Within a few moments she heard Patsy's footsteps on the landing stairs, then approaching her bedroom door.

The handle turned and Patsy's head poked into the room. 'I thought you'd be watching *Prime Suspect*?' she asked with surprise.

'I've got a headache,' Nancy mumbled with feigned indifference.

'Mmmm – me too, in fact I feel awful! Do you want some cocoa?'

Patsy avoided her sister's eyes, choosing instead to appear tired, and concentrated on heading towards the kitchen. It was obvious that she didn't want Nancy to adopt big-sister mode and question her most recent whereabouts.

'No, thank you – good night. Leave the landing light on in case I need to get my pills from downstairs.'

'OK then, I'll have an early night too in that case.' Patsy retreated, concealing a relieved expression as she closed the door.

It took about half an hour for Nancy to hear the loud snoring of her sister penetrating the silent house. Patsy was a heavy sleeper, and her snore was as deep and resonating as her voice. Nancy knew that once she was out for the night, there would be no waking her until morning.

Satisfied that all was safe, Nancy climbed out of bed. She was still fully dressed. She crept quietly onto the landing and down the stairs, careful to miss the squeaky seventh step on her way down. In the unlikely event that Patsy called out, she had already set the scene by mentioning her headache and need for pills.

She took her mackintosh back out of the understairs closet. It was a rare new purchase, as she normally wore her mother's old clothes, or at least her own until they literally fell apart. This was a smart coat from the sale at Boden in Bury St Edmund's. She felt put together wearing it. In control. She grabbed her door keys and slipped quietly out through the back door and onto the dark alley. It had thankfully stopped raining, although the thunder was still rumbling in the distance. There were large puddles everywhere, which she needed to avoid for fear of slipping, and the moon drifted in and out from behind the clouds which gave her enough light to see where she was going.

She didn't know whether Charles would still be at the allotment, but she had a feeling that he wouldn't be heading home any time soon. It wasn't her intention to have it out with him that night, but she could tell that there may be some ammunition to be had if she found out what had happened between him and Augusta.

It must have been nearly 10 p.m. by now. As she finally approached the allotment through the spread of undergrowth cloaked in darkness, with only the occasional glimmer of moonlight to guide her way, she could see that one of the potting sheds had a light on. She knew that it would be Charles's and she began to walk in the general direction, being careful not to slip on any mud or make any noise that would alert him to her presence. She wasn't quite sure what she expected to see, say or do. She remembered Patsy's hesitation to approach Charles earlier that evening, but even worse, she recalled a much younger Patsy's distressed face staring horrified and panicked at Charles over forty years ago. She could never forget the fear in Patsy's eyes. The fear of being taken advantage of and abandoned in favour of Augusta. The outrage she had felt for her sister would never, ever disappear. In fact, the outrage she felt for *both* Warburton sisters being rejected was as intense today as it ever was . . . and the incandescent anger that she had held within her for so many years began to build up in her once more.

Chapter 5

In the ten months that Daphne and her family had resided in Pudding Corner, a few things had become rather apparent, Daphne thought to herself.

Firstly, life was, as she had hoped, far quieter and slower paced in the countryside, giving her the mindful respite that she had so eagerly sought and enabling her to slow down and enjoy the more important things life: primarily her family.

Secondly, although the pace of things was slower, the relationships between people were just as complicated and intertwined as they were anywhere else, and a backdrop of rolling fields filled with wire-haired sheep did not make petty disputes disappear or allow difficult conversations to feel any easier – regardless of how quaint they made the world of Pepperbridge parish appear.

Thirdly, Daphne had realised, you can take the girl out

of south London, but you cannot take south London out of the girl, and Daphne's inbuilt desire to root for the underdog showed no signs of abating – despite the rather less confrontational nature of their day-to-day happenings in these apparently genteel parts.

Even paradise had its bullies, and it was clear to see how tightly residents such as Augusta and Marianne held control of innocent would-be victims.

It was the morning before Charles's death, and the residents of Pudding Corner had no idea what the next 24 hours would hold. For Daphne, despite the hope for a dose of much-needed jollity at Silvanus's party later on, today was also going to be a day for uncomfortable conversations. She was not one to go searching for problems, but there were certain things that needed to be addressed. Her main mission was to organise a meeting with Augusta and Charles Papplewick to discuss Black History Month next year. Having politely enquired about it after a recent parent assembly, to be met with a blank expression followed by a patronising pat on the hand and an empty reassurance from Augusta that they would 'sort something out, dear', Daphne knew that she would have to get the two of them together in order to get going in advance of next year.

It was only just past 8.30 a.m. and in the rare absence of their neighbour simultaneously leaving for the village surgery, her own departure for the school run with three children in tow had been surprisingly easy. The sky had looked ominously dark that morning, and the light outside had the curious yellow tint that she had learned to recognise as a sure sign that a storm was on its way. She looked across to the doctor's gate. He had obviously left early.

Truth be told, Daphne wouldn't have minded a short delay or at least a minor distraction before arriving at school to confront Augusta Papplewick about her Black History Month proposal. Organising the meeting to include the headmaster was one thing – he seemed affable and sensible and open to ideas, and she regretted not having approached him in the first place. However, she also wanted to check that Augusta had received the recommended textbooks that Daphne had previously left at reception, and if not, she intended to hand one straight to her.

Daphne wasn't usually one for unwarranted confrontation. She was also quite aware that as a relative newcomer to the parish, it probably wouldn't be seen as seemly to push her opinions and ideologies on the good people of this enclave of sleepy, unchanged villages. Naturally life would be far easier to leave things as they were. However, when it came to education, whether welcomed or not, it felt like she had a duty to help the parish. Not just for her own children, but for the generations of children to come who would otherwise be naively cocooned in a world lacking in diverse thinking and inclusiveness. (She had nervously rehearsed her reasonings in front of an encouraging James on more than one occasion – wanting to get the wording perfectly correct and persuasive.)

She smiled wryly to herself as she drove along the calm and winding road towards Pepperbridge, passing the broad and green fields between the two villages, some filled with sows and their piglets, and others bright yellow with rapeseed. For a moment or two she floundered. Perhaps she shouldn't be getting on her soapbox so early on such a beautiful morning.

She looked up at the rear-view mirror to observe the children sat giggling and prodding each other happily on the back seat.

'Mummy, the Coraline lady stuck her tongue out at Mrs Papplewick yesterday – and I saw her do it. Then she winked at me!' Immy called to her from the back seat.

'Immy, I've told you already that her name is Miss Warburton – not the Coraline lady!' Daphne replied, attempting to change the subject while inwardly trying not to laugh as she imagined Nancy Warburton getting caught sticking her tongue out at another adult by an eight-year-old.

'She doesn't look like Coraline!' shouted Archie. 'Coraline is a little girl – perhaps she's Coraline's "Other Mother"!' he said with a playful grimace. He pulled his scariest face and crossed his fingers over his eyes, causing his twin, Fynn, to start laughing uncontrollably.

'Mummy, Oscar Towbridge brought a toad into school yesterday and it had black spots on its back,' chirped Fynn, suddenly remembering the fun of yesterday's show and tell.

'Yuck,' declared Immy. 'It was probably poisonous – did you lick it?'

Daphne couldn't help but smile. They were so happy and carefree; she didn't want to cause any problems in their otherwise seamless integration into village school life. But what would be worse – for their counterparts to live in polite ignorance, or a discussion that could potentially prompt an uncomfortable but necessary awareness? She sighed heavily to herself. Perhaps there were certain things that remained easier to deal with in a city after all.

*

Arriving at the school playground ten minutes before the first bell, Daphne paused to watch the children run merrily towards their various playmates, before heading straight to the school office and asking after Augusta Papplewick. There was no delaying it now, and she could sense her knuckles whitening with unexpected tension as she grasped the book tightly by her side. She wasn't nervous, exactly. At least not of confronting Augusta – she knew that some things were worth rocking the boat for, and this was one of them.

'Good morning!' she said brightly, the words *kill them with kindness* resonating in her mind. 'Is it possible to speak with Mrs Papplewick? I believe that she said she would be in attendance with the headmaster today?'

'I've only just come in, so I'm not sure whether she's in today, although someone is in with the headmaster . . . Is she – sorry – are they expecting you?' the school receptionist enquired.

She always seemed so jolly, although Daphne had noted that, like so many of the other staff at the school, even she would suddenly deflate in the presence of Augusta Papplewick, yet quickly unfurl like a spring flower after a storm, all smiles again, once the headmaster's wife had wielded her authority and swept on by.

'Errrr . . . not exactly,' Daphne admitted. 'Although, she knows what it's about and it *is* important . . .'

The receptionist looked down at the book held tightly by Daphne's side. *Let's Talk About Race* was written in colourful jaunty letters on the front, surrounded by a sea of illustrated stylised faces of all shades. The receptionist had seen that book before, alongside the others that Daphne had previously left. She looked back up with a mixture of guilt and pity in her eyes.

'Would you like me to pass the book on?' she asked tentatively, knowing that her attempts to pass it on to Augusta would probably be in vain.

'No thank you, I'll wait.'

'All right then, go ahead and I'm sure that Mr Papplewick's secretary, Mrs Musgrave, will let you know if they're available.'

The receptionist gave her a friendly wink and buzzed her in, and Daphne walked through the entrance hall, its walls covered with garishly bright drawings and hastily Pritt-Sticked offerings created by proud pupils (and in the better cases – even prouder parents, Daphne suspected). Unintentionally grotesque papier-mâché faces loomed down on the approach to the headmaster's office, making for a rather foreboding path, where Daphne could just make out raised voices as she grew closer.

She sat down on one of the four grey plastic chairs directly outside Mrs Musgrave's office. Their position meant that she had a clear view of the staffroom when the door was opened, and she could hear every word emanating from the headmaster's office – whether his door was open or not. Surprisingly, she recognised the highest pitched voice in the highly charged 'discussion'. Oh lord no, just her luck – it was definitely the voice of Marianne.

'I'm warning you just one last time,' Marianne roared, 'Just pick up the bloody phone or write the damn letter and I'll be out of your hair for ever, because so help me God, if you don't do *something* to get my child into that school then I promise that you'll be sorry!'

The screeched warning was followed by a thump, and then a smash, and Daphne could only imagine that Marianne had thumped her hand down hard on Mr Papplewick's desk.

Daphne hesitated for a second, her bottom hovering uncertainly over the uncomfortable surface of the seat, not quite sure whether to get up and quietly retreat, or whether to make an attempt at nonchalance and pretend that she had heard nothing at all. At the same time, she felt compelled to keep on listening – this was unexpectedly juicy stuff coming from the enclaves of a tiny village school.

It seemed that Marianne had lost the plot with her angry threats. Daphne had always known that Marianne was highly strung, with an inordinate sense of entitlement, but she had always had a calm aloofness that morphed into manipulative charm when and where necessary. But the person who was threatening the headmaster right now sounded like someone who had finally snapped.

'You think that this poxy little nothing of a school is where I want my children to be? You think that THIS is what I want them to be defined by? You are a NOBODY, Mr Papplewick, and this school is NOTHING. It means NOTHING to me. It matters to NO ONE. How DARE you tie us up in this godforsaken nowhere of a so-called education system with no way out? We are BETTER than this, so sign the letter or so help me I'll—'

'You will what, Mrs Forbes?'

It was the first time that Daphne had heard Charles Papplewick speak in the past few minutes, and to his credit he sounded surprisingly calm and controlled.

'I'll make you rue the day you met me, Charles Papplewick. When I'm finished, I'll have you struck off the teacher's register. I'll make you regret the day you were born.'

'I think that you should stop right there Mrs Forbes – don't you?'

And then came the resounding sound of a firm slap landing on skin.

Daphne sat in shock for only a second before she realised that now would be a prudent time to depart. The book could wait for another moment. Was Augusta even in the room? She didn't think so, otherwise surely she would have intervened and put her twopence worth in – or perhaps she caused the slap? No, Daphne decided. She would leave now and find Augusta another time. Perhaps she'd drop the book off at the cottage with a note. This was not the best time for a discussion after all. Not a good time at all.

Within minutes she was back at her Morris Traveller, panting in her effort to avoid bumping into Marianne. She hastily clipped herself into the seatbelt, looked around to make sure that the coast was clear and, once she was reassured that Marianne wasn't close enough behind her to delay her escape, drove off down School Lane and towards Pudding Corner.

Relief flooded over her as she passed the familiar golden fields. Marianne had a bad habit of trying to coerce people into supporting her own selfish endeavours – and Daphne had no intention of being Marianne's bitter sounding board on that day or any other for that matter.

The next job on the agenda was to return home to collect and then deliver the freshly painted vintage bed to Minerva in time for this afternoon's tea party. She would also be bringing some sandwiches and a three-tiered Victoria sponge cake that she had baked last night but was yet to be filled, since Minerva seemed to be as nervous as a bride on her wedding day about the whole thing. It was obvious that Minerva's real fear was that nobody would turn up for her son's party, and so Daphne fully intended to ensure that even if she and her children were the only guests, the whole event would still feel as festive and as joyful as possible. This was in part for Silvanus's sake, but just as much for his mother too.

Daphne arrived home to find James chatting affably with Doctor Oates on the driveway. The two men got on surprisingly well, although Daphne suspected that her husband took great pains to accommodate their neighbour's longer 'lectures' out of good-natured politeness. Today the doctor was cheerfully but passionately attempting to convince James of the mediative merits of fly fishing at the local stream.

'You see, there are considerable health benefits to the sport itself that many people overlook. It's a physical workout, it reduces stress, and it improves concentration and focus . . .'

Daphne smiled to herself, seeing that James was nodding his head with feigned interest. An athletic man more drawn to the physical exertions of off-road cycling and rugby, James would have absolutely zero intention of standing and staring at a river – of that Daphne was quite sure.

Doctor Oates was a constant and calming presence in this tiny village. He had been welcoming from the off and was never one to indulge in idle gossip or salacious chitchat. He was like the jovial grandfather figure from a Hans Christian Andersen fairy tale – or perhaps a less acerbic Toad of Toad Hall. All boiled sweets, tweed waistcoats and home-grown vegetables with a few historical ramblings thrown in for good measure. Daphne felt that he would make a good Santa Claus at Christmas, although she imagined that he would 'accidentally' remind the children of the true origins of St Nicholas, the pious monk born in Turkey around AD 280 – an important and necessary historical fact perhaps, but one which would be somewhat of a festive buzzkill.

Although Daphne was eager to tell James of the shocking conversation that she had just overheard in the school office, she also needed to get a move on with the party food and bed delivery, and she really didn't have time to be drawn into an extended – albeit juicy – round up. Sensibly resisting the urge to immediately dissect Marianne's rant – that pleasure could be saved for another time, she thought – she swept past the two chatting men, avoiding James's pointed stare that may or may not have been silently pleading to be saved from the fish talk. With a quick wave, she determinedly went about ticking off her list of chores for the day. The first task may have been scuppered by Marianne, but she fully intended to place the book directly into Charles and Augusta's hands by stopping by the Papplewicks' cottage later that day. If Augusta wished to sidestep the discussion on race by pretending that she hadn't received the previous books, she would surely find it far harder when it was on her doorstep, staring her in the face . . .

It was rather magical driving up through the avenue of low-land pine that made up the bulk of the trees in the forest at Cringlewic. The area was home to several species of deer, including the small squat muntjac that frequented Daphne's own garden to indulge in her courgettes; as well as rabbits and their larger cousins, the hares, with their comically huge ears.

Pulling up to Minerva's cottage filled Daphne with a

particular kind of childish joy. As with much of the area, the house resembled a scene from a fairy tale. A modest size building made of flint and wood with a higgledy-piggledy roof and a sweet little working chimney, it originally formed part of a group of gamekeepers' cottages. It was certainly befitting of a so-called witch in a 'Hansel and Gretel' way, although any sinister implications had been erased by Minerva's use of tall swathes of cottage flowers and herbs, and the timeworn but neat picket fence surrounding the building. For someone who liked to hide behind a mound of dark and voluminous clothes, Minerva's cottage was exactly the opposite of her Gothic appearance. Despite being hidden among woodland, the house was pretty, quaint and obviously well loved. A truly enthralling place for a child to grow up.

Opening up the double doors at the back of Aggie, Daphne pulled the bed slats out first, followed carefully by the head-board and footboard, which were both adorned with her handiwork of swirling vine leaves, magical toadstools and stars with the name 'Silvanus' written as though growing from the roots of a tree.

Hearing the car pull up, Minerva was soon by Daphne's side, marvelling at the beautiful upcycled bed.

'Oh my goodness, Daphne! It's perfect – thank you.' She had tears in her eyes as she spontaneously hugged Daphne. Minerva was an unusual creature, Daphne thought. So closed, reserved and contained – almost fearful, but with a heart of gold when you got to know her better. When she felt comfortable, she was fun to be around. Thoughtful and surprisingly humorous. Daphne felt at ease in her presence; there was no pretention, no oversized ego to navigate, and no ulterior motives to decipher. Just a shy and grateful hand of friendship.

'It's been my absolute pleasure. Such a fun piece to work on. Thank you for trusting me with it. Oh – and did I mention that I have cake?' Daphne swiftly changed the subject before the tears threatened to spill over from her own eyes.

Daphne breathed a huge sigh of relief seeing how delighted Minerva was with the bed and together they made up the tiny bedroom, decorating it with hanging stars and paper dragons – Silvanus's favourite. Next, Daphne helped Minerva tidy the kitchen and prepare the table for Silvanus's first ever birthday party.

'Better late than never,' Minerva sighed sadly. She had never invited friends of her son to their modest home before out of fear that no one would turn up.

'Don't worry about that,' Daphne reassured her kindly. 'Children are resilient things, and the six of us will have a wonderful time regardless of who else comes along.'

It was just after 3 p.m. before Daphne once again found herself in her car, trundling bumpily away from Minerva's cottage. She pulled into a parking space opposite the school gates, and sat for a while in the car, waiting to hear the bell that would mark the end of the school day. It had been a funny afternoon with Minerva. The atmosphere had been slightly tense, and Minerva had been decidedly jumpy. On more than one occasion, Daphne had caught her glancing anxiously at her phone and responding to a few messages that were obviously unnerving her. At first, she'd tried to pretend that she hadn't noticed. But when, after the third or fourth time, Daphne had asked if she was OK, Minerva had merely given her a startled look, shoving the mobile phone deep into her skirt pocket. Perhaps it was just a case of party nerves ...

It was Daphne's job to collect the four children from the playground. Her own three plus Silvanus, while Minerva stayed behind at the cottage in case anyone happened to show up early. The buzz of anticipation from the children was infectious, and Daphne couldn't help but laugh out loud as they bundled together, chirping loudly with excitement into the long back seat, with Immy – the eldest and tallest – electing herself the 'most mature' enough to take pride of place in the front passenger seat alongside her mother.

Meanwhile, back in Cringlewic, Minerva had set up party bags, hung a piñata donkey from a tree in the front garden and placed clues around the immediate wooded area for a little treasure hunt. She looked around the enclave that she called home and tried to see it through the eyes of her would-be guests. It was unusual in that there were no visible neighbours – just a road that was really a track, and trees as far as the eye could see. It was rather like living as a modern-day Robin Hood among the great oaks of Sherwood Forest. There was no traffic noise and not even the sound of a tractor within earshot. Just birdsong and the calming sound of the wind rustling the tree's leaves. To Minerva it was perfect, and she could see that Daphne saw the beauty in it as well – she just hoped that the other parents would 'get it' too.

Inside, the tiny kitchen table was laid out with a selection

of homemade sandwiches and cupcakes, plus the larger birthday cake that Daphne had made. There was orange squash
and homemade lemonade cooling in two jugs in the fridge.
She felt nervous. Was it enough? Now she just had to wait
and see if any of the other parents were decent enough to
show up . . .

In the end it wasn't so bad a ratio. Four extra children, beyond
Daphne's, with three no-shows – including Marianne's daughter. Marianne's absence did not surprise Daphne (although
her rudeness in not responding to the original invite did), and
she imagined that Minerva was secretly quite relieved to not
have her barbed presence there anyway. It wasn't the children who Daphne feared would let Silvanus down, it was the
parents, and Daphne could sense that even the parents who
had shown up were most likely there to have a gawp around
the so-called commune belonging to the strange characters
reputed to practise witchcraft.

From time to time, Daphne would look over at Minerva
to see her nervously fussing with the table decorations or
pretending to adjust the tablecloth – anything but engaging
with the other parents who seemed so intimidatingly at ease
with each other – and she would smile reassuringly or draw
her into a conversation.

'Are you all right? It's going well, isn't it?' Daphne said
confidently, nodding towards the children playing happily
around the house.

Minerva nodded gratefully, clearly appreciative to finally
have a friend on her side.

The children were currently running around searching for

clues, squealing in delight, small fists filled with cupcakes, while the other four school mothers sat gossiping and laughing with mugs of tea (thankfully, Daphne had brought some Yorkshire tea bags with her after she'd noticed that Minerva only had random tins of loose-leaf herbal tea on her makeshift kitchen countertop).

It all seemed to be going rather successfully, and the children were growing close to tiring themselves out from running around the immediate woodland and hunting down 'hidden' treasure. Each of the parents seemed to be relieved by that particular result and the mood was relaxed and buoyant, with thoughts of soon-to-be sleepy children ready to be put to bed when they got home. One or two of the other mothers had even initiated conversations with Minerva, which Daphne took as a good sign. Daphne had no problem making small talk with anyone, but she knew how hard it was for an introvert like Minerva.

Finally, approaching 6 p.m., it was time for the party to come to a close – the signs were all there. The children were flagging, their limbs growing heavy and weary as they flung themselves onto the grass or against their parents' legs, and for Daphne there were only so many cups of tea she felt she could offer before it would start spouting from everyone's ears. She had just excused herself from a less than scintillating conversation about the school tortoise and was looking around for Minerva. She wanted to ask if she needed help slicing up the birthday cake and thus mark the time for party bags and the end of the event, when she realised that the unassuming host was nowhere to be seen.

Seeing that the other mothers had one eye on the children

outside, Daphne first called upstairs to see if Minerva had escaped for a moment's peace, before wandering out through the back door of the little cottage, where the garden led a snake-like path towards more woodland. Daphne marvelled at how isolated the house felt. Moving to sleepy Pudding Corner was enough of a drastic change from the hustle and bustle of the big city for her, but this little slice of heaven called Cringlewic was something else altogether. A sea of green Corsican pine, Douglas fir, larch and Weymouth pine, the trees formed a dark canopy that only allowed twinkling shafts of sunlight through the leaves the deeper you went.

Daphne peered around, squinting her eyes and trying to spot her friend, who was evidently no longer in the house or the garden. Perhaps Minerva was a secret smoker and had wanted to hide away for a quick cigarette? Daphne couldn't think of another reason for Minerva to leave the party, but what she did know was that it was getting late, the other mothers were ready to go home and Daphne still had the book that she desperately wanted to hand deliver to the Papplewicks's before it got dark.

She was just about to turn back to the cottage when she heard voices coming from beyond the back gate. In fact she could now hear two distinctive voices filtering though the overgrown thicket of the woodland just a few hundred years in front of her. Could it be Minerva on her phone? But why could she hear two voices if that was the case? She didn't want to disturb her, but at the same time she didn't want the party to creep on endlessly or they'd all have exhausted and ratty children on their hands later on.

She walked slowly along the path, straining her ears towards the darker area beyond the low fence. The air had turned thick, the earth beneath her was soft and covered in leaves, and she'd rather not walk out much further without her wellies. *It's going to rain*, she thought, and was just about to call out Minerva's name when she suddenly saw two figures among the trees. One was clearly Minerva, but the other figure – a tall man – was harder to make out immediately. Minerva was shaking her head as the man walked tensely up and down in front of her, and they were both firing urgent words at each other. It took Daphne a few moments before it became obvious that she was looking at Charles Papplewick – the last person that Daphne expected to see deep in the woods with Minerva. What on earth could they be discussing? Whatever it was, they seemed to be having quite an intense conversation and Daphne sensed that she was intruding on something personal. It wasn't an argument exactly, that much was clear. Minerva didn't appear to be intimidated or fearful, in fact she appeared to be the more in control of the two.

Deciding that they were best left alone, Daphne was about to retreat backwards when they launched towards each other and embraced. Daphne's mouth hung open, unable to tear her eyes away. It was a strong hug, Minerva's head resting tenderly on Charles's shoulder. Not for the first time that day, Daphne slunk away quietly in shock.

Will wonders ever cease in this supposedly sleepy village? she thought, as she began to run towards the gamekeeper's cottage and out of the rain that was starting to fall properly now.

'Everybody in!' she called out, deciding to take matters into her own hands in the absence of an 'otherwise engaged' Minerva. 'It's time for the party bags.'

Minerva came in through the back door not long behind Daphne, to find everyone putting on coats and claiming party bags. Her expression seemed to be a mixture of relief and guilt. She looked over towards Daphne with a grateful smile as Daphne simply shrugged her shoulders and continued to thank the mothers for attending. It was Minerva's job, but they were both aware that Minerva preferred it this way. Lost in their own thoughts, both women chose not to say a word about Minerva's absence from the party.

An hour, some polite conversation and a clear-up later, and the three children were almost fast asleep on the back seat of the car. Daphne had left a subdued but grateful Minerva and a sleepy Silvanus at the flint cottage in Cringlewic a few minutes earlier, and she was now pulling out of the road that led out of the Oxwold Overy estate. It had taken a while to fully get started but by now the rain was bucketing down in what looked like sheets of water. 'It's raining cats and dogs,' she murmured, more to herself than to the dozing children she could see through the rear-view mirror. Windscreen wipers swiping furiously in their attempts to clear the rain from her vintage car, Daphne was eager to get home. Aggie was never at her best in heavy rain – but she had one more job to do. She had to deliver the book.

She wasn't sure that she really wanted to see Mr Papplewick so soon again that evening, but she also felt that since he hadn't seen her in the woods, she could pretend that she hadn't seen him draw Minerva into his arms only a couple of hours earlier. Perhaps there was a good excuse? She hoped so, but – regardless of whatever that might be – what dark horses they both were.

She deliberated driving straight home right up until the second she pulled up on the side road adjoining the home belonging to the Papplewicks. With a quick look at the sleeping trio on the back seat, she made a mad dash up the rain-soaked path until she found herself standing at the entrance to Wellingborough House, sheltering from the torrent of water under the porch, book in hand. The children may have been fast asleep, but she wanted this to be quick so they could all get home for a speedy supper and then bed. She sighed and braced herself, plastering on a faux smile as she raised her hand. Just as she was about to knock, she looked to the left and found herself with an unintentionally clear view of the sitting room through the rain-misted window. Charles Papplewick was standing, mouth firmly closed, in front of his wife, who was standing equally as still and silent, staring straight back at him. There was a palpable pause before Augusta lifted her hand slowly, and with a force that seemed unnaturally strong for her slight frame, gave Charles an almighty slap across the side of his face. It was hard enough to make him stumble, and even from the other side of the glass, the sound of the 'whack' resonated horrifyingly in Daphne's ears.

For the third time that day, Daphne made a swift and soundless retreat. This was becoming a pattern. Why oh why was her timing so bad – or was this 'normal for Norfolk', as the saying went? She wondered what it was about the quietly spoken Charles Papplewick that seemed to make women want to either hug him or slap him.

Chapter 6

It is said that there are five phases of grief. Denial, followed by anger, then bargaining, depression and finally acceptance. Augusta was quite sure that she had been firmly stuck at stage two for a large proportion of her married life. Oh, the irony that now she was expected to return to phase one of the mourning process when she had been mourning the life she'd wanted for over thirty years.

Of course, it went without saying that she was sad to find herself sitting in a private room at Downham Market police station, a cup of cheap weak tea in an equally cheap mug balanced precariously in hand. The only female police officer had been shipped out to sit expectantly by her side, a box of tissues waiting redundantly in her lap while she shifted uncomfortably in her seat. There was an air of slight disappointment that her presumed calming presence and sympathetic ear were not needed . . .

A widow. Augusta was now, quite unexpectedly and quite prematurely, a widow, and the truth of it was that it infuriated her rather more than it upset her. For decades she had prodded and poked her husband into expressing some sort of impassioned emotion, only for him to be dead within hours of having finally done so.

Oh yes, her grief had started long before her husband had drawn his last breath. Her grief had started the day she realised, thirty years ago, that she would never be able to conquer her husband's emotions. At first, she had indeed been hit by denial and its errant cousin – avoidance. She'd avoided the fact that she had emotionally blackmailed her husband into marriage and now she had to lie in the frosty bed of her own making. She had loved him in her own controlling way, and she had hoped that despite tricking him into a marriage with someone he was not in love with, he would at least begrudgingly settle down into a loving companionship.

Except Charles had not played ball. He had quietly accepted his fate and proceeded to live a half-life with her, or at least with half of the emotions. To her despair Charles had become almost zombie-like in his state of surrender. Thus, immersed in denial as to why the marriage had got off to such a poor start, she had tried to be a good wife. After the initial denial swiftly followed anger – and anger is where she had remained.

'Would you like another cuppa?' the police officer asked in a desperate attempt to fill the silence.

'No thank you, Maxine – another "cup" of tea will not be necessary.'

Augusta remembered Maxine from her schooldays at Pepperbridge Primary. A bright girl who had achieved all her badges in Brownies despite challenging family circumstances. It was no surprise that she had joined the police force, but that was no reason for her to talk patronisingly to her old headmaster's wife. She could sense that Maxine was rather bewildered by Augusta's apparent lack of emotion. Perhaps she ought to squeeze out a tear or two if only to keep up appearances? Yet she couldn't.

She was a bag of emotions, but not for the reasons that everyone would assume. She was still seething, literally taut with anger, about the previous evening's events, and even the knowledge that Charles was dead could not retract what had been said. Perhaps she was still in shock? Perhaps at some point it would hit her, and she would break down in a wet and sobbing pile of despair.

The door to the small office eventually opened, and a dishevelled looking Inspector Hargreaves walked in, followed by a shell-shocked looking Daphne – eyes wide and cheeks flushed – turning towards Augusta.

Daphne had been asked to give the inspector a brief statement about why she'd been at the Papplewicks' house that morning – choosing to omit having recently seen the deceased man being embraced by one woman and slapped by another to preserve the dignity of all involved; not that either event bore any relevance to a suspected heart attack. The statement was a formality, nothing serious, but just being in a police station had made the whole surreal situation feel very real. Charles Papplewick, who had only yesterday had been very much alive, was indeed now dead.

'Are you all right, Augusta? Would you like me to give you a lift back to Pepperbridge now – or perhaps I can call someone?' asked Daphne.

All three pairs of eyes turned towards Augusta expectantly, each of them uncertain of how to read the mood of the poker-straight-backed and newly widowed woman. Augusta's lack of emotion certainly appeared strange, but perhaps it was not unusual under the circumstances – the poor woman was probably still in shock, assumed Daphne. After all, it wasn't every day that one lost one's husband to a heart attack in the middle of an allotment in the middle of the night. At least, a heart attack was what everyone was presuming. Now that the body had been formally identified, it would be up to the coroner's office to give the exact cause of death.

'Yes, thank you, Daphne, I'd like to go home now.'

There was an almost imperceptible release of tension in the room as the two police officers silently communicated their relief – the formidable Mrs Papplewick was no longer their responsibility.

The four of them walked towards the station exit in silence before Augusta turned, looked pointedly at Inspector Hargreaves and said, quite matter-of-factly, 'Of course, you know that Minerva Leek was responsible for it, don't you?'

You could have heard a pin drop in the quiet that followed, and not for the first time that morning, Daphne wondered how on earth she had found herself playing carer to Augusta.

When Daphne had been about to knock on the front door

of Wellingborough House earlier that morning, in a second attempt to deliver the book, she had not been prepared to stumble across the sight of Augusta in her nightgown alongside PC Maxine Clarke. The officer had just delivered the shocking news that a person fitting the description of Charles Papplewick had been found dead among the allotment cabbages at approximately 7.30 a.m. that morning.

The front door to Wellingborough House had been slightly ajar as Daphne approached. As she had raised her hand to knock, in a moment that almost mirrored the night before, it had swung open. She had been intent on delivering the book directly into Augusta's hands this time. Whatever had taken place the day before was none of Daphne's business – she was erasing it from her mind and focusing on the task in hand.

'I'm so sorry – I was just delivering a book ...' Her words had trailed off as she saw the strangely solemn look on both women's faces. 'Er – I'll leave it for another time – I didn't mean to intrude.' She was half turning in retreat when Augusta had said, 'No – please stay, Daphne.'

Daphne had turned back in surprise and looked enquiringly at the police officer.

'Are you a friend? It might be best if you stay,' PC Clarke had said almost pleadingly, with her eyes as well as with the tone of her voice. Clearly neither of them wanted to be left alone with the other. 'I'm afraid that she's had some bad news ...'

A few minutes later, Augusta had retreated upstairs to change into more suitable attire to accompany the policewoman first to the mortuary to identify the body, and then to the police station to make a quick statement. It was a

Saturday morning and James was at home with the children, so Daphne had been designated involuntary 'babysitter', at Augusta's request, and would wait outside the station to drive her back home again. At first, she had gently protested that surely there was someone closer who would make the whole ordeal more bearable, but Augusta had said that there wasn't. Daphne hadn't argued again. Augusta may not have been a particularly warm individual, but she was at least democratic in her coldness and Daphne had never felt singled out. Staying with her in her hour of need was the least she could do – wasn't that what village life was all about?

Poor Augusta, it must have been such a shock to have been woken up to find her husband gone and the police knocking on the door.

'I can't believe that he's dead!' Daphne had exclaimed in quiet shock. 'He seemed absolutely fine ... oh, I ...'

She had been about to reference her presence the previous night and belatedly thought better of it. Her eyes had suddenly filled with tears. She hadn't known Charles Papplewick for long, but if one could forget the events of the day before, in the short time that she had known him he had always been kind and welcoming and extremely pleasant. In fact, meeting with the headmaster had been the reason behind the decision to send the children to school at Pepperbridge Primary, rather than the bigger school in the local town.

In a poor attempt to shield her sudden tears, Daphne had walked towards the back door while PC Clarke diplomatically pretended to look elsewhere. The idea of a person being present one day and then gone the next was still quite unfathomable to Daphne. After more than forty years of living in the UK, her own parents now lived abroad on the tiny Caribbean island of Grenada and the fear that one of them would succumb to ill health was ever present. She was stood next to the coat rack in the boot room, looking towards the back door and staring out through the four square panes and into the drizzle. The rain had been non-stop for the past twenty-four hours. An aptly sombre backdrop for such unexpectedly sad news. It had taken her a few moments to realise that the arm of her jumper had become soaked after absent-mindedly leaning against the coats. 'Damn,' she'd muttered, broken out of her thoughts. The coat hanging up was absolutely sodden and even the inner lining looked wet, as if it had just come in from the rain. In fact, it was still dripping and forming a murky puddle on the floor – which, Daphne noted, was thankfully flagstones and not carpet.

She'd bent down to push aside the short pink wellies that were soaking up the larger drips in their fleecy lining. No one wanted sodden inner boots, after all. They too were slick with rain and covered in freshly gathered mud and ripped grass which she could see had recently left moist footprints from the back door.

'I'm making more of a mess than helping,' Daphne had muttered to herself in frustration, deciding to leave it all well alone.

Just then Augusta had called out, 'I'm ready – shall we go?'

Daphne had returned to the kitchen, where PC Clarke and Augusta were about to exit into the hallway. Augusta had still seemed strangely subdued and calm. No sobbing, no crying – in fact no tears at all. She had rolled her hair into a neat chignon and had put some make-up on, including a delicate slick of pink frosted lipstick and a bit of blusher. Now neat as a pin, dressed in a matching twinset and form-fitting slacks, she had pulled on the tartan mohair coat that she was holding in her hands, helped by Maxine who was evidently feeling relieved to have something to do.

'You might want to wear something a bit more waterproof than that or at least you'd better bring an umbrella – it's been raining non-stop and it's due to last all day, I'm afraid,' Maxine had said kindly – her arm hovering over Augusta's shoulders, unsure as to whether her attempt at comfort would be welcomed.

'Oh, is it raining . . . ?' Augusta had replied, dodging Maxine's touch as she bent to grab an umbrella from the stand and walked through the front door. 'I haven't left the house since yesterday afternoon, so I'd hardly noticed.'

'If you could drop me at the back door when we arrive at the house please,' said Augusta now, tearing Daphne away from her surreal thoughts of earlier that morning. 'I'd rather not bump into anyone if possible.'

They had sat in silence for the entire journey to Pepperbridge. Daphne was still half confused, half seething with anger at Augusta's entirely unsubstantiated accusation about Minerva, and had felt it better not to say a word. After all, the woman was surely just in a state of shock at losing her husband . . . Or did she know something about the – what on earth was it? – the 'relationship' between Charles and Minerva? Was that the reason behind the slap?

'Of course,' Daphne replied as she continued driving,

indicated right and took the turn along the alley that led to the back of the house. The narrow passage had a Dickensian feel, with Victorian gas lamps that, despite having been converted to electricity during the last century, still had an air of yellow low light that cast an eerie rather than a particularly useful glow at night.

As Daphne drew up to the kerb at the back of Wellingborough House, she kept the engine running. She felt sympathy for Augusta and in any other circumstance would have offered to come in to comfort her and get her settled, but not after this. Not after making such a wild accusation about her new friend. Even the two police officers had been unable to respond for a few shocked moments after Augusta's dramatic statement. Inspector Hargreaves, whose biggest case to date thus far had involved a tip-off about a cannabis farm operation in nearby Billington – which had turned out to be sixteen-year-old Connor Matthews utilising his grandfather's greenhouse – was so unsure of what to do with the information that he'd decided simply to send Augusta home with a mumbled promise to look into it, subject to the coroner's findings.

Augusta unclicked her seatbelt, thanked Daphne politely and walked around the front of the car to towards her back gate. The rain had finally stopped. Just before she left the pavement, she turned back and lent down towards the driver's window before Daphne had a chance to pull off again. Daphne reluctantly but obligingly rolled down the window.

'She's not what she seems, you know – your friend. She's a grasping and grubby little witch,' said Augusta, a scowl on her face.

Daphne remained silent for a moment as she watched Augusta turn back towards the gate. She felt conflicted about what she'd seen the day before at the party, but she also knew that Minerva wouldn't harm a fly.

'I'm so sorry for your loss Augusta. Truly I am,' she called out from the car '... and do be careful with the puddles on your path, it's muddy and you might slip – perhaps you ought to have worn your pink wellies again.'

She wasn't quite sure why she had said it, and she didn't know why it seemed significant, but there had been something niggling in the back of her mind all morning. Something about Augusta claiming to not have left the house. She pulled off from the kerb, but not before she had seen Augusta's back stiffen in surprise – a second before she had closed her back door with a thud.

Daphne pulled into her own drive just a few minutes later, just in time to see Doctor Ptolemy Oates, returning from an apparent trip to the Pudding Corner garage shop during the break in the rain. He waited for her to pass and waved as she slowly crawled the car onto the gravel drive and up towards the garage. She wasn't really in the mood to talk to anyone else but James after her unexpected morning, and she hoped that the ever-jovial doctor would have continued along to his own house by the time she had walked back to close the gate. However, just as she'd sensed he might be, her neighbour was still standing at the gate, smiling cheerily as she approached.

'I was hoping that I might see you today,' he began. 'They accidentally gave me your Saturday paper at the shop, and I thought that I'd drop it in rather than leave ...' He paused, suddenly, concerned as he saw the sad and exhausted expression on her face. 'Oh dear, Daphne – is everything tickety-boo?'

'No. No, I'm afraid it isn't, Doctor Oates. It isn't at all,' replied Daphne. 'Charles Papplewick was found dead of a suspected heart attack this morning and I've just been with Augusta. I was there when she found out and to be honest, it's all a been a bit of a shock.' She realised that she was babbling, and suddenly she could feel a hot prickle of tears forming behind her eyes. She really did feel completely exhausted. Emotionally wrung out, in fact.

'Oh, my word – that's a terrible business!' he said, his eyes rounding. 'How is Mrs Papplewick? What a shock for her indeed.' He had placed a consoling hand on Daphne's shoulder and was fishing for a handkerchief with the other, which he duly found and handed to her. It was clean and pressed and smelled of lavender. 'Would you like to come over to mine for a cup of tea before heading in to see the children? You can tell me all about it,' he said with an understanding tone.

Daphne considered whether it would be wise to compose herself before seeing the children whom she had left to finish eating their breakfast cereal while James had a lie in at least four hours ago. How were you supposed to tell children that their headmaster had passed away so suddenly? Should she tell them straight away? How did one navigate a situation like this?

She was about to take him up on the offer – the past two days had taken their toll and she really just wanted to be comforted with tea and cake – but then she heard the crunch of fast-approaching footsteps along the gravel from her house.

'Mummy, Mummy – where have you been?' Archie looked up at her, eyes wide and inquisitive.

There was no time for reflection or sadness, it was time once again to be 'Mummy'.

She turned to Doctor Oates and regretfully said, 'Too late – but thank you. You're very kind to offer.'

And with that, she turned towards her children and James, who was following behind with a concerned expression.

Chapter 7

Things in the English countryside did not move fast, and it seemed that things in the sleepy parish of Pepperidge and the surrounding villages moved even slower still. As there had been no obvious cause of death by illness registered by his doctor, a hospital or otherwise, the body of Charles Papplewick would need to undergo a statutory autopsy. The coroner's office only performed autopsies on a Friday, but both senior coroner Janice Clancy and the area coroner Yvonne Clapton had requested annual leave during the same week, which was currently causing chaos. As Charles's body had been discovered on a Saturday morning, there was no chance of exploring Augusta's unsubstantiated slurs against Minerva (which she had noted vocally to all who passed by to pay their respects) for at least another week . . . Neither was there any particular sense of urgency from the powers that be that the body would require anything as un-Pepperbridge as a potential crime-related forensic post-mortem.

Within the parish it was widely accepted among those who had heard the news that there was little or no plausibility in any accusation of foul play. Despite the fact that Charles had seemed fit and healthy, and that to the casual observer he could have passed for a man at least a decade younger, he was also a man approaching retirement age, and it was therefore not unlikely that, unbeknown to himself, he may have had something nasty and undiagnosed lurking in the background.

It's not that the villagers were unsympathetic to the possibility of Augusta's claims, more that nothing 'really bad' ever happened in Pepperbridge, and a death result-ing from suspicious circumstances was as unlikely as the local vicar admitting to having had a passionate affair with Veronica Tamworth – the artist, potter, life model and self-proclaimed 'raging atheist' who lived on the corner of School Lane. (Although the Warburton sisters had their own suspicions, knowing what they knew about Reverend Duncan and his secret aptitude for penning surprisingly 'indelicate' anonymous prose.) Besides, everyone appeared to have a first-hand anecdote about a relative or neighbour who had seemed healthy one day and then dropped down dead the next. It was a regrettably tragic yet common symptom of the rigours of modern life – one only had to listen in on church yard conversations after Sunday service or better still, to read the *Daily Mail*, to know so. Forget the mean streets of London, where there could be 'a fatal mugging around every corner', to display rude health in the vicinity of villages like Pepperbridge after the age of fifty was to unwittingly gamble with a mischievous grim reaper waiting to pounce.

The truth was that the people of the parish did not want to take Augusta's claims seriously – although they weren't brave enough to say so to her face. There were a few members of the school council who sycophantically acted as Augusta's unofficial henchwomen. Tending to her every need, bringing forth Royal Albert 'Old Country Roses' teacups filled (regrettably, for Augusta) with sweet tea, and nodding in agreement at her every barbed utterance. When local residents made the obligatory visit to pass on their condolences and to proffer flowers, cake – or in some cases, a tad less diplomatically, boxes of vegetables gathered from the very same allotments where Charles had met his unexpected fate – they would stand awkwardly, nodding mutely while the newly widowed woman embellished her unproven suspicions for dramatic effect. Most of them would stand shuffling and wide-eyed like rabbits stuck in headlights, desperately trying to find their excuses to leave quickly. The all-too-recent allure of finally being invited into Wellingborough House – the Papplewicks' heraldic domain which, until now, had been a rarely accessed and much coveted social prize, was fading sharply and quickly with the headmaster's passing. Augusta's tyrannical power may have been fast diminishing, but its long-held impact was still far reaching enough to dampen any rebellious dissidence.

Augusta had held a certain status in the community as the wife of the highly respected Charles for over thirty years, but even though his absence had been just a matter of days, the

long-held grip of her vicarious authority appeared to be loos-
ening rapidly. Just like the henchwomen, none of the visitors
were brave enough to challenge Augusta's claims to her face
or make any attempt at a more balanced discussion surrounding the events of Friday night or Saturday morning. As far as
Augusta was concerned, Charles's death had been caused by
Minerva – and not as the result of a heart attack – although
she refused to give a motive behind her reasoning and sat
tight-lipped and angry eyed if the question even appeared to
draw near. Equally, in the rare moments that anyone deigned
it polite to converse beyond saying how sorry they were, they
would be met with a sudden cold silence, left to sweat and
twitch under her unflinching Medusa gaze.

The news had spread thick and fast on the Monday after
Charles's discovery. Daphne had wrestled with her conscience
immediately after leaving Augusta's on Saturday afternoon.
Her first instinct was to tell Minerva what had happened, but
she hadn't wanted to broach the subject of what she had seen
in the woods, and wouldn't Minerva wonder why Daphne had
thought to tell her so quickly and specifically? On top of that,
there was the topic of Augusta's accusations about Minerva
and Daphne wasn't sure that she wanted to nominate herself
to reveal that particular nugget of information. It had the
ingredients to be quite the messy web of lies and deceit, and
as a relative newcomer, Daphne wasn't sure what her place
should be in it all.

Even James had suggested that she keep her thoughts to
herself – at least for a while.

'After all, we are the newcomers here. These people,

whether they are friends with each other or not, have all known each other for years, and whatever has been going on, it would all still be taking place whether or not you were here to observe it!'

He was right of course; who was she to interfere? But try as she might, Daphne still couldn't get the surprise embrace between Minerva and Charles out of her head. When Daphne thought long and hard about it, she knew that Augusta's claims may well have something to do with a possible 'relationship' between her late husband and Minerva after all, and Daphne certainly didn't want to get entangled in that. Yet, at the same time, their body language in the woods had indicated that there was a genuine affection between Minerva and Charles, and if they had indeed been having an affair, then didn't Minerva deserve to know that her 'special friend' – Daphne couldn't bring herself to say the words that might best describe their unlikely pairing – was dead?

In the end, Daphne decided to wait and see Minerva at the school gates on Monday morning. Her plan was to loiter far longer than normal after the school bell had sounded, ready to lend a shoulder to cry on if necessary. She knew that she was running the risk of bumping into Marianne, whom she hoped would at least have the decency to quell her spiteful tongue under the present circumstances – although she feared that was unlikely.

The weather over the next couple of days seemed to mirror the tumultuous feelings hovering around Daphne's mind, veering from rain and wind one moment to warm and humid sunshine the next. The school gates were quiet and subdued, and she never seemed to spot Minerva or Silvanus, thus dashing her hopes for an innocuously spontaneous reunion.

There was a sense of reserved quiet around the local villages. Losing such a prominent member of the community had been quite a shock. The police had already been in contact with the school governors, who had in turn had informed the teachers and staff at the small village school. They had been offered the opportunity to close the school for the day as a sign of respect for their much-loved headmaster, but they had mutually agreed to keep the school open with a reduced timetable so that the children could have time to come to terms with what, in many cases, may have been their first direct contact with death – an especially shocking one too, as Mr Papplewick had appeared to be in full fettle during the assembly on the day he died.

The impact of Charles Papplewick's loss on the community was huge, and so it was naturally assumed that it must have been an unimaginable blow for his widow. No one would have been surprised if Augusta had laid low for a few weeks – it was a tragic loss after such a long marriage, after all. However, having sensed that losing her husband potentially meant losing her hold on village affairs, Augusta had deemed it necessary to ensure that she was as impeccably dressed as ever, and above all, ready and present at the school gates. In addition to the necessary optics of being the village matriarch, it didn't do any harm for her to be there to receive the embarrassed condolences from those who had avoided doing so in person at her home. She had taken a note of those who had sent cards or flowers and how soon after the events, placing them on the rung beneath those who had delivered tokens of their sympathy. On the very last rung of the ladder were those who realised that their avoidance of visiting the formidable Mrs Papplewick would backfire within forty-eight hours, as she stared them squarely in the face and made sure to enquire pointedly how *they* were a millisecond before they could stutter out their belated condolences.

She also wanted to keep an eye out for Minerva. They may have stopped burning witches and cuffing harlots into the stocks on Pepperidge Village Green several centuries ago, but the ritual of trial by gossip had steadfastly remained, and Augusta wanted to make sure that she was there to fan the stake flames if and when Minerva Leek dared to show her face.

By Wednesday morning, with still no sign of Minerva and Silvanus (or indeed Marianne, for that matter), Daphne decided to bite the bullet and drive over to where Minerva lived. It felt like a lifetime ago that she had been at Silvanus's sweet birthday party, and she had even started to question whether she really had seen an intimate tryst between Minerva and Charles Papplewick.

Pulling up at the cottage, Daphne noted that there were tendrils of smoke twisting from the gamekeeper's cottage's crooked chimney – a sure indication that someone was using the woodfired stove in Minerva's little kitchen.

Walking up the grass-tufted cobbled pathway towards the front door, Daphne wondered what she should say. In fact, she now wondered why she was even there. Their fledgling friendship was still in its early stages and she suddenly felt rather silly. She had only been a member of this community for six months, while Minerva had apparently lived here all her life. If, as Daphne suspected, Minerva was still in the dark about Charles's death, who on earth was Daphne to be knocking on her door and bestowing the bad news about someone that Minerva clearly knew far better than Daphne? And yet there was something so vulnerable and innocent about Minerva – despite them both being round about the same age. Minerva seemed like someone who needed protecting, and Daphne was – she smiled wryly to herself remembering the time she confronted a group of rowdy teenagers on a south London bus – going through her crusader phase . . .

In the end, she needn't have feared. The door was yanked open and a tear-stained and red-faced Minerva appeared merely a foot away from Daphne. She looked dreadful. Unkempt and wild, distraught and tearful, with dark puffy shadows creating heavy bags under her red rimmed eyes. For a split second, the two women stood staring at each other, before Minerva let out what could only be described as a gut-wrenching moan and collapsed, crying into Daphne's now open arms.

'There, there . . . It's all going to be OK – I promise.' Daphne didn't quite know what she was promising, but she simply held Minerva's convulsing head on her tear-soaked shoulder.

It had taken quite a while for Daphne to get to the bottom of Augusta's claims. Without her husband's cloak of protection, it really wasn't Augusta's place to be sweeping through the school corridors and entering the headmaster's office at will – but few were willing to confront her. The official line was that she was deep in the throes of mourning, and as such, she ought to be allowed to spend time in the office where her husband had spent so much of *his* time. There would be personal items and mementos to clear out before the end of term, and before thoughts of introducing the new headmaster would be discussed. That was the 'official' line. The truth was that no amount of mourning had dulled Augusta's ramrod-straight back, her arrogant sense of entitlement, or the sharp delivery of her cutting tongue. Therefore there was no one brave (or stupid) enough to deny her entry.

Daphne had heard via the school gates that Augusta's primary accusation was that Minerva and her clan of 'Wiccan harpies' had been blackmailing Charles for several months, leading to his eventual poisoning. It was a wildly eccentric notion, and what they might have been blackmailing him about, no one seemed to know. How they had come to poison him was lesser known still. The facts were comically thin on the ground, the motive completely unsubstantiated and the entire idea wildly fantastical, but that hadn't stopped more than a few eyes looking out for Silvanus and his mother to arrive at school over the past few days.

Daphne immediately felt guilty for not having visited her friend sooner. Minerva's reaction to seeing her had been instantaneous and emotional, and truth be told it had caught Daphne off guard. True, she was growing fond of Minerva – hence her presence at her front door now – but she had also assumed that after the initial delay in reaching her, there might also be other, closer friends or family members who would have been shielding her from the vicious tremors of village gossip. What about the other women in the enclave of Cringlewic Woods? Daphne hadn't seen any of them at Silvanus's party.

Daphne ushered the runny-nosed and red-faced Minerva into the tiny kitchen, made her sit down on a crooked farmhouse chair covered in chipped yellow paint, and checked if there was a pot of boiling water on the stove – another ancient range that seemed to feature in all country kitchens regardless of how big or small, this time a small Rayburn – so that she could make a cup of strong tea. One thing Daphne had realised about country life is that a cup of hot, strong tea proffered in an old-fashioned farmhouse kitchen seemed to be everyone's initial answer to most situations – that or a strong G&T, depending on the time of day.

Daphne knew how Minerva liked her tea without needing to ask. The familiarity of that realisation cheered Daphne somewhat as she handed the drink to Minerva in her favourite mug – another thing that she had noted. She had already stirred in the required one-and-a-half sugars and the small dash of semi-skimmed milk, and Minerva had accepted it gratefully. The two women sat in companiable silence for a while, until Minerva had gathered herself together enough to stop the half sobbing, half gulping and was breathing at a normal rate. Daphne looked around for evidence of Silvanus's presence before beginning to speak, meeting Minerva's eyes as her friend nodded silently towards the little boy's bedroom, indicating that he was out of earshot enough for them to talk discreetly.

'I guess that you've heard the news then ...?' Daphne asked tentatively.

'Yes.' Minerva's response was barely audible, yet wracked

with such sadness and thick with such emotion that the single
word seemed to transmit a thousand thoughts.

'I'm so ... sorry.' Daphne was at a loss for what to say. It
was clear that Minerva was hurting, but Daphne didn't want
to pry into the relationship between Charles Papplewick and
her friend until she was ready to reveal it herself.

'What are they saying?' Minerva eventually asked, cutting
through the silence that had fallen once more.

Daphne knew that Minerva was asking what was being
said at the school gates. She was a woman who had tried so
desperately not to stand out for the sake of her young son, and
now her name appeared to be on the tip of everyone's tongue.

'Well ...' Daphne began, 'there's just a lot of silly nonsense
that Augusta is spouting. She's clearly still in shock and of
course, no one is taking it seriously.' *How many ways could
one skirt a topic?* Daphne wondered. She couldn't quite bring
herself to articulate what Augusta had been saying, but judging from Minerva's reaction, she seemed to have a pretty good
idea that whatever was being said was negative enough to
keep herself hidden away from the peering eyes and wagging
tongues of Pepperbridge.

'I didn't do anything, you know,' she said sadly, not looking
directly at Daphne and instead sipping her tea as a means of
distraction.

She bent her head down and sighed with such sadness that
Daphne believed Minerva's heart to be broken. *She really must
have loved him*, she thought to herself.

'I ... that is he, he was ...' Minerva's voice trailed off into
silence again, and then suddenly, almost as though a mask
had slid over her face, she sat up straight and looked Daphne

directly in the eyes for the first time since she'd arrived. Her voice now sounded far more measured than her bewildered hesitance of the previous half hour. 'He . . . was a nice man. A kind man and a good headmaster . . . but, I, I hardly knew him really. In fact, the last time I saw him was in the school playground last Thursday, with you . . .' She faltered, and her eyes flickered around the room, suddenly unable to settle on a single point. Minerva continued with what sounded like a rehearsed conversation. 'Why would she lie about me to everyone like that? Why would she say I had anything to do with his death? I hardly knew him.'

Daphne sat stock still. She hadn't been expecting that. She had quite clearly seen Charles and Minerva embracing in the forest during Silvanus's tea party on Friday evening. Why would Minerva lie to her – and what was she concealing? There were so many questions, but Daphne sensed that now was not the time to ask them. Whatever relationship they'd had was Minerva's business, and Minerva's business alone . . . As she watched Minerva start to cry all over again, Daphne hoped with all of her heart that it wasn't also police business.

On the other side of the parish, there was another school mother sitting wide eyed, nervously peeking through the drawing room window that overlooked her front drive. Throughout the chaos of the weekend and the subsequent gossip, most people (aside from Daphne) hadn't particularly noticed that there was another set of absentee children and parents at the school gates.

Marianne Forbes sat biting her lip and staring through the distorted glass of her twelve-pane Georgian sash windows, onto the brick path that led to her front door. The unseasonably wet weather looked as gloomy and grey as her mood. Her eyes were uncharacteristically moist with tears and her fidgeting hands had wrung themselves raw.

'But what if someone saw us . . . ?' she uttered with strained despair, not once taking her eyes from the glass.

From behind her, her husband responded with barely contained impatience and a distinct lack of sympathy. His eyebrow raised at his wife's use of the word 'us'.

'Well if they did see *you*, we'll just have to deal with it when we need to, won't we?' he answered scathingly.

Chapter 8

There were few things that Marianne Forbes didn't like about herself, but her inability to contain her anger and frustration at the unfortunate hand fate had dealt her was definitely one of them. It was a rare occurrence, but sometimes – in the face of a perceived threat to her relentless quest for social progress – she just saw red and blew a gasket. When that happened, all thoughts of being a 'lady', and feeling superior to the residents of Pudding Corner, were thrown out of the window with her elocution-lesson-mastered RP vowels.

Last Friday morning had been one of those rare moments when she had completely lost all rational thought and words had simply come tumbling crudely out of her mouth. Not just words, she was embarrassed to say, but a few vicious threats, several rather fruity profanities and – horror of horrors – a slap ... Not that Charles Papplewick hadn't deserved it, with his poker-straight face, calmly refusing to budge an inch on his decision. That had been bad enough, but from the very beginning of the heated exchange, she had sensed that the headmaster's concentration hadn't even been fully engaged in the conversation. If there was one thing worse than being refused her demands, it was to be ignored.

The morning had started off well enough. Marianne had just left a group of parents chatting in the school playground, having dropped a few major hints that Silvanus Leek's party, which was due to take place later that evening, was one that 'no responsible parent or upstanding member of the Pepperbridge community would allow their child to attend. Of course, it's a safety issue you understand – nothing personal towards travellers ...' There had followed an awkward silence where the mothers who had indeed intended to take advantage of a birthday tea which would absolve them from cooking when they got home, weighed up the repercussions of non-compliance on either side.

Despite missing the irony that Minerva Leek had lived in the parish for her entire life – which was thirty-six years more than she herself had – Marianne nevertheless felt satisfied that she'd taken control of a minor opportunity for social mutiny among her minions. One had to keep on top of the social ranking, even in a village playground filled with Boden mums. She had looked around for Daphne, to see whether she too could be 'encouraged' to boycott the tea party – although judging by the budding friendship that seemed to be sprouting up between her and Minerva, she doubted her chances. It was a strange choice of friend really; what possible gain was there for Daphne to become friends with the likes of Minerva? Life was all about 'sides' and it paid to choose the correct one. Was it an 'outsider' thing? Perhaps poor Daphne hadn't yet realised that there was a social cachet to having a Black friend these days – especially a well-spoken one up from London, and as such, Marianne was more than willing to keep her among her group.

Regardless, Marianne had been a woman on a mission that morning, and she'd slipped away from the group of mothers and swept into the school reception, demanding to see Charles Papplewick. The end of term was looming, which meant that another year would be wasted. She had already passed the deadline for September entry, but she was willing to try anything to get her child into the best school around – even if it meant tearing her darling Giles prematurely away from his new friends at Pepperbridge High and disrupting his academic year by starting him afresh for a second time the following January.

The school receptionist had asked whether she had already made an appointment directly with the headmaster's secretary, Mrs Musgrave.

'You do need one, you know. You can't just pop in whenever you feel like it or everyone would be doing it!' Her disapproving tone had made it clear that she wasn't a big fan of the pushy parent with the supercilious attitude standing in front of her.

Marianne's eyes had narrowed as she peered at the receptionist, who stared back smugly and unflinchingly at her. Neither woman liked the other and they were both fully aware of it. Unfortunately for Marianne, the woman behind the reception desk appeared to hold all the cards. The 'stand-off' was broken when a phone from inside the office began to ring.

Raising an eyebrow, the receptionist said curtly, 'If you'll excuse me, I have to answer that, but I will pass on your request to the headmaster ... when he's available.'

It was a clear dismissal followed by a fake smile to indicate that the conversation was over.

Marianne had slowly turned on her heels towards the exit. It was only when she had dashed past reception and darted quickly into the school corridor, out of sight, that she lifted the mobile phone from the pocket of her waxed Barbour jacket. She smiled to herself as she saw the words 'School Office' at the top of her recent calls list. With the receptionist momentarily occupied, Marianne headed determinedly towards Mr Papplewick's office. She'd hesitated only for a moment, leaning her ear against the door to make sure that he was alone before she confronted him. God forbid his awful wife was in there with him. Even Marianne reluctantly had to admit to herself that she was no match for Augusta Papplewick. Augusta had ruled the roost in Pepperbridge for almost as many years as Marianne had been alive. In some ways Marianne almost admired her ...

With her ear up against the door, she had heard silence at first, and then a soft response from Mr Papplewick. He must have been on the phone.

'It's all right my darling, it will all be fine,' she had heard him say. 'I'm telling her tonight. She needs to know, and I can't live a lie any longer. I only wish that it hadn't taken this long. Just remember that I love you and please stop worrying.'

The old goat! Marianne had been thrilled that she would catch him off guard in the midst of some sort of deviant behaviour. At best this might have been a piece of information that she could use as ammunition, and at least it might crumble his reserve in the next few minutes. She'd turned the handle and marched in – ready to fight by using any means necessary.

She couldn't have imagined that just a few minutes later, her own far more raucous conversation would be similarly overheard by a shocked and decidedly less invested Daphne Brewster.

When Marianne had stormed out of Charles Papplewick's office, she was furious. The conversation hadn't gone as well as she'd hoped. In fact, it was safe to say that it had been a disaster. A one-sided argument that had reduced Marianne to a screaming and caterwauling harridan. No amount of cajoling, threatening and eventual attempts at blackmailing had made him budge. He did not feel that the eldest of the Forbes children was the right choice of pupil for the highly rigid and academic St Jude's. He could not stop them from sending their child there if they had the financial means to do so, but he could not in all conscience write a recommendation that would mean lying about the boy's academic prowess. If that was all Mrs Forbes had to say, then the matter was, regrettably, now closed.

That had been when Marianne had decided to use the ace up her sleeve that she had accidentally stumbled across.

'I'm warning you just one last time ...' she had roared, 'just pick up the bloody phone or write the damn letter and I'll be out of your hair for ever, because so help me God, if you don't do something to get my child into that school then I promise that you'll be sorry!' She had thumped her hand on the headmaster's desk, ostensibly to emphasise her anger but mainly because if she didn't hit something inanimate in the immediate vicinity, then Charles Papplewick's face – the true intended target – would surely be next in line. A framed wedding photograph featuring a smiling young Augusta and a rather more strained and serious-looking Charles had toppled onto the floor upon impact, shattering its glass into hundreds of pieces.

The crash had made Marianne laugh maniacally. The fear of being stuck in this restrictive world of insincere politeness and forced manners incensed her. Oh, the irony of the smashed wedding photo of this holier-than-though philanderer and his frigid little stuck-up wife.

'You think that this poxy little nothing of a school is where I want my children to be? You think that THIS is what I want them to be defined by? You are a NOBODY, Mr Papplewick, and this school is NOTHING. It means NOTHING to me. It matters to NO ONE. How DARE you tie us up in this godforsaken nowhere of a so-called education system with no way out? We are BETTER than this, so sign the letter or so help me I'll—'

She vaguely remembered being shocked at how calm he had been when he eventually spoke.

'You will what, Mrs Forbes?'

Marianne had desperately tried to put two and two together, coming up with five, six and even twelve – whatever it took to take down this monster in charge of her child's future. She quickly calculated that surely it must have been a mistress he was speaking to – perhaps someone she knew, a teacher perhaps? Someone in the village? What if it had been a parent – wasn't that illegal? Yes, it must be a parent for him to mention consequences and risk. That was it. She had him!

'I'll make you rue the day you met me, Charles Papplewick. When I'm finished, I'll have you struck off the teacher's register. I'll make you regret the day you were born.' Her voice had been thick with furious triumph, and yet Charles Papplewick had still looked unperturbed as he stared back at her.

'I think that you should stop right there Mrs Forbes – don't you?' he had said with a patronising sigh, nodding his head towards the door and indicating that now would be a good time for her to leave.

That was when Marianne had leaned over and, without thinking, given him the hardest, most unrestrained slap across his face that she could muster. She had even shocked herself with its force, and they had stared at each other in startled silence for a few moments. Enough time for Marianne to see the imprint of her fingers appearing red and raw on Charles's left cheek, and to realise that, even then, he hadn't flinched.

'Good day, Mrs Forbes,' he had said finally, and with that Marianne had turned slightly wobblingly on her feet and exited the room.

She had had to steady herself against a wall immediately after she'd left the office. Hearing voices and feet coming en masse from just around the corner, she had ducked through a door that read 'Toilet', only to find herself inside a set of children's loos where the cubicles reached just above her shoulders. Nowhere to hide or catch her breath. Nowhere to collect herself together and think about what to do next. After a few minutes, she'd heard the bell ring for first assembly. Registration was obviously over, and the children would all now be meandering towards the main hall for the last assembly of the week. She had given it five more minutes for good measure and then the voices had grown increasingly fainter. The corridor was deserted and empty, and Marianne slipped out as quietly as she had slipped in. Her resolve may have dented slightly, but her rage was still bubbling beneath the surface.

That ought to have been the end of it. The Marianne that now stood staring anxiously out of her drawing room window desperately wished that she had simply accepted defeat and resigned herself to the fact that her three beautiful children would be attending the local high school after all. But the Marianne of last Friday was still smarting with the indignity of it all, and she hadn't left it there at all. What was worse was the fact that she knew that her privately educated husband didn't seem to care either way.

No, the Marianne of last Friday was still boiling over with bile and spite. She would continue to sort this mess out herself, and she had a hunch that the answer lay in whatever it was that Charles Papplewick was up to outside the boundaries of his marriage vows.

Daphne sat back in the battered leather driver's seat of her Morris Traveller, having just driven from Minerva's house in the woods. The discussion – if one could call it that, had come to a close when Silvanus entered the room looking solemn and concerned for his teary-eyed mother. Daphne felt dreadfully sorry for the little boy. She was acutely aware that children picked up on all sorts of things, whether a parent wanted them to or not, and Minerva wasn't making a very good show of concealing her despair. Silvanus had asked if the school was open yet, and Daphne realised – catching Minerva's startled eyes turn quickly towards her – that her friend had lied about why he hadn't been able to attend school so far that week. Daphne, not wanting to be caught up in another lie – particularly where a child was concerned – made her excuses and left, but not before promising that she would bring her own children to play with Silvanus very soon.

She had given Minerva a reassuring hug at the door, reminding her friend that she was there for her, and that she could tell her anything, with no judgement forthcoming. Minerva had smiled sadly but had not imparted any more information before slowly closing the door, and that was that.

Now, pulled up on a grass verge a few minutes down the lane that led out of Cringlewic Woods, Daphne was taking a few minutes to think over the conversation that had just occurred. The woods were as dark, enclosed and dense as they had been on the evening of Silvanus's birthday. The evening that Daphne had seen Minerva and Charles Papplewick with her own eyes. Not only had she caught Minerva in a lie about the last time that she had seen the headmaster alive, but she was also concealing the fact that they knew each other rather well indeed. Daphne could well understand that Minerva would want to hide a potential affair, but now was not the time to be lying about when you last saw the deceased person that you're accused of poisoning, regardless of how outrageous, unfounded, and lacking in any such evidence of wrongdoing in the first place.

Daphne sighed and turned the engine back on to continue her journey home. All she could do was be there for Minerva if and when she needed her. As most of the rational residents of Pepperbridge parish presumed, the coroner's report would in all likelihood state that Charles Papplewick had died of a sudden heart attack or a stroke, and that would be the end of the ridiculous speculation. Then Minerva could get on with mourning the loss of ... whatever it was that Charles Papplewick had been to her.

It was barely lunchtime by the time she drove back past the gates of Pepperbridge Primary School and towards the little unit on the high street that she had so recently claimed as her own. 'The Country Mouse' – named after her feeling of being a city mouse transformed into a country one – was going to be a shop split into two parts: a front section where she would display her painted and restored vintage furniture, decorative antiques and vintage linens, and a back section that would be the workshop where she intended to do her restoration, wood sanding, fixing and painting. There was also a handy storeroom, a small toilet and a galley kitchen. Out back there was a convenient parking space for Aggie and a place where she could display her vintage garden items and pots.

All in all, the set-up was rather perfect, and such a result for a woman who a few months earlier had had no idea about what direction her career would take now that she had extracted herself from London and was ensconced into village life. It felt frustrating that, within the rush of excitement she got every time she had driven past the small shop over the past few days, there were now also tendrils of anxiety surrounding the death of the headmaster and the connection that he may or may not have had with her new friend. Life had an odd way of keeping balance, she thought, as she turned the key in the lock to the shopfront door. Excitement often tempered by anxiety; happiness slightly dulled by loss.

Moving from the stress that they had felt in London to the comparatively calm countryside had had its challenges, but it was definitely the best decision that they'd ever made. A move such as this inevitably came with stresses and worries of its own, including negotiating one's way through new attachments, and accidentally stumbling across new people to care for and worry over. Daphne's heart was a big one and she also had an inbuilt need to right petty injustices – even those, according to her husband, that shouldn't concern her – and especially those where people didn't have the strength or ability to stand up for themselves. She hadn't changed as a person just because she happened to change her postcode, after all.

The storefront being just a little way down the road from the grocery shop belonging to the Warburton sisters was a fact that had initially concerned her. But having got into the habit of popping in for a few basic sundries when absolutely necessary (at incredibly random and often inflated prices) she had slowly come to appreciate the novelty of having the two eccentric and slyly humorous sisters nearby. The elder of the two, Nancy Warburton, would usually be at the helm of the store, peering over her glasses and standing silently behind the old-fashioned countertop. To the untrained eye, she looked harmless enough, but Daphne had no doubt that

Nancy was as sharp as a pin. She reminded Daphne of the West Indian aunts at church during her childhood, who would start their conversations with over-enthusiastic compliments, only to end the discussion with a sharp and sudden sting of criticism that had obviously formed the entire purpose of the conversation.

Daphne had witnessed such 'stings' on several occasions at the Warburton sister's shop, as unwitting 'victims' would attempt to engage in friendly conversation. The most toe-curling scenarios would usually begin in a patronising fashion towards the 'ladies' as the shopper complimented the 'fresh produce' displayed alongside the eclectic variety of Mr Kipling cakes, McVitie's biscuits, basic bleach, wrapping paper that must have dated from 1972 and overpriced, regal-looking toothpaste usually found at Harrods all held on the same shelf. Depending on the level of condescension, these conversations would culminate in an abrupt crash-landing, with the offender's tail tremoring between their legs. Nancy Warburton, having waited patiently to impart a particularly sensitive piece of information about the person themselves, delivered her ace card in the most innocuous way, all the while slowly wrapping the customer's purchases in brown paper bags and watching them squirm from behind her glasses.

Daphne had come to realise very early on that Nancy and Patsy Warburton appeared to know something about everything and everyone. The sisters had lived in the village for their entire lives and there were no secrets – either historic or recent – that were safe from their all-seeing gaze. Daphne wondered what they would have to say about the 'not so secret' accusations that were flying around about Minerva, and as she'd forgotten to bring any white spirit from home to clean oil-based paint from her brushes that morning, she was going to have to see if the shop was open and then regrettably find out.

Chapter 9

It was uncharacteristically restrained for the Warburton sisters not to position themselves as the all-knowing oracles at the centre of a wave of local gossip. What Pepperbridge's most well-informed matriarchs didn't know about the goings-on among the residents of the villages usually didn't warrant knowing about in the first place.

During one recent conversation with James, Daphne had likened the sisters to her own Grenada-born Aunt Hilda, who would make a habit of turning up uninvited to private events and celebrations (family weddings, funerals, birthday parties ...) for the specific intention of getting a free slap-up meal, but would then complain bitterly about any food not slathered and bathed generously in hot pepper sauce. Daphne had rationalised that the similarity lay in the fact that the Warburton sisters weren't interested in any old bland, run-of-the-mill gossip. Indeed, they were only interested in the spiciest and well-seasoned of secrets – the sort that its participants had hoped to remain buried, made bland by time, distance and concealment. In the event either sister deigned it interesting enough to selectively distribute information about a particular situation, there was sure to be added seasoning to the tale – one that others had yet to be party to and that would burn the reputations of the unwitting subjects like a large dollop of hot pepper sauce.

If Nancy and Patsy Warburton were drawn to gossip like a Grenadian drawn to a bottle of hot pepper sauce at a picnic, then under the present circumstances, one would have assumed that not only would the sisters be imparting the most salacious details of events, but they would also be taking bets on the outcome of the eventual autopsy and the cause of death.

However – to the chagrin of those who had tried and failed to prise even a slither of information from the sisters on the pretext of purchasing a bag of sugar that everyone knew could be found at the nearby garage for at least half of the price – both women remained completely tight-lipped.

When Daphne eventually and rather reluctantly entered the inconveniently priced convenience store to buy white spirit, she overheard Mr Laverley, who lived at Foxglove Cottage with his long-term lodger, Cedric, enquire to the sisters (who both stood behind the shop counter) as to whether a cause of death had been made known.

'I mean, it has been several days now, hasn't it? That's rather a long time to simply announce a heart attack, wouldn't you think?' The question was asked with a frisson of excitement, and it was clear that as far as Mr Laverley was concerned, the topic of Mr Papplewick's death was simply the best excuse for spreading gossip that he had had in months if not years.

Curious to hear what the Warburtons' response would be, Daphne momentarily stopped browsing the shelves and pricked up her ears in dreaded anticipation of hearing her friend's name maligned unfairly once again.

The enquiry was met with a sudden pause in what both women were doing, followed by a wall of stony silence that filled the air weightily, until Mr Laverley was forced to repeat the question under the mistaken assumption that neither of the sisters – standing a mere three feet across the shop counter from where he was standing – had heard him.

Daphne moved closer with what she hoped implied a nonchalant indifference. She bent over to scan the bottom shelf in front of her, giving her a direct line of vision towards the till. She even used her pointed index finger to theatrically indicate that she was shopping and not listening intently, surreptitiously watching everyone's next move.

Patsy, the younger sister of the two, had immediately stopped packing groceries into the awaiting brown paper and turned as white as a sheet. After the ensuing pause where she had stood stock-still, wide-eyed and mannequin-like, she pivoted to face the rear shelves, with her back to Mr Laverley. She was now – it seemed to Daphne at least – pretending to look intensely at a shelf filled with headache pills, Tampax and condoms while mimicking Daphne's finger pointing. As far as Daphne had heard, Mr Laverley had not asked for a three pack of Ribbed and Dotted, yet Patsy was nevertheless scanning bottles, packets and tins as though her life depended on it.

Nancy, on the other hand, remained stony faced, staring through her bifocal lenses directly at Mr Laverley without acknowledging or responding to the question. While she appeared less flustered than her sister, Daphne could also see that her left hand was gripping the countertop ... and was that an almost imperceptible throb of a vein at her temple? It was clear to Daphne that not only had both women heard Mr Laverley's enquiry quite clearly, but that the two women were not as calm as they were attempting to convey. It was all very curious, and Daphne was left desperately trying to think of an excuse to continue perusing the shelves.

It was almost disappointing when the shop bell went, indicating that someone else had entered the grocery store. The spell was broken, and a rather confused Mr Laverley paid for his shopping, leaving without an answer to his pertinently asked question.

Daphne was only a second or two out of the shop, white spirit in hand, when she turned and noticed that Nancy Warburton had closed and locked the door behind the last customer who'd followed closely behind Daphne. The 'Closed' sign was quickly turned to face the street. Daphne hesitated, wondering whether she ought to enquire as to whether the ladies were all right. It wasn't at all unusual for them to close the store at any time of day that they chose. They made a habit of closing at the most inconvenient of times – often lunchtime, which made one wonder whether they were burdened by the needs of commerce at all or whether the store was just a means of accumulating and spreading gossip . . . Although not today it seemed. Today was evidently not a day for spreading gossip, or indeed chewing the cud of speculation – and Daphne was more than a little interested to find out why.

Before she knew what she was doing, she had turned back to the shop and was now knocking on the door. She was just in time to see Patsy still behind the till counter and yet to retreat through the back door and up the stairs to the living quarters above. Patsy looked up to see who had the impertinence to be knocking and Daphne mimed an apology through the glass and pointed to the shelves, attempting to indicate that she had purchased the incorrect item.

Patsy hesitated – it was obvious that she was in two minds whether to simply ignore Daphne and pretend that she wasn't there. In the end, she begrudgingly walked over to the door, opened it only a few inches and barked the words, 'What do you want – can't you see we're closed?'

'Oh yes, I do apologise,' said Daphne, 'but I've only just realised that I've bought the wrong thing. You see, I needed sugar soap – not white spirit . . .'

Patsy rolled her eyes and opened the door further, letting Daphne in. She walked towards the hardware shelf that Daphne had been hovering at only a few minutes earlier and grabbed a bottle of the yellow solution. 'This?' she snapped impatiently.

'That's the one,' Daphne acknowledged with feigned gratefulness. 'Is everything OK, Miss Warburton? Is anything the matter . . . ?' she asked innocently.

Patsy Warburton looked up at Daphne. Her face was etched with sadness, and it was clear that she was hiding some sort of distress. She was just about to speak when her eyes filled with tears. Daphne was shocked. In the short time that she had lived in the village, she had never seen any signs of vulnerability or indeed empathy from either sister, so the possibility of a sudden burst of pent-up emotion was an intriguing turn of events indeed.

The women were barely a couple of feet from each other, and Daphne felt a wave of compassion come over to her as she watched Patsy Warburton's human side come to the fore.

'Are you sure? If you'd like to talk about something ... anything at all, I'd be happy to lend an ear, or even a shoulder – you know – to cry on?'

With that, the tears started streaming down Patsy's face. She still held the bottle of sugar soap in her hands, all thoughts of the transaction gone.

Daphne offered Patsy a clean tissue that she had in her pocket. 'I mean it, you know ... if you ever need to talk, I'm—'

'PATSY!' the voice of Nancy bellowed as she came charging down the stairs.

As she flung herself through the back door, Nancy appeared to assess the situation in a split second, immediately ushering Patsy behind the counter, while simultaneously grabbing the bottle from her sister's hand and shoving it into Daphne's.

'We're CLOSED!' she practically snarled.

Daphne looked down at the two bottles now at her chest. 'But I haven't paid for—'

'IT'S ON THE HOUSE – NOW OUT!'

Daphne left the shop quickly and increasingly perplexed. If their behaviour had seemed strange before, it was now positively bizarre. The Warburtons would *never* pass up the opportunity to squeeze a few extra pence out of a sale under normal circumstances ... which meant that these were not normal circumstances. Something had clearly rattled the sisters, and Daphne had a fair idea that it was something to do with the death of Charles Papplewick. She intended to make it her mission to find out what.

Upstairs, Patsy immediately locked herself in her room to avoid any further interaction with her elder sister. She knew that she'd made a mistake by crying in front of Daphne Brewster, but overcome with emotion at Daphne's kind words, she hadn't been able to help herself. She felt so incredibly guilty, and every time a customer brought it up, she felt even more guilty – but sadly it was too late to do anything about it now. If only she could turn back the clock and act differently on that night, then perhaps Charles wouldn't now be lying cold, stiff and lifeless in a dark hospital mortuary. She couldn't quite believe that he was no longer alive. No longer the living, breathing, compassionate entity that had played such an important part in her life. She tried and failed to choke back another sob. She really needed to pull herself together. The Warburton sisters didn't cry. They hardly ever showed any emotion at all. That was their superpower ... To remain calm, controlled and to observe other people's angst – not to display their own. It was the accidental slips of other people's emotions that they had learned to carefully watch out for. It was the main source of their currency in the parish. (That and the fact that, in the absence of another 'convenience' store in the village, they had a monopoly on everyday essentials.) They saw everything and knew everything, and to be quite honest that had given Patsy a darkly perverse and satisfied thrill over the years. A thrill that made up for the emptiness and longing in her heart that she knew was unlikely to ever be fulfilled. Not while she lived in this village and not while certain people were still around, anyway . . .

She sensed her sister hovering outside the locked bedroom door.

'Here's a cup of tea for you.' Nancy spoke gruffly, although it was evident from the softness of her knock that under the harsh exterior lay concern for her sister.

Patsy hesitated to speak, not wanting to get into a discussion, but eventually acknowledged the peace offering with a quiet, 'Thank you – just leave it outside on the hall table – I'll be out in a minute.'

Nancy had retreated to the sitting room and turned on the radio. Her head was throbbing and her hip was playing up. She was feeling stressed, and she was feeling anxious – although perhaps nothing that a slice of cherry and almond fruit cake wouldn't fix. She pushed herself back up from her armchair, trying to ignore the pain in her hip as she made her way to the cupboard above the draining board in the kitchen. She pulled out an old cake tin that had a faded image of King George V in full military regalia and a large handlebar moustache staring back from the lid. Inside was a quarter of the remains of a particularly good brandy-infused Dundee fruit cake.

'That'll do,' she muttered to herself. She wished that *The Archers* was on to provide some comfort listening, but it was far too early in the day, so setting her plate to the side, she adjusted the settings until it was playing a kind of Bing

Crosby-esque crooning. The DJ said that it was Michael Bublé or some such silver-tongued crooner. He would do too.

The slice of cake, washed down with some hastily made tea (from teabags rather than loose leaf for speed, unfortunately), provided a slight reprise from her thoughts, but it was short-lived. Nancy was worried. It wasn't a familiar feeling, and it certainly wasn't a nice one either. Things had gone too far last week and had eventually taken an unexpected turn for the worse. She had been so angry on behalf of her sister. Years of pent-up frustration had come spewing out in one furious outburst. The truth was that she didn't even know if it had been Charles who she had been angry at. She was ashamed to admit that, in retrospect, perhaps it had been years of emotions towards other people that had formed layers of swirling fury, and ended up being misguidedly focused on one person.

Not that she didn't have a right to be angry at Charles, of course. He had played with Patsy's heart and messed up her dear sister's life. Poor, foolish, broken-hearted Patsy. Didn't she know by now that *all* men were scoundrels, unworthy of even the most basic imaginations of love or loyalty? They would all end up betraying you in the end. Nancy had tried to teach Patsy over the years that, on the whole, people were rotten to the core. Both men and women, although she felt that men had the edge. Each and every piece of gossip that they had gathered, stolen and eked out of the village's unsuspecting victims had proved her point a dozen times over and counting. She had tried to show Patsy that it was often the most innocent-looking ones – like the vicar, for instance – who had the darkest, most abhorrent secrets. No man was to be trusted. Not even Charles Papplewick – although at least he wouldn't be a problem anymore.

Anyway, what was done was done and there was no room for regret. She just wanted to put the whole thing behind her and to move on. She wanted Patsy to move on too. As far as Nancy was aware, there were few residents in the parish who knew of any history between her sister and Charles, and considering the current circumstances, that's exactly how she wished to keep it. The less anyone knew about any type of connection between the Warburton sisters and the dead headmaster, the better.

She grabbed the final slice of fruit cake, shoving it into her mouth greedily and swallowing it almost whole. Sadly, it didn't prove to be as satisfying or as distracting as she had hoped. It seemed that no amount of fruit cake or tea would be enough to take her mind off the memory of Charles's silhouette walking alone last Friday evening, unaware that he was being followed through the torrential rain. It was an image that kept her awake at night, and an image that woke her up with a start even on the rare occasion that she had been able to fall into a disturbed slumber since that night. No regrets, she repeated to herself. No regrets ...

Chapter 10

It was finally the weekend, and for the first time in over a week, Daphne was able to enjoy the benefits of having a lie-in. James had taken the children, along with Byron, out for an early walk followed by breakfast in town, ostensibly to curb the inevitable energy that miraculously appeared at 7 a.m. on a Saturday, unlike the feigned lethargy on a school-day morning. The truth was that James could see how the events of the past week had affected his wife. Her concern for her new friend, coupled with her questions over the unusual behaviour from a few members of the community after Mr Papplewick's death, were troubling her deeply. James couldn't quite understand why it was affecting her in this way, but he knew better than to dismiss her concerns. When Daphne had the bit between her teeth, it was impossible for anyone else to rein her in.

James had been shocked by the death of the headmaster of course, but he had rationalised the entire situation in his usual level-headed and logical way. 'Intrigue' didn't appear to be a word that featured in James's vocabulary.

'It's a distressing business all round, but the man had been approaching retirement, and life is stressful for most people at the best of times, let alone for a headmaster in charge of a village school whose future probably depends on positive Ofsted reports . . .' He'd peered over his laptop as he said it, watching for Daphne's reaction. 'Maybe he'd been juggling – what, judging by the news, I would assume would be – inadequate budgets, plus a myriad of sticky village politics. Was it any wonder that the poor man suffered a heart attack?'

In James's opinion, that was all that had happened, and the rest of the nonsense that was circulating was pure small-minded tittle-tattle.

Deep down, Daphne agreed with James's summation, but as she lay alone in bed with the house still and quiet, a cup of tea brought up by James much earlier growing cold on the bedside table, she couldn't help but feel that despite the probable cause of Charles Papplewick's death, there was a bumpy road of confusion and speculation ahead.

She attempted to close her eyes and force a few extra minutes of sleep, but with her head spinning with theories and a cacophony of thoughts buzzing about her brain, Daphne realised that a lie-in was going to be highly unlikely. It was time to get up and do something constructive to take her mind off things – albeit at a more leisurely pace than she could command during the week.

A shower had reinvigorated her troubled state somewhat. Now dressed in a floral prairie dress and mini wellington boots – not unlike the ones that she had seen covered in wet soil at the back entrance in Augusta's house (she really must stop remembering such minute details that probably meant nothing beyond evidence of her own over-active imagination) – Daphne was about to go out into the garden and tend to the raised beds that had been left neglected for far too long. She was standing in the laundry room, the trolly maid above her with Immy's long school socks dangling down and almost touching her head, the pie crust butler's sink directly behind her with a pile of Doctor Oates's yet-to-be scrubbed new potatoes piled high next to three courgettes. Minutes had passed before she realised that she was still absent-mindedly looking down at the boots; it took a few more minutes to realise that a panting and muddy Byron was sat on his small haunches, staring straight up at her.

'When did you get back?' she asked as though expecting a comprehensively explained answer.

He cocked his head to the side in a questioning manner as though sharing her roaming thoughts. His inquisitive whiskery expression made her laugh out loud and instantly brought her mind back to the present and the job at hand. James must have dropped him back after the walk before heading off for breakfast with the children.

'Don't look so concerned, Byron – it's only Mummy's mind running riot again.'

She was an amateur gardener, although even that sounded far too grand for a woman who had only recently moved up to the country from a tiny terraced garden in south London, and was now slightly overwhelmed with the vast expanse of verdant space surrounding their historic property. She looked back from the laundry room and into the kitchen with its huge flagstones and large windows. The house was a beauty. A well-proportioned Georgian farmhouse that had needed work, but whose bones were solid and attractive. From the front it looked like a doll's house, but at the back – where the original footprint of a smaller, less symmetrical building was, built before the grander Regency façade was added in 1822 – it rambled along in beautiful, twisting chaos. She wanted to do the house justice and create a tra- ditional cottage garden as well as cultivating an area filled with raised beds where she could grow her own produce. The garden had become an unexpected passion of hers now that the initial overwhelm was subsiding. She was keen to learn as much as she could and do as much of it herself as she could too.

In the past she had often wandered up to the allotment where Charles Papplewick had been discovered dead only a week ago, searching for inspiration on what might grow easily and abundantly in the Norfolk climate. She had spotted Mr Papplewick himself there on more than one occasion, pottering about his potting shed, or on his knees with his hands deep in the soil. He had always seemed to have had a contented expression on his face in that environ- ment. Very different from his slightly strained and serious look when he walked up the aisle in church with his wife on a Sunday morning. It was clear that the allotment had been his happy place – perhaps then a befitting place for his final hours?

'Rrrruff!!' Yet again Byron dragged her back from her thoughts.

'What's that? You'd like a treat now that you've had your walk? Well, why didn't you say before!' she laughed at the wriggling pup who was now beyond excited at her use of the word 'treat'.

'I'm rather peckish myself. Let's see what we can find for us both, shall we?'

Back in the kitchen, wellingtons still on her feet, she was just shovelling the remains of some sourdough toast topped with almond butter into her mouth when she heard the distinctive sound of the letterbox flap close with a loud clatter – cutting sharply through her musings. *I'd better pick up the post before the dog gets to it*, she thought absent-mindedly, walking into the hallway and towards the front door. The post was comprised of the usual clothing catalogues that would immediately be relegated to the recycling bin – how on earth they kept getting her details was anyone's guess. There was a leaflet offering gardening services that made Daphne pause and then smile ... If only, she thought, although she instantly acknowledged the satisfaction of creating the garden herself. And not that finances allowed her a choice, in any case! There were a few other letters, mostly brown envelopes, and not much else, but at the bottom of the pile lay the most interesting item to be slipped through the letterbox in a while. It looked as though it had lain there for longer than the recent delivery, and without a postal mark, it had certainly been hand delivered at some point. It was the *Village Pump* – the parish newsletter that covered everything from charity events and local car boot sales, to

diary dates for the villages, shop opening times, local advertising services, the church calendar, and words of comfort
from the vicar featuring a summary of the month's Sunday-
service sermons.

Then there was the 'Grumpy Old Man' column. A supposedly anonymous column simply signed off 'with best wishes
from the Grumpy Old Man', which would often rib a few
locals with embellished anecdotes, spill a few secrets about
who had been unceremoniously turned down for planning
permission or which neighbours were in conflict with one
another – and why. On good months it was all clean harmless
fun ... but some months ... the months where perhaps there
had been an unexpected death in the village? Well, on these
months, the Grumpy Old Man would turn slightly darker
with his humour, teasing just enough to drop a hot potato of
speculation or two ...

Today his letter was short and, on the surface, it was an
obituary to Charles Papplewick ...

By all accounts, the untimely death of our dear
beloved headmaster is an epic tragedy of Macbethian
proportions. We have lost our moral guide in a man
of genteel spirit, whose nature was full of the milk
of human kindness, who served this village well and
remained amongst his own people for more years than
many of those less selfless would have offered. For this
we must be eternally grateful on behalf of our children
as well as ourselves. We can all agree that we in the
parish of Pepperbridge were blessed to have the services
of a man of such education and commitment for so many

years, and it will undoubtedly be a lesser place without him. Some would say that he was a man "not without ambition, but without the illness should attend it", as the saying goes – a rarity in the world these days. May we all join in offering our greatest sympathies to his widow, Augusta Papplewick, in the hope that the spirits that tend on our mortal thoughts will give her peace of mind and comfort during these challenging times.

Daphne re-read the piece at least three times, not quite sure what to make of it. Was it serious? Was it meant as a joke, and if so, how had it passed the scrutiny of the *Pump*'s editor? On the surface it was a tribute to Charles Papplewick and his newly widowed wife, and yet – to those who knew their Shakespeare – the hints to *Macbeth* were quite clear. What an odd thing to liken Charles to Macbeth ... For of course, if he was Macbeth then surely the implication was that Augusta Papplewick must be *Lady* Macbeth ... and everyone knew how shady her character was. A scheming and ruthlessly ambitious wife with an appetite for violence. Who was the author keen to point a finger of suspicion to the wife of the dearly departed? Whoever the Grumpy Old Man was, they fully intended to drop the seeds of treachery into readers' minds – and as far as Daphne was concerned, joke or not, they had succeeded.

Despite still wearing her gardening boots, suddenly the draw of her unkempt raised beds didn't feel so strong. She had hardly made it back from the hallway to the kitchen before Daphne's mind was once again focused on the details surrounding Charles Papplewick's death, and why it hadn't already been wrapped up as a straightforward case of death by cardiac arrest. What could be holding the post-mortem result up? Were the coroners on holiday and if so, wouldn't they have holiday cover anyway? If they would only just release the inevitable findings of natural causes then all of these accusations would disappear, and for the most part – although obviously not for Augusta or Minerva – things could go back to normal. Right now, nothing seemed quite normal. Here was someone insinuating that Augusta was the counterpart to Lady Macbeth, while Augusta herself was unabashedly accusing Minerva of being the cause of her husband's death. Meanwhile, she had witnessed Marianne haranguing the headmaster the day before his death, and then there was the odd behaviour of the Warburton sisters who were acting as though they had something to hide. What on earth could be going on with everyone?

Daphne's mind was drawn back to the morning of Charles's discovery. To the moments after she had entered Wellingborough House and learned – apparently minutes after Augusta – that Charles had been found dead in his potting shed. Apart from the obvious shock and distress of hearing such news, something had been bothering Daphne about the morning ever since. It was to do with Augusta's wellington boots. Outside, the rain had been bucketing down since the night before, and the boots had clearly recently been used. Not only had they been wet but they were covered in mud. Red clay soil to be precise. The sort of mud that you see in the surrounding fields of Pepperbridge and Pudding Corner and the rest of this enclave in West Norfolk. The sort of mud that Daphne should by now be digging through in her raised beds ... the sort of mud that one would have to trail through to walk to any part of the allotments on a rainy day. A rainy day exactly like it had been last Saturday morning.

It shouldn't have meant anything, but Augusta had still been in her nightgown with mussed-up bed hair, as if she had just been woken up. Indeed, she claimed that she had been woken by the knocking at the door from the policewoman who had arrived to break the bad news. It was Augusta herself who'd been adamant that she hadn't left her house all morning. For that matter, she'd insisted that she hadn't left the house since the previous afternoon when the school day had ended, which by Daphne's calculations must have been some time around 4.30 p.m. These were her own words, so why on earth would Augusta Papplewick's wellington boots have been completely sodden and covered in thick wet mud that left a trail to the back door? Who had been out in the boots if not Augusta herself (Daphne estimated they were around a size four, which meant they could hardly have been borrowed by her husband who had been at least six foot), and what did she have to gain from pretending to have remained indoors?

Daphne stopped herself. Speculating when there was no reason to speculate was a pointless endeavour. There was no claim – as yet – that Charles Papplewick had died under any sort of suspicious circumstance, and the only reason that the idea had entered into her mind was because Augusta herself had fuelled the flames. Until there was a definite reason to speculate – and Daphne sincerely hoped that there wouldn't be – she would attempt to quash all thoughts of intrigue about how Charles had died.

Maybe she was better off driving into Pepperbridge and spending a few hours at the shop pricing up some vintage items that she had ordered from eBay? Opening boxes filled with treasures was always a pleasurable experience, and as much as she loved working in her garden, right now what she really wanted was the dopamine thrill of opening packages. She put her gardening gloves down, grabbed her market basket and keys, and quickly left the house.

Just a few miles down the road, in Daphne's intended destination of Pepperbridge, and only a week after her husband had been discovered dead in his allotment, a less than tearful widow stood seething with rage in her formal sitting room resplendent with mismatched chintz, brown furniture and antiques. She was jamming her index finger onto the buttons of a landline telephone and repeatedly calling the editor of the *Village Pump*. Her fiery mood was in direct contrast to her genteel surroundings. Augusta was incandescent with rage, and she intended to find out exactly how on earth the most recent edition of the local newsletter – only posted through the letterbox that morning – had been allowed to be circulated with such a damning column from the so-called 'Grumpy Old Man'.

It didn't take a genius to read between the lines. *She*, Augusta, was Lady Macbeth, a scheming, manipulative wife, and therefore in some way she must be responsible for her own husband's demise. How *dare* they! Who did they think they were toying with? She demanded a retraction – *each* and *every* copy of the *Village Pump* would need to be recalled and destroyed, and an immediate apology printed and handed out. Furthermore, whoever the Grumpy Old Man turned out to be, well she would have him exposed for the nasty slanderer that he was, then hung, drawn and quartered, and threatened with legal action.

After what must have been the seventeenth attempt, she eventually slammed down the receiver and stormed towards the back door to grab a lightweight jacket. If she couldn't get through by telephone, then she would damn well turn up at the editor's front door. Grabbing her keys and flinging open the door, she jumped back with a start to find Inspector Hargreaves standing directly in front of her. Behind him loitered a nervous looking PC Clarke.

Inspector Hargreaves cleared his throat awkwardly and began to speak. He in turn was clearly startled at finding Augusta Papplewick flinging open the door with such force. They were almost nose to nose.

'I'm afraid we have some news Mrs Papplewick. May we come in.'

It was more of a statement than a question and Augusta immediately felt faint with fear – an unusual feeling for her, especially when faced with the likes of Hargreaves and Clarke who were no more than 'rude mechanicals' dressed up in uniform, in her opinion . . .

'Well actually, I was just on my way out . . .' she attempted far more feebly than was characteristic of her.

'Well, I'm afraid not, Mrs Papplewick. You see, we have a few questions concerning the death of your husband . . .'

Daphne was just pulling Aggie into the road that dipped down Canberwick Heath and entered the village of Pepperbridge. It was a sunny morning and the village looked quite beautiful in the dappled early-summer sunlight. The varying roof lines of the village houses created a stunning stage set in front of a clear blue sky. The chocolate-box houses built from a variety of Norfolk flint, honeyed gingerbread stone and oak timber, meandered along roads that were always on a curve and never seemed to appear straight. For once it wasn't raining and there was no morning mist. She looked down at Byron, who was snoozing happily in the wicker dog seat beside her, before turning the steering wheel and rounding the corner that led towards the high street. But for some reason, just as she neared the junction towards the village green, she felt a compulsion to take the adjacent turn.

It was a small and narrow road that eventually ended up passing the school and then the Church of England church (one of two in the village – the other being Catholic), finally snaking its way back to the opposite end of the high street. She rarely drove this way as the road was slight and there was often a tractor coming in the opposite direction, which meant that you had to either mount the pavement to one side or choose to drive into the grass verge – neither of which was particularly appealing considering the height of the sloping verge and the cobbled pavement. Thankfully, on this particular Saturday morning, all was quiet and there wasn't a tractor in sight.

After a few minutes, Aggie the Morris Traveller reached the real reason that Daphne had dipped into the lane, if she was being truly honest with herself. This was the road that led to the allotments. Daphne didn't know what was compelling her, but she felt the urge to take a look around the place where

Charles Papplewick had so recently taken his final breaths. She pulled up to one side, locked the car and walked up the narrow walkway towards the open field of allotments beyond. The allotments were hidden out of sight from the road by two high hedges, but once you had walked up about fifty paces, the space opened out to a veritable feast of pastoral loveliness. There were willow obelisks and bamboo plant supports topped with tiny terracotta flowerpots; brightly painted chicken houses with runs that bordered neatly planted rows of leeks and carrots. Buff Orpingtons roamed alongside rescued battery hens; large swathes of rhubarb leaves billowed in the breeze alongside overgrown pyramids of runner beans and lush fountains of chard heads. It was a truly beautiful sight. Everyone took great care of their own individual patches, but as a whole, the allotment was a perfect mix of flowers, vegetables, mushroom theatres, rustic fencing and all manner of flora and fauna. Every so often there was a greenhouse, or a potting shed made up from the most innovative of construction solutions. Old windows secured together to create the most fanciful greenhouses, water butts made from huge old whiskey barrels, vintage chests of drawers holding twine and garden tools; specially converted wardrobes that served as garden storage and makeshift tea-supply areas; corrugated iron structures with haphazard seating formed of old crates adjacent to smarter patio sets arranged around sweet peas and sunflowers.

Daphne always found it a delight to visit, but on this early crisp and clear-skied Saturday morning it was all but empty, and Daphne knew exactly where she was heading. She wanted to take a look at Charles Papplewick's plot. Specifically, the potting shed where he evidently collapsed and died. She didn't know what he was hoping to find, but she had a hunch that it might prove useful to look – although she had no idea of what it would be useful for.

The shed was unassumingly basic but as neat as a pin, just as she had expected. Charles had been the sort of man who would make a concerted effort to be tidy in all of his endeavours – even when it came to his allotment and gardening tools. One wouldn't have said that he was humourless, exactly; Daphne had come to realise that that particular assertion completely depended on the company he kept. She had seen Charles looking warm and carefree in the company of children at the village school, as well as laughing heartily with many of his staff. There seemed to have been quite a jovial fraternity among the small number of teachers, assistants and helpers that made up the teaching staff at Pepperbridge Primary ... that was unless Augusta happened to be within the vicinity. Like a cold northerly wind, Augusta brought with her the distinct chill of formality and frigidity. People stood up a little straighter, and the laughs – if any – were a tad more subdued.

Charles's border had been clearly mapped out with a short picket fence and a neat gate. On one side of a grass walkway that led to the shed were his prized vegetables, still growing bountifully despite the lack of attendance over the past week, and on the other side were his flowers, a compost bin and water butt. It was quite a large plot which wrapped around the shed. Daphne hesitated for a second – this was, after all, the scene of a man's death. But she was here now, so why not just investigate a little, she thought, determinedly shrugging away any doubts as she looked around before opening the gate and walking in. There didn't appear to be anything out of the ordinary. She noted that there was a broken flowerpot and some plants that looked to have been squashed and bent backwards towards the side of the shed. Daphne wondered if that was where Charles had been discovered, doubled over on the ground.

She gingerly pushed open the door to the shed. It wasn't locked, and despite the bright morning, it was dark inside. She wasn't sure whether there would be any electricity on the allotment, and in the absence of a light switch anywhere to be found, was pleased to see a battery-operated lantern as well as a torch on a small farmhouse table. The space was modest, but as well as garden tools hung neatly on pegs along one side, there was a small armchair, a shelf with books and a tabletop camping stove on which sat an old-fashioned whistling kettle. She could just imagine Charles retreating here of an evening, after a tiring school day. She envisioned that he would work in the allotment until the sun began to set and then sit in the peace and quiet confines of his shed with the door flung open as the light started to fade.

She was just about to leave when she noticed the edge of some paperwork to one side of the table, slightly hidden behind a sack of little potatoes that appeared to be sprouting shoots in all directions. Chitting potatoes, she thought, with a silent nod of acknowledgement to Doctor Oates's exemplary vegetable talk over the garden gate. The papers would have been easy to miss being just out of sight of the door entrance as you entered, and half concealed under a box of what she presumed were onions judging by the strong smell emanating from the container. Despite glancing around, the papers hadn't been obvious at first due to their position wedged between the two lots of slowly decaying produce, but the crisp, stark whiteness of the paper had momentarily stood out against the dark wood of the table and the rough fabric of the potato sack.

She knew that none of this was any of her business. They were probably just receipts for garden compost or new tools. Yet she couldn't help herself . . .

Picking the papers up from the table, she squinted and tried to decipher what was on them. She would need to bring them closer to the open door to read the exact wording, however, she could already make out, 'Last Will and Testament of Charles M. Papplewick' at the top. If that wasn't bizarre enough, what was even more surprising was the name Minerva Leek, clearly written underneath.

Daphne stood still with shock. It seemed that Charles had been intending to leave the bulk of his worldly goods to Minerva – but why? What hold – if any – did Minerva have over Charles Papplewick, who had been at least twenty years her senior? Did Augusta know about this? Was that why they'd been arguing the night before Charles had been found dead? The questions swirled around her head, dizzying her.

As Daphne turned the short distance towards the door, her eyes acclimatising to the brightness outside, she realised that she was no longer alone. Shielding her eyes from the sun with her hand as she peered towards the entrance, she could just make out the appearance of two darkly clad figures peering back at her through the shed door.

'What the . . . ?' she gasped out loud, startled by the sudden appearance of other people.

'"What the", indeed – Mrs Brewster, isn't it?' Inspector Hargreaves stood directly in front of her, scanning her face inquisitively. 'Find anything interesting, did we?' he asked, nodding towards the papers that were still grasped firmly in her hand.

'I . . . er . . .' She wasn't quite sure how to answer the question. If the fact that she held a copy of Charles Papplewick's will in her hands was a huge surprise to herself, then there was no doubt that it would be an even bigger surprise to other people. 'Oh, it's nothing – at least, I don't think that it's anything important,' she mumbled, in an attempt to gain some thinking time. She wished that she could ask Minerva what all this meant before handing over private details to the police.

'On the contrary, madam, I think that it may be something very important indeed. This is now after all . . .' he paused for effect and raised his eyebrow, 'the scene of a potential murder inquiry – and you, Mrs Brewster, are not only trespassing, but are also attempting to withhold what could be important evidence.'

Daphne gasped in shock and the pile of paper fluttered down and out of her hands.

'Did you just say murder?'

'Yes, Mrs Brewster. A murder inquiry, and I think that you'd better accompany me down to the station to answer a few questions about your reason for being here this morning – wouldn't you agree?'

It was only then, as she stumbled to think of an answer – she honestly couldn't think of a reasonable explanation for her presence in Charles Papplewick's potting shed, even for herself – that Daphne noticed two other police officers bordering the perimeter of the allotment entrance with ominous neon yellow police tape.

Daphne stumbled out of the shed, wide eyed and aghast. Filled with immediate regret at the impulsiveness that had come over her this morning, when she ought to have been sipping tea in bed, she suddenly felt that perhaps living in south London hadn't been so bad after all . . .

Chapter 11

The rural vistas seemed inordinately tranquil with their large expanses of land filled to the brim with rows of arable crops alongside fields of heavy sows and their blissfully ignorant piglets. The bucolic theme continued with even more acres piled high with cylindrical hay bales, neat hedging separating each stretch from another, their eventual borders leading to tiled barns and ancient 'gingerbread' buildings made from local flint and carstone which created scenes straight out of a fairy tale set against a backdrop of hazy afternoon sunlight.

Similar to any other rural community across the country, the countryside set the scene for change, and perhaps somewhat inexplicably to exhausted city dwellers, the academic summer term in the parish of Pepperbridge was always awash with the buzz of relief at the thought of escaping this patch of seeming paradise for a few weeks. As the end of the school year drew to its inevitable close, even the teaching staff would develop a slight bounce in their weary heels as the finishing line crawled into sight. Relief was relief and challenge was challenge – regardless of the environment one woke up to – and an escape from the challenge of a school year brought with it waves of blessed relief crashing through sagging defeatism like the North Sea on Holkham beach. Yet this year there was the charge of something else in the air . . .

The cornfields were still golden, the sun was as pleasingly high in the sky as one could hope for, but not one person in either Pepperbridge or Pudding Corner was thinking about holidays. This year, there was no talk of which parents would help out at the tea tent for carnival, nor was there mindless chatter about which vacation destination was proving more popular than most. No, the talk of the parish focused on one thing, and one thing only. The ongoing investigation to discover whether Charles Papplewick had died under suspicious circumstances was like a soap opera brought to life, and everybody wanted a front-row seat to watch the story unfold.

Trying not to be the main focus of the front-row seats was why Daphne was currently huddled in bed under the covers while James sorted out the children downstairs. Byron lay on top of the duvet, pinning her down as he stretched his long body out beside her. Every now and then when she came up for air, she would find him staring at her with one eye open, and one eye still presumably sleeping. Thank goodness for non-judgemental dogs, she sighed.

Since the police car had turned up at the Papplewicks' house on Saturday morning and then proceeded to tape up parts of the allotment, it was the talk of the entire town.

What was even worse, in Daphne's personal opinion, was that she was somehow embroiled in the centre of these discussions – and she had no one else to blame but herself. By being discovered snooping in the apparent 'victim's' potting shed, she had inadvertently positioned herself as the prime topic of gossip.

As a Black woman from south London, she had never been under any illusion that her mere presence in some parts of this rural, mostly white area of sleepy England might cause the occasional stir of interest. But nothing could have prepared her for the feeling of exposure that came from being led through rows of cabbages and kale into a waiting police car as a gaggle of locals, rescue hens and the odd child on a bicycle looked on with intense scrutiny.

She hadn't been arrested of course; Inspector Hargreaves had made that extremely clear. She was being asked a few questions about her reason for being at the allotment, and rather more to the point, why she had been in Charles Papplewick's potting shed where (and she was aware of this) she had no business loitering at all.

At the station, Daphne had vaguely thought about using the excuse that she was hoping to claim an allotment plot for herself, and knowing that the recently departed Mr Papplewick would regrettably but quite evidently have no need for his space any longer, she thought that she might as well go and have a look ... But even Daphne felt that the heartlessness of that explanation was worse than the far less explicable truth.

The real truth, as she'd attempted to explain to an increasingly perplexed Inspector Hargreaves, was that the events surrounding Charles Papplewick's death and the subsequent accusations of his widow, hadn't sat well with her from the start. She had purely been attempting to clear the good name of her friend from idle gossip.

'But how did you think searching his potting shed would clear your friend's name?' Inspector Hargreaves had asked, quite clearly confused, particularly since the papers that had had fallen from Daphne's hands had done anything but proven her friend's innocence.

If anything, evidence of a close enough relationship between the pair, where Charles willingly signed over the bulk of his estate to Minerva, confirmed Minerva as a person of distinct interest in this newly opened case. Why would he have left anything to someone who was, until now, assumed to be a random member of the extended community? Why had he not wanted his estate to go to his own wife? What was the relationship between Minerva and Charles? Had they been lovers? Were Augusta's accusations true – had Minerva been blackmailing Charles?

The questions had been wracking Daphne's brain. Charles and Minerva's closeness in the woods had been without dispute – Daphne was quite sure about that. Perhaps they were just jolly good friends, she'd wondered? Unlikely. 'Jolly good friends' don't have a tendency to studiously ignore each other when others are around to witness their interactions while hugging passionately when said others are not. There must have been something more to it. However, determined to stay loyal to her friend, Daphne had decided not to disclose any information about what she had witnessed that Friday evening to Inspector Hargreaves – despite it having occurred only a matter of hours before Charles was found dead. Perhaps there was a connection and perhaps there wasn't, but she would leave that for Inspector Hargreaves to find out.

In the meantime, she wouldn't actively assist in redirecting the investigation towards suspicions of Minerva's involvement. Her lips were sealed. In the short period of time that she had known her, Daphne felt in her gut that Minerva didn't have a bad, or indeed violent or vindictive bone in her body. However, now that the situation had turned into a case of potential murder, Daphne intended to confront Minerva about what she had witnessed at Silvanus's party, along with asking the reasoning behind Charles's will. Confronting Minerva would be done with the sole purpose to help protect her – it would be an act of friendship, and as soon as she could find the energy to drag herself out of bed and out into the public arena again, it would be her main focus. The problem was that Inspector Hargreaves had every intention of doing the same thing – and in his case, friendship had nothing to do with it.

Three people had been politely asked to attend the police station for informal questioning that Saturday. Augusta Papplewick, Minerva Leek and, unexpectedly, Daphne Brewster. No one had been arrested, and no one had been accused of anything. At this stage it was simply an investigation to clarify the cause of death, due to a few anomalies in Charles Papplewick's post-mortem.

It had only been a slight issue, the coroner had said. Possibly nothing of any real value at all, but it would need to be investigated further by a criminal pathologist to rule out any foul play.

He had died of a heart attack, that much was very evident, but it had been a heart attack that had shown no physical warning signs prior to its occurrence, and no obvious medical evidence as to its cause. This was unusual, but not unheard of. Yet there were no blockages in his coronary arteries, no narrowing or atheroma (build-up of fatty deposits), no signs of blood clots or historical damage to the artery wall. He had no history of diabetes, nor high cholesterol and he was certainly not obese. In fact, for his age, he had appeared to be in perfect health. It was as though he had had a sudden and violent reaction to a toxin, the coroner had suggested. Like a car with a flat battery, his lights had suddenly failed, and he'd died, and yet the motor had not been damaged or left running beforehand. Just a sudden extinguishing of a life – like a bulb blowing.

It was a frustrating situation for Inspector Hargreaves. Almost a murder case but not quite a murder case. Until further investigation they were going to have to treat it as such, but it had started off as a paperwork-led formality. One that would hopefully be cleared up by the criminal pathologist. Everyone knew that nothing suspicious ever happened in the parish of Pepperbridge. An investigation would be a waste of time and resources, plus they were about to embark on the tourist season, where city types descended on the English countryside in droves. It was not a good time to have a potential murderer on the loose.

Inspector Hargreaves had started the morning off going through the motions of a half-hearted investigation. He hadn't anticipated finding Daphne Brewster bang in the middle of the 'unexplained death's' scene. Discovering her there, caught like a rabbit in headlights, had set the course of the investigation on a different tangent altogether. What with Mrs Brewster being caught mid-snoop, finding a copy of the will with its surprising beneficiary, coupled with the accusations being fired out by the deceased's widow (which now made far more sense) – well, it was turning into a far more complicated situation than the inspector would have liked. Murders simply didn't occur in this small and sleepy part of England, and he rather hoped things stayed like that.

Daphne had now proceeded from her bedroom to the kitchen table. It was some sort of progress, she felt. There had been no further communication with the police apart from a call to ask if she knew of Minerva's whereabouts, and they had seemed to have taken her word that she had only been at the allotment out of concern for her friend's reputation.

She herself had attempted to contact Minerva immediately after her interview and every day since, but yet again her friend had gone to ground and was refusing – or so it appeared – to answer or return any calls. To James's despair, Daphne had even made him drive over to Minerva's house in the woodland on Sunday morning (his Land Rover Discovery was far less identifiable than her darling Aggie), but to no avail. Neither Minerva or Silvanus were anywhere to be found, and on questioning one of the other residents in the small coterie of self-proclaimed Wiccans that made up the little commune, Daphne had been met with a blank, although not unfriendly response. No one seemed to know where Minerva or Silvanus had gone or how long they would be gone for. Or at least, none of the residents of the commune were willing to tell her if they did.

*

James had been furious. He couldn't understand why Daphne had been at the allotment on Saturday morning when he'd left her alone for a much-needed break from the village and a lie-in ... or so he had thought.

'How was I to know that it would turn into a murder investigation?' she had said, attempting to defend herself.

'It makes no difference; you had no business being there because it's none of your concern – murder or not!' he had retorted, frustrated. 'You hardly know the woman, and she's hardly your friend if she disappears without a trace and fails to tell you.' He slapped his own forehead while talking to emphasise how ridiculous the situation was, and Daphne couldn't help but stare at the red impression his handprint had left afterwards as he continued. 'She couldn't give two hoots about you – obviously – so why on earth are you attempting to play the saviour? She's going to get you into trouble Daph, and she's not worth it.' His tone had changed from one of frustration to one of abject pity as he calmed down, and his hands descended from gesticulating furiously in the air to resting on the back of a kitchen chair as a result.

His words had hurt. Was she really being silly trying to help her new friend? Were they even really friends? For the first time since their arrival in Pudding Corner, Daphne didn't feel entirely certain about her new life, and it wasn't a nice feeling at all.

During the following week, walking into school to drop the children off felt like an endurance test. Word had obviously travelled round the village about Daphne 'breaking into the murder scene' and there were a few whispers and several comically theatrical averted eyes in the playground.

By the Thursday, Marianne Forbes approached her after the morning bell had been rung. Daphne, seeing no obvious escape route, groaned inwardly. It was another crisp and clear day, and not for the first time, Daphne wished that a heavy downpour would suddenly erupt and give her the excuse to run quickly back to her car. She couldn't bear the idea of a smug-faced Marianne grilling her for all the 'juicy details' or worse still, crowing a few 'I told you so's about her friendship with Minerva. As it happened, Daphne was pleasantly surprised when Marianne showed an almost sheepish restraint. She asked if Daphne was all right, which allowed Daphne to relax a little, although that was quickly followed by an almost skittish questioning of what details the police had wanted to know at the station.

'Did they mention anything specific about why or how he died?' she questioned Daphne agitatedly. 'Was it definitely a heart attack? They don't think anyone ... I mean, anything else caused it, do they ...?'

Her attitude perplexed Daphne. Marianne remained watchful, her eyes flicking around her, uncharacteristically displaying no signs of obvious relish or enjoyment while digesting Daphne's response – not that Daphne had filled her in completely of course.

It was only when Marianne had left that Daphne realised that she had hardly seen her for over a week. Daphne considered it for a moment, realising the last time she recalled seeing Marianne was on the Friday morning of Charles Papplewick's death. The morning when Marianne had been screeching insults and hostile ultimatums behind the ever-patient head-master's office door.

Where had Marianne been for the past week? Had she – or the children – been unwell? Her interest piqued, Daphne turned to watch Marianne get into her car. There was something different about her, she noted belatedly – a lack of her usual polish. Her hair was slightly unkempt, her blouse was crinkled and, together with the nervous air she'd exuded throughout their brief conversation, she appeared to be harassed and troubled. Marianne's smartly co-ordinated appearance was usually a badge of honour. Wearing a pair of shoes that did not match one's handbag was normally anathema to her ... However, that morning, Marianne was wearing gym shoes, an old shirt and a pair of jeans that looked as though they might be her husband's. What on earth had happened since Daphne had last seen her?

Daphne knew that James wouldn't approve, but since when had she waited for her husband's approval before acting on a hunch? Despite her previous resolution to give Marianne a wide berth, Daphne decided that today was the day to renew their friendship – at least until Daphne could find out why she was acting so strangely.

She decided that she would casually drop into Marianne's house on her way home – perhaps on the pretence of giving her more information about the investigation. First, she'd pop into the Pepperbridge convenience store for some biscuits and a box of Earl Grey. Surely Marianne would take the bait if Daphne arrived on her doorstep wielding tea and biscuits?

This morning, the convenience store was thankfully open.

It had been kept shut for longer and longer periods of time over the past week, and one could never be sure when it would live up to its name.

As Daphne entered the shop, the doorbell tinkling, Nancy Warburton was standing alone behind the counter. Her face was sombre and still, and her eyes were staring straight at Daphne, as if she had been expecting her arrival. Daphne felt a sudden flush of self-consciousness; after all, she was now widely known as the woman who had been picked up by the police only a few days ago. She wondered whether that particular piece of gossip had reached the 'Oracle sisters' – although, in all likelihood, the sisters had probably informed most of the village about the incident themselves ...

'I hear you had a meeting with the police on Saturday, Mrs Brewster.' Nancy had gone straight in without hesitation or pleasantries, and despite half expecting it, it still made Daphne squirm uncomfortably.

'Yes, it was just a misunderstanding ...' Daphne responded as she hastily scanned the ever-changing aisles for the biscuit section, which occasionally sat next to the teabags – but not always. Finally her eyes rested on what she wanted – thankfully this time conveniently placed together – before she picked them up and reluctantly approached the shop counter.

'I'm actually quite interested in signing up for a plot at the allotment for myself ...' She trailed off, hearing her own lack of conviction as she started to perspire under the unflinching gaze of Nancy Warburton.

'I see,' the older lady said with obvious scepticism. 'You have about three quarters of an acre over there at Pudding Corner haven't you – no space for a veg patch of your own then?'

She started to package up the biscuits – McVitie's Fruit Shortcake – and teabags that Daphne had brought over from one of the aisles, all the while staring directly into Daphne's eyes.

'Er – yes, you're quite right – I didn't realise that you knew the house?'

'I know lots of things,' she responded without any visible emotion.

Daphne felt unnerved. She had been caught out in her lie, but she wasn't quite sure whether it mattered, or whether Nancy cared in the slightest. She had the same expression and tone regardless of the situation.

There was a long silence as Nancy slowly totted up the total – writing the prices down on a small paper bag and adding them up using long arithmetic before entering the figures into the till. With only two items, it was an unnecessarily drawn-out transaction, and Daphne couldn't help but feel that Nancy was purposefully trying to make her feel on edge.

Daphne suddenly felt desperate to fill the silent space, eventually mumbling something about heading over to Marianne Forbes's house for tea. *Too much information*, she groaned internally – she knew better than most that not everyone liked Marianne Forbes.

On hearing Marianne's name, Nancy Warburton's eyes sharpened their glare. 'Marianne Forbes, you say?'

For the first time, Nancy looked down as she spoke, taking the ten-pound note that Daphne had proffered. She went on with a clearly contrived casualness, 'I do hope that she has recovered from getting caught in the storm?'

'The storm?' repeated Daphne, confused.

Despite the troubled nature of the news in the area, the past week's weather had been idyllic, filled with clear blue skies and sunshine. They were deep into beautiful British summer season. In fact, the last time it had rained was the weekend that Charles had died – and that was over a week ago ...

Daphne looked up to see Nancy peering intensely back at her once more.

'Yes, the storm a week ago, on the Friday. I saw her driving up towards the allotment. Quite late it was. I was putting the bins out when I saw her get out of the car. Funny little thing she is. Looks like butter wouldn't melt – but my, does she have a good pair of lungs when she wants to use them. I thought that she was going to burst a vessel the way she was screaming at him. What a temper! Anyway. I hope that she didn't get too wet. She could have caught her death prowling around the village at night like that ... although I imagine that the brandy or whatever it was she'd been drinking was keeping her warm ...'

Daphne stood paralysed and wide eyed at Nancy ... but Nancy had handed over the change – what there was of it – and was now silent again. The conversation was over.

'Good day Mrs Brewster. Enjoy your tea.'

Daphne thanked the shopkeeper and walked slowly out of the store – slightly reeling from what to make of such an unexpected conversation. Nancy had clearly wanted to tell Daphne that Marianne Forbes had been arguing with Charles on the night that he had died, but why had she not told the police? Was the implication that she had murdered him? Surely not ... Marianne was many things, but a murderer?

It was all getting far more complicated than Daphne could have imagined.

Outside, under the bright blue of the sky and suddenly feeling reinvigorated, she opened Aggie's driver's door and threw the paper bag with the tea and biscuits onto the passenger seat. She was on her way to pay Marianne a surprise visit, and hopefully she'd find out more about the events of that night. If nothing else, she could gather a timeline of events that might help Minerva.

As Daphne started her car, she looked back at the grocery store through her rear-view mirror just in time to see Nancy Warburton turning the 'Open' sign to 'Closed'.

Chapter 12

How many times could one knock on a front door knowing that the person inside was pretending not to be in, without seeming crazy or desperate? The tall and narrow town house was extremely handsome in an elegant and prim way. A smart and shiny carriage-black front door with a large swan-necked carriage lamp above a shallow portico that sat almost flush to the outer walls, it was an impressive frontage for a house that was in reality quite modestly sized inside. It was a perfect example of how much the Georgians valued kerb appeal, accentuated by a twisting, turning wisteria vine which covered the front and was a thing of pure beauty for the short few weeks that the wisteria's lilac blooms flourished in the spring.

Daphne's arms were growing tired from cradling the biscuits and box of tea, while banging on the dolphin-shaped brass knocker. She had literally just seen Marianne – or someone she assumed was Marianne – dash away from the curtain of her drawing room window as she'd walked up to the Forbes's front door. Marianne's car was even conspicuously parked in front of her house. If she was trying to pretend that she hadn't returned straight home from the morning school drop off, then she wasn't doing a very good job of hiding it. Daphne was almost certain that if she stood very still and listened carefully, she'd be able to hear Marianne's frantic breathing through the front door. What was she hiding from, and what had spooked her? Rather than clearing anything up, the visit had simply provided another layer to the growing mystery of Marianne's involvement – if any – in Charles Papplewick's untimely death. Marianne was obviously scared about something. That much was clear, but after a few more minutes of knocking, it seemed that now was not the time to find out what exactly she was scared about.

It was only a few minutes journey back to Cranberry Farmhouse, and as Daphne pulled into the sweeping gravel drive, Doctor Oates was pulling his recycling bin onto the roadside. He gave her a friendly wave and waited for her to wind down her window as she turned towards the garages.

'Good morning, Daphne!' he called out in his reliably cheerful manner.

If there was one thing that felt reassuring about life at Pudding Corner at the moment, it was the constant upbeat presence of Doctor Ptolemy Oates – possibly the jolliest neighbour that Daphne had ever encountered.

Doctor Oates was an unexpected benefit of their move to the countryside. On countless occasions prior to the move,

Daphne had wondered what the villagers would think of their multicultural family moving into the area. It was 2023 of course, and it was hardly groundbreaking for a Black person to take up residence in any part of the United Kingdom that they chose to. However, Daphne, and anyone else who had cared to take note of the Black Lives Matter movement that had grown with increasing momentum over the past few years, was aware of the lack of racial diversity in many areas of the British countryside. It had even been the been the topic of a *Countryfile* documentary on the BBC, and if there was anything that the population of Pepperbridge and Pudding Corner could agree on, it was that *Countryfile* was one of the last bastions of safe viewing and common sense on the television these days.

As it was, all fears were assuaged the moment she met the welcoming doctor, and she was more than happy to give him some of her time.

'Good morning, Doctor Oates,' Daphne replied. 'I have an apparently unwanted packet of biscuits and some fancy tea – care to join me in a quick cup? I need to ask your opinion on my rhubarb if you have a spare moment?'

She had seen him eyeing up the biscuits with distinct interest as he'd leaned down to proffer his good morning through the car window. She hadn't seen him at the gate that morning before dropping the children off at school. In fact, she now realised that their morning chats had been slightly erratic over the past few weeks, due to her preoccupation with chasing down errant friends and exploring crazy notions. She owed nothing to her new neighbour of course, but he was a kindly gentleman of a certain age, who lived alone, and she felt slightly guilty that she had so unceremoniously discarded their friendly rapport in the two weeks since Charles Papplewick's death.

The older man instantly perked up – if that was possible with his already buoyant nature. It seemed that tea and biscuits were the secret to most people's hearts after all, she smiled wryly to herself – or perhaps that was only when said people had nothing to hide. Her mind went fleetingly back to Marianne, before she decided to concentrate fully on the good doctor and his encyclopedic knowledge of plant-to-soil compatibility.

Inside Cranberry Farmhouse, the kettle was whistling gently along on the range and the biscuits were plated. Doctor Ptolemy Oates, uncompromising in his tweeds, waistcoat and bow tie – despite the warm summer sunshine – was seated quite happily at Daphne's kitchen table with the dog by his feet waiting patiently for any dropped crumbs. It brought a moment of calm to a mind otherwise filled with chaos and intrigue for Daphne. She really didn't know why she was so invested in Minerva, Marianne and Charles, but what she did know is that it wasn't bringing her the relaxation she had hoped for after the family's move to the countryside. She couldn't even claim that she was bored – now with the shop and painting and sourcing furniture in between running after the children and maintaining a far larger house and garden than she was used to, she had a lot more to get on with besides playing amateur sleuth.

She brought her attention back to her neighbour, who had been patiently explaining how her rhubarb needed to be in a sunny, open site with moist but free-draining soil – hence why positioning it under her overrun apple trees had caused the young plants to fail to thrive, let alone produce any fruit.

'You see, rhubarb prefers a slightly acidic to neutral soil, and a soil that's consistent with its moisture and high in organic matter,' he explained. 'Moreover, you mustn't over-water as the crowns can rot in wet soil. A good rule of thumb is to water when the top inch of soil dries out, you see . . .' he continued as he munched enthusiastically on his fifth Fruit Shortcake in as many minutes.

Much of what he told her was obvious, really, and could be found in the numerous gardening books that she had collected over the past few months, but as a relative novice to garden-ing, she delighted in listening to Doctor Oates, and Doctor Oates clearly delighted in being listened to in turn. He had the voice of a stage actor, the face of a grown-up Billy Bunter and his capacity for knowledge seemed boundless. Having an abundance of fruit and vegetables in the field that lay beyond his cottage, Doctor Oates had no need of an allotment in the neighbouring village, unlike many of the residents in the older part of Pepperbridge where the original houses were several hundred years old. There, the outbuildings, barns and stables had long since been converted into other homes, resulting in the larger gardens being carved up into more modest patches to go with each new dwelling.

She sighed contentedly as he spoke on, switching topics every so often, but always remaining on pleasantly neutral and wholesome territory. With a rare break in the gardening conversation, both she and Doctor Oates sipped on their cups of tea in companionable silence, lost in their own thoughts.

'Well . . .' Doctor Oates took a final sip of his tea to wash down his sixth biscuit – not that Daphne had been counting – and then stood up, brushing a regrettably meagre number of crumbs from his trousers in the direction of the eagerly awaiting Byron. 'This won't get the baby bathed!'

Daphne grinned at the old adage – Doctor Oates enjoyed peppering his conversation with aphorisms which often left the children in fits of giggles and always caused Daphne to smile.

A cup of tea with her neighbour was 'just what the doctor ordered'. It had been a welcome treat to sit in a world that wasn't concerned with death or post-mortems or disappearing friends. The doctor had proclaimed, from the beginning of their acquaintance, that village politics and local gossip was not 'his thing' – a fact that she had been very pleased about.

James called shortly after Doctor Oates had left. He had spotted what he believed to be an ornately carved mahogany Arts & Crafts chair with a seat that needed to be reupholstered discarded in a skip, and wanted to discuss whether it was worth the inconvenience of bringing it home on the train.

'I can't be sure that it's an original, but it looks a lot like the one that you pointed out to me at the auction in Tottenhill, and it's FREE,' he exclaimed, hardly believing his luck in spotting it.

'Well, if they're willing to part with it, and you're sure that you can manage it on the train, then yes please!'

Daphne was delighted that they had moved past the topic of her 'almost arrest', but she was also thrilled that James was so on board with the idea of her workshop. It was a passion project, to say the least, but if she could keep getting commissions and a few sales, things would tick over nicely and she'd hopefully make a successful business of it eventually. She had set aside a small portion of her rainy-day savings to secure the lease of the small shop, but thankfully, the rent on Pepperidge High Street was a fraction of what a similar unit would have cost in London – and it was much prettier, with its crooked little Victorian façade and nineteenth-century bullseye windows. Although at this point it was mainly a workshop, she was grateful to have a dedicated space that made her feel like her initial nugget of an idea was now a fully-fledged business. She was a vintage hunter, not a homicide hunter – or at least that's what she told herself . . .

It was 2.15 p.m. before Daphne thought about attempting to visit Marianne again. By her calculations, Marianne would be thinking about leaving the house to collect the children soon, and Daphne wanted to catch her before she did – at a point when she couldn't possibly avoid her.

Daphne pulled Aggie out of the drive for the second time that day and made the short journey across Pudding Corner to Marianne's house. This time she was in luck. Parking a little way down the road, so that her car would not be visible enough to spoil the element of surprise, Daphne walked to the Forbes's house just in time to catch Marianne signing for a FedEx delivery.

Daphne could tell from the panic in Marianne's eyes that she felt trapped. Her body language had turned unmistakably stiff and from the sudden gasp of breath that Daphne heard before she'd even reached the gate, her mere presence seemed to have propelled her 'friend' into fight-or-flight mode. Unfortunately for Marianne, the delivery man had taken his sweet time and now there was nowhere for her to run.

'Marianne!' Daphne called out, waving cheerfully.

'Daphne . . . ?' Marianne responded – a slight question in the tone of her voice.

Daphne could sense the chink appearing in Marianne's armour, and pressed on. If she could bamboozle her with words, then she'd have to let her come in.

'I was just passing and realised how early I was for pick-up, so I thought I'd pop in for a cup of tea . . . we haven't done that in such a long time, have we? In fact, I did try calling in on you earlier, but you must have been in the garden . . . ?'

Marianne hesitated for a fraction longer than was entirely comfortable before taking a quick glance at her watch and realising she was cornered. Sighing under her breath, she allowed Daphne to follow her through the front door.

The two women walked towards the kitchen at the back of the house. The route was familiar to Daphne, who had delivered Marianne children's home on more occasions than she cared to remember. The hallway was narrow and long but extremely tall. The stairs to the right were equally as narrow and incredibly steep, ascending the entire four stories and seemingly even tighter the higher you got. The house was elegant, yes, but certainly not a practical abode for anyone with even the mildest of mobility issues.

The kitchen was the largest room in the house, but even then it was on a more modest and cosy scale than one would have imagined from the grandeur of the exterior. Marianne walked resignedly towards the kettle and flicked the switch on. She turned around to face Daphne who by now was sitting at the farmhouse table in the centre of the room.

The two women eyed each other – one looking apprehensive and suspicious, the other feigning cheerful innocence as she watched the other squirm.

'I'll be honest with you, Marianne . . .' Daphne eventually began, 'I'm here because I wanted to know how you are? You seemed rather out of sorts this morning. Jumpy even. Is everything OK?'

She could see Marianne's chest begin to rise and fall that little bit faster and harder. She was clearly nervous . . . but why?

Marianne's mouth simply opened and closed noiselessly for a few seconds, resembling a goldfish that had unexpectedly found itself out of water. Daphne stared at her with what she hoped was a concerned rather than just inquisitive face. She could practically see the mechanisms of Marianne's brain whirring for a suitable explanation.

'I . . . I . . . ' she began promisingly.

Daphne realised that she was quite literally sitting on the edge of her seat. She subtly composed herself, sliding her bottom back. Marianne's eyes were flickering towards the open kitchen door, as though she was hoping to be rescued by someone.

'Yes . . . ?' Daphne tried to stop her voice from showing any signs of impatience. She was meant to be here under the guise of being Marianne's 'friend', not as her interrogator. Perhaps a nudge in the right direction was needed?

'Is it about the circumstances surrounding Mr Papplewick's

death ...?' Daphne probed gently. She glanced at the clock above the Aga – time was ticking by. 'I remember that you were rather upset that morning ... in the school office ...?' Daphne let the sentence hang in the air.

Marianne's head snapped up at the mere mention of Charles Papplewick. She had exited the school hastily that morning, still shaking with anger after her terse exchange of words. Despite her rage, she had assumed that no one had seen her enter or leave.

Her shoulders sloped down in defeat. She had been seen after all. There was no point pretending that the altercation hadn't happened. Daphne had obviously witnessed – or heard – it all.

'It was just words!' she finally cried out – almost wailing, her voice cracking as the words spilled out in abject despair. 'They were just idle threats – they meant nothing and what else could I do? What would you have done? He refused to help me, he refused to help my children. He refused to help with anything! It was nothing more than that.'

By now Marianne was crying: big ugly, gulping sobs with her nose streaming and her arms flailing, narrowly missing scalding her arm as it waved perilously close to the still steaming hob kettle.

'Nancy Warburton said that she saw you with Charles again later that evening?' said Daphne. 'Outside in the rain ... she said that you were screaming at him ... she said that you seemed slightly ... er – out of control?'

Pain seared through Marianne. 'Oh god! Oh my god – she saw me? Oh my god – please – I didn't know what I was doing, it wasn't me, I mean, it wasn't who I am – I'd, I'd been drinking!' she finally blurted out and sobbed again. 'I don't remember – I was drun—'

'MARIANNE!' Timothy's voice came out of nowhere and cut through the air like a knife.

Marianne's wailing had been abruptly and obediently stopped in its tracks.

'STOP TALKING. Stop. It. Right. Now!'

Daphne had never seen the slightly gormless Timothy look so angry before. His face was contorted with fury and for the first time since she had known the couple, the tables of power seemed to have turned. It was usually Marianne who took control, with Timothy resignedly falling into line. Something had obviously changed in the dynamic of the relationship over the past few weeks. Marianne meekly lowered her eyes at the sound of her husband's command, did as she was told and didn't utter another word.

Timothy turned to face Daphne with a face like thunder. He no longer looked like the overgrown public schoolboy that she was familiar with – all floppy hair, toothy smile and self-deprecating charm. His demeanour was far more menacing, and his darkened, furious eyes stared at her with suspicion.

'She's talking rot. Ignore it.' It was more of an order than a request, denoting the end of the conversation. Daphne – not wanting to challenge him in this mood – sensed that it was time to go. She stood up with forced brightness, smiled at Marianne, thanked her for the chat, and walked towards the open kitchen door as though nothing untoward had happened.

'I'll see you at the school gates!' she called out as she casually passed Timothy, and calmly headed out. Once out of sight, she practically ran towards her car like a bat out of hell, her heart pounding so rapidly she felt as if it would burst through her ribcage.

So, Marianne had been drunk that night. Drunk *and* driving no less! How awful, although it explained why she'd felt it appropriate to be screaming at Charles in the darkened streets of Pepperbridge on a Friday night. Was that all that had happened though? Had Marianne followed him into his potting shed and killed him? It didn't seem likely . . . From the sound of it, he didn't have any physical trauma about his body that would imply a scuffle or a fight. There were no stab or gunshot wounds. No evidence of blunt objects whacking him about the head, and yet despite all roads leading to a probable heart attack, there was still the faint prospect of foul play.

It was ten past three when Daphne parked her car near the school gates. She had five minutes before the bell rang to announce the end of the school day at three fifteen. The children would then routinely take at least a few minutes more to find their bags and get themselves organised into class lines, which gave Daphne a few minutes more to contemplate whether Marianne may have unwittingly caused Charles's death by screaming at him only a short while after an argument with his own wife. It was enough to have given anyone a heart attack, Daphne mused wryly, absent-mindedly chewing on her bottom lip as she tried to figure everything out.

The sudden trill of the bell pulled her sharply out of her thoughts, and she jumped out of Aggie and walked towards the school gates just in time to see Timothy pulling up in his battered old Range Rover. It seemed that he no longer trusted his wife not to blab at the school gates. Was Timothy Forbes frightened that his wife would be in trouble for drunk driving, or was he frightened that his wife would be held responsible for the death of Charles Papplewick? Daphne had a flashback of his face filled with anger only fifteen minutes ago. Maybe he wasn't worried about his wife at all. Perhaps the Timothy Forbes that she had witnessed a glimpse of was the unexpected villain in this scenario. His son had been refused help with the scholarship bursary, after all. But was that enough to murder someone?

A glowering Timothy walked through the gates and was now within a few feet of Daphne to her left. The knowledge that he was there, pretending, as she was, that they hadn't just seen each other made her feel instantly and uncharacteristically nervous. Daphne gathered her emotions together, studiously avoided eye contact with anyone in the vicinity, and plastered on a fake smile as she looked for her children.

Chapter 13

According to James, there were only two reasons why someone would willingly involve themselves in a criminal investigation that had nothing whatsoever to do with them. The first was a result of friendly – but misguided – concern for a family member or friend, and the other was down to plain old-fashioned nosiness. Much to Daphne's annoyance, James had rather unhelpfully declared that he was inclined to believe she fell into the latter camp.

'Don't real friends reveal their deepest, darkest secrets to each other?' he had asked on more than one occasion.

'Not past the age of twelve,' she had replied curtly. 'Besides, it's only been eight months. We're friends, but not lifelong soulmates – yet . . .'

Yet it had been two and a half weeks and Minerva had not returned any of her calls or text messages. Not even the ones that asked for no more than an indication that she was simply safe and well. If that was friendship, it was more than a little one sided.

> Hello Minerva, It's Daphne. I just wanted to make sure that you and Silvanus are OK? I haven't heard from you in a while. Sending love. xx

> Hi Minerva. Just checking in. I'm sure that you're OK, but it would be nice to know that all is well. x

> Hi Minerva. Please just send an emoji if everything's OK. I'll leave you alone now though. Hope all is well.

Every single message had been steadfastly ignored.

Inspector Hargreaves had called to ask about Minerva's whereabouts twice over the past week, and Daphne had promised (with a metaphorical finger crossed behind her back) to let him know the minute she got in touch. Apparently, Minerva wasn't a suspect as such, but thanks to the accusations being spread about by a certain member of the parish, they did want to have a chat with her.

Meanwhile, unlike the long defunct Pepperbridge flour factory, the village rumour mill had been working overtime, with more and more fantastical stories about why the police were unwilling to release Charles's body so that he could have a proper burial. Naturally, the *Village Pump* was leading the way by providing a running commentary of what was quite obviously a plethora of exaggerated daily events. At least, it was claiming to be the *Village Pump*. The highly coveted newsletter was now being unofficially produced as a single-page supplement that was randomly circulated a few times per week, much to the chagrin of the official editor (and principal soloist of the church choir, she liked to remind everyone), Mrs Freestone. Mrs Freestone claimed to know nothing of these mini editions being hastily printed and distributed without her consent. Somebody was obviously having an immense amount of fun with their poisoned pen.

> ... *Did anyone actually see a body? Could it be that the long-suffering husband has in fact done a John Darwin and is currently hightailing it as far away as possible on a canoe to South America?*
>
> *Rumour has it that said headmaster had an insurance policy that was worth a six figure sum to be left to his beneficiaries – of which there is one ... Let us now take a moment to lament the 'not so poor' or grieving widow for her loss ...*
>
> *Why has a certain resident of Cringlewic gone mysteriously missing? Has she fled in haste on her Vroom Stick or is that just witchful thinking for a certain Pepperbridge resident?*

Had it not been for the fact that Augusta had featured in most of the issues, then one would have assumed that she was behind the whole thing. She was, after all, the primary accuser when it came to the supposed involvement of Minerva in Charles Papplewick's death.

Her narrative now implied that Minerva had been blackmailing the headmaster over a period of years and had ultimately chosen to murder him in an act of revenge.

Augusta had failed to comprehend that her version of events didn't portray either her husband or her marriage in a good light, and the rumour mill had exploded into an abundance of scandalous theories about illicit affairs and deadly betrayals.

Having already spoken to Marianne to gain some insight into the fateful night, Daphne planned to speak once more to Augusta regarding her accusations. It was ironic really, since, beyond the odd occasion when their eyes had met briefly at school, Daphne had avoided Augusta as much as possible since returning her home a few weeks ago. Daphne was a huge believer in innocent until proven guilty, and she would rather hear the truth straight from the horse's mouth – or in this case the elusive Minerva's. Even if James, upset that his wife's new friend had inexplicably disappeared without any explanation, didn't think she deserved her unquestioning support . . .

Daphne doubted that anyone else would have been brave or silly enough to confront Augusta – she'd even witnessed the police jump to attention at the sound of her clipped tones and dismissive attitude. Yet, here Daphne was, pulling up to the back entrance of the Papplewick house, with the sole aim of interrogating Augusta. Daphne was reminded of the other occasions of heightened emotion that she had walked up this very same path. Unlike today, those times had been filled with a lot of rain and a healthy dose of foreboding – if you believed in that sort of thing. Today it was thankfully bright and sunny, with another cloudless Norfolk sky. Surely Augusta's 'bite' would be less intense when the sun shone – or did that only apply to vampires . . . ?

As luck would have it, if one could call it that, Augusta was at home. She was apparently spending much of her time alone at home these days. It had been suggested that perhaps it was better if she didn't spend so much time in the headmaster's office at Pepperbridge Primary School, attempting to pick up where her husband had left off with no official jurisdiction given by the local authority to preside over school affairs. It had taken the deputy head almost a fortnight to gather the courage to politely evict the domineering matriarch from the office that she herself should have been occupying.

According to the rumour mill, Augusta sat at home most days with her vodka Martinis, having graduated from delicately footed teacups and saucers to larger but equally pretty china mugs. There was little point in holding back now.

Augusta opened the door to Daphne with her usual sense of authority. She was evidently loath to play the broken widow for anyone's benefit, and her anger remained intact. Hers was not a smouldering rage, but a freshly stoked firepit, and Daphne almost regretted her decision to be there.

Augusta held the door open before turning on her heel and allowing Daphne to enter with a commanding 'Come in'.

Daphne did as she was told; after all, she reminded herself, this is what she had wanted – some time alone with Augusta.

'Sit. I don't suppose that you'll require a cup of tea,' Augusta said pointedly as she sat down on her chintzy sofa, having led Daphne through to the formal sitting room with its perfectly placed cushions, French-polished antiques and immaculately laid out silverware on a high mahogany sideboard at the end of the room – as if waiting for the perfect retro dinner party to begin. It was a statement and not a question, the tone of her voice ensured that much was crystal clear.

Augusta may have had no intention of making Daphne any

tea, but as a stickler for the rules of polite society, she was forced to at least make a pretence at civility.

Daphne felt more bemused than uncomfortable. It was a miracle that Augusta was willing to have her within ten feet of her house, let alone be sat opposite her.

'Well?' Augusta broke the silence.

Her petite hands were clasped in her lap, her knees together and legs slanted elegantly to one side in the manner of a debutante freshly out of finishing school. There was nothing accidental about how Augusta Papplewick presented herself. Each glance, each clipped enunciation, and even the way she sat down, projected the uncompromising vibe that she was superior to you.

'I'd like to ask you a question, if you don't mind,' began Daphne with steady confidence as she looked straight back at Augusta without hesitation.

As much as she loved it in Pudding Corner, one of the best things about growing up in south London was that she had a self-assurance that couldn't be diminished by the self-imposed hierarchy of the village's born and bred residents. Daphne had never felt the need to vie for social dominance in the way that Augusta Papplewick and Marianne Forbes did. The combination of city street-smarts and the pride instilled in her from her immigrant parents was a hefty defence for a Black woman taught to be comfortable in her own skin from an early age.

'Go on,' Augusta responded, nodding her head.

Daphne paused for a moment before asking, 'Do you really believe that Minerva Leek murdered your husband?'

'I do,' Augusta replied calmly.

'And ... why is that? Do you have any evidence, did you see something?'

Daphne didn't even know if the police were taking Augusta's accusations seriously, but regardless, she wanted to know her reasoning behind them.

Augusta stood up abruptly and walked over to the door which led towards the kitchen.

'I think that I'll make us some tea after all. Would you care for some?'

It was a few minutes before Augusta returned holding a tray carrying a teapot, one single Royal Doulton cup and saucer, a jug of milk and a sugar bowl filled with white cubes and a silver pair of tongs. At first, Daphne assumed that Augusta was really following through with her decision not to offer Daphne any tea, but after Augusta enquired as to whether her guest would prefer milk or lemon, Daphne realised that even the queen of the dismissive put-down wouldn't be that rude. She exited again quickly but returned almost immediately with her own mug, and sat down once more opposite Daphne.

'Herbal,' she stated when she noticed Daphne look towards the cup enquiringly, wondering why she had not simply brought it in with the tray.

They sat in silence for a moment as both took a sip of their drinks. Daphne's tea was hot to her lips and she pulled back, almost scalded – Augusta's apparently not so much.

'We'd had a perfectly pleasant evening together ...' Augusta suddenly resumed unprompted and out of nowhere, causing Daphne to jump inwardly. 'I'd had a headache that afternoon at school – I feared that it would turn into a migraine, so I decided to return home early. It was raining quite heavily, I remember.' Augusta paused and took another sip out of her mug. 'Charles arrived home rather later than usual – he'd had a meeting with a parent, I believe. I'd made him his supper – one of his favourites – a cottage pie with garden peas, swede and mashed potatoes – all from his allotment. It's a winter meal of course, but the weather was so unseasonably cold and dreary that week that it seemed appropriate.'

Daphne kept very still and listened as she noted Augusta's eyes looking into the distance beyond her shoulder, as if visualising each detail in her mind.

'We were having such a lovely time. My headache had abated, and we were just about to settle down to the second course – a rhubarb crumble with crème anglaise – when Charles remembered that he'd left the door to his shed unlocked at the allotment. It was very out of character for him you see – he's usually very careful with security . . .'

Daphne didn't move. She knew full well that the picture Augusta was painting was a false one. She'd seen Augusta screaming furiously through the front window that evening with her own eyes.

'I remember he said that he'd only be a little while as he dashed out into the rain. He stored some personal items as well as his tools in the shed, and he didn't want anything disturbed, or for the door to be blown open and everything inside drenched with rain. It was blowing quite a gale that evening.'

Daphne's mind went to the documents she'd discovered tucked away behind the chitting potatoes on the desk.

'It was at least an hour later when I started to get worried.

He hadn't returned and he wasn't picking up his phone. The crumble was drying to dust in the Aga – he prefers it with a bit of juice in, you see – so after another hour or so I thought that I'd go and see what was keeping him. Plus, I needed a bit of fresh air – after the headache and everything.'

'So you went out into the downpour?' Daphne asked. She was thinking about Augusta's wet and muddy boots the morning she'd denied leaving her house since the previous afternoon.

'Yes,' Augusta was looking directly at Daphne now, as though examining her face to see her reaction. She knew full well that Daphne had questioned the wet state of the wellingtons.

'But why did you tell the police that you hadn't left the house, Augusta? Why did you lie about that?'

Augusta took another sip from her mug. This time, she tilted it so far back that it was obvious she was draining the cup. It must be good herbal tea, Daphne thought to herself, as Augusta once more excused herself to, 'Top up her cup . . .' leaving Daphne impatiently hanging on for the answer.

She returned to her seat and, as was becoming habit now, picked up directly where she had left off.

'. . . that's just it. I didn't tell them because I was still in shock. You see, that's the reason I know it was Minerva.'

Daphne was on the edge of her seat again. What had Augusta seen that had made her so sure that Charles had been murdered by Minerva?

'I arrived at the allotment and it was almost pitch black – I could hardly see. The rain was still coming down, in fact the conditions were quite horrific. I could just make out the light coming from his potting shed – the only light on in the area. There's no electricity there so he uses a gas light and a camping stove. I was about to call out when I saw her ...'

Augusta paused for what Daphne was certain was a flourish of dramatic emphasis.

'Saw who?' Daphne felt compelled to ask the question even though she already knew what Augusta's answer was going to be.

'Minerva Leek, of course.'

Daphne sighed and took a quick sip of her own only slightly cooling tea. In her eagerness to hear the story, she'd almost burnt her tongue twice without thinking. Augusta eyed Daphne's curled lip as she attempted to drink the scalding liquid.

'Shall I put get you some cold wa—'

'No!' Daphne practically spat – she didn't want any more gaps in the conversation. She wanted to know exactly what Augusta had seen that night. 'No, thank you – it's fine. Delicious even,' she lied, quickly composing herself as she continued to sip through a suppressed grimace. Boiling hot tea was a small price to pay ... 'What was ... Minerva doing?' she asked.

'She was arguing with Charles. They were in the potting shed, and she was shouting at him.' Augusta sounded vaguely irritated, as though the answer ought to have been obvious.

Daphne thought about it for less than a minute. It didn't make any sense.

'... But if Minerva was shouting at your husband, why didn't you intervene? Why didn't you go and find out what was wrong? Or try to stop it ... or her ... or something?'

'That's exactly what I intended to do, but ...' Augusta stopped and sighed, and took another long gulp of her 'herbal tea'.

'But ...?' Daphne prompted her.

'... But – that was when they kissed.' It was the mic-drop moment and Augusta knew it.

Daphne looked on, eyes widening. 'They, they ... were actually kissing?' she stuttered out eventually.

'Yes indeed. Kissing. What I thought had been an argument, with her fists pounding on his chest, well, it all turned very quickly – before I could reach the shed – into a passionate embrace and, and a kiss ...' Augusta looked down into her cup and for the first time Daphne felt a little sorry for her.

Unfortunately, her description of events confirmed what Daphne had seen in the woods. It was a cliché as old as time. The older married man and his much younger lover embracing in a few illicitly snatched moments. It was very disappointing. Daphne didn't want to be a prude or cast moral judgement, but she had hoped that this wouldn't be the conclusion ...

'To be honest, I couldn't believe that he hadn't seen me – or heard me. He was facing my direction the entire time – they might have heard me stumbling about in the dark, but I suppose that they were otherwise ... engaged.'

There seemed to be no stopping Augusta now. Whether recounting the story was proving to be cathartic or whether there was something in the 'herbal tea' that had 'relaxed' her, she seemed eager to continue.

Daphne sat puzzled for a few moments. Something wasn't quite adding up.

'How close were you?' she asked.

'How close?' Augusta seemed confused. 'How close was I to my husband? We had a very loving relationship, or so I thought ...'

'No, I mean, how close did you get to the potting shed that night? You said that it was dark, and presumably muddy in the rain, and you needed to call out? How close did you get if you needed to as you say, "call out"?'

Augusta raised an eyebrow, clearly calculating her response. 'Close enough,' she replied curtly.

'Yes, of course ... but had you reached the window, or were you a distance away? You said that he was facing you the entire time, did you actually see Minerva's face? If you were at a distance, how did you know it was ...'

'ENOUGH,' Augusta boomed and stood up, violently capsizing her mug. 'This entire experience has been traumatic enough as it is without having to relive it over and over again!'

They both looked down at the mug that had crashed down onto the wooden floorboards and smashed into several pieces, its clear liquid contents spilling out onto the edge of an antique rug.

'I'm so sorry,' Daphne cried out as she instinctively stood from her seat and bent down to help pick up the mess.

'LEAVE IT!' Augusta practically screamed, but it was too late.

As both women crouched down, it was quite obvious to Daphne that the clear contents had been neat vodka. She hesitated before standing up, a fragment of the mug still attached to the handle in her hand.

'I'm sorry, Augusta. I really didn't mean to upset you,' she offered gently. 'It must all be so awful, regardless of what they were doing, you've been married for such a long time. It must be hard.'

Daphne thought of her brief glimpse of Charles's will, leaving the house that Augusta had shared with her husband throughout their married life to Minerva and Silvanus. She was being completely genuine when she'd described it as 'hard', as she wondered whether Augusta was yet aware of that particular detail.

Augusta remained crouched on the floor, dabbing at the liquid with an embroidered handkerchief that she'd pulled from her pocket with one hand, while holding several pieces of broken china in the other. She was mumbling to herself as she dabbed the floor aggressively – staring down rather than at Daphne.

'All this time! All these years. I sacrificed everything. I gave up EVERYTHING – and for what? That little BITCH.'

Daphne was frozen, aghast and mesmerised at the jumble of words pouring from the incoherently babbling Augusta.

'She poisoned his mind. She POISONED him! Poisoned him against me. We were fine. He was about to retire. We were going to travel. To DO things. We were supposed to leave this godforsaken prison and DO things. She killed him. She killed US!' She was crying now, her shoulders jerking with each sob.

Daphne kneeled down and put her arms around Augusta as she rocked in despair. The older woman seemed suddenly small and broken. It was all very sad. *This* was obviously what Augusta had meant by Minerva 'poisoning' Charles. She hadn't meant that she had murdered him – she had meant that the younger woman had poisoned his mind. It sort of made sense now. Almost. It still didn't explain why Charles had been found dead the next morning.

Augusta's sobbing had stopped, but she was still quietly rocking in Daphne's arms.

'I think that we should get you to lie down for a nap, Augusta,' Daphne said. 'Is that OK?'

Augusta nodded her head almost imperceptibly, and then looked down at the broken shards that were still left on the floor.

'Don't worry about the mess, Augusta, I'll clear up and then let myself out.'

She helped raise Augusta to her feet, and they made their way to the stairs and walked up, Augusta leaning on Daphne's side and held up by her arms the entire way.

'Which bedroom is yours?' Daphne asked, before guiding Augusta in the direction that her finger had limply indicated.

It was a very neat and tidy bedroom, tastefully decorated with an antique half tester bed and a window seat in a bay window that overlooked the rear garden. Daphne sat Augusta on the bed, helped to remove her shoes and swung her feet up so that she was reclining with her head on the pillow. It was a warm day, but still Daphne pulled up a blanket that was folded neatly across the end of the bed, and gently covered Augusta with it. Whatever her thoughts on Augusta, the woman appeared to have no one to comfort her.

Daphne's eyes flickered across to the nearby dressing table. As well as the expected brush and comb and various bits of make-up and bottled perfume, it was also home to a wedding photograph in a heavy silver frame. It showed a much younger and serious-looking Charles Papplewick dressed in a morning suit, standing next to a very youthful and deliriously happy-looking Augusta. They appeared to be leaving the village church in Papplewick – Daphne recognised the tiled lychgate that marked the entrance to the attractive church that was now presided over by Reverend Gerald Duncan.

Even in his twenties, there seemed to be a hint of sadness to Charles's eyes. It should have been the happiest day of his life, but it was evident – even through this millisecond snapshot of their wedding day – that he wasn't a happy man.

Daphne was just about to turn back to Augusta when she saw another picture almost hidden out of sight behind the first frame. It showed a smiling Augusta on her graduation day, in a robe and mortar board. It hadn't occurred to Daphne that Augusta had attended university. She hadn't appeared to have pursued a career beyond being the wife of a headmaster. Augusta looked happy in the photograph. She had someone's arm around her, but the person's torso was cut off by the frame, leaving Augusta alone in the image with a floating arm about her shoulder. Daphne looked peered a little closer. The hand around her shoulder was square and large and had a signet ring on its little finger. A boy. You rarely saw rings like that on men these days. She glanced back at Augusta in the photograph. She looked like someone who was filled with joy and promise and the excitement of life to come. What had happened to turn her into the spiky and uptight bully that she was today?

'Will you be OK?' Daphne asked, her attention now back to her dozing companion.

Augusta was drifting in and out of sleep, but she seemed settled at least.

Daphne knew that it would be cruel to interrogate Augusta any further in her current state, but she wanted to ask one final question before she left.

'Augusta?'

'Mmmmm?' Augusta's eyes were open and vaguely focused on Daphne as her head rested against the pillow.

'Did you actually see Minerva's face that night – in the potting shed?'

'No,' Augusta murmured sleepily. 'I saw the back of her head, but it must have been her. He said that we should never have married – because of *her* . . .' and then she was asleep.

Chapter 14

The Pepperbridge village fete was held annually on the first Saturday of July. It was one of the highlights of the parish calendar and was kept to the same reliably quaint format every year. Despite the recent sad events, this year was set to go ahead as planned. The stall holders, the fairground rides and the entertainment had been organised several months in advance, and it was expected to run like clockwork, held in the late headmaster's honour. Most of the school staff, residents and parents agreed that Mr Papplewick would have wanted it that way and, being the selfless headmaster that he was, would have been aghast at the thought of his passing causing a disruption to such a stalwart Pepperbridge tradition. Augusta had even agreed to hand out the prizes again this year, despite her loss being so recent that the headmaster's body had yet to be laid to rest. It was all settled. No one was in any doubt that the village was in dire need of something uplifting, and a village fete, with its bunting, maypole dancing and cream teas, was just the ticket.

Naturally, the children of Pepperbridge Primary were in a frenzied state of excitement that would rival even the most toxically intense sugar rush, and every long-suffering parent – whether willingly or not – had been pulled in to prove their creative acumen by designing costumes or building and decorating the increasingly more elaborate floats. No one wanted to be accused of the harshest criticism known to Pepperbridge parenthood: the horror of *buying* a costume.

The PTA authenticity police made it their annual mission to weed out and publicly shame any parish resident who dared to circumvent the unspoken rules of 'friendly competitiveness'. Those who were not interested in children's activities were preparing themselves for the battle of the best home-grown flowers, the largest organic vegetables, or the fluffiest Victoria sponge cake. Even the all-ages prize for the bonniest bonnet, which the women of the WI took incredibly seriously, and which often ended in vicious accusations of stolen intellectual property and angst-ridden tears, was being eagerly prepared for among the more senior residents. The collective excitement was palpable – and despite Daphne's preoccupation with Charles Papplewick's death, even she was beginning to get caught up in it.

It had been quite a few days since Daphne had left Augusta sleeping off her afternoon 'tea' in bed. She had called in to check on her that same evening, wanting to set her mind at rest that Augusta hadn't fallen off the bed or choked in her sleep. When a composed and unruffled Augusta had opened the front door, Daphne had seen that the grand dame of Pepperbridge had returned to her habitual haughty self, making no reference to the earlier events. Over Augusta's shoulder, just down the entrance hall, Daphne spotted two of Augusta's village henchwomen waiting at the kitchen table. With relief, she had gladly left the older woman to her entourage, made her excuses, and departed in the knowledge that her questions had caused no lasting damage.

Much to Daphne's disappointment, there had been no more revelatory inroads into the night Charles Papplewick had died. She feared that without confirmation from Minerva herself as to whether it had been her (kissing? arguing?) with Charles in the potting shed, any further speculation was a moot point, but Minerva was still missing, and even Daphne felt that trying to send her more than the occasional text might constitute harassment at this point. What was reassuring was that all of her messages had been read – the twin blue ticks confirmed that – and once she had even noticed the pulsating dots of a reply about to be typed back. Minerva then obviously thought the better of it, and didn't commit to pressing 'send'. Regardless of any confirmation, Daphne felt in her bones that Minerva was not the type to go around kissing married men in darkened sheds at night, although perhaps she was naively and conveniently failing to count the tryst that she saw in the woods as proof otherwise. Yet there was something off about the whole situation. Daphne knew that Minerva would not have willingly left her sleeping child alone in order to meet up with a lover – and surely, Silvanus hadn't been there with her? Minerva was fiercely protective of her son and would not have abandoned him for even half an hour in favour of an illicit meeting – of that, Daphne was certain. Perhaps Augusta had seen a still tipsy Marianne in the potting shed, confronting Charles for the third time that night?

There had been a brief conversation, due to the light drizzle threatening to turn into proper rain, with Patsy Warburton in the street outside of Daphne's little shop, where Patsy had seemed far more composed than the time Daphne had caught her uncharacteristically off-guard when questioned about Charles Papplewick's death. They had even managed to laugh about the atrocious weather that day considering Norfolk was supposed to be the driest county in England. It had taken a while for the feeling to be reciprocated, but Daphne had warmed to Patsy Warburton and her tongue-in-cheek humour hidden just below the surface.

As harbingers of local gossip, the sisters had been accused of being the perpetrators of the *Village Pump*'s rogue issues. It was common knowledge that neither sister could stand Augusta Papplewick, who was consistently being hinted at as the person most likely responsible for her own husband's death. The underlying tone that an 'unlikely love interest' may be involved only added to the sense that whoever was behind the unsolicited issues was more concerned with causing mischief for Augusta than helping her to mourn her loss. However, although the sisters claimed to have a good idea of who the true culprit might be, they vehemently denied all responsibility, claiming quite reasonably that *if* they had an accusation, they would gladly say it to the suspect's face.

Patsy had been restocking the Victorian jardinière that they used as stock display in the front of their grocery shop when Daphne had shouted a cheerful 'hello' after parking in front of her own shop a few doors down. Patsy had paused to check who had called out before her stern features softened, returning the wave in good-natured acknowledgment.

Unlike her smaller, bespectacled older sister, Patsy had an almost formidable presence to her height. Almost always dressed in battered overalls with a striped T-shirt underneath, she was the outwardly intimidating yin to Nancy's unassumingly granny-like yang. However, woe betide anyone who imagined that Nancy, with her Mrs Pepperpot looks, was the more affable half of the pair. Nancy Warburton definitely had the deadlier sting in her tail.

On the other hand, Patsy might look as though she could take you out with one right hook, but she preferred to stealthily build up to the knockout rather than waste her punches. That morning she had been surprisingly talkative, choosing to walk the few short yards towards Daphne's store and enquire how everything was coming along. After exchanging a few pleasantries about footfall, the conversation had turned unexpectedly to the topic of Minerva.

'How is your friend, Minerva, from the commune?' Patsy had enquired politely.

'Oh gosh – Minerva, well ...' Daphne had stumbled on her words, unsure how much to admit to Patsy, who was obviously well known for gathering information.

'I do hope that she's all right. All this nonsense that bully Augusta and the village are spouting!'

Patsy had sounded far more impassioned than Daphne would have expected, and she believed that Patsy was speaking with sincerity, rather than fishing for gossip.

'To be honest, I'm rather worried as I haven't heard from

her for a while,' Daphne reluctantly admitted, unable to keep up a pretence about her friend who had seemingly disappeared into thin air.

Patsy looked Daphne directly in the eye with sudden compassion. 'Look after her, please. They're a nice bunch up at Cringlewic. They've been unfairly treated over the years.'

Daphne had looked back in surprise. Of all the people whom she had expected to defend the 'Witches of Cringlewic', one of the Warburton sisters had not been one of them.

'Do you know them up there? I've hardly seen any of the others – apart from Minerva. I did rather hope that she had a good support network, but it always seems so quiet – and empty.'

'Mmmm. That's a shame.' Patsy was looking past Daphne into the distance, as if recalling a long-forgotten memory. 'There used to be a lot more of them. It's historically been the site of a Wiccan coven, although it was just a woman's commune when I knew them. Lots of yoga and chanting and emotional support. One or two were trained midwives turned doulas. I think there were a few who had run out on abusive marriages or something, and some brought their children to live with them. It was all harmless really, although everyone thought it was scandalous back in the day and they've always had a hard time fitting in.' Patsy had sounded rather sad at this point. 'Nonsense, really. They're no different to you or me. Probably better than most in Pepperbridge, in fact,' she ended knowingly.

Daphne could have sworn there was a tinge of sadness to her voice – and something else too – was it regret? It was the most that Patsy had ever said to Daphne in one sitting, and it confirmed what Daphne had thought: Patsy was a good sort after all.

The conversation had ended abruptly there at the sound of Nancy calling her sister's name. Patsy had looked at Daphne with a smile and rolled her eyes before walking off.

The Saturday morning of the carnival had come quickly, and Cranberry Farmhouse was a hive of frantic activity, with all three children calling out for help in finding additional bits of costume and discarded paraphernalia. Immy had been asked to be a 'princess' on the carnival king and queen's float, and was taking her role as handmaiden to the eleven-year-old queen extremely seriously by repeatedly applying thick swathes of pink shimmery lipstick on her lips every time Daphne had wiped the last vetoed application off. Fynn was dressed as a playing-card soldier from *Alice in Wonderland*, complete with painted cardboard diamonds balanced sandwich-board style over his body, and a pair of Daphne's favourite black Wolford tights covering his beanpole legs. Archie was dressed as Willy Wonka – happily resplendent in a vintage purple smoking jacket that Daphne had found in a local charity shop, with hastily pinned up sleeves and an antique top hat that kept falling over his eyes. Byron was joining in with the excitement by gleefully getting tangled up in discarded clothes and attempting to grab hold of Archie's top hat with his mouth.

For the first time in weeks, Daphne felt carefree, her mind on things other than solving crimes that weren't officially crimes. Throwing herself into the joyful atmosphere of her deliriously happy children as they prepared for their first village fete and carnival parade was a pleasure after the previous weeks. It was a defining moment that they were so involved with the Pepperbridge parish institution. Even James had been called upon to man the coconut shy stand for half an hour, and he was also down for the Pudding Corner tug of war. It was a rite of passage.

They would need to leave the house within the next twenty minutes in order to get the children to the carnival floats at the north end of the village on time. Then the parents would follow along slowly behind the parade through the village, led by a local marching band, the more mobile members of the WI in their bonnets and sashes, a procession of vintage steam tractors and members of the Girl Guides and Boy Scouts. All the while, the children and teachers would be high up on their decorated floats, waving at the onlookers who lined the narrow, winding cobbled streets.

'Is that the doorbell?' Daphne vaguely heard James call out from Archie's room in the attic.

'What?'

She was on her hands and knees in Immy's room searching for a lost lace glove, although she had a sneaking suspicion that the culprit may be a four-legged long-haired miniature dachshund.

'The door – was that the door?' James repeated.

Daphne retreated her head from beneath Immy's bed and strained to listen. Sure enough, she could hear the tinkling of their ridiculously delicate Georgian doorbell that worked with the assistance of a small brass bell pulled by a string. They could only hear it fifty per cent of the time, depending on what part of the Cranberry Farmhouse they were in, but its authenticity and history added to the charm of the house. As ineffectual as it could be at times, they would never swap it for a more modern alternative.

Trrrrrrrringgg, it went.

'Damn,' she grumbled to herself. 'I'll get it then!' she called up to James with only a hint of sarcasm. They were both busy, she knew, but *he* had heard it first.

Daphne leaped down the stairs two at a time, aware that she had told the children not to descend this way on more than a dozen occasions. She looked up as she reached the bottom, to make sure that none of them could use the evidence against her.

'I'm just coming,' she called out to the other side of the heavy double doors.

The faux patient smile that she had plastered to her face soon turned to shock as she saw who was responsible for the ringing. She had assumed that it would be Doctor Oates, but there stood the one person whom she had least expected.

A distinctly nervous and bashful-looking Minerva Leek was on her front doorstep. She was holding the hand of a child whom Daphne could only assume was Silvanus since his head was covered in a medieval knight's helmet and he wore a full suit of cardboard armour covering his little body.

'Hello, Daphne,' she said with palpable embarrassment. 'I'm *so* sorry that I didn't return your calls.'

Daphne was aware that her mouth was literally hanging open in shock. She had called Minerva so many times and left her so many messages that she had begun to think that their friendship was a figment of her own imagination and desperation to connect with someone – anyone. Yet, here

was her 'friend' with tears in eyes which were just about to
flow down onto the dark circled rings that lay beneath her
red, puffy eyes. Her hair, dishevelled and hastily scraped
back behind her ears, looked as though it hadn't seen a brush
in weeks. She kept her head slightly bowed, her red-rimmed
eyes flickering up occasionally as she spoke with a voice that
was thick and heavy, filled with sadness, shame and regret.

Daphne was still quite unable to speak. She wasn't angry at
Minerva, simply shocked to find her on the doorstep.

Minerva, sensing that she had caught her friend off guard,
held her hand out towards Daphne's shoulder, 'I'm so, so
sorry,' she repeated again quietly, 'I didn't mean to leave
your messages unanswered. I just didn't know what to say.
It's been such an awful time – I just had to get away, and . . .
and . . . I also needed to get some legal advice. Away from
here . . .'

Daphne was about to say something, but Minerva's eyes
glanced down to Silvanus's head. Silvanus who was squirming
and shifting around while attached to his mother's hand. She
had never seen him so agitatedly excited. He was obviously
desperate to see his friends.

'Mummeeeeeee!' Daphne heard from the top of the stairs
'I found the glove, Byron had it in his bask— SILVER!'

There was a heavy clamouring down the stairs while Immy,
closely followed by an equally-as-excited Fynn and Archie,
came barrelling down the stairs and launched themselves
at their friend. A yapping Byron followed on afterwards,
jumping up while desperately attempting to include some
welcoming licks in the happy reunion.

It was a few minutes of thunderous laughter and

enthusiastic shouting before, through the chaos, Daphne turned back to Minerva and said apologetically, 'We need to talk, but I have to get the children to the floats first.'

'Yes, yes, of course,' replied Minerva. 'But Daphne, would you please do me a favour? Could you possibly take Silvanus with you? I don't want to spoil his day by drawing unwanted attention to myself, and I think it would be easier for him to blend in if he arrived with you. I'll be there discreetly in the background, of course. I didn't want to come back in this way or to do it like this, but he was so upset about missing the carnival, and he missed his friends so desperately that I . . . I couldn't bear to disappoint him . . . not again . . .'

Daphne could see the tears once more forming in her friend's eyes and she felt a wave of compassion. No matter what she herself was feeling right now, no matter how disappointed she was in Minerva for not letting her know what was going on, she couldn't deny her – or her son for that matter – the chance of doing something fun.

'Of course he can come along with us. The children would love it – they'd insist anyway.'

Daphne looked over at her own children playing happily with Silvanus and immediately understood the choice of costume. Whether Silvanus knew it or not, Minerva had been cleverly discreet by dressing her son up as a medieval knight in armour complete with a fully enclosed helmet. His distinctively narrow and pale face was totally concealed. It was a genius idea for Silvanus to feel like he was part of it all without prompting questions about where he or his mother had been. Or so Minerva hoped.

*

The day since then had gone incredibly smoothly – the sun had shone brightly, the predicted winds hadn't been too strong, the atmosphere had been buoyant and the crowds bountiful. There were only a few items left on the programme of events and the day was almost winding down. The three Brewster children had been having a whale of a time, completely at ease in their 'not so' new community in the English countryside. Silvanus had had a marvellous time too. His helmet had stayed firmly on – even when Daphne handed him a hotdog and she'd watched with impressed amusement as each bite had disappeared into his helmet as if by magic. James was crowing about his part in 'Pudding Corner Eight' claiming the winning title in the dads' tug of war – insisting seriously that it was all 'in the angle – and *not* just the grip'. Daphne had completed her shift on the tea tent and had managed to win a coffee and walnut cake in the tombola which – in the absence of any coffee and walnut cake lovers in her family – she intended to donate to Doctor Ptolemy Oates who, despite his age, seemed to be working all hours. They had invited him to accompany them to the Pepperbridge village fete, but he had good-naturedly declined, stating laughingly that his days of dancing the maypole at village fetes were long over.

'Ladies and gentlemen, now we come to the final event of what has been an absolutely wonderful day at the Pepperbridge annual school fete and carnival – wouldn't you all agree!'

The compere spoke into the microphone and was met with loud and enthusiastic cheering as dozens of sun-kissed faces, both young and old, stared back into the large showring which had been the centre stage for most of the day's big events.

'Can all the children joining in the primary-age fancy dress competition enter the showring now please!'

Daphne was leaning against James's arms contentedly. It really had been a lovely day, but she was looking forward to a few hours' peace with a nice, chilled glass of wine and her feet up on the sofa. She would have to speak with Minerva soon of course, but for now she would enjoy the final moments of this quaint country carnival before heading home. Archie was sitting on the grass at her feet, and she could see Fynn still dressed as a playing card in her tights playing a particularly boisterous game of 'tag' with a few friends off to the side behind the large crowd now gathering at the ring.

'Where's Immy?' she looked down and asked Archie.

'She went to the fancy dress,' he offered, staring intently at a bug that was crawling over his thumb.

Daphne looked up just in time to see her daughter boldly making her way through the rows of villagers sat in deckchairs towards the showring for the final competition of the day. She smiled to herself. She had brought up three very self-assured children who thankfully found it easy to make friends wherever they went. There wasn't a shy bone in Immy's body.

'Oh my gosh. Where's Silvanus?!' Daphne stood bolt upright and started to scan the area. A little way behind her confident daughter, who was skipping happily along wearing her sparkling tiara, lace gloves and princess dress, was an equally joyful skipping medieval knight. His helmet was still covering his face as he was walked, like all the other children, towards the centre of the ring where the compere stood next to the guest of honour, who was about to judge the competition. For a split second, Daphne felt that the scene resembled 'The Pied

Piper', where the village children were led blindly off towards the mysterious pipe music and into the emptiness of the night. Except instead of a pied piper, there was Augusta Papplewick, looking very serious in her duties as she stood, clipboard in hand, examining each child as they walked past her.

Daphne looked around her panicked. She'd noticed Minerva hovering discreetly on the outskirts of the large field where the fete was being held. Silvanus had even run up to her a few times, but Daphne was quite sure that no one else had noticed. Scanning the edge of the crowd, it didn't take her long to lock eyes with a terrified-looking Minerva. They both knew that it wouldn't end well if Augusta realised that Silvanus was there.

The two women turned their eyes back to the ring. The kids were all lined up, and Augusta was walking along the children of varying heights and ages. Augusta kept scanning the line, keeping everyone in suspense before turning to walk back towards the compere. There was a slightly awkward pause as Augusta began to speak, and they realised that she needed to be mic'd up.

'Just a second, ladies and gentlemen, boys and girls. Our guest of honour, Mrs Augusta Papplewick, will be announcing the winners in just a minute.'

A moment later, Augusta had a microphone clipped to her blouse lapel, and was speaking to the crowd.

She had maintained the role of guest of honour for so many years that her speech thanking all parents and children alike for their incredible work on this year's annual fete was meticulously delivered and performed without the need of a script or prompt cards.

'It gives me great pleasure to be here in attendance at the 125th annual Pepperbridge School fete, although I must hasten to add that I have not been present at all 125 of them!' There was a polite tittering from the parents at the predictable joke that she made every year, and then silence as she went on, adding a sombre dedication to her late husband whom she knew 'would be looking down and wishing everyone well'. Then all that was left was to hand out the three prizes in reverse order.

Daphne glanced towards where she had last locked eyes with Minerva, but this time her friend was nowhere to be seen. She turned back to the ring in time to see a small boy dressed as a rooster walking up to receive the third-place prize of a book token. The child shook hands with Augusta under the guidance of an adult who was presumably the mother, then a photograph was taken with Augusta and the little boy was walked to one side.

Daphne's heart was beating fast as she gripped James's hand. By now, James had been filled in on the close call that was unfolding slowly and painfully in front of them, and they both held their breath as Augusta called out the second prize.

'Second prize goes to – STONEHENGE!' Augusta pointed to a girl who stood within a papier-mâché replica of the heritage site, her torso encased in the middle third of three sarsen standing stones topped with a horizontal cardboard lintel. Despite her angst, Daphne had to admit that the costume was incredibly impressive. The child, with her face painted grey to match the stones, walked up to Augusta, grinning broadly as she accepted her book token prize and took a picture with the judge.

'We have one final prize to hand out, but before I do, may I just take this opportunity to say that each one of you is a winner. You have all made a marvellous effort and I am sure that your parents, parent figures and grandparents are all extremely proud of you. Well done!' There was another burst of applause from the audience. 'And now, the moment that we've all been waiting for. The winner is ... drumroll please!' Augusta paused for emphasis as Daphne's intestines felt like they were being twisted.

Please God let this be over soon so that we can go home! She squeezed her eyes shut and crossed her fingers behind her back, acknowledging without embarrassment that she was resorting to childish tactics to get her through.

'The winner is – our wonderful MEDIEVAL KNIGHT IN SHINING ARMOUR!' Augusta boomed through the microphone.

There was much cheering and clapping as all eyes turned to the awkward looking child in the knight's costume who seemed to be refusing to budge an inch. Daphne saw Immy look towards Silvanus, urging him to go up for his prize. The little boy walked slowly towards Augusta; his helmet still firmly over his head. Daphne's heart hammered as she watched it unfold in slow motion.

Augusta bent down and held out her hand in order to formerly shake the boy's hand.

'Well done young man, I presume, or are you a young lady?' The audience tittered as they watched the 'sweet' exchange.

'I'm a boy,' Silvanus said quietly.

'Ahh – a boy, I see, then well done young man it is then. Where are your parents?' Augusta bent back up to look around for any parents or guardians. No one seemed to be coming forward, so instead she went back to the child. 'Now we just need to take a photograph and then I can let you all go.' Augusta addressed all the children. 'Now, take your helmet off and hold it next to you so that we can get a nice picture for the paper.'

'No,' replied Silvanus.

Watching the exchange, Daphne was sure her racing heart could be heard from the stage.

'I said, take your helmet off for the photographer.' Augusta had now slipped into command mode.

Silvanus shook his head and once again refused the request.

'I said TAKE IT OFF!'

Daphne had edged closer to the ring, preparing herself to rush in to rescue Silvanus. She had no idea where Minerva was but she wanted to be ready. Even the crowd and most of the children had hushed their chatter around the ring, realising with quiet fascination that Augusta was about to lose her temper, enthralled to see what would happen next.

Once again Silvanus refused and it was obvious from his body language that he was about to turn and run, when suddenly Augusta, in an uncontrolled fit of anger, clasped her hands around the boy's head and yanked off the helmet. The audience gasped in shock as the small boy stood wide-eyed, looking up at Augusta, and Augusta, aghast, looked down at the small boy.

When she finally registered that the child who had challenged her authority was the son of Minerva Leek, she let out a screech that, with the stereophonic help of the microphone on her lapel, sounded so deranged and distorted that the entire field stopped what they were doing and looked towards her, many clamping their hands to their ears.

'YOUUUUU!' she screamed.

She grabbed Silvanus's shoulder and managed to catch his escaping sleeve just as both Daphne and Minerva practically pole-vaulted from opposite ends of the showring.

'CALL THE POLICE!' Augusta yelled. 'SOMEBODY CALL THE POLICE! THIS BOY'S MOTHER IS A MURDERER!' She was still gripping the small boy's shoulder, and he began to cry in shock as well as pain.

Daphne reached him first, tearing him from the grasp of Augusta, while on her other side Minerva grabbed Augusta's arm and shouted, 'LET GO OF MY SON!'

There was a collective gasp around the arena as the residents of Pepperbridge watched the dramatic scene unfold. Of course, being a tight-knit community, there had been a multitude of conflicts and feuds in the villages over the years, but never had one been played out so publicly – in the middle of a showring . . . in front of an audience . . . with microphones!

Augusta, forced to release Silvanus as Daphne pulled him from her grasp, swung around and turned to face Minerva with an expression contorted with fury.

'YOU! YOU WHORE!' she screamed, raising her hand to slap the younger woman with as much force as she could muster. Her face was still a mask of hatred, distorted to the point of being almost unrecognisable as the prim and proper maven of respectability that she normally presented to the world.

Minerva flinched slightly but said nothing, managing to catch Augusta's hand just before it made contact with her face.

She held it there as Augusta struggled, continuing to scream at the top of her lungs, which in turn was emphasised by the microphone blasting each of Augusta's words in glorious stereo.

'YOU KILLED HIM! YOU SEDUCED HIM AND THEN YOU KILLED HIM – YOU SCHEMING BITCH! YOU TOOK MY HUSBAND AWAY FROM ME AND NOW YOU WANT TO TAKE MY HOME AND EVERYTHING ELSE! WASN'T SLEEPING WITH HIM ENOUGH? WASN'T BEING HIS MISTRESS ENOUGH?' Spittle was visibly flying from her mouth. All thoughts of keeping up appearances had been cast aside as Augusta flung her accusations and insults at Minerva without a care for who might be witnessing her uncontrollable and verging-on-violent outburst.

The crowd had remained silent throughout. Their heads turned in mesmerised wonder from one woman to the other – as though mimicking an audience viewing the most thrilling tennis performance.

It was Minerva's turn to respond now. She was desperately trying to keep Augusta's hands from clawing at her face, but each time she attempted to release her grip, Augusta's remarkably strong hand, despite its diminutive size, boomeranged back towards her.

'Augusta, I was not having an affair with Charles.' Minerva was trying to speak calmy and normally, but she was also trying to keep Augusta's flailing arms down by her side.

Daphne had run out of the showring with Silvanus under her arm and a shocked Immy following swiftly behind. She'd reached James who was standing with the other two children, looking on horror-struck at the commotion.

'Take the children home to ours. I'll come back with

Minerva.' Daphne looked pointedly from James to Silvanus who was currently quivering in her arms.

James nodded and they transferred Silvanus gently from Daphne's arms to James's, with Immy holding on to her friend's arm supportively on the other side. The small boy clung on to James willingly, refusing to look up, but happy to be led out of the crowd to safety.

Daphne went back into the ring; she hesitated, not knowing what to do. Should she try to pull Augusta and Minerva apart? Should she ask for help to separate the two women? She looked around to see if there were any likely helpers. The captivated 'audience' had not budged an inch and all eyes were on the entertainment in the middle of the ring.

'WHAT DID YOU SAY? ARE YOU DENYING IT? ARE YOU DENYING THAT YOU WERE HAVING AN AFFAIR? I FOUND THE PAPERS. HE SIGNED EVERYTHING OVER TO YOU. I SAW YOU. I SAW YOU WITH HIM. I HEARD YOU ON THE PHONE. DID YOU THINK I WOULDN'T FIND OUT? YOU KILLED HIM. YOU WERE BLACKMAILING HIM. YOU ARE A DIRTY LITTLE SCHEMING WHOR—'

Augusta stopped abruptly as a slap from Minerva resonated against her cheekbone, but despite the split-second pause in shock, Augusta continued to rage and scream.

'AUGUSTA! AUGUSTA – PLEASE!' Minerva pleaded for the older woman to calm down.

'MURDERER! MURDERER! WHORE! MISTRESS!' Augusta continued to repeat manically.

'AUGUSTA – I WASN'T HIS MISTRESS! I AM HIS *DAUGHTER*!'

For the first time in almost fifteen minutes there was silence. Augusta Papplewick's jaw swung open in shock and remained hanging, mirroring Daphne's incredulous expression as she stood just behind the woman.

The equally stunned village residents didn't know whether to remain silent or whether to clap and cheer. One woman later claimed to have heard Biddy Merriman – the oldest member of the Women's Institute – inform her friend that it was the best amateur dramatic performance that she'd seen in years.

Chapter 15

There were many reasons for the crowd still hovering on Pepperbridge Green to believe that the drama which had just unfolded so dramatically in front of their eyes had reached its climax. However, no one seemed to be ready to relinquish the prime ringside 'seats' and miss out on a potentially exciting curtain call . . .

The crowds that had moments earlier been watching, quietly enthralled, were now awkwardly hovering with one eye still on the trio of ladies standing at the centre. They were slowly exiting shocked mode and becoming a bubbling hotbed of gossip and wild intrigue, with accusations of torrid affairs and spousal grudges thrown about carelessly like confetti. Despite that the fact that the two women were within hearing distance, decorum was forgotten, voices were raised in exhilarated faux whispers, and a dozen varying opinions and theories were being traded. 'But who is her mother?' 'How old is she – when did it happen?' 'The old dog!' 'I knew he was too good to be true!' 'But I thought that *she* was the mistress?' It was the most fun many of them had had all year – better than previous village carnivals, that much was certain.

At the centre of the chattering crowds stood a silent Augusta, immobilised by shock and staring directly at Minerva. Minerva had hardly moved either, unwilling to be the first to back down after the public name-calling, and staring defiantly back at Augusta. Like her father, she was a person of few words. Quiet, stoic and contemplative – and under normal circumstances as non-confrontational as anyone could possibly be. Yet she could not be the first to retreat. She had done nothing wrong but admit to the secret that Charles Papplewick had intended to tell his wife on the night of his death. It wasn't her fault that Charles had kept such a huge secret from his wife – although to be honest, she had begged him not to tell Augusta earlier that same evening. Anyway, she had no reason to be ashamed and wasn't it more suspicious that her father had died on the same night as revealing who his daughter was?

Minerva could sense Daphne standing behind her and for that she was incredibly grateful. She was relieved when Daphne had taken Silvanus out of earshot of the ensuing havoc and she had seen her son disappear along with James and the Brewster children to what she imagined was the safety of Cranberry Farmhouse. She was sure that Daphne had returned to make sure that the two women didn't actually start to fight and wrestle each other to the ground, and although her own inclination was to turn, run and hide again, her pride made her stand fast. Now that her secret was out, she wasn't a hundred per cent sure that Augusta wouldn't choose the wrestling route, but she'd have to take that risk.

Daphne slowly edged herself towards where the two women stood facing each other.

'Perhaps we ought to go somewhere a bit more private?' she asked tentatively as she nodded towards the gawping crowds that were still dawdling unsubtly around the perimeter of the ring.

For the first time in what seemed like a lifetime, Augusta seemed to become aware of where she was and rather belatedly registered that her every action was being surveyed. She was under a microscope of ill-concealed village interest. They – she – had just made a spectacle of herself in front of the entire village and now the village was hanging around to see more.

She turned to look at Daphne with an expression of slight bewilderment, registering that she had just said something about going somewhere more private while simultaneously nodding her head vigorously towards Augusta's chest. Augusta looked down to see the microphone still clipped to her blouse.

'OH SHI—' she said instinctively – almost letting a final cherry-topped expletive slip out before Daphne lunged towards her and ripped the mic off.

Twenty minutes later, the unlikely trio of flustered women were sitting in Daphne's shop on the high street. The walls had been recently limewashed and the beams had been scrubbed and stripped to create a modern, rustic setting filled with both polished and painted furniture, all surrounded by vintage treasures and decorative antiques. It provided a welcome neutral backdrop to the continuation of the 'discussion' that had started on the school field, and was of course, far more discreet – 'rather like Switzerland' Daphne had offered up with zero humour intended. Augusta had refused to allow Minerva anywhere near her house, and Minerva had refused to invite Augusta anywhere near the cosy enclave of Cringlewic ... but they both knew that they had to talk. There were too many unanswered questions and untied loose ends for them to retreat into silence again.

Daphne had disappeared for a few minutes to make everyone a cup of tea that none of them had requested or felt like drinking. However, there was something faintly comforting for Daphne in the mere action of making the tea, and something equally as grounding in the ladies accepting the mugs and having something to hold in their hands as they considered who was going to speak first.

Augusta bit the bullet, her expression still strained, but far less aggressive than it had been less than half an hour ago. Daphne could see that the older woman was exhausted by the emotional toll that her public outburst and the shock revelation had taken.

'So, Charles is – was – your father?'

'Yes,' Minerva replied and took a sip of the scorching hot tea.

'... and you've known that for all of your life? Have you both been laughing at me the entire time?' Augusta's eyes had grown large and round and were filling with angry tears that she steadfastly refused to let overflow.

'No. I only found out from a letter that my mother had written to me before she died. It had been kept by one of the women at the commune. She'd been told not to give it to me unless there was an emergency.'

From the close sidelines atop a small chest of French-grey-painted drawers, Daphne tried not to shift around too much. It had been a poor choice of perch, due to its diminutive scale and her far more ample bottom, but it would be a distraction to move now, and she wanted the conversation to continue. For the sake of both women. She was also keenly aware of her own conflicting emotions at being here. She felt a combination of discomfort at being party to such intimate personal information, but also enthralled to be finally hearing the answers to so many of her unanswered questions.

'Emergency?' Augusta asked pointedly. 'What sort of emergency?'

'Well, as it happened, she felt that being pregnant with Silvanus was that emergency. She felt that my mother would have wanted me to know once my child was born.'

They sat in silence for a few more minutes, quietly sipping at their tea and lost in their own thoughts.

'And did Charles already know? Did he know about you?' Augusta asked calmly.

'No. He didn't. My mother hadn't told him about ... me,' Minerva replied quietly. 'To be honest, I hadn't intended on telling him myself. In fact, I had no intention of enrolling Silv at the school in Pepperbridge at all. I was furious when I found out. I went to school at Pepperbridge Primary myself. All those years of feeling awkward and lost and not knowing that the man I called my headmaster was actually my father.

I have so many awful memories of being ridiculed for being the child of a single mother and not knowing who my dad was – and yet there he was all along. Teaching me, even reprimanding me at times and watching me grow up without saying a word to help or to comfort me.' The words were tumbling out of Minerva's mouth now. 'For the first few years I was furious. I didn't want to know him. I didn't want him to know Silvanus – his grandchild!' Her breath was quickening, and she too was beginning to fight back tears.

'So why didn't you just leave? Why did you stay and put Silvanus in his school?'

'Because I've lived here all my life. It's my home. My mother died here. Why should I have been pushed out of my home just because my father didn't want to know me?'

'He didn't *want* to know you?' Augusta looked up sharply.

'That's what I thought at first . . . but then I came to realise that he had no idea about me. I realised that he hadn't even been aware that I'd been born . . . I don't know what's worse. Having a father who rejects you and doesn't acknowledge you – as I had initially thought – or having a father in such close proximity who has no idea of your existence at all,' she finished sadly.

'Both cruel.' Daphne couldn't help interjecting. She had tried to remain out of it, but she felt such compassion for Minerva, who still sounded as lost and sad as a little child.

Minerva looked over to Daphne and gave her a sad but grateful smile.

'What changed?' Augusta clearly didn't have time for compassion. At least, not for anyone but herself.

'He took notice of Silvanus. Purely by coincidence at first.

It was like he saw something in him somehow. Something familiar. He always seemed so sad – I mean Charles. He had this expression that always seemed as though he was lost in a well of despair.' Minerva looked up suddenly, realising that her description was probably not the most diplomatic thing to be saying to his wife.

Augusta raised her chin defiantly. Her eyes were still shiny with unshed tears but determined in their focus to hear the full story. She evidently wouldn't let emotion hinder her need to know what had happened. 'Go on.'

'I only say so because Silvanus often has a similar look. Old before his years – too sad and too knowing. I've often worried that it was because he didn't know his father either. That made me feel that it was unfair to deny them a relationship.'

All three sat thinking about the similarity between the late Charles Papplewick and his grandchild, Silvanus. The same narrow face. The same large and serious brown eyes. The same willowy frame with a rarely seen but charmingly crooked smile that only took up half of their face. Now that Augusta and Daphne knew what they did, it seemed obvious. Silvanus was just a younger, identikit version of Charles. What was even more ridiculous was that now that they thought about it, they saw the same features in Minerva's face too. If it wasn't for the hooded cloaks and long hair that almost always covered her face, then perhaps they would have seen it long before now.

'So, when did Charles find out?' Augusta asked eventually.

'Two years ago,' Minerva replied. 'Silv had been at the primary school for a year and a half, and I'd seen how patient and gentle Charles was with him. Without even knowing who he was. I . . . I saw how kind he was, and I suddenly missed him, if that makes any sense? I missed having him in my life – even though he'd never really been in my life – apart from as my headmaster. I wanted him to know that I was his daughter. I wanted him to know Silvanus. I wanted us to have some sort of relationship, like . . . a . . . a real family.' She looked down at her hands in embarrassment as she gave this last admission. 'I know that it might sound juvenile, but I'd envied all the children who'd known their father when I was at school. It's such a small village that even the ones who had split up or divorced still knew who and where their fathers were. Some even lived with them or stayed with them for half of the time. I'd never had that. I thought that my father had abandoned my mother – just like I was abandoned when I got pregnant. I didn't want my boy to think that everyone had abandoned him, and so I made the decision to confront Charles and tell him about his grand-child.' She'd barely paused, but both Augusta and Daphne sat listening, their expressions urging her to continue.

'It was one evening during the week – after school. I knew that he went to his allotment most evenings, and so I knew that I would catch him there. He was surprised to see me when I knocked on the potting-shed door that day, but he welcomed me in without question and allowed me to speak. I don't think that he'd believed me at first, but then he began to cry – and then he gave me a hug. It felt like coming home.' She looked up, obviously saddened by the memory. 'I remember that he had been present at my mother's funeral.' She began to blink rapidly as she spoke, fighting back tears that were apparently very close to the surface. Daphne leaned over and offered her a tissue from her pocket.

'It's all right – I'm fine. I still miss her, but it was over a decade ago now ... Anyway, it was just a small pagan forest funeral, nothing grand or in a church, and so it was weird to see him there. It was before I knew who he was – or at least what he was to me. I remember thinking that he was just being courteous – with me being an ex-pupil and all. I hadn't realised that there had been a, a ... connection between them.' She trailed off, allowing the others to lose themselves in their own thoughts as they digested her words.

'Ten years ago?' Augusta was clearly desperately trying to remember what had been happening in their lives at that point. 'Who was your mother?' she asked flatly. 'What was her name? Would I have known her?' She looked directly across to Minerva for the first time in minutes, the pain and humiliation of finally realising why her husband had never really loved her evident in her eyes.

'She kept herself to herself,' Minerva replied, choosing defiantly not to say her mother's name. 'She rarely came into the village – if at all, and we travelled to Somerset a lot when I was young. She had family there. A brother – my uncle. He has a campsite. It's where we've been since ... since Charles died.' The words were proving difficult to get out. This time the tears began to slowly fall, and she looked down at her hands.

'So, he'd known about you for two whole years before he died,' Augusta finally acknowledged, allowing Minerva a few moments to grieve before restarting the conversation from where they had left off.

'Yes, but he was always going to tell you. He'd said so from the beginning. He just didn't know how to, and then after a while, I didn't want him to tell you and I made him promise not to. After all, you knowing made no difference to me.' Minerva looked Augusta directly in the eyes. 'I didn't ask for anything, you know. I didn't want anything from him apart from an acknowledgement that Silvanus was his grandchild in private. I didn't want him to leave you. I knew nothing about the will.'

'And yet he wanted to give you all of it.' Augusta looked back at Minerva without any empathy at all. She wasn't going to give her blessing. 'We wanted children of our own. But it didn't happen.' Augusta's eyes suddenly narrowed. 'How old are you? Thirty? Thirty-five? When were you born?'

'No, no!' Minerva exclaimed vehemently. 'I was conceived before you came to the village. He didn't have an affair. He was faithful to you throughout your marriage!'

'How do you know?' Augusta spat out bitterly.

'He told me.'

'How sweet,' Augusta replied, her voice dripping in sarcasm. 'The problem is, Minerva, that my husband is dead, and his will was changed without my knowledge. Now I have no doubt that you are indeed Charles's daughter – until now I'd obviously chosen not to see it, but the truth is that any fool can see the resemblance between you all. But Charles is no longer here, there's a gaping hole in his bank account, and the police are currently investigating the cause of his death . . . and so my question is this, Minerva. Did *you* murder my husband that night for his money?'

Form the corner, Daphne let out an uncontrolled 'No!'

The other two women stared at her.

'It wasn't Minerva in the potting shed the night that Charles died.' Daphne was speaking to Augusta.

'There was someone with Charles in the potting shed the night that he died?' Minerva exclaimed incredulously, turning back to Augusta. 'Who was it?'

Augusta squinted at Minerva. 'I'd assumed it was *you*.'

'Me? Why would I have been there? The last time I saw Charles was at my house that afternoon – towards the end of Silv's party.' Daphne nodded in agreement, remembering seeing them together when she was looking to cut the birthday cake. 'He explained that he was going to tell you about me once and for all. He said that he was fed up with keeping a secret and living a lie and that you deserved to know. I begged him not to say anything. It was fine just the way it was.'

Augusta seemed nonplussed; she had been so sure that it was Minerva who she had seen through the potting shed window that night. 'You were wearing a dark coloured mackintosh with a bright yellow lining – *I saw* you!'

'But Augusta, I promise you – I wasn't there. The last time that I saw my fath— Charles, was at my home in Cringlewic during the party. It was the afternoon, and it had only just started to rain. Besides, I don't own a raincoat with a yellow lining. I also loved my father very much. Yes, I used to feel angry, but by the ... by the end we had a wonderful – if secret – relationship. He loved us too. It's why he didn't want us to be a secret anymore.'

'So, who *was* in the potting shed with Charles?' Daphne wondered to herself, belatedly realising that she had spoken the question out loud. The two other women turned again to her and looked at her blankly. 'The kiss, Augusta? You said that you had seen them kiss? Obviously, that couldn't have been Minerva ... now we know that, well ... you know ...'

The three women took a moment to reflect on the certainty that it couldn't have been Minerva that Augusta saw kissing Charles in the potting shed.

Augusta shuffled uncomfortably in her seat. 'Well, now I come to think about it, perhaps I didn't see an *actual* kiss. They were so close, I just assumed . . .' Augusta's voice trailed off guiltily as she belatedly realised that she may have jumped to the wrong conclusion.

So, who had she seen talking with Charles? That was now the number one question.

Daphne had taken a moment to leave the two other women and put the kettle on again. She wanted time to think. There was something niggling her at the back of her mind. Firstly, Augusta had obviously been lying about how close she had been to the potting shed that night. She had been close enough to see the yellow lining of the rain mac. That wasn't something you saw from a distance in the dark. She also knew that there had been at least two other people out and about in the rain that night. Two people who had both admitted to seeing Charles on his way to the allotments. The first was Marianne, whom Daphne already knew had threatened Charles that same night. She was the obvious answer as to who would have been in the shed with him. However, was it obvious? Shouting at someone in a drunken fit of rage was one thing, but following them to their allotment then killing them was another thing altogether. It was too extreme and didn't make any sense. How would killing Charles Papplewick advance either Marianne's social progress or help her efforts to get her son into a smarter school? If Marianne was going to go beyond verbal threats, surely, she would have tried to blackmail him properly first as she'd already threatened to do during their earlier heated 'discussion' in the headmaster's office. Marianne had obviously discovered that Charles had a secret, although she couldn't possibly have known what it really was, could she? Had she her own suspicions about the closeness between Minerva and Charles? Although she would have had the wrong end of the stick about the exact nature of their relationship – as would most people. If that was the supposed ace up her sleeve, wouldn't she have used that as leverage before resorting to violence?

And then there was Nancy Warburton. So eager to tell Daphne about witnessing Marianne arguing with Charles in the darkened street. Why had she wanted Daphne to know about it? She had obviously been hoping that Daphne would spread the word.

Of course, there was also the question of whether any of this mattered. As far as anyone had been informed – Augusta included – Charles had died of a heart attack and any further speculation was a moot point until they had been told otherwise.

Daphne sighed as she stirred the last mug before transferring the teas to the tray. She was just about to open a packet of biscuits and spread them on a plate when she heard the wailing of police sirens.

Chapter 16

'Please remain silent. You are being arrested on suspicion of the murder of Charles Papplewick.'

The three women had practically jumped out of their skins when the four police officers, including a red-faced and out-of-breath Inspector Hargreaves, had dramatically entered the little vintage shop, only seconds after abruptly sweeping their cars up onto the kerb outside with blue lights flashing and sirens blaring noisily.

Although all three had heard the police cars entering the village, it hadn't occurred to any of them that they might have been heading straight for them. It was an unusual enough occurrence to hear the sound of police sirens at all in the sleepy village of Papplewick, but to then have said sirens screech to a halt within feet of you was quite the surprise.

It had been a highly surreal moment – almost like

something out of a television programme, Daphne had thought as she had stood trembling with shock at the kitchen door, her hands tightly gripping the tray of tea and her now familiar McVitie's Fruit Shortcake biscuits. As a city girl born and bred, she was not unused to hearing the shrill sound of sirens at all times of the day in her old life, but this was the Norfolk countryside – south London it was not.

Augusta and Minerva, who had been sat opposite each other, mouths agog, had stood up instantly in a panic and were now side by side, facing the door, where Inspector Hargreaves had his badge held out aloft. To his left, two police officers were gingerly and – quite frankly – bashfully, in Daphne's personal opinion, circumventing the inspector and approaching the women with a set of handcuffs which they then equally as apologetically indicated that they would have to use.

'What on earth?' Daphne exclaimed from the kitchen door, moving a few steps forward. They clearly believed the foolish rumours, and were here to arrest Minerva. 'Are you mad – is this really necessary? She hasn't done anything!' In her furiously trembling hands, the three mugs of tea had slid to the side of the tray. They were about to topple off, causing Inspector Hargreaves to adjust his gaze towards the plate of biscuits that he obviously feared would end up crashing to the ground if Daphne wasn't careful.

'Mind the biscuits!' he shouted in her direction as he simultaneously held out his hand as though attempting to halt the potential slide from across the room.

Daphne noted that this action had been performed with far more conviction than he had displayed during his mumbling statement of arrest upon entering the shop just a few moments earlier.

Meanwhile, Minerva had been staring at the handcuffs, too shocked to say anything, her voice having apparently yet to catch up with what her mind told her was happening.

'I, I, why . . . ?' she eventually stuttered.

The inspector's eyes reluctantly dragged themselves away from the 'endangered' biscuits, and he continued awkwardly.

'This is necessary to allow the prompt and effective investigation of this offence and to prevent escape and/or injury.' He was obviously reciting from memory – clearly never having used these particular words before. 'You do not have to say anything, but it may harm your defence if you do not mention, when questioned, something which you later rely on in court, and anything you do say may be given in evidence.'

There was a large pause as everyone slowly took in the enormity of what was going on. It was broken only when an uncharacteristically quiet Augusta asked, 'So he was murdered after all?'

Minerva and Daphne looked at each other in horror. This was the moment that Daphne had feared. They were arresting Minerva for a crime she hadn't committed – and Daphne was certain of that now.

For the first time, the flustered inspector looked Augusta straight in the eyes. 'I can't say much at this stage, but yes, I'm afraid we now have firm evidence that your husband was indeed the victim of foul play, and we are investigating several leads.'

'But this is ridiculous,' Daphne called out again as she saw a defeated looking Minerva hesitatingly hold out her wrists towards the waiting police officer. 'It couldn't – wouldn't have been Minerva. She wasn't at the potting shed – tell him, Augusta!'

She looked pleadingly over towards the older lady who was still stood beside Minerva, watching the situation pan out before her with anxious eyes.

'What's that, Ms Brewster?' He turned sharply to look at Daphne again and then immediately back to the two women standing in front of him with horrified expressions. 'No, no – I'm afraid that perhaps I haven't made myself quite clear. Augusta Papplewick, we are arresting *you* on suspicion of the murder of Charles Papplewick. *You* have the right to remain silent . . .' The words tumbled out of his mouth with high-pitched embarrassment as he nodded gruffly at one of the police officers to hurry up and administer the cuffs.

With that he turned and instructed the accompanying police officers to guide a visibly shaken and dismayed Augusta out of the shop and into one of the two awaiting police cars as Daphne and Minerva looked on in astonishment.

'We'll need to speak to you both at some point as well, I'm afraid,' he said as he looked back at Daphne and Minerva standing in the shop entrance. They both nodded their acquiescence, promising to drive up to the station. Reeling, the friends watched the police cars leave.

Nothing newsworthy can be hidden for long in a small village, and before the hour was up the story of Augusta Papplewick's arrest for her husband's murder had been circulated among even the most gossip-averse residents of the village – of which there were not many.

Daphne and Minerva had remained behind in the shop for a while longer, struggling to understand what had just happened.

'Augusta? Murdering my father? I just can't believe it!' Minerva had kept repeating over and over again.

'Then you're a more generous woman than she is – two minutes ago she was accusing *you* of being responsible for it.' Daphne had reminded her, although she too felt that Augusta, for all her supercilious put-downs and propensity for catty, bullying remarks, didn't have it in her to murder her own husband. However, if it wasn't Augusta, and it certainly wasn't Minerva – his daughter for heaven's sakes – then who was it?

'If you're sure that James will still be fine with looking after Silvanus, then I'll drive us both up to the station?' Faced with Daphne's quizzical look, Minerva continued, 'For questioning? Like Inspector Hargreaves said. There's no time like the present, plus I really need to know what's going on and why my father died.'

Daphne nodded. 'James will be fine, but bear with me for a few minutes. I just need to pop to the grocery store – I'll be right back.' She knew that it might seem like poor timing to visit the store now, but something had been playing on her mind. Why had Nancy Warburton wanted her to know that she'd seen Marianne Forbes haranguing Charles Papplewick in the pouring rain? Was it a smokescreen to force suspicion towards someone else? Whatever the reason, Daphne wanted to try to tie up a few loose ends before attending the station for questioning.

For some reason she had a hunch that Augusta hadn't been responsible for her husband's death. Augusta may have been many things, but on the day that Daphne had had to tuck her up into bed, she had sensed a vulnerability and hurt that didn't align with someone burdened by the weight of guilt for murdering her own husband.

The sun had stayed shining like an intense spotlight on a stage until late afternoon, but now the light – as well as the day's drama – was losing its intensity. Daphne entered the shop as Nancy and Patsy Warburton were shutting up. It had been an unsurprisingly quiet day due to most people being out on the green where there had been stalls and stands selling both food and drink. In truth, the Warburton sisters could easily have closed the shop and attended the carnival themselves without causing any harm to their business. However, true to their very contrary nature when it came to opening times, they chose carnival day – a day they historically knew to be quiet to the point of empty on the small high street – to be stubbornly open from dawn till dusk.

'Hello,' Daphne attempted cheerfully, looking around as the bell tinkled her arrival in the shop.

'Hello indeed,' replied Patsy from the fifth rung up a step-ladder behind the door where she was restocking a corner shelf with boxes of Ritz crackers situated 'conveniently' next to piles of blue and white striped jay cloths and tinned Spam. 'I hear that Augusta's little gossip train backfired and she's now been arrested for the very crime she was accusing Minerva of committing!' Patsy couldn't help herself from chuckling quietly.

'Yes, apparently so,' said Daphne non-committally.

Patsy kept on stacking her boxes as Nancy walked onto the shop floor behind the counter to ring up the till.

'She poisoned him then. I always knew she had it in her,' Nancy interjected matter-of-factly, without skipping a beat to say hello or acknowledge Daphne as she emptied the till drawers.

'Did you?' responded Daphne as she pretended to peruse the shelves for an imaginary necessity.

'What are you looking for?' Nancy asked with a hint of suspicion, clearly having noticed that Daphne was distractedly running her finger over everything from Daz washing powder to tins of chickpeas and nappies.

'Oh.' Daphne tried to think on her feet – what on earth was she meant to be looking for? 'I need some insect repellent. We're supposed to be taking a day trip along the Broads tomorrow. Last time we were there in warm weather it was full of mosquitos – although I think that rain has been forecast . . .' She was babbling, but she was unclear of what she was trying to achieve and talking nonsense seemed to be buying her time to process what she was really after.

'Yes,' Patsy continued pleasantly. 'I hear that we might be due for a summer storm – possibly electrical with thunder and lightning. I'd be careful if I were you – take your waterproofs.'

RAIN MAC! – the words entered Daphne's head suddenly. 'You're right. Annoyingly, we don't have proper waterproofs – I don't even have a good rain mac – you know, a proper one with a hood . . .' she said innocently as she put a packet of plasters and a can of fly killer in her basket. She looked up to see if anyone would take the bait.

'You don't own a raincoat? Really? You Londoners are a

soft bunch! We have a few between us don't we, Nancy – do you want to borrow one?' said Patsy.

'Oh, yes please – that would be amazing – if it's no bother. I can get it back to you first thing on Monday morning.'

Nancy had remained quiet during the exchange and Daphne could tell that the elder sister was peering directly at her, obviously wondering what she was up to. Nancy had borne witness to enough badly concealed secrets in her time to sense when somebody was saying one thing but meaning another.

Patsy retreated down the stepladder having emptied the contents of her box onto now perilously overstocked shelves. 'Just a second,' she said over her shoulder as she walked through the door that led to the residential side of the shop. 'You're probably more Nancy's size than mine, aren't you?'

Nancy continued to watch Daphne while her hands counted some coins without looking down at them. Daphne could feel a warm trickle of sweat making its slow descent down her back between her shoulder blades. She was beginning to feel rather uncomfortable under Nancy's unbending gaze.

'Still warm, isn't it,' said Daphne. 'Close even. I think Patsy is right – it really does feel as though there's a storm coming.'

Nancy remained silent as the sound of Patsy's heavy footsteps descending the stairs from the maisonette above could be heard getting closer.

'I thought mine might be a bit too long – unless James needs one too, so I've bought you some of Nancy's to choose from,' Patsy said as she returned to the shop floor.

Daphne looked at the pile of coats hanging from Patsy's hand. There was an old Barbour with a hood that looked as though it would swamp anyone under the height of 6 foot 7, then there was a thin-looking cagoule with wooden toggles. On the bottom of the small collection resting directly on Patsy arms was a navy-blue rain mac. It was unremarkable except for its bright yellow lining.

'That one will do nicely – thank you.' She looked up at Patsy and held her hand out towards the navy-blue mac. She could still feel Nancy Warburton's eyes on her.

'Oh yes, that's Nancy's. Probably better for your height. Did you need any for your husband or the children?' Patsy continued.

'No thank you – this will do nicely.' Daphne took the coat, trying hard not to snatch it too eagerly. Her heart racing, she thanked Patsy again and turned to exit the shop.

'DAPHNE!' The sound of Nancy Warburton's voice made her jolt to a stop at the door. 'Don't you want to pay for your things?' The older woman was eyeing her curiously.

'Oh gosh, I'm so sorry,' Daphne exclaimed breathlessly. She fished out a ten-pound note from her pocket, walked over to the till and practically threw it on the counter before turning to walk quickly out. All the while, she was still holding on to the rain mac tightly.

She didn't look back, even when she heard Patsy cry out to her disappearing back, 'But your change . . . ?'

Seconds later and she was back in her own shop a few doors down.

'Let's go – now!' she shouted with urgency to Minerva, who was in the little kitchen washing up the tea mugs.

Minerva looked up, startled, but immediately put down the mugs and left the shop. Daphne quickly locked up.

Within minutes they were in Minerva's car, and heading off in the direction of the police station. As they'd pulled off at speed, Daphne saw the image of Nancy Warburton getting smaller and smaller as she stood in the entrance of her shop watching them go. As they drove, Daphne was still clutching the rain mac in her hands, its yellow lining glowing almost fluorescent against her dark trousers.

Daphne was sitting in a small interview room waiting for Inspector Hargreaves to enter for their 'talk'. It was a square box of a room with walls she suspected may once have been white, but which were now unmistakably and depressing grey. The lighting was unnaturally harsh and far too bright, providing a direct contrast to the warm evening sunshine attempting to filter in through the high slit of window which faced the wall where she sat. On a metal table covered by a peeling Formica wood-grain effect sat an open box of Kleenex tissues. It was the least welcoming room that Daphne had ever found herself in. No wonder people may have been reduced to tears – or making confessions – in their desperate haste to get out of it.

Minerva had been led into a different interview room twenty minutes earlier and the women hadn't seen each other since. Augusta, she assumed, was being held in custody somewhere in the same station. Despite the shoe now being on the other foot, Daphne still felt sorry for Augusta. The woman had just lost her husband of forty years and was now accused of being the cause of his death. True, there could be an element of karma coming to slap her in the face after her own accusations towards Minerva, but regardless, she must have been feeling pretty bleak at that moment.

Inspector Hargreaves entered the room, characteristically red and flustered.

'So ...' he began.

'So ...?' Daphne repeated. She was met with silence as the inspector contorted his face into a series of expressions that ranged from confusion to annoyance. She decided to be the first to talk. 'If you don't mind, I have something here that may be of interest? I'm not sure what Augusta has told you, but on the night of Charles's death, she went to look for him at the allotment. She saw somebody in the potting shed with him.'

'Yes ... we already know that to be the case,' Inspector Hargreaves replied with a slightly irritated air, 'and before you try to tell me, we already know that it wasn't Ms Leek as we have witnesses living in the area who are able to prove that she was at home all night. In fact, we now believe that Mrs Papplewick was making the entire thing up. There was no one else at the potting shed that evening apart from herself and her husband,' he ended smugly. After leaning back in his chair with great aplomb, the inspector continued with what he clearly intended to be a flourish of rhetorical finality. 'You see, Mrs Brewster, we do know how to follow up allegations without resorting to the help of amateur sleuths poking around ...'

'Oh,' replied Daphne suddenly made uncertain by the exasperation in the inspector's tone. 'Well, then I suppose you already know that it might have been Nancy Warburton that Augusta saw with Charles in the potting shed that night ...' she added, holding up rain mac that had remained grasped in her hands ever since Patsy Warburton had handed it to her an hour earlier.

Inspector Hargreaves's mouth dropped open for a milli-second and then snapped closed as he reached over and grabbed the rain mac. 'Thank you, Mrs Brewster. That will be evidence and may I ask you not to concern yourself with the gathering of it in future, please.'

'But don't you want to know why it might have been Nancy Warburton and how I got the rain mac?' Daphne asked quietly, torn between feeling rather proud of her powers of deduction and chastened by the police officer's not-so-subtle reprimand.

'Go on,' the inspector continued with obvious reluctance.

Delighted that she had permission to elaborate on her theory, Daphne went on. 'Well, it was after my daughter kept calling Nancy Warburton – not to her face of course – "the Coraline Lady".'

'Coraline?' Inspector Hargreaves queried. 'What on earth is "Coraline?"'.

'She's a fictional character in a children's animated film – but she wears a yellow mac with a yellow hood. In the film . . .' Daphne could see that Inspector Hargreaves was growing even more confused at the mention of cartoon characters. She tried to get to the point swiftly. 'You see, during the bad weather a few weeks ago, when I was trying to get my shop ready for opening, I would sometimes bring the children along while I sorted things out. We're only a few doors down from the Warburton sisters' shop, and we would often see them outside clearing the pavement area in the rain – they had a blocked drain filled with leaves at the time . . .'

'Please, Mrs Brewster, what is the point of this story?'

'It's the rain mac. Nancy Warburton was always wearing a

fisherman-style rain mac with a hood. A sou'wester I think it's called. I didn't pay much attention to it at the time, after all, it's just a coat, and you see children in them all the time, but it's more unusual to see them on grown-ups I suppose – unless they are fishermen maybe? Anyway, it was my daughter mentioning Coraline that made me remember it. Although at first, I didn't think about it – it's just one of those things that children say, isn't it? But then Augusta mentioned that she had seen someone in a mac that night, and after Nancy mentioned that she had been out in the rain that same evening and had seen Marianne screaming at Mr Papplewick . . .' She stopped, realising that she was babbling.

'Marianne screaming at Charles Papplewick? Is that Mrs Marianne Forbes?' Inspector Hargreaves looked up sharply. Evidently, rather frustratingly, Daphne Brewster had just given him more information in five minutes than he had managed to collect himself in a fortnight.

'Yes, they'd had a few arguments in the build-up to his death – but I don't think that it was her,' Daphne said matter-of-factly.

'Oh, do you not indeed?' Inspector Hargreaves replied with a raised eyebrow. 'Well, thank you, Mrs Brewster, you've given us a lot to think on.' The inspector rose from his seat, motioning towards the door with his head to indicate that the interview was over.

Daphne stood up reluctantly. She was rather enjoying the chance to discuss the possibilities with someone other than James, although she was begrudgingly aware of being met with a similar vibe from both men that she was sticking her nose into places where it was not needed.

'May I ask you something before I leave?' she asked, before she was ushered out.

'It depends on what it is, Mrs Brewster.'

'How did Charles Papplewick actually die – and why do you think that it was his wife who was responsible? Which I don't believe is correct by the way,' she couldn't help adding.

'Well, Mrs Brewster. That is of course police business, but what I can tell you is that Charles Papplewick died from a heart attack brought upon by the ingestion of a poisonous substance in large quantities.' With that he shuffled the papers on his desk and gave a parting shot. 'No more meddling, Mrs Brewster. We are more than capable of concluding this case ourselves, thank you.'

As Daphne was escorted through to the front desk towards the exit, she was met by Minerva. The two women instinctively embraced each other with relief before leaving to walk to Minerva's car. The sun was lower in the sky, and the wispy pink beginnings of a perfect Norfolk sunset were just beginning to form, although the main event wouldn't be visible for a few more hours yet.

'They believe that he was poisoned,' Minerva said with tears in her eyes, as she turned the key in the ignition. 'They think that it was a plant-based poisoning – cardiac glycoside plant poisoning they called it. It's why they were looking for me initially.' Minerva looked over at Daphne in the passenger seat beside her. 'We make all sorts of herbal remedies and plant-based healing tinctures up at the commune. We've done it for generations, in fact there have been healers on the site for several centuries. We make face creams and beauty products too. It's how most of the ladies earn a living. Some read tarot cards or do psychic readings too – that sort of thing.'

'I did wonder,' Daphne said quietly.

'Anyway, we know our stuff too well to make mistakes. We are all taught which plants are safe from a young age, and we don't dabble with poisons or anything dangerous, although we do know how to make them,' she admitted. 'It's no secret. It comes with the territory – having to learn what to avoid for our own safety as well as for the safety of others.'

Daphne nodded her head slowly. She groaned inwardly, remembering the history of the area. How sad yet predictable that after so many centuries had passed, the small community still blamed the 'Cringlewic Witches', who knew as much about poisons as they knew about herbal remedies and cures. Surely, like Daphne, they knew that the local area was prevalent with all sorts of plants filled with toxins that could kill if one didn't know how to identify them. Dianthus barbatus – commonly called sweet William, angels's trumpet, digitalis, or foxglove, deadly nightshade, and even lily of the valley, oleander and yew – they were all filled with natural chemicals that could affect the heart's rhythm, and lead to a heart attack if ingested in large enough quantities. The children had been taught about it in their country-safety classes at school – to stay away from certain wild plants and certainly never to touch them or put them in their mouths. Daphne shuddered in her seat at the thought of anyone accidentally coming into direct contact with a 'killer' plant.

'But why do they think he was poisoned by someone else? Couldn't it have been accidental? Wasn't there that thing on the news a few years ago about a gardener who came into contact with – what was it – monkshood, mullswood or something?' asked Daphne.

'Monkshood – also known as wolfsbane and devil's helmet,' Minerva corrected her.

'That's it – monkshood flowers. That wasn't a case of murder, was it?' Daphne asked, genuinely not wanting to believe that anyone could have wanted to end Charles Papplewick's life on purpose. 'And Charles was already upset. Anxious even – perhaps his heart was already weak?'

'The thing with these plants is that a little will make you feel unwell. Cause a rash, usually, or if you're really unlucky you'll have vomiting and diarrhoea – but you have to eat a lot or have it in concentrated form to cause an instant heart attack. That's why they've held Augusta. I suppose they want to know what she fed him that night – especially after he told her that he was leaving her. I suppose they feel that it was a bit too much of a coincidence.'

Minerva looked over to Daphne who was deep in thought, thinking about Augusta's shepherd's pie – which she had privately questioned at the time – and the two women drove along in silence for a while.

'She had mentioned cooking his favourite meal that night, which seemed unlikely considering their mood even before everything unfolded.' She looked at Minerva from the corner of her eyes, trying to read her expression before continuing. 'Do you really think that Augusta killed him?' Daphne finally asked.

'No. No I don't. She's a dreadful woman, a snob and a bully, but I don't believe that she's a murderer.'

They continued the rest of the journey in contemplative

silence against a backdrop of puffy clouds and hazy pink skies before eventually turning in to Daphne's drive at Cranberry Farmhouse, just in time to see Nancy Warburton wobbling up to the front door on her ancient black bicycle.

'We need to talk,' Nancy said menacingly through the passenger side window.

Chapter 17

The evening was warm and quiet, with only the faint sound of the odd car driving in the distance breaking the serenade of evening birdsong. The air was thick with the heady scent of the sweetly fragranced jasmine that climbed up and over the front door of Cranberry Farmhouse. It was the most beautiful backdrop to what was likely to be a rather uncomfortable conversation, Daphne mused to herself, as she shuffled slowly from one foot to the next, wondering whether Nancy could tell that she was nervous. Nancy Warburton was most likely the person who'd been arguing with Charles Papplewick in the potting shed the night that he died. She was therefore likely the last person to see him alive. Was Nancy Warburton the unlikely murderer, and if so, what had been her motive?

As a result of her recent interview at the police station, Daphne assumed that it would only be a matter of time before

Nancy was 'invited' in for questioning herself. The question was, if Nancy was indeed responsible for the murder of Charles Papplewick – then what she was doing here? Daphne sighed to herself, waiting to see what Nancy would do next. She was still holding on to both handlebars of her ancient Pashley bicycle, which at least meant that her hands were currently occupied. Having nodded with feigned reassurance to Minerva that she should continue into the house without her, she had to admit to a slight feeling of nervous tension now that she was alone with the older woman.

'You took my raincoat. Why?' The sound of Nancy's voice interjected Daphne's erratic train of thought.

'I ... err ... well, you see ...' Daphne began, trying to consider whether she ought to tell the truth, or whether telling Nancy the truth would give the woman time to make up an alibi.

'You know that I was there, don't you!'

It was more of a statement than a question, and Daphne felt rather relieved. Nancy knew that Daphne had pieced together who had been in the potting shed with Charles Papplewick just before he died – there was nothing more to hide. With that relief brought a wave of tiredness, and on impulse, Daphne dropped her legs and sat down on the front doorstep. It seemed to catch Nancy off guard for a moment, before she flicked the bicycle stand on, and joined Daphne on the step.

The view from the doorstep was as pretty as it was looking towards the farmhouse. Underneath the increasingly deep pink sky was a wide expanse of neatly clipped lawn, bordered by box hedging and large round box balls acting as sentinels framing the gravelled drive. Beyond the lawn were all manner of colourful shrubs and flowers, with magnificent hydrangea bushes with their white, blue and pink heads bobbing lightly in the breeze like giant pompoms, while above them stood a host of impressively tall and voluminous trees, many planted at the same time as the house was being built three hundred years ago. Daphne often wondered what mysteries these trees had seen in their time. The different families meandering in and out. What did they make of the current mistress of the house being a Black woman from south London? She doubted that it would even warrant a stirring of their leaves. After all, these trees had witnessed far more interesting cultural changes over the decades than an influx of different skin colours. She imagined their thoughts on the two women sitting on the flagstone steps this evening. One a possible murderess, the other a woman who didn't know when to stop asking questions.

Tiredness caused Daphne's caution to melt away. 'I knew that you had been there as soon as Augusta mentioned the raincoat. It was niggling in the back of my mind for ages, but eventually I remembered – I think that I'd always realised, but I had to make sure.'

'It was me, but I didn't mean to cause him a heart attack. I was just so angry. I've been so angry about it for years!' Nancy's voice had gone up a few octaves until it somehow now matched her diminutive frame. It seemed that despite her anxiety, the evening's air had melted away her own usual reticence too.

'What were you angry about, Nancy?' Daphne asked cautiously, not wanting to seem too eager and frighten any forthcoming answers away.

'It's Patsy. Patsy has been in love with Charles for as long as I can remember.'

Perhaps spooked by her own surge of anger, Nancy kept her face expressionless as she stared out into the distance, eventually focusing intently on the trees at the far end of the garden. She was obviously attempting to keep her emotions in check, but Daphne could tell from the softening of her voice as it turned from shrill anger to a gentler, thicker tone that she was very emotional.

'We all grew up together in the village. Same school, same church, same socials. Our parents all knew each other. Patsy and Charles were inseparable as children. There was a trio of them all the same age. The Three Musketeers, we used to call them. Always up to no good and escaping down to Cringlewic Woods to play with the commune children. No matter what our parents said about not hanging around the 'witches' coven' and their good-for-nothing children, those three would always be down there getting up to mischief. I think she'd always been in love with Charles, even as a young girl. When they grew up and became teenagers, I suspect the hormones started raging. I noticed that Patsy was withdrawing more and more into herself. She only lit up when she was around Charles. They would disappear into the woods, and she'd come out laughing and happy. It was obvious that they were courting, but whenever she was at home, she would become secretive and looked desperately unhappy. She'd never been particularly academic, so when it came to university she didn't get in anywhere – to be honest, I don't think that she actually tried. Art was her thing – and she's incredibly good at drawing. There was talk of art school, but our parents weren't having any of it. There was a shop to run, and after our father died it was left up to us girls . . .' She paused, clearly realising that she had gone off track.

Daphne smiled. It was good to hear the backstory. She didn't mind how long it took for Nancy to tell her. 'Go on . . .' she encouraged gently.

The older woman sighed, tilting her head back and looking up to the sky, which was only now starting to get dark. She closed her eyes and remembered. 'It was the year that Charles was supposed to go up to university in Cambridge. He was all set when he suddenly decided to defer it by a year. His parents were furious, but Patsy, who wasn't going anywhere, was absolutely overjoyed. Charles's parents were so ambitious for him. His father was the headmaster but wanted so much more for his son. Charles was incredibly bright, and they felt that the world could have been his oyster – especially after Cambridge. I think he stayed for Patsy. I believe that they were in love . . . but then that love waned. He must have grown bored realising what he was giving up and decided to end things. There was one particular night when Patsy had stayed out very late. My mother had sent me out in the car to look for her as her tea had been sitting getting cold for over an hour. There'd been a dreadful storm and it was still raining, and we were beginning to worry. I tried to see if she was at Charles's parents' house and they said that he wasn't home yet either, so we knew that they were together. I was intending to return home in the hope that she was there, when something told me to drive towards Cringlewic Woods. That's when I saw that she was sobbing – howling in Charles arms. I don't know what had happened exactly, but she was absolutely distraught. He looked pretty grim too.'

'Did she say what had happened? Had he broken up with her?' Daphne asked.

'She refused to say. I don't know whether he tried to take advantage of her, or whether it was just the fact that he broke up with her, but she's not spoken about it since. When we got back to the shop that night, she went up to her bedroom without eating anything and locked her door. She remained inside her room for about ten days, only coming out to use the loo and then scuttling back in. She changed after that. When she eventually came out, she'd hacked all of her beautiful long hair off. She refused to wear dresses or make-up or anything that would make her look attractive. He ruined her, you see. If she couldn't have him then she didn't want any man to look at her. She gave up all of her artistic ambitions too. Threw herself into the running of the shop and refused to look at another man. He broke her heart, and then he broke it again when he came back after Cambridge and brought a stuck-up wife back with him. His parents were terribly disappointed, they'd hoped for so much more, but he joined the staff at the village school and worked his way up until he was headmaster and remained there for the rest of his life.'

'But what has all of this got to do with the night that Charles died?' Daphne asked, puzzled.

Nancy looked down at her lap. 'My life has never amounted to much. My romantic history, I mean. Oh, I had a few flings here and there, but it never bothered me too much. I can see how relationships can twist the knife in and bring out the worst in people. I've never wanted any of that. Patsy, however, Patsy is another thing all together. Patsy wanted – needed more. She lives a half-life – she always has done, and she didn't deserve that. She tries to hide it, but she has a huge capacity for love – it's plain to see and were it not for Charles Papplewick breaking her heart at such a young age, she may have gone on to have a wonderful life, with a husband and children and all the trimmings. I'd have loved to have been an auntie. I can't stand children myself, but I would have loved to have spoiled Patsy's . . .'

Daphne understood. The softer and more playful side of Patsy that she herself had glimpsed had become more obvious the longer she had known her. She nodded her head in agreement. 'I can imagine that.' She smiled in understanding, as a slightly surprised Nancy in turn gave a fleeting smile to show that she was grateful for that acknowledgement before continuing.

'Anyway, that night, the night Charles was killed, it was raining, a dreadful downpour, just like that night a long time ago when I found Patsy sobbing in the woods. It was a Friday evening, and we would normally have our supper in front of one of those gameshows, but Patsy was taking ages putting out the bins. It was still raining so I couldn't work out what could be taking her so long. I went downstairs and saw that she had gone out further than the bin yard and it brought the hairs up on the back of my neck. It was strange, you see, for her to just disappear into the night like that, so I put my coat on and went to see where she was. That's when I saw her . . .'

'What was she doing?'

'I didn't notice at first, but she was almost in a trance, walking slowly towards the allotments. It was only as I rounded the corner that I saw what – or who – she had been following. Charles was a little further up the road. He clearly hadn't noticed her, and I could just see the longing in her body language. She looked bereft. Tearful even ...'

'You could see her crying?' Daphne asked, confused.

'Well, no – I was too far to see her crying exactly, but I could tell from her demeanour that she was. It brought that other night back to me. Patsy sobbing in Charles's arms as he ripped her heart into shreds. It made me furious. I wanted to confront Charles and ask him if he knew how he'd ruined my sister's life.'

'And so that's what you did? You confronted Charles that night?' Daphne remained still and tried to ensure that the tone of her voice remained calm. Her expression was encouraging – was this some sort of confession?

'Yes – although not straight away. When I saw Patsy stop following him and begin to turn around, I ran back to the shop and pretended that I hadn't left at all. I didn't want her to know that I'd seen her being so pitiful. She would have been embarrassed, you see. She's always tried to play down her relationship with Charles, but I've seen the sadness in her eyes when she doesn't realise that I'm looking. She's a woman with a face filled with secrets and regrets – I can see it clearly in her eyes.'

Daphne wondered whether Nancy was inadvertently describing herself as well as her sister, but instead she asked, 'So, you went back to find Charles after Patsy had returned home?'

'Yes. I did. Once Patsy had returned home, she didn't want to do anything other than go to her room to bed. She was crushed, and it broke my heart for her all over again. Her heart hasn't healed in over forty years – isn't that tragic?' Nancy looked over at Daphne, with teary eyes filled with sorrow.

Daphne simply nodded. 'What happened next?'

'I crept back out into the pouring rain. Once we go to bed, we never disturb each other again until the next day. Sleep like logs, we do. I knew that Patsy wouldn't check on me until the Saturday morning, so once I heard her snoring, I doubled back out. I knew exactly where I'd find him. Moping about in his potting shed where he always escapes to. He was always moping about on his own when he thought that no one could see him – but I noticed. It serves him right, if you ask me. Augusta was never the woman for him. Any fool could see it. She hated living in the village from day one – she was always stuck-up and holier than thou. Thinking that she was better than the rest of the village – we're too provincial, apparently. Too unsophisticated. I've never known what on earth he saw in her. They never seemed happy – even at the beginning. Patsy would have made him happy. Patsy would have made him laugh.'

Daphne could see that Nancy was getting riled up and she wanted her to remain calm and finish her story. 'What happened when you found him?' she asked gently.

'Well, it was almost pitch black, but I know my way to the potting shed like the back of my hand. My father had a plot there for years. I could find it in my sleep. I walked along in the darkness – I wanted the element of surprise, you see. I walked along until I came to the potting shed. It had a little light on – a gas lamp. I could see him dimly lit as I peered through the window. He was sitting there on his chair at the table, just looking through some papers. He stood up when I entered. I'd startled him when I opened the door. I imagine that I was the last person he expected to see suddenly appear at that time of the evening.'

'Yes, I imagine so. What did you say to him?'

'It all came out. Years of frustration and anger. It all came out in an instant. I even tried to hit him – but luckily, he grabbed my hands before I got the chance to make contact with his face.' Nancy looked over to Daphne, her face filled with remorse and shame. 'I've no idea why I was so het up about it all. It's been so many years ... but seeing her there standing in the rain – it brought it all back. It was just instinctive – you know?'

Daphne nodded, trying to understand, although she still didn't quite know why Nancy had taken it upon herself to be so angry on Patsy's behalf. What she did now know is that Charles holding Nancy's hands to avoid him slapping her is probably what Augusta had seen through the potting shed window and interpreted as a lovers' tiff.

'The truth is that was all over and done within a few minutes. There was a sound outside – an animal rustling or something – it startled us both and it brought me back to my senses. I realised that I was probably making a fool of myself. After all it wasn't really my fight, was it? It's not as if he was ever mine.'

She looked up sadly, and Daphne instantly understood. Nancy Warburton had been in love with Charles Papplewick all along. Not simply the same unrequited love as her sister, but a much sadder version. A secret, unrequited and lonely type of love that she had kept hidden from everyone. Even Patsy – or perhaps *especially* Patsy, who she believed had had more of a right to Charles's love. What a sad and complicated situation that they'd all found themselves in. Is this what village life was all about? Falling in love with your neighbour's sons and keeping the dating pool only puddle-deep? Daphne made a mental note to ensure that her children enjoyed a rich and varied life that included looking beyond the boundaries of Pepperbridge parish – regardless of how safe and wholesome the idea of keeping the modern world out might seem.

'I left him after that. I left him alive and well in the potting shed. A bit surprised, perhaps, but certainly not unwell or even hurt.' Nancy's voice had turned from sadness to urgency. 'I know that it doesn't look good, but I honestly had nothing to do with Charles's death. He was fine when I left – I swear!'

'I believe you, Nancy. Honestly, I do, but you're going to have to tell Inspector Hargreaves exactly what you just told me. Unfortunately, he already knows that it was you in the potting shed that night, but now he needs to know why you were there, and exactly what happened. Is that OK?'

Daphne reached over and touched the older lady's hand. She didn't flinch or pull away but allowed Daphne to squeeze her hand reassuringly and suddenly Nancy Warburton didn't seem so stubborn or confident anymore. It appeared that even the most formidable of Pepperbridge and Pudding Corner residents had a soft underbelly hidden just beneath the surface.

Despite her protestations, Daphne offered to drive Nancy home. It was dark now, and having eyed up the creaky old Pashley bicycle – which looked more like an antique befitting of a museum than a working bit of pedal-driven engineering – she didn't fancy Nancy's chances of arriving home with either the bicycle or herself in one piece. Talking to the police could wait until morning, although Daphne had a hunch that Inspector Hargreaves may come looking for her first.

'It's a Pashley – they're indestructible. I'll have you know that I've been riding that bicycle since my teens!' grumbled Nancy, although she allowed Daphne to fold the bicycle into the back of the Morris Traveller and collapsed into the comfort of the passenger seat quite willingly.

'Since your teens? Now that I believe,' replied Daphne looking at the handsome and slightly battered bicycle with a smile.

When they arrived back in the village of Pepperbridge, Patsy was waiting anxiously outside the front of the shop. Daphne had called Patsy to alert her to her sister's whereabouts half an hour earlier, but had not expanded on the reason for Nancy visiting her. That was Nancy business for now, although she imagined that she'd have to address the situation with Patsy before Inspector Hargreaves hauled her in for questioning.

The three women retrieved the bicycle from the back of Aggie and stood in the dim light of the pavement in front of the shop. The evening was still warm and balmy. A perfect summer's night.

'Thank you for delivering my sister safely, Daphne, although lord knows what you were doing out on your bike when you knew it was getting dark!' Patsy looked pointedly at Nancy.

'I'm not a child, Patsy. *You're* the baby of the family. I'm quite safe out and about on my own – unlike you!'

'Ha – baby my backside, you're only as tall as my armpit . . .'

With that, Daphne chose to leave the two women to fall back into their familiar squabbling and retreated to her car. She'd already decided that she would call in on Nancy the following morning on her way into the vintage shop to ensure that everything was all right, and that Nancy had spoken to Inspector Hargreaves. There was no point trying to cover tracks in this situation – Nancy may have been the last person to see Charles alive ... No one could deny that these were suspicious circumstances, and it was far better to face things head on. If, as Nancy claimed, she was innocent of any wrongdoing beyond having a few terse words with Charles Pepperbridge the night that he died, then she had nothing to worry about.

Chapter 18

Doctor Ptolemy Oates opened his front door on the second ring of the doorbell.

'Come in, come in!'

He ushered his neighbour through the oak-topped porch and into the narrow entrance hallway of the cottage. It was a handsome old house, quite dark inside but atmospheric and quaintly beautiful to those who appreciated the sort of period style that had lain almost untouched in aesthetically pleasing aspic for several generations.

Daphne hadn't often received an invite into the hallowed interior of the doctor's house, although she'd always wanted to explore the Tardis-like cottage which seemed to have a multitude of unexpected and multi-levelled rooms that ran on from each other through endless interconnecting doorways. His home, which had apparently belonged to his

parents before him, was obviously his oasis of calm and comfort, and that is exactly how he wanted it to remain. Daphne
respected his preference for privacy and orderliness; she
knew that a boisterous house filled with noise and children
didn't appeal to everyone – goodness, at times it didn't even
appeal to her!

When she had visited on previous occasions, they would
usually take their tea and conversations into the back garden.
Today, however, the doctor pointed her in the direction of
the kitchen and requested that she put the kettle on while
she waited for him to locate his National Trust card so that
she could gain entry to Oxburgh Hall as his plus one. He
remembered last seeing it in a striped blazer – he was quite
sure of it. He had an old-fashioned stove-top whistling kettle
which was very much in keeping with the charm of the rest
of the house. She turned the gas dial for the small back ring
burner and pressed what she assumed was the ignite button.
Nothing happened. She pressed again, but all she could hear
was a slight clicking and the faint hiss of gas. Turning the dial
back off, she returned to the front hallway to call upstairs.

'Doctor Oates? Doctor Oates – is there a special tech-
nique for turning on the stove? I can't get the ignition button
to catch?'

From upstairs, the doctor's voice called down. 'Oh yes –
silly me, you'll need to use the matches!'

'Matches? Where are they?' she called back, approaching
the bottom of the staircase so that she could hear better.

'They're in the flubbyy shollleer,' is all that she
could decipher.

'I'm sorry – they're in the what?'

'The flobbery schole!' His voice was muffled, as if communicating a through a tunnel.

'The fluuby? The Study? The what?' she mumbled to herself. 'Don't worry – I'll find them.' She gave up – whatever he was saying didn't bear any resemblance to the name of any room she'd heard of before.

Daphne went back to the kitchen and started opening the drawers. Everything was obviously old yet still tidy and neat – cutlery, scissors, nails, batteries – but no matches. Perhaps the pantry, she thought to herself. All houses of this age had some sort of pantry or walk-in larder, she was sure of it. She walked towards another door leading on from the kitchen leading into an area that she hadn't been to before. She hesitated for a minute just before she pushed the door open.

It led to a smaller corridor lined with a clay-tiled floor, with three more doors. Gosh, talk about original features. She knew that the house had once been the stable block and coach house to the farmhouse, and she could see quite clearly from the flooring that it had been well built with local materials. She opened one door which turned out to be a cupboard filled with shelves. Each shelf was filled to bursting with jars of preserves – everything from pickled cucumber to strawberry jam and onion relish. She looked at the dates – some of the jars dated back to 1997. She let out a faint gasp. Note to self, do not wolf down any gifts of home-bottled preserves from the good doctor!

Daphne closed the door and turned to the next. It was a larger room, filled with a deep ceramic sink – almost big enough to bathe a child in – a Sheila's Maid hung from the ceiling, and more wooden hanging rails and an ancient-looking washing machine sat in the corner. There were a few pairs of what appeared to be long johns hanging along a line across the centre of the room. Daphne quickly stepped back and closed the door. She would try the final door and if she still couldn't find any matches, she'd just wait for the doctor to come back downstairs before boiling the kettle.

The final door was slightly ajar and stiff due to warping. It had a large old-fashioned key in its lock that didn't look as though it had been used for years, and with a little bit of effort she pushed it open only far enough to poke her head around as it scraped along the flagstone floor. It seemed to be a study or an office – although there wasn't a computer screen in sight. This was promising – she walked in. It had floor-to-ceiling shelves on either side of a large lawyer's desk which was clearly an antique, although Daphne imagined that it probably hadn't been an antique when it had first made its way to its current location as it fit the space perfectly.

On the shelves were row upon row of medical books, encyclopedias and files. Many of them were leather bound and most likely out of date. She imagined that a medical journal from 1986 probably wouldn't have a huge amount of relevance today, but who was she to judge what people liked to keep – perhaps there were articles and cases that were interesting to read over. What little space that was left on the walls was filled with what appeared to be vintage anatomical posters. They were fascinating and she wondered whether the doctor possessed any vintage treasures that he would like her to sell on his behalf – old posters were all the rage for gallery walls these days. There were also carefully placed piles of medical pamphlets, newsletters and more journals laid out on the floor. It was like a medical museum. Doctor Oates was obviously a hoarder of medical literature, Daphne mused, still scanning the room for matches.

She turned round to look back at the door that she had just come through and noticed a bureau to the left of it with its front unlocked and open. On top of the gleaming writing ledge and the worn inlaid green leather, she spotted a small box of matches; however, it was something resting inside the bureau that caught her eye. In one of the cubby holes above the matches was a trio of old-fashioned glass syringes. Two were clear and empty of fluid and one had a small amount of dark liquid in the vial. All three rested unassumingly in the bureau, their glass glinting in the shafts of light that were filtering through the window. The syringes were things of peculiar beauty with their brass handles and large size. Gosh, they must have been painful to use, thought Daphne. Nothing like the small disposable syringes that were used today. She shuddered.

She lifted her gaze a little higher to the top of the bureau, where a group of photographs in silver frames sat. They were a collection of black and white images featuring groups of students at a university graduation. One image showed a young man on his own, clutching a scroll as he smiled proudly at the photographer. She grinned, remembering her own graduation photo that hung on the wall in her parents' retirement house in the Caribbean. This must have been at least twenty years before her own graduation. How funny, it seemed that every generation had been instructed to sit in that same side profile position, clutching a fake scroll to represent their degree, with the same cheesy grin directed towards the camera. She peered at the young man in the single photo. His cheerful smile and full face were familiar, as were his round spectacles. A young Ptolemy Oates! She laughed out loud. He looked so proud and happy. His face was unmistakably familiar, and just as jovial. He appeared in most of the other images too, and it was easy to spot him every time.

There was something else familiar in the group shots. The buildings in the background – she'd seen them before. It was Oxford. How wonderful – Doctor Oates gained his medical degree at Oxford, but it wasn't just that ... The precise location was familiar. She was sure that she'd seen it in another photograph before. She tried to remember where, and just when she was about to give up, grab the matches and go, it came to her. It was exactly the same backdrop as the graduation photograph Augusta had in her bedroom.

Daphne thought back to that day when she had left Augusta sleeping off a mild hangover in her bedroom. After settling the covers around her, and making sure that she was safely lying on her side and not liable to choke in her sleep, she had looked at an image in a similar silver frame on the dressing table. The photograph had been of an extremely happy and laughing Augusta standing on her own, but for the disembodied arm draped casually around her shoulder belonging to someone who had once appeared on the other side of the photograph. At the time, Daphne had assumed that the picture had been bent in half to accommodate the smaller size of the frame.

She looked back in surprise at the photos on the doctor's bureau. It really was Augusta – but why had she not known that they were old friends before now? On closer inspection,

she realised that she could find Ptolemy Oates and a young
Augusta among the group in every image. What was more
interesting was that in each image that they appeared
together; a fresh-faced Ptolemy was staring directly at
Augusta with the soppiest, most lovestruck look that Daphne
had seen on anyone outside of a Hollywood romantic comedy.
Not merely friends then, after all. He was clearly besotted
and couldn't hide it – not even for a photograph. She noticed
one final silver frame that had fallen down onto its front. She
picked it up, already predicting what she was going to see.
It was the original photo of Augusta – identical to the one
in Augusta's bedroom – but this time it was the full version
with the owner of the arm in plain view, staring at Augusta
in the same loving and longing way, with his hand caressing
her shoulder tenderly, its little finger adorned with a crested
signet ring. It was clear that he couldn't tear his eyes away
from her, let alone his body. He was pressed up against her or
touching her in almost every shot. Ptolemy Oates had clearly
been infatuated with Augusta on their graduation day and
possibly even since then considering he still kept so many of
their photographs on his desk. It ought to have been rather
sweet really, but something had begun to niggle at Daphne
thoughts – why did this all seem so odd?

Still holding the frame in her hand, she glanced back down
at the three glinting syringes. They were huge. Like something from a Victorian apothecary shop in a Dickens novel.
The type where you would have found jars filled with arsenic
and glass phials filled with strange remedies. She noted a
vintage looking box with the screw-on needles to go with the
syringes sitting inside it. She remembered reading that the

needles would have been sharpened by hand. The thought made her grimace.

'Daphne?' The sound of the doctor's voice made her jump, instantly pulling her out of her assessment of the photographs.

She grabbed the matches quickly and exited the room at top speed, closing the door swiftly behind her and re-entering the kitchen that resembled a period set from a 1950s kitchen sink drama from the little hallway.

'I'm here – I found the matches!' She smiled at the doctor across the kitchen.

He remained silent and looking at her for only a split second too long, but it was long enough to add a slightly different frequency to the atmosphere. Daphne sensed it immediately. He was obviously not happy that she had come through the door leading from the three rooms, and she tried to think quickly about why that might be before saying anything. She knew that Ptolemy was a private man. Yes, he could talk the hind legs off a donkey when it came to local history, but he rarely spoke about himself or his private life. In fact, hadn't he once said that he didn't have any interest in what was happening in the village at all? Recalling his lovelorn expression in the photographs, was that because Augusta had married Charles and he'd decided to keep himself separate?

Her mind began whirring. If Ptolemy had gone to university and been in love with Augusta, then how had Charles come to be the one who had ended up marrying her? It was all rather curious. James's disapproving face suddenly popped into her mind. *Daphne, don't ask. Don't ask. Don't ask.*

Doctor Oates finally spoke. He was rubbing his chin slowly with his head slightly cocked to one side. All traces of good humour had vanished from his expression, making Daphne feel uncomfortable in his company for the first time since she'd met him. 'I said – tea?' he repeated.

She realised that she had missed his question the first time. She also realised that he had a distinctive signet ring on the little finger of the hand that was currently rubbing his chin. The flesh of his finger was bulging out on either side of it, as though it was now far too tight, forty or more years since the graduation photo was taken. Why had she never noticed it before?

'Perhaps we should be going – they've probably got a café there?' Why had he claimed to not know anyone in Pepperbridge particularly well?

It occurred to her that it might be best to leave the small kitchen which was strangely now beginning to feel more claustrophobic than cosy.

'No. I think that we'll have a cup of tea here first if you don't mind. I'm parched.' His smile didn't quite reach his eyes in the same way that it normally did. He put out a hand towards her and she flinched away from it slightly without thinking. 'The matches?' he cocked his head sightly in question.

'Oh – yes, of course. The matches,' she repeated – handing them over to him. Why did she feel so jumpy all of a sudden?

He nodded in thanks and walked over to light the stove. 'Of course, you could have just used these ones ...' He pointed to a small, tiled alcove flush to the wall to the left of the stove that she hadn't noticed until now. Inside was a box of matches and a tin of lighter fluid. With his back still to her he said, quietly but firmly, 'Do sit down, Daphne.'

Daphne did as she was told, although she couldn't help

glancing towards the doorway as she did so. *Stop being so silly, Daphne,* she told herself. *Nothing has happened. You saw some photographs and a piece of vintage equipment. An antique syringe which is perfectly in keeping with a doctor who enjoys talking about history. Why on earth has that spooked you?* But she knew exactly why. Seeing the antique syringe had jogged her memory back to her first few weeks in Pudding Corner and her first few chats over the garden gate. Doctor Ptolemy Oates had warned her to inform the children about various potentially harmful and poisonous plants. He had told her how the seventeenth-century so-called 'witches of Cringlewic' had started off as midwives and herbalists and then been accused of witchcraft by male doctors like himself who wanted to strip them of their increasing power. The 'witches' had sought to defend themselves by using untraceable poisonous plants to outwit their persecutors. It had been fascinating stuff, but at the time it was simply one historical story in a long list of historical stories. Now, however, his repeated mention of and fascination with phytomedicine and ethnobotany stood out with glaring clarity. And now that she had seen the picture of him with a young Augusta it seemed obvious really. In hindsight, it made sense that Charles Papplewick had received a large enough dose of a toxic substance that it had induced an instant and fatal heart attack. It was through an expertly administered prick from a syringe filled with a perfect cocktail of poisonous plants. An injection so covertly done that it could only have been administered by someone who was a self-proclaimed steady hand, someone who was so expert at taking blood that his patients had often marvelled that they'd hardly noticed it had happened until it was over.

'Biscuits?' the doctor asked her as he stirred a teaspoon of sugar into her teacup before placing it in its saucer down in front of her.

'Errrr – no thank you.' Her heart had started to race a little, and her mouth had become so dry that she doubted a biscuit would have been able to pass through her lips.

'Are you certain? That's unlike you, Daphne. They are your favourites, I made sure to have them in especially for you ... Fruit Shortcake?'

Daphne shook her head a tad too vigorously.

'No, honestly I'm fine. In fact, I'm really sorry to do this, but I've just remembered that I have to collect a couple of chairs from a lady in Shipdham. I'm so silly, but I organised it last minute and it totally escaped my mind. Do you mind if we take a rain check and do this another time?'

She was aware that she was babbling and that there was a faint edge of panic entering her voice, but she couldn't help it. She needed to get out of there and she needed to do so immediately.

She was halfway out of her chair when Doctor Oates commanded her to '*sit* down – please!'

Once again, Daphne instantly did as she was told. The tone of his voice had altered the meaning of every polite word that was coming out of his lips. The subtle hint of a threat was laced within it and now was obviously not the time to challenge him.

'All right then,' she forced out with feigned cheerfulness as her bottom slammed back down into her seat. 'Just one cup and then I really must be going.'

She felt it was necessary to keep up the act that she was in control. The truth was that she could feel her heart thumping wildly against her ribcage – she only hoped that he couldn't hear it from the other side of the kitchen table.

'So, Daphne,' the doctor said quietly. 'It appears that we may have a problem.'

'A problem, Ptolemy?' It was rare that she had ever used his first name and she hoped that it wasn't too obvious a blatant attempt at appearing calm. In all the months that Doctor Oates had tried to insist that she call him Ptolemy rather than the more formal Doctor Oates, Daphne had always refused, feeling it impossible to resort to such familiarity with such a cartoonish character. With his bow tie, battered old brogues and tweeds; his ruddy face and usually jovial manner, he'd always reminded Daphne of Toad of Toad Hall, and she'd joked privately with James that a character like that suited an appropriately grand title.

'Wouldn't you say so, Daphne?' he continued quietly with what Daphne imagined he thought was a smile, but which came out as more of a grimace.

'I'm not sure what you mean, Ptolemy, unless you're talking about me having to reschedule our tour of Oxburgh Hall? As I said, I'm ever so sorry, but it's completely unavoidable – the meeting ... er ... my appointment – It completely slipped my mind. Silly me!' She finished with an unnecessary flourish, using her finger to gesticulate in a circular motion while pointing at her head to indicate a temporary ditziness.

They both knew it to be a lie. Daphne was neither forgetful, nor ditzy, and as a Black woman who had given up her formal career to retreat to the English countryside, she had been at great pains to prove to all and sundry that she was not only extremely clever and very capable but also a match for anyone who dared challenge her competence. It was probably one of the reasons she had so happily entered into conversations that covered history, social issues, politics and everything in between over the garden gate with the 'friendly neighbourhood' doctor. A second-generation immigrant transplanted to the unfamiliar and far less diverse surroundings of Norfolk, it was built in to her DNA and upbringing to prove that she was the exact opposite of anything that could be called ditzy or incapable. Perhaps there was an automatic desire to prove that one belonged without question. Reducing herself to a mindless simpleton now was a survival instinct that she hoped would get her out of what she was now realising might be a less than safe situation. She prayed that she was wrong, but she wasn't prepared to take any chances. If her hunch was indeed correct, and Doctor Oates had played some part in the mysterious death of Charles Papplewick, then it wouldn't do her any favours to express her powers of deduction at this particular moment.

'Which is it, Daphne? A meeting, an appointment or a chair collection? Or none of the above?'

His question was met with silence as she tried to remember what she had said originally. He was staring at her intently and it was making her feel incredibly nervous. She didn't want to say the wrong thing . . . and so she said nothing. Not until she could get her story straight in order to leave.

'What did you see in my study, Daphne?' His sudden change of the topic caught her off guard.

She attempted to feign ignorance. 'Your study? Surely

you mean your pantry – the one filled with homemade jams and pickles?'

'STOP LYING, DAPHNE!' The doctor's voice had risen to such a level of anger that Daphne had practically fallen off her seat with the shock of its resonance. This was a side to the doctor that she had never seen before, and to be honest, if she hadn't been caught in her current predicament, she probably wouldn't have believed him capable of it.

Exasperated, he shook the matches violently with his left hand as he continued to half talk, half shout at her.

'The MATCHES, Daphne! You found the MATCHES in my STUDY! What else did you see in there?'

'N-Nothing!'

He had morphed from Doctor Jekyll to Mr Hyde in the space of a few sentences and she instantly regretted that particular analogy popping into her head, as it only served to increase her barely concealed anxiety. 'I'm really not sure what you want me to say. I went to look for matches – you told me to look in your study, and I did – and we were just supposed to be having a nice cup of tea, weren't we. Is everything all right? Are you feeling unwell?'

She bit her lip anxiously, praying that he would take the bait. It wasn't too late. Nothing had been said or admitted or alluded to. He could easily feign illness now and put this very intense conversation down to a migraine. It was just a blip. If only she could pretend that the last twenty minutes had never occurred.

'Cubby.' He sighed.

'I'm sorry?' Daphne had no idea what he was talking about and she wasn't sure that she wanted to know at this point.

'I said cubby . . . when I called down. I told you to look in the cubby. The CUBBY HOLE!' he shouted. He pointed once more towards the small alcove by the side of the stove where a box of matches still sat.

Daphne's mouth formed a silent 'oh'.

'You saw the photographs?' His tone had changed once more as he returned to the original topic of conversation. This time he sounded tired. Almost defeated. Daphne watched as the doctor slumped down in his chair with a sigh and closed his eyes.

Daphne looked at the kitchen door and then back at the doctor who still had his eyes closed and was now rubbing his temple with his hand – the signet ring flashing intermittently as it rhythmically moved back and forth. She adjusted the pressure on her feet from the heel to the ball, ready to spring forward. Her heart was really racing now, the way it had raced when she had tried out for the Crystal Palace Harriers athletics team aged fifteen. *Heel, ball, spring. Heel, ball, spring.* She remembered the familiar old mantra she had recited before pushing off for a race. *Breathe.* She kept her eyes on his head, where his hands remained, and started to count. *One, two three . . .*

She propelled herself forwards and ran towards the door and into the hallway. Narrowly avoiding a clutter of obstacles in her way – a coat stand and standard lamp being the most tricky to circumvent while attempting to sprint; she had made it to the door leading to the porch when she felt a rough and powerful grip on her upper left arm, forcing her to stop dead in her tracks and boomerang back into the hallway, almost toppling them both over. The tips of her fingers on her right hand had been on the door handle but her entire arm was now flailing around, knocking a pile of post from the hall table to the floor.

Facing him again, she was met with a look of fury. His bow tie was slightly askew and his cheeks had transitioned from red to almost purple, his teeth were clenched and spittle formed at the corners of his mouth while his lips remained open in a strained grimace.

'Please, Doctor Oates – I didn't see anything! You're really scaring me!' She was shouting too now as he dragged her forcibly back into the kitchen, flung her towards the seat furthest away from the hall door and sat himself down opposite – but not before he made sure that he had closed the door behind him first with a slam.

'Please, I really don't understand why you're keeping me here,' Daphne tried again once she had caught her breath. 'What is it that you think I've seen?'

'Scaring you?' the doctor responded mutedly. His breathing was still slightly laboured but his eyes had lost their anger now. 'You're scared of me?' He sounded wounded, disappointed, upset even. 'That's what she said too . . .'

'That's what who said?' she asked tentatively. What were you supposed to do in these situations? Keep talking to him? Continue to feign ignorance? Unfortunately, deep within her fear was also a growing curiosity. She couldn't help herself.

'Who do you think?' he asked with more than a dose of melancholy.

Daphne felt torn. The time for pretence was over, that much was obvious, but was it really safe to indulge him in this conversation? One thing she was certain of was that he wasn't going to let her walk out of the kitchen at this precise moment in time, so perhaps she may as well attempt to dis-covering what on earth was going on.

'Augusta? Did Augusta say that she was scared of you? Did you do something to hurt her?' Daphne dug her fingernails into the palm of her hand. She sighed inwardly. Betrayed by her own inquisitiveness.

'Yes,' he acknowledged sadly. 'But I didn't hurt her. I wouldn't ever hurt her. I love her, you see. Augusta is the love of my life.' His face was still slightly purple and sweating. He was staring straight at her now as he sat closest to the door. His eyes looked huge behind his round spectacles as they pleaded with her to believe him.

'I see.' Daphne nodded, watching the doctor intently while also gauging the distance between him and the door. His words came as no surprise – she had seen his expression in the photographs as he looked at Augusta all those years ago.

She noted another shift in his mood. From the slump in is shoulders, she wondered whether admitting to his feelings for Augusta was a cathartic experience for him. To finally get it out – to talk to someone.

'But why – as you say – was she scared of you then?' she asked, hoping that she wouldn't regret probing further.

Doctor Oates looked up with a sigh as he slowly rose to his feet and picked up a tea towel from the table. He absent-mindedly wrung it between his hands.

'Tea?' he asked affably, as though they were sitting down to a friendly cup and Daphne had a choice in the matter. Tea seemed to be the answer to everything in Norfolk.

Daphne decided that it was probably best to go along with the pretence that they were having a normal conversation.

'Yes please. That would be lovely.' She attempted a smile as she watched him walk over towards the range cooker.

His back was to her while he once again filled the kettle and lit the stove. Although highly tempting, she knew that attempting to make a second dash for the door would probably prove pointless and could tip him over the edge.

By the time Doctor Oates had made the tea, Daphne was genuinely ready for a cup – although something stronger would have been far preferable under the circumstances. Not that she was complaining – surely nothing bad happens when one is drinking out of a china cup, she thought, grasping at any straw possible. Wasn't there a social rule about that?

She took a sip, ignoring the temperature. It was sweet and hot and slipped down her dry throat with ease. She looked up to find the doctor staring down at her and watching her drink her tea with an odd expression. She looked down at the contents of the cup, which was now half empty. Suddenly uncomfortable, she rested the cup in its saucer on her lap.

'She was scared because I tried to protect her,' he finally said, sitting back down. 'All these years, I watched over her. I was her protector, her guardian angel.' He smiled to herself. 'I promised her that I would look after her, and I kept that promise – always. Do drink up.' He was staring at her again.

'How did you keep that promise, Ptolemy? Why was she scared of you?' Daphne wanted to keep him talking – her teacup poised at her lips as she pretended to sip its remaining contents. She could tell that whatever he said next could be of great importance.

'I, I just . . . I watched over her. I kept an eye on her, but she didn't always like it. In the beginning she did. In the beginning she promised me that she would leave him if she ever became unhappy. She asked if I would be there for her if she ever needed me. She made me promise – and I did so willingly. I've always been there for her. She knows that.' He stopped.

'Then why was she scared of you, Ptolemy?'

Doctor Oates looked down to his hands that were once again wringing the tea towel in his lap.

'It wasn't from the beginning. In the beginning I avoided them. After they married, I did my medical foundation training at the university hospital and stayed well away. But then my family wanted me to complete my final years and take up residence at Pepperbridge Surgery. First, I worked as a locum there, just to see if I could handle being near her. She would still flirt and ask me to pop in for tea when he was at work. I felt guilty. He had been my best friend, but I suppose he had betrayed me first, so ...' He paused again and looked up at Daphne as if to gauge her reaction. 'In my defence, it was obvious that they weren't happy from the beginning. I think that she had seen this big, brooding, unfathomable prize who wasn't interested in her. Everyone was interested in Augusta at university. This was new to her. She always said that I was like an over-eager puppy. The exact opposite to Charles. I suppose that he was more of a challenge. Challenges excited her, and so she refused to give up until she got what she wanted. She was a spoiled little rich girl – I always knew that, but I didn't mind. We made each other laugh – but that wasn't enough for her.'

Against her better judgement, Daphne was enthralled by this description of a young Charles, Augusta and Ptolemy.

She could imagine each one of their characters in their mid-twenties. She nodded for him to continue.

'I'd originally brought her home at the end of our degree. She was my girl then. We'd both studied medicine and had plans to eventually have a little country practice together. She was top of her class – far brighter than me. We had such a future ahead of us. And then I brought her home and introduced her to *him*. I didn't notice at first. I was just so proud to have her on my arm. Then she kept making excuses to come home with me, but only when she knew that Charles would be there. I just thought that she wanted to get to know my parents – except she never wanted to stay at home. She thought that the village dances were all so parochial and quaint, making fun of the villagers and calling them inbred – and yet she kept on wanting to go to them. It seems so obvious now. The morning after she got together with Charles, she claimed that we had never been serious and certainly never exclusive, and that it had all been just a silly student romance. I was devastated. She told me that I needed to grow up, that I was too clingy and suffocating. Then she stuck to Charles like a limpet.'

He suddenly turned to look at Daphne as though to emphasise the sense of irony and betrayal. The sudden break in the story made her jump, but she indicated for him to go on.

'He didn't even want her. He claimed it was all a drunken mistake. It didn't stop her though. It was like torture watching her pursue him. She was relentless – like a steamroller. The worst thing is that she dropped everything for him. It's as though his indifference drove her completely insane!'

The words *pot*, *kettle* and *black* instantly entered Daphne's mind, but she passed no comment.

'Five years of study and then she threw it all away by insisting on marrying Charles – a man who never even loved her! It was shocking. She gave it all up to become a bored housewife. She lost her purpose after they married. She had him, yet she didn't "have him" – do you see?'

Daphne nodded. She could see very well indeed.

'Despite her begging him, he refused to leave Pepperbridge and she didn't want to admit defeat and acknowledge that she'd married the wrong person, so they stayed . . .'

Daphne was slowly taking it all in. She was finally beginning to understand the strange dynamic between Charles and Augusta. Had they ever really loved each other?

'That explains why Augusta married Charles, but if he didn't love her, then why on earth did Charles marry Augusta?' she asked.

'Because she told him she was pregnant . . .' Doctor Oates didn't hesitate for a second before imparting this important bit of information. The missing link in a chain of miserable events.

Daphne's mouth formed into a silent 'oh' before asking, 'But they were childless, weren't they? What happened to the child?'

'Charles did the decent thing and married her of course – we weren't as progressive as people are today – and then a few weeks after the wedding, she told him that she had lost the baby.'

'Oh gosh – how sad . . .' In that moment Daphne felt a genuine sorrow for Augusta. No one deserved to feel the loss of a child.

'Except there never was any baby. She used it to force him into marriage. He didn't want to marry her – he'd told her that he had no intention of it, in fact – but she knew that he would never leave her if she were carrying his child.'

Daphne's mouth was now hanging open. She hadn't seen that coming. Not even from Augusta. 'When did Charles realise that she had lied about the baby? And why did she not just try to really get pregnant after they were married or was she unable to conceive?' She continued to question the doctor, for a second almost forgetting that she was sitting at his kitchen table against her will. She already knew that Charles had been able to conceive a child – Minerva was testimony to that.

'He never did know the truth – or at least he never knew for sure. I believe that he always had his suspicions about it, but he hated knowing that Augusta might have been capable of deceiving him like that, so he never asked, and she told him that it pained her to speak about it. So, they never did. As for having children – she was on birth control for the majority of their marriage.'

'You mean she didn't want to become pregnant?'

'No, she didn't. She told me that she refused to destroy her life with children.' Doctor Oates looked over at Daphne with tears in his eyes. 'She always joked that she was incapable of loving anyone more than herself – not even a child. I didn't believe her at first, but she was telling the truth all along.'

'And how do you know that she took birth control to avoid getting pregnant?' Daphne's face had gone from surprised to incredulous. How had she kept up the lie for so many years?

'Because I administered it to her. She was registered at my surgery under a false name. She said to pretend that she was discussing fertility issues if anyone ever asked – but nobody ever did.'

Daphne leaned back in her seat; the remnants of her tea (thankfully) having now grown too cold to drink. 'Goodness,' she exclaimed. 'But you still haven't said why she was scared of you, Ptolemy.' She wasn't sure whether she wanted to know the answer to the question, but it was the elephant in the room. The unspoken issue that tied Ptolemy to the death of Charles Papplewick. Of that, Daphne was certain.

He began slowly, before getting more and more riled up before Daphne's eyes. After the first few sentences, she almost began to regret asking him . . . almost.

'As I said, I would visit, just a few times at first. Then more over the years. It started off as just a comforting ear, but then it turned into more . . . She told me how lonely she was. How unappreciated she felt. I made her feel wanted, loved. I never stopped loving her, you see,' he repeated again, this time more vehemently, as though trying to convince himself as well as Daphne that his actions had been justified. 'She made me promise to always be there for her – and I kept to my word. She would give me a sign when she was alone. Two flicks, pause, one flick of the light. Always when he had left to go to his bloody allotment and potting shed. Can you believe that he would have rather been with his dahlias than with Augusta?' he exclaimed incredulously. 'I would sneak in and . . . well, let's leave it at that. It was exciting. Thrilling. I knew that she regretted being with Charles, and I didn't understand why she refused to leave him when what we had was so good.'

Probably precisely *because* it was exciting and thrilling, thought Daphne to herself.

'I earned a robust living and despite not continuing with

her degree, she's a woman of independent means; she's an only child, and after her father died when she was at university he left her with the bulk of his estate.'

While the source was news to Daphne, she realised that she had heard rumours of Augusta's personal wealth hinted at before, and it now made complete sense why money hadn't ever seemed to be an issue.

'As I said, she was spoiled and entitled – but she was also wonderful and fun and charismatic and beautiful ...!' His eyes had lit up for a second, before growing sorrowful again. 'But after several years she started to make excuses. She couldn't see me for long or wouldn't open the door when I arrived. It was obvious that whatever it was we were having – a relationship? A fling? A love affair? – was over in her eyes, and to this day I have no idea why.'

Boredom, Daphne suspected. It was hard to imagine a less 'thrilling' man than Doctor Oates. He had probably been on borrowed time since the day their affair started.

'But I never stopped loving her, and despite her rejection of me, I promised that I would be there for her, and I was. Every evening at 6.30 p.m., I would be there watching her, watching him leave to go to his allotment or potting shed or whatever. I would be there making sure that she was all right – even when she wouldn't let me in. I could see when she turned the lights off in the drawing room and I could see when she walked up to bed, and I would watch him return later. Sometimes she would leave the light on when she undressed for bed. I know that she knew I was there. I knew when the cocktails started spilling into daytime hours. I used to stand outside the kitchen window, seeing her pour vodka into teacups. She caught me looking once. It made her jump out of her skin and she came out to confront me. She told me to stop, but I said that I was there to look after her. It was my job to keep her safe. That was when she told me that she was scared of me.'

'Ptolemy, when did this start? Do you still watch her? How many years have you been standing outside Augusta's window and watching over her for?' Daphne asked gently.

Doctor Oates didn't hesitate. 'Oh, I don't know, perhaps about twenty-five years? Give or take a year or two.' He looked over at Daphne, who had just taken a sharp intake of breath, with a defiant look in his eyes.

'I know what you're thinking. That I was obsessed with her. Well, maybe I was.' He corrected himself: 'I still am, a little. But it was necessary. She needed me – even if she didn't realise it. They were an unhappy couple from the start, and I could tell that Charles was miserable and angry and disillusioned. I knew him like he was my own brother. We were friends as children, you see. We would hang out together and cause a riot. There was a group of us. They called us "the—"'

'The Three Musketeers,' Daphne completed, putting two and two together before he could finish.

Doctor Oates looked at her surprised and then smiled. 'You've done your homework.'

'Just a conversation I had with someone recently. They mentioned how you, Patsy Warburton and Charles had been inseparable as children.'

'So, you know more about us than you've been letting on!'

'Not at all!' Daphne protested. 'Only a few things here and there. I know that Patsy was in love with Charles, but I hadn't known that you were the third musketeer, to be honest.'

Doctor Oates snorted. 'Patsy in love with Charles? Who told you such nonsense?'

'Oh, but I thought that ... well that is, I heard that she was upset one night ...? More than upset ... heartbroken even ...' She didn't want to give too much away.

'No, no, no. Patsy wasn't in love with Charles Papplewick, good heavens, not at all. Patsy was in love with a girl from the commune! Seraphina or something.' Doctor Oates looked over at Daphne, who was looking back with faint surprise. 'Oh, you didn't know? Well, I suppose that it's nobody's business but hers, but let's just say that Patsy has never been interested in either Charles, or me, or any other man for that matter, as far as I know.'

Daphne thought back to the night she'd spent sitting on her front doorstep with Nancy Warburton. Nancy had been under the illusion that her sister had been pining for Charles for all these years, when all along, it wasn't Charles she was mourning the loss of at all. Charles had simply been a good friend of Patsy's – but a woman called Seraphina had broken her heart. The irony was that if Nancy had known the truth back then, she wouldn't have found herself in the potting shed on the night of Charles's death and then subsequently been accused of playing a part in it. She may even have taken a punt at letting Charles know her true feelings for him. Nancy Warburton and Charles Papplewick. Even in her current state of anxiety, Daphne could see how unlikely that pairing would have been. Although judging by everything Daphne had learned over the past week, half of the people entangled in this intricate web were not living the life that they claimed. Who would have thought it of this quaint and quiet country town? The icing on the cake was the local village doctor. Like Charles as headmaster, the village doctor was the epitome of a highly respected and trusted member of the community.

Yet the truth was that Doctor Ptolemy Oates was not only holding Daphne in his kitchen against her will, but had stalked, watched and obsessed over Augusta after she had ended their affair. An affair that she had clearly used to make herself feel better about her own unhappy marriage, until her unhappiness drove her to alcohol and vodka became her bed partner of choice instead of the increasing inconvenience of her old friend Ptolemy. It was all very sad.

'But it was necessary – and it was worth it – SHE was worth it. She needed me – even if she didn't realise it.'

'What did you mean by "It was worth it"? You said being obsessed with her was worth it? What did you mean by that?' she asked – suddenly jolted out of her thoughts by the stark realisation of how odd that phrase sounded. What had been worth it? Watching her through the window every evening for more than twenty years? Risking his career by straining to catch a glimpse of a woman who had told him to leave her alone? Reducing himself to being a peeping Tom?

Doctor Oates remained silent for a few minutes and for a moment Daphne was acutely aware of how surreal the conversation they were having was. They had almost slipped back into a companionable level of discussion, an almost amiable exchange of questions followed by facts – just like the exchanges that they had at the front gate. Almost, except this conversation made a shiver run down her spine.

'I meant that it was worth watching over her. Taking care of her. She was far too fragile, far too needy and yes, far too spoiled for him. He didn't know how to cherish her like I did. I understand her, you see; I've known her since she was eighteen. I knew that it would come to a head one day. I knew that I had to be in the right place at the right time to save her – and I was. He didn't deserve her. He'd never even loved her. What a waste. I knew that she would be happier without him, I just had to wait until she could see that too, and after that night – she knew. All I ever wanted was to help her see that he wasn't worthy of her. To make her realise that it was *my* job to *save* her.'

The doctor seemed exhausted after his emotional outburst, but he was still forthcoming. He seemed so willing to share his emotional baggage with Daphne. He had always struck her as a lonely man, despite his amiable nature. Now she knew she hadn't imagined the air of loneliness to him, and she knew the reason behind it.

'And so how did you "help her to see it", Ptolemy? How did you save Augusta?' Daphne wasn't sure whether she was ready to hear the answer to this question while there was nothing between herself and the doctor but an antique pine table and a bone china teacup ... but the conversation was reaching a natural conclusion and she wanted to keep him talking. She also couldn't deny how compelled she felt to ask the inevitable question. 'How did you "save" Augusta, Doctor Oates?' she repeated.

'Why – I disposed of Charles, of course. Just as she asked me to.'

Chapter 19

August 1983

'Pregnant?'

Charles sat miserable and cross-legged opposite Clo on the floor of the cramped makeshift bedroom. It was the furthest that they had sat apart from each other all summer, but he had been instructed that this was to be a 'hands off' discussion, where touching and kissing were strictly off limits. He'd known that it must be serious as they had hardly been able to keep away from each other since they had left the local sixth form the previous year, having worked incredibly hard to find the most imaginative and covert ways to spend time together, away from the disapproval of their families. Not that Clo's mother was particularly against their relationship per se – and there was no father around to speak of – rather, she was worried that her daughter would be hurt by this conservative young man from the village who appeared to be masquerading as a free spirit for a summer or two, before he 'buckled down and got serious at university with a nice girl from a proper environment', as his own mother described it.

Both mothers had been wrong of course. Charles was utterly and completely committed to Clo. He hadn't realised that being in love would make him feel so strongly about another human in the way that he felt about Clover right now, and had hardly believed his luck that she'd deigned him worthy of her attention in the first place. Despite the stigma attached to the community who lived at the Cringlewic commune by the adults of Pepperbridge parish, the younger generation had seemed incredibly cool and mysterious to the youths in the area – or at least those who chose to attend lessons at the school. As the son of the headmaster, the academic, polite and always smartly dressed Charles Papplewick had possessed the opposite attributes of anyone who could be deemed cool or funky. Clover had said so herself when they first sat next to each other in A level English. She had laughingly called him 'square' because his ties were always pushed up to the hilt of his neck and his shirts were always unnecessarily stiff and starched – especially for a boy of his age.

Several months later, as he had lain with his head nestled comfortably in Clover's lap in the cow parsley-covered woodland at Cringlewic, he had explained that his uptight exterior was to do with his mother's obsession with keeping up appearances. She insisted on dressing him up as the person she wanted him to be and, as there seemed to be little else that made her happy, he was obliged to keep the peace.

In fact, for as long as Charles could remember, his parents' marriage had been about putting on a good show, and concealing the reality of what was actually a hollow shell of limp politeness.

There had never been much emotion in the Papplewick household – no arguments nor any passionate reconciliations. Just a blandness that remained on an even keel, which felt almost worse in Charles's eyes. Nothing to rebel against, no evidence of spite or hatred: in fact, there seemed no intensity of feeling at all beyond a hope for a similar life for their only son. A mild acceptance of a life based on made-up social rules. He'd always longed for the day he could escape and live the relaxed and carefree life that had evaded his rigid and stagnating parents. With a maturity beyond his years, he had vowed that he would never enter into an emotionless marriage like his parents'. He wanted the angry passion, the happy kisses and the wild laughter that he'd seen at his friends' houses – and he also wanted a noisy and chaotic house filled with children.

Now Clover seemed to be offering that chance to him. Yes, they were only young. Yes, he would have waited if he could have planned it better, but now that the 'issue' had presented itself, he couldn't help but feel a bubbling excitement welling up within him. He would marry Clover, of course, and attending university in September was now out of the question. He'd have to get a proper job – or perhaps they could travel around Europe, baby in tow. He'd already deferred a year before university to spend more time with Clover. He couldn't bear the thought of being parted from her and so had begged his parents to allow him a gap year on the pretext of helping his father out at the school and offering maths and English tutorship to earn money. They had reluctantly agreed – not knowing the true reason.

'I'm not keeping it,' Clover said with a quiet finality that sent a chill down Charles's spine.

'What do you mean? I want us to keep it, I want to be a dad – I love you!' He tried to launch himself across the room to hold her but was stopped in his tracks when she put out her hand in a silent command.

'Don't be ridiculous, Charlie. We're kids ourselves, and you've already compromised your life by staying back a year. Besides, I want to travel and make music and do other things. Things that don't include having a baby.' She looked directly at him then, her face expressionless and her eyes unmoved, if a tad shinier than normal. 'I'm serious. I'm not having it, and Mum has agreed.'

Charles was convinced that he could feel the sound of his heart beginning to crack a little as they sat in silence. Could she hear it too? He didn't know what to say or do. Was this a moment to stay polite and accept her decision, or should he fight? He'd never been taught how to fight. He'd never learned how to allow his emotions to run free and express what he really felt. He'd had a beautiful year of coming close to that with Clover, but now he could feel the constraints of his upbringing start to enclose him again. He could almost feel the tight knot of an imaginary tie at his neck. The stiff scratching of a non-existent shirt against his arms.

'I think you should go. It's raining and Mum says that it's only going to get worse – and Charles … I won't change my mind, so don't ask.' Her face expressed an unflinching and stubborn determination that showed clearly that the matter had been decided and was now closed.

He didn't know what to do. Beg her? Force her? He had never felt so powerless as this in his young life. He had no right to force her to do anything. He knew that. He was dismissed. No longer required. He could tell from her tone that this was it – the end. This was the break-up that he heard so much about in books and films. Was it really supposed to be this quick – this simple? There would be no baby and with that there would be no more Clover.

He stood up numbly and walked down the narrow staircase and straight out through the back door, narrowly avoiding Clover's mother in the kitchen who was tapping her foot along to the raspy tones of Rod Stewart singing 'Baby Jane'. Ironic. He wasn't ashamed to see her because of the baby situation – he would have proudly left with Clover there and then if anyone else had challenged his desire for them to remain together and keep the baby – even her mother. No, he was leaving because Clover had told him to do so. He simply didn't want her mother to see how much he had been hurt by the decision. How much his inability to fight Clover for what he wanted was hurting him right now.

Why had she not wanted to keep the baby? They could have done it together – not without a few hardships, but they would have been fine. Was it her mother – did she not approve? Hadn't she been in exactly the same situation herself? Or perhaps that was it. She had been through it herself as a young mother, and didn't want the same life for her daughter.

The sky turned slate grey and thunder had started rumbling

just as he was leaving – matching his darkened mood perfectly. Even in the gloom, he could tell that the clouds were low due to the absence of stars and the oppressive thickness of the air. A heavy downpour had followed shortly after while he walked and kicked at tufts of muddy grass, childishly launching his steel-capped Dr. Marten boots against fallen branches just to hear them snap. He'd cycled there that evening and was just making his way over to the ancient oak tree where he had left his bike propped up, when he saw another figure emerging from the dirt track that led to the other properties in the Cringlewic enclave. The figure was tall and willowy, hunched over and visibly drenched by the downpour.

'Patsy?' he called out, 'Patsy, is that you?'

Patsy looked up from her folded arms and rounded shoulders.

'Charles?' Patsy acknowledged, hardly looking up.

'Are you OK?' As devastated as he was about his own situation, he was suddenly aware that he had been neglecting Patsy over the past few months, and here she was looking like a drowned rat, with an expression as miserable as he felt.

Patsy tried to put on a brave face, but at the last minute her face crumbled and she began to sob, taking in huge gulps of air as she tried to find the words to explain.

'They're leaving, Charles! Did you know? They're all leaving to go and live with family in Somerset – and Seraphina and Clover are going with them! Did she tell you?'

Patsy and Seraphina had been going out with each other for far longer than Charles and Clover. It was an open secret within the Cringlewic community, but not widely known among the members of the Pepperbridge parish community, or indeed to Patsy's own parents or older sister, Nancy. Patsy had come out to her close friends when she was fifteen years old. She had told them that she had known about her sexuality her entire life, but that she wanted her two closest friends, Charles and Ptolemy, to be the only people who knew until she was ready to tell her parents. Unfortunately, that moment had not arrived before her father had died prematurely, and as the years went by, Patsy had simply chosen to keep her two lives separate, dividing her time between home life and her authentic life known only to a few select friends. Despite her mother's reluctance to support the idea, Patsy knew that one day she would go off to art school in London and, in a dream that mirrored Charles's own dreams of small village emancipation, she would be free to be the person she'd always known she was without hiding anything ever again. For the moment though, she needed to stay and help her mother and sister with the village shop until they were on their feet again. Dreams would come later, and besides, she had fallen in love with one of the girls from Cringlewic who loved her just as passionately back. Her dual life had been easy enough to negotiate until now.

Wordlessly, Charles hugged his old friend close. No words were needed. He knew exactly how she felt. Their silent embrace was meant to comfort himself just as much it was intended to soothe Patsy, and they stood getting drenched by the rain and clutching each other, crying in mutual empathy. Their shattered dreams were accompanied by a dramatic symphony of thunder and lightning, as though emphasising the despair they both felt at being deserted by their first loves.

It was during this embrace that that a desperately worried

Nancy drove along the woodland lane towards Cringlewic and discovered her clearly heartbroken sister sobbing and gasping for air in Charles Papplewick's arms.

August 1987

Ptolemy couldn't help but congratulate himself as he neatened his bow tie and straightened his collar in front of his parents' dressing room mirror at the family home in Pudding Corner. For the first time in years, he had the upper hand over his best friend Charles Papplewick. Charles had always been taller, fitter, better looking and far more likeable than him – despite starting out as the nerdier of the two (that girl – who was it Clover? – had supervised his transformation) while Ptolemy had stopped growing at fifteen and ended up as the 'runt' of the pack. The bespectacled joker, the unsexy one. Well, wasn't this a turn up for the books? Ptolemy would be turning up to the Pepperbridge school reunion with the most beautiful girl that the village had ever seen on his arm. Not only that, but she also had class and beauty as well as brains.

Augusta Churchill was training to be a doctor just as he was. The village would surely be in awe at these two shining beacons of respectability and intelligence. Two young doctors in love – they would be the pride of the town, just as everyone had assumed that Charles would be when they were growing up. Charles, who had apparently been destined for great things, who had been teacher's pet (not hard when your father is headmaster) and even Ptolemy's own mother's favourite.

'When is Charles coming over again, Ptolemy?' she would

ask him. 'Why not invite young Charles over for lunch? How is that fine young friend of yours doing – did I see him in the village the other day?'

Well, look at him now. Charles had returned home with his tail between his legs to teach at the same small village school they had attended. Imagine that! Getting all those A levels, being accepted into Cambridge and turning it all down to become a teacher back where he started, and under his own father too. Not that Ptolemy wasn't still fond of his old friend, of course. Charles had never been anything but kind. It was just that, in a small village, people tended to be stuck with labels for the rest of their lives, and as someone who had once been known as the awkward one within the Three Musketeers, it was a joy to be the one who came out on top for once.

Tonight, he would show everyone what success outside of Pepperbridge looked like. With Augusta Churchill on his arm and a medical degree firmly in his pocket, this was his time to shine.

He twirled his signet ring around on his pinkie finger absent-mindedly while thinking of another ring – his mother's engagement sapphire, which she had so kindly given him – that was safely hidden in a box in his bedroom. There was also a bottle of champagne chilling in the freezer back home. It was going to be a perfect evening. He was sure of it.

August 1990

'Do you have the rings?' Charles asked Ptolemy for the third time in a row and with such solemnity that one would have questioned whether they were about to take part in a funeral rather than a wedding ceremony.

'Of course I do. Just as I had them five minutes ago, and again when I checked five minutes before that,' Ptolemy replied pointedly.

If he wasn't feeling so wretched inside, then the whole thing would be laughable. Here he was acting as best man to his so-called best friend, who was about to marry Augusta Churchill – the great love of his own life. The very person he had proudly brought home three years ago now to show off to the village on the assumption that *he* would be the man that she would be marrying today. Not Charles Papplewick – his miserable, humourless, angst-ridden friend who had shown little to no interest in the instantly smitten Augusta.

It had taken Augusta three years to break down the tightly clamped emotional defences of the non-committal Charles. Three years of using the unwittingly gullible Ptolemy as an excuse to return to the village with the specific intention of flirting with his oldest friend.

Even then it hadn't started out as some great romance. Augusta had simply been obsessed with making Charles want her. Being ignored wasn't something that Augusta was accustomed to – especially by someone who came from a tiny village in the middle of who-knows-where. Charles had started out as a challenge, of that Ptolemy was sure, and Augusta liked nothing more than proving people incorrect. Charles had shown not a flicker of interest in Augusta on first meeting her, and that infuriated her to the point of needing to conquer him like a climber conquering Everest. It was as plain as it was simple – Augusta was a spoiled little rich girl who refused to take no for an answer and despised the monotony of things that came too easily. Unfortunately, Ptolemy in his gratefulness had presented no challenge at all. He had been a willing puppy, eagerly accepting Augusta's occasional crumbs of affection, showing himself to be far too easy and willing to do her bidding. Not only had he kicked himself on numerous occasions for having worn his heart so clearly on his sleeve since then, but Augusta had joined in and given him a kicking too – especially when she was feeling particularly infuriated by Charles's inattentiveness.

His greatest weakness was that he kept coming back for more abuse from the very people he knew could hurt him the most. Even now, when the two people that had meant more to him than anyone else in the world had betrayed him, here he was playing one of the most important roles at their wedding. He hated himself for it – and yet, like to a moth to a bonfire, let alone a flame, he couldn't tear himself away from them.

Only that very morning, when Augusta had requested that he bring some aspirin to her in her dressing room, then purposefully pressed herself up against him wearing only a sheer silk dressing gown, he had been ready to do anything for her in that moment. Anything at all. Her hand had lingered far too close to the top of his inner right thigh. She knew what she was doing. Always promising, always manipulating. Occasionally delivering – when it suited her. He had become unsteady on his feet as he felt her warm breath on his ear and she had made him promise to always look after her and never leave her.

'You still love me, don't you, Tolly?' she had said finally and breathlessly, her tongue close enough to flick his earlobe with its tip.

He had nodded quickly.

'Say it. Say it out loud for me.' There was an urgency in her voice that was unfamiliar to him: a yearning. She sounded far younger than her years and he turned his head to look directly at her. She had tears in her eyes. Sad tears – and for once they were real.

'Tell me that you love me,' she demanded petulantly, her eyes turning from sad and fearful to fiery.

'I love you. You know I do.' He caved in as she knew that he would.

'Yes. I know you do . . . I just needed to hear it from at least one person today.' And with that she turned away, her barriers back up as she dismissed him before her mother returned from the hotel bar.

Through the haze of his confusion, he had become acutely aware of three things in that moment. The first was that he was able to see that Augusta wasn't as sure of herself as she pretended to be. Even now, on the cusp of saying 'I do', she knew that her soon-to-be husband was hardly besotted by her, and it scared her. She hadn't conquered Everest after all, she'd simply fooled herself by getting to base camp. In fact, if it hadn't been for her being in the early stages of a supposed pregnancy, they would not be getting married at all. She knew that. Charles knew that and Ptolemy now knew that too.

The second thing he realised, with absolute clarity, was that despite knowing he was being used, it would be his lifelong job to look after Augusta. To make sure that he was available for her should she need him. It was a visceral feeling in his bones – potentially helped by the hand resting on his crotch. A feeling that he was unable and unwilling to defy.

He belonged to Augusta and in some small way – even if only in his imagination – Augusta belonged to him.

The third and final thing that he realised, was that it was possible to feel intense hatred for someone at the exact same time as feeling intense love.

July 2023

6.30 p.m. The night of Charles's death.
Augusta had sensed Ptolemy watching. Just as he did most evenings. She'd felt his eyes all around them tonight. A feeling that he had been peering in through the front window and then through the back, as though watching her in a play. It had been so many years now that she was used to it. Almost comforted by it. The only time that it had really proved to be a problem was when she had been worried that he would tell Charles about their five-year affair.

However, tonight she was pleased that Ptolemy had been here; had seen it. She had never seen Charles so angry and so distant. She knew that this time she had truly lost him. The sense of duty and loyalty that had kept him with Augusta had finally been shattered by his feelings for someone else. She could feel it in her bones although she had hardly let him get the words out of his mouth. All she knew was that it had something to do with that strange-looking witch of a woman – Minerva Leek. Of all the women that he could choose, a woman who dressed in black rags, hardly combed her hair and fancied herself to be some sort of white witch. It was extraordinary, but not only that, it was an absolute insult to Augusta after she had presented herself as the picture-perfect and dutiful village wife for over three decades. He told her that it wasn't what she thought, but he'd already revealed that he wanted to leave and that it was because of Minerva, so who was he trying to kid now?

She had slapped him around the face, calling Minerva every name she could think of under the sun. He had grasped her hand violently and flung it away from his face before she had time for a second swing. They had stood staring at each other in shock before Charles had left the house to go – she imagined – to the allotment to cool down. It had never got to such a heated stage before, and she sincerely hoped that Ptolemy had seen that bit. She wanted him to see how little Charles valued her after all these years of her self-sacrifice and martyrdom.

Despite knowing that he had been watching, she still jumped when there was a knock at the back door a few minutes after Charles has left. Sure enough, it was Ptolemy standing drenched in the rain. His face was tense with concern and his round glasses were steaming up. His bow tie was still present but he was bedraggled, and she could smell the strong odour of wet and musty tweed emanating from his jacket.

'Are you all right – did he hurt you?' His voice was stressed and tight, which comforted her for a second. She had no desire for him to cross the threshold into the house so she kept him on the doorstep, with large drips from the porch tiles falling onto on his head.

'No, Ptolemy, I'm not. It's awful. He's been having an affair. He's been sleeping with a slut from Cringlewic. How could he, Ptolemy – after everything I've sacrificed! I gave up my

LIFE for him. My entire life. I didn't want to live here in this village with these people! I did it for *him*!'

Ptolemy raised his arms and stepped towards Augusta to comfort her, but she immediately pulled away, into the house. She didn't want him to touch her. Not anymore.

He sighed and retreated, frustrated. He looked down at his sodden shoes. 'Is there anything I can do to help?'

'Anything you can do? Perhaps just turn back the clock. Wave a wand and take me back to a time before I met Charles Papplewick. Can you do that, Ptolemy? Can you make Charles Papplewick disappear for me – and return all my wasted years? I wish I'd never come here. I should have married you, Ptolemy.' She smiled at him sadly and closed the door in his face.

9.45 p.m.
It was several hours and several shots of vodka later when Augusta belatedly realised what she had said to Ptolemy and how he might have interpreted it. He had left immediately. No hovering, no loitering.

I'm being silly ... she thought to herself. *I was just being metaphorical.* Yet Charles had failed to return, and the rain was unrelenting.

Augusta toyed with the idea of calling Ptolemy and checking that he had returned home, but decided that it would be best not to involve him any further. She grabbed her rain mac and her wellington boots and made her way quietly and quickly out of the back door and along the lane. There were only occasional street lamps, but she had the light of her mobile phone to guide her through the areas that she couldn't see properly. By the time she got to the allotment, the rain was bucketing it down and she regretted her decision to leave the house. She was sure that Charles would just be brooding alone in his potting shed, sitting out the rain before returning home. It was only as she got closer that she could make out the faint glow of lamplight coming from one of the buildings at the allotment. She knew it must be Charles as nobody else would be stupid enough to be out here in the middle of the night and in the pouring rain.

She was closer now, and as she looked up she could see that there were two people in the potting shed. One was undoubtedly Charles but the other she couldn't quite make out. She felt the faint taste of bile rise into her mouth for a split second as she imagined Ptolemy confronting Charles and revealing their own affair that had carried on for years.

'Please, Ptolemy, please don't tell Charles anything,' she mouthed silently as she simultaneously crossed her fingers and attempted to get closer. If there was one thing that would be worse than having her husband of thirty years abandon her, it was the thought of not being able to claim the moral high ground as he did so.

She was only yards away from the side window now, the light from her phone facing down towards her feet. She just could make out the back of the person who was with Charles. By now, she could see it wasn't Ptolemy. It was very obviously a woman with dark hair wearing a mackintosh and gesticulating with her hands. The coat was flapping as she waved her arms about. What were they doing – arguing? Laughing? The rain was too loud to hear whether they were shouting or talking. Who was it? She peered closer. Did she recognise the coat? What was it – was it navy blue? Sou'wester style, with a flash of bright almost fluorescent yellow lining. She saw the dark hair again. Minerva? Minerva Leek – his bit on the side. The other woman.

Incandescent with rage and humiliation, Augusta turned on her heel, slipping as she did so, covering her hands with mud as she held them out to break her fall. It had come to *this*. Her husband had obviously been sneaking around, conducting an affair in his allotment and had probably been doing so for quite a while. How could she have been so stupid? So blind to what was going on? And there she was worried about herself and Ptolemy. She had a mind to start it all up again with him. He would look after her. He would never have treated her like this – abandoning her for a woman twenty years her junior.

She walked the rest of the way home, crying miserably to herself and shivering from the cold rain, her wellingtons covered in mud and feeling as though they were wet from the inside out. She never normally cried like this – even when she had finished half a bottle of vodka and her emotions tried to get the better of her. She had spent too many years being strong and pretending that she had a heart of stone to break down now, but this was too much. Even for her. She rarely admitted it to anyone, not least herself, but she did love him in her own way. The problem was that she'd never really had him. She'd always known that and so had spent their marriage toying with him, testing him and torturing him for not loving her back, when perhaps all she'd needed was to be honest with him and tell him what she felt. Perhaps she could try tomorrow? Perhaps she could convince him before he actually packed up and left. Yes, she would try that. What did she have to lose? After all, on the one hand she now finally realised how much she loved him and didn't want to lose him – on the other hand, she couldn't possibly lose out to that bitch Minerva.

10.58 p.m.
Charles was exhausted. Everything that could have gone wrong *had* gone wrong today. He was officially the most hated man in Pepperbridge if the onslaught of anger and accusations that had been directed to him today was anything to judge by. Here he was in what was supposed to be his oasis of calm, his potting-shed shelter, his retreat from the world, surrounded by his flowers and vegetables, his most treasured books and small mementos of the parts of his life that he was most proud of. Things that he didn't want to keep in the house that he shared with his wife for fear that she would ridicule or destroy them. Photos of the Three Musketeers in primary school, a book of love sonnets that Clover had given him over forty years ago, old maps with plotted-out routes of the places that he'd once wanted to visit and travel to. Then there were the more important things. The copy of his will which he had changed twelve months ago to include the family he hadn't been aware of. He had transferred everything over into Silvanus's name under the guardianship of Minerva. It was only right that the house that had belonged to his parents and grandparents before him should go to his own daughter and grandson. He knew that Augusta would feel hurt by this, but they had not had any children of their own, and Augusta was still in possession of a very healthy inheritance of her own that she had hardly used, having lived in the Papplewick family

home for her entire married life. It might even be the best thing for Augusta to go somewhere other than Pepperbridge in the long run – especially after they dealt with the issue of a divorce. She wouldn't want to stay here after that particular indignity, he imagined, and she had always complained that she despised having to remain in the village, after all.

He looked around again and made the sad decision to contact the council tomorrow and let them know that after thirty years he would be handing over the lease to his allotment plot. It was time to give someone else the escapism that it had brought him. For the first time in decades, it no longer brought him peace. It was time to leave behind this life. It was time to leave Pepperbridge.

He began to pack up a few things with the intention of returning to pack up properly when he knew where he was going to go. He would return to Augusta tonight, but he would go to one of the spare rooms, and hopefully he and Augusta cold talk more sensibly tomorrow. He wanted to put the record straight. She had jumped to conclusions about Minerva, and he had seen red when she had accused her of being a 'dirty trollop'. He regretted his actions but that wasn't good enough. He really wanted to apologise to Augusta. He knew that he had been a miserable husband. He knew that his heart had never been in their partnership and the truth was that he should never have married her. He knew it when Clover had returned to the area with a daughter he had devastatingly assumed had been from another relationship. He had been deeply hurt seeing her playing happy families with another man's child. A man whose child she had evidently wanted to keep so soon after she chose not to have his own.

Still, he'd continued to love her regardless, and had strained to catch rare glimpses of her over the years. Always keeping a watchful eye over her daughter, and then on Minerva's son when she eventually grew up to have a child of her own. When he had heard that Clover had died from cancer, he had been as devasted as though they were still in love and had seen each other every day from the beginning. He had turned up to the woodland funeral and stayed at the back, hoping that he wouldn't be seen, but he had noticed when Minerva had caught him watching silently with tears in his eyes.

The feeling he'd had on the day that Minerva approached him in this very potting shed to reveal to him that she was indeed his own daughter was immeasurable. Clover had disappeared but she had kept his baby safe and well after all. How he hadn't deduced that fact he didn't know, but having home-schooled Minerva until she was nine years old, Clover had chosen to register her daughter as a year below her real age, thus concealing the true year that she had been born. Possibly on purpose, or possibly as a genuine concern about the gaps in Minerva's formal education, but whatever the reason, it took a letter left for Minerva from her mother for both Charles and Minerva to realise the truth about her real parentage. It had given them both the missing link of happiness that they'd so needed throughout their lives.

Through Minerva, he'd found out that Clover had never had any intention of giving up their child. She had felt horrified and guilty that Charles had been considering giving up his place at Cambridge and his aims to further his education for her and the baby. Even Clover's mother had tried to reason with her to tell him the truth, telling her that she would regret not giving them a chance. Of course, in the end, he hadn't risen to great things anyway. He had needed Clover by his side to achieve that.

11.38 p.m.
The rain had stopped, leaving large and noisy occasional drips drumming down onto the roof, and he knew it was time to face the music and return home to Augusta – for a while at least.

The potting shed door began to open before he had reached it, startling him. He jumped. *Who now?* he thought with a resigned inward groan, steeling himself for another angry onslaught. Who could it be? Augusta come to find him? A drunken Marianne returning for another swing at him, or Nancy with her forty-year-old grudge?

It was none of them. His unexpected visitor was probably one of the few people that he was genuinely pleased to see after the events of earlier on that evening. Dear old Ptolemy Oates, his school friend, his best man and his long-time best friend, although he hardly saw him these days.

'Hello old friend.' Charles sat back into his chair with relief and smiled at the familiar face. 'Long time no see! How's the world of medical science treating you and what are you doing up and out at this time of the night, old boy? I thought that you were a "jammies on and in bed by ten with a mug of cocoa" type of man!' He chuckled amiably.

The drip, drip, dripping continued slowly on the roof, each drop echoing slightly quieter than the last as it eventually came to a stop, with just a faint low rumble of thunder still present in the distance.

'Oh, you know. I was passing on a late call out and I saw a light coming from over here. I realised it must be you. Thought I'd give you a bit of company before I head home.' Ptolemy's face remained impassive, the apparent jollity of his tone not quite reaching his face.

'Well, that's good of you! I'm afraid there's not much space in here, but if you're prepared to perch, I can knock up a quick pot of tea and we can catch up.'

The two men sat in comfortable silence for a while, listening patiently to the kettle ascend to its slow whistle.

'Charles?'

'Yes, Ptolemy?'

'Did you know that I was in love with Augusta when you slept with her?'

Charles hesitated. It had always been a topic of deep guilt and shame for him. One that they had never before brought up in conversation, and his face hung suddenly weary and filled with regret.

'Tolls ...' Charles began, reverting back to his friend's childhood nickname. 'I honestly didn't mean for any of it to happen. I was drunk that night, I wasn't thinking. I know that it's no excuse, but I can honestly say that it was never my intention to come between the two of you. I swear to God. It just, it just happened ...' Charles finished lamely.

He remembered the night horribly well. There had been a party at the social club. Charles had started drinking far too early and had excused himself to return home to sober up. Much to Ptolemy's surprise, Augusta had nominated herself to chaperone Charles while Ptolemy, who at the time was driving a little red two-seater MG, dropped off two of his female friends who lived in a village in the opposite direction. He would then drive back through Pepperbridge to collect Augusta and return to his family home in Pudding Corner.

By the time Ptolemy had returned, Charles had passed out in bed and a naked Augusta, wrapped in a sheet, had come to the door telling Ptolemy to pick her up the following morning. To this day Charles wasn't aware what, how or why it had happened. He had hardly any memory of the events that night at all.

'Honestly, Tolls, I know that we've never spoken about it, but I've always felt dreadful . . . I—'

'No hard feelings, Charles,' Ptolemy said quietly.

Charles sighed with relief. He hadn't realised how much the guilt of that night had troubled him for all these years.

'Let's put it behind us. I've just always wondered about it and wanted to ask. Let's shake on it and vow never to speak about it again.'

Charles smiled gratefully, eager to put it all behind him. He could see that Ptolemy's eyes were thick with emotion, almost tearful, and he genuinely felt awful that one moment of madness may have tarnished his relationship with his old friend.

The two men stood up to shake hands, but Ptolemy pulled Charles in for a proper hug, cupping the back of Charles head and resting his own head on Charles's left shoulder.

'I've missed you, Tolls,' Charles exclaimed, surprised but grateful for this unusual show of affection. He stiffened as he felt a sharp prick to the side of his neck within the lower part of his hairline – close to where Ptolemy's right arm had awkwardly remained resting on his shoulder. 'Ouch!'

He stepped back and looked down at his chest. Why was it thumping so visibly? He could feel that his heart rate was increasing, as he tried to raise his right hand to feel whatever it was that was on his neck. Had he been stung? He felt no raised area, no wetness of blood, and even if he had been able to look, there was hardly a mark to be seen by the naked eye under the short wisps of hair. His hands felt numb and floppy, as though he had been sitting on them, and he looked up to ask Ptolemy if he could see anything on his neck. Except Ptolemy was suddenly blurry, and when Charles tried to speak his tongue felt heavy and swollen. His heart was really racing now. 'Tlghh tlghhhhth!' was all that his mouth, with its swollen tongue taking up all of the space, could manage. Through the blurred shapes, he could just make out the outline of Ptolemy walking towards him. Thank goodness, his friend was coming to help him. Ptolemy raised his hand to Charles's neck and appeared to pull something out of it. Thank goodness for his dear old friend.

12.07 a.m.
The last thing Charles saw before he hit the ground, was the feet of Doctor Ptolemy Oates disappearing into the wet darkness of the Pepperbridge community allotment.

Chapter 20

Doctor Oates's story had come to an end. There was nothing left to say, and Daphne's time was limited. She now knew that Ptolemy Oates had murdered his old friend Charles Papplewick, and she also knew that murderers didn't tend to leave evidence of their crimes lying around. Least of all witnesses to either crime or confession.

Daphne looked over at the doctor's impassive face staring unmoved back at her. He didn't look upset or even slightly contrite. He showed no signs of inner angst or moral struggle. She even suspected that he somehow inwardly rejoiced at having a captive audience for one more dramatic monologue as he described the events leading up to Charles's death in his wonderfully melodic, deep tones. He had always enjoyed beguiling her with his wealth of historical facts and informative stories over the garden gate. Until now, she hadn't realised how much he enjoyed the sound of his own voice – almost as much as he had enjoyed the thought of 'educating' a woman twenty years his junior. It seemed so blatant now. She had been so eager to make friends with her new neighbour, to be accepted into this new and alien territory by everyone she met and particularly those that she saw on a daily basis. So eager to protect her children and for the family as a whole not to be judged or critiqued for their newness or differences, that she had allowed him to embrace the role of self-appointed educator bordering on the pedagogue. She had allowed him to patronise her in a way that she would never have allowed a neighbour to do back in London. Not knowing what to expect when they got to Norfolk, she had accepted his unexpected friendship with the gratefulness of a lost and relieved puppy. It was, after all, far preferable than to regress to her London ways and allow only the occasional wave and distracted nod of the head.

As abhorrent as the thought seemed now, with her eyes wide open to his true character, she realised that any connection they had made over the past few months could work in her favour now. Despite his recent admission, he liked her. He appreciated her company and her ever-willing and responsive ear. If she could play to his ego, boost his levels of conceit and lessen her viability as a threat, then she could buy more time before he decided what to do with her.

She knew that it would be several hours before James would question where she was. She had asked him to collect the children just in case she wasn't back from her little excursion with their friendly neighbourhood doctor in time. That would mean that he wouldn't feel the need to call her until around 4 p.m. And her handbag was still sitting on the hallway console table with her phone inside it . . .

'Ptolemy . . .'

'Yes, Daphne?' They had sat in silence for the past five minutes. Each lost in their own thoughts and contemplating separately what was going to happen next.

'Would you mind if I used your bathroom, please?'

The doctor hesitated and gave a slow sigh from deep within his chest. She could see him battling; he was reluctant, but he also considered himself to be a gentleman, and a gentleman could hardly refuse a lady that type of request – regardless of how questionable her timing might be. Daphne knew it; Ptolemy knew it. They both knew that he wouldn't say no.

'Yes, Daphne, you may use the bathroom, but let me direct you to the one upstairs.'

'Oh, that's fine – any loo will do,' Daphne replied with faux cheerfulness, trying to keep the atmosphere light. She imagined that he was thinking that she might have attempted to escape through the ground floor toilet window, which now she thought about it, would have been a good idea.

'If you don't mind, Daphne, I'd like you to go first.'

Doctor Oates was standing directly in front of Daphne, indicating towards the door with his arm. She took her cue and stood up smiling at him, leading the way into the entrance hall and towards the bottom of the staircase. The front door was mere feet in front of her and she contemplated making another mad dash for it, but hesitated when she realised that while one door may have been possible, she would still need to get through the porch door beyond it.

'May I have my bag please? It's my time of the month.' She looked at him innocently.

The doctor looked from Daphne to the bag and back to Daphne again, assessing the likelihood of this new piece of information.

'Of course.' He nodded towards the bag. 'But I'll have your phone first, please.'

Game over, Daphne groaned silently, while doing as she was asked. She handed over the mobile phone to the doctor as though it were an object of no consequence, taking the handbag upstairs with her to the bathroom that she had been directed to.

Sat safely on the toilet seat, she was engulfed by a wave of momentary calm. With a door in between them, she was safe. For the moment. She could hear him breathing on the other side of the door, and she wondered how long she could feasibly take pretending to use the loo, or perhaps she ought to simply barricade herself inside until help came?

'Daphne? Daphne? Aren't you finished yet? If you don't come out soon then I will have to come in to get you ...' he said determinedly and without a hint of jest or sarcasm. She realised that he wasn't bluffing, flushed the toilet, ran the tap quickly and exited the bathroom.

'Thank you for letting me go,' she said politely.

'Why on earth would I not let you go to the bathroom?' he asked incredulously.

'Well ... I, you know – I don't know?' she ended, confused. 'I mean ... will you let me go home now?' she asked hopefully.

'Of *course* not!'

'Well, *that's* exactly the reason why I questioned whether I'd be allowed to go to the loo. I want to leave and go to an appointment, but you won't let me, so why should I presume that you would let me use the toilet!' Her voice was getting higher and was now closer to whining than she intended, but she couldn't help it. Despite her outward attempts at remaining unflustered, inside she was feeling very frightened indeed – but there was also something else. She was feeling more than a little angry. Angry at being fooled by someone that she had thought was harmless. Angry at being held here against her will. Angry that they had moved all the way from south London to a tiny village only to move next door to a stalker and a killer. Angry that this man had just told her that he had committed murder and yet showed little to no remorse. Angry that she had found herself in this situation in the first place, when she had young children who depended on her. Why, oh why couldn't she leave things well alone? Why did she have to go snooping every time?

The doctor made her lead the way back downstairs again and back through to the kitchen where they resumed their places, although this time he remained standing and agitatedly started to pace the floor. She noticed that at some point during their excursion upstairs, probably while she was in the bathroom, he had collected a small bottle containing a colourless liquid that he now held in his hand along with a small piece of cloth. The hairs on the back of her neck stood up and a trickle of sweat had formed at the nape of her neck, sliding slowly down towards the dip between her shoulder blades. What was in the bottle? She tried to see if she could read the writing on the front, but his hand was masking most of it.

She wondered whether she should just keep her mouth closed and play the waiting game, or whether she ought to keep him talking. There was something in the way that the doctor had suddenly become so quiet and lost in his unsettling pacing that unnerved her. The bottle meant something; she was sure of it. What was it? Chloroform? She could sense that he was thinking hard about what to do with her, now that he had divulged his secret.

Searching for a distraction, she looked over to the kettle sitting on the hob – she couldn't bear the pretence of drinking more tea and so they sat in silence, lost in their own thoughts as the kitchen clock ticked loudly from above the range.

If only she could rewind the clock. To be stood at the garden gate with the friendly version of Doctor Oates before he revealed himself to be the heartbroken ex-lover of Augusta waiting pathetically in the shadows. Right now, she would gladly draw the scales back over her eyes, returning to a time when she believed the man standing opposite her was simply wanting to impart weird and wonderful titbits of historical information to his captivated audience. Toad of Toad Hall indeed! Although there was one similarity, she supposed. Both were as selfish as each other, with a tendency to exult in their own exploits. Vain and conceited with a love of the sound of their own voice . . . Daphne looked up at the doctor for a second. She had an idea.

'Doctor Oates?'

'Yes, Daphne?'

'The books in your study. The really old ones on local herbalism and botany. Did I see that some of them were first editions?'

The doctors face lit up. This was a welcome distraction.

'While we're – er, waiting here, would you mind if we had a look at some of them? They looked like the most beautiful books. Would you be able to tell me a little bit about them please? I think that I may have something similar in my shop. They're a series of leather-bound botanical books, I just wanted to check to see if the illustrations are similar. You know, while we . . . er, wait?'

The doctor didn't hesitate for a second and even appeared relieved by the diversion. He was always happy to have a ready and willing audience, even if she was here under duress. He put down the bottle and the cloth next to the kitchen sink, and Daphne felt a millisecond of relief.

'Ladies first,' he said with an unexpectedly gracious flourish as he motioned for Daphne to walk through to the back lobby where the pantry, the laundry room and his study resided. The study that had put her in this mess in the first place.

As she walked towards the door, she took note again of the large and antiquated key that remained in the lock. Did it work? Was it stiff? Would she even be able to turn it and lock him in if she got the chance? She walked into the room first and stood in the middle, closely followed by the doctor.

'Right, Daphne – which particular books were you interested in?'

'Those ones over there.' She pointed randomly at a potentially interesting seeming pile.

'Ahh – you have a good eye, Daphne! Now this one is entitled *Insectivorous Plants* and it's a Charles Darwin first edition, second thousand. It was published in 1875 by John Murray and is quite a rare find. Now the hardback is made from green cloth and gilt with ...' He continued sermonising about the book while Daphne listened with half an ear, her heart thudding almost visibly in her chest, her eyes scanning the room to see if there was any obvious means of escape, or failing that, a heavy object that she could use in defence. Behind her was the bureau with the photographs from Ptolemy and Augusta's university days ... and below them lay the three oversized Victorian syringes – one still with its needle attached.

'... while this lovely little one is *The Flowering Plants of Great Britain* by Anne Pratt – which comes in six volumes and may be similar to the ones ...' He was really hitting his stride now, lost in a world of original decorative cloth bindings and gilt lettering, intricately describing what to look out for when it came to searching out first editions. He was fully immersed, just as she had hoped, in describing the joys of his covetable book collection.

'What about those over there?' Daphne pointed at some red volumes in the corner of the room. It was the corner furthest away from the door. She continued to point and walk towards them, hoping to gain his trust as she purposefully strode further away from the door.

He relaxed visibly as he saw her walk away from her only exit route.

'Be careful, Daphne!' he said with an indulgent smile on his lips and a wagging of his finger as though speaking to a child. 'Those ones are truly special – you really do have a keen eye, don't you?'

'Oh gosh – do I need to wear white gloves to hold those ones? I'd love to see inside?' she recoiled as she spoke, as if nervous about spoiling the beautifully bound scholarly tomes, then looked over to him with what she hoped were eager eyes.

The doctor chuckled good-naturedly. 'Not at all Daphne, I trust you to be careful with them. Here, let me.' And with that, he lent down towards the shelf that held the pile, leaving Daphne just a little behind him for the first time since they had entered the room. The shelf was low and he had to stoop and bend one knee slightly to balance as he reached towards them.

Daphne's heart was thumping so hard in her chest she felt that it would come up through her mouth and fall onto floor in front of her. It was now or never. As he lent down, she leaned forward and used all of her force to shove him face downwards, pushing him as hard as she physically could towards the piles of books and medical magazines that were piled precariously all around the edges of the room. She then spun on her heel and fled towards the door, upturning the chair and toppling over another pile of magazines to land behind her as she went.

As she reached the doorway, she pulled desperately on the handle. The door was stiff and catching on the wrinkled rug, she remembered belatedly, but the key was still in the lock. She could hear the doctor clambering up from the floor as she tugged to get the door shut. She wasn't sure that her strength would be a match for his if he got to the door before she managed to close and lock it, so she turned and ran into the kitchen and across the room towards the hallway.

The hallway now felt narrow and dark and claustrophobic. All thoughts of its prior cosiness and period features diminished into a cramped and oppressive tunnel that seemed endless in her desperation to outrun the doctor. She slammed her way through the first door, reaching the locked porch door just as she could hear the doctor exiting the study and pounding his feet on the hard tiles in the back pantry hall.

'DAPHNE!' he called out in a deep and rage-filled voice, bellowing through the house like a large and wounded wart-hog. He caught up with her just as she had managed to turn the latch to the second door, grabbing onto her arm just as she desperately stretched and yanked it away from him, managing to get half of her body out through the front door and into the open air. The sky had remained blue, and the light was still bright. So terrifyingly normal, she thought momentarily, realising how dark the inside of Doctor Oates's house had felt by comparison.

'Heeeeelllp!' she screamed, praying that James would hear her – or if not, then at least Byron would alert her husband or one of the other neighbours might hear her anguished cries.

She screamed again as he wrenched at her arm, dragging her back towards the house as she yanked and pulled and kicked, hooking her foot around anything she could and continuing to scream. She kicked backwards, trying to catch his hand and release herself from his grip, writhing and twisting, but his grasp was firm, and however hard she contorted and bent her arm and body, his hand remained tightly gripping on as he gradually and, with great effort, dragged her back, slow step by slow step.

She could see that he was out of breath, but he was like a juggernaut, and she realised that she was no match for his strength.

'I really wish that you hadn't done that, Daphne.' He

puffed with laborious effort. 'Now I'm afraid I'm going to have to restrain you to keep you quiet. I was hoping that it wouldn't have to come to this. We were getting on so well. I thought that you were enjoying the books!'

His voice was a mixture of anger and disappointment, but mixed in there was a sense of wounded male pride. She had hurt his ego, his need to show off, mansplain and impress her with his endless knowledge. More than revealing to her that he had killed a man; more than the admission that he had stalked and watched a woman through her window for over twenty years; eclipsing the implications of any of these shameful revelations was the overwhelming anger that she was no longer entranced by his pseudo-intellectual swagger, his brandishing of facts and figures, his parading of enlightening hypothesis. Daphne saw him now for what he was: a sad and lonely old man who had delighted in the idea of flaunting and parading his 'wisdom' to a new and gullible audience. She saw clearly now how patronising and condescending he had felt towards her all along, and she was engulfed in a new rage of her own.

Her head was throbbing, but through her desperation not to be dragged back into the house, a myriad of thoughts began to grow in her mind, fuelling her determination and powering her not to give up. *I moved here for safety*, she thought furiously. *How dare this man destroy my rural calm, my rustic dream. I've coped with armed robbers and talked down angry youths. I'm from south London for goodness' sake! Dig deep, Daphne, dig deep. He may be strong, but I'm no simpering milk maid. You can only take the girl out of Streatham …*

She placed her hand on the antique syringe that she had

managed to slip into her jacket pocket while Ptolemy had been mansplaining the first selection of books.

She stopped screaming and allowed herself to go limp, for just long enough to watch him turn back towards her, surprised and then pleased by her sudden acquiescence.

'That's right Daphne – no one can hear you anyway, you may as well give u—'

She chose her moment, keeping still while leaning away from him and jamming her foot into the front doorstep to give herself leverage. Still holding on to her left arm, he was now close enough that she could almost smell his breath as they stared at each other in the eyes, both panting and both equally as exhausted.

She gasped for air, finally able to speak. 'I give up . . .' she said between breaths.

Hearing her words, the doctor relaxed his grip for a split second and smiled.

Daphne continued. 'I GIVE UP PRETENDING THAT I WAS INTERESTED IN ANYTHING YOU BLOODY WELL SAID, YOU ARROGANT TOAD – AND FOR THE RECORD, YOUR CHARLES DARWIN BOOK IS AN OBVIOUS FAKE, YOU PILLOCK!'

Shouting, she brought herself towards him, raised her knee into his groin and stabbed the glass syringe into his shoulder. As the doctor doubled over, not knowing whether to clutch his groin or shoulder, Daphne gave him a final kick just below his kneecap. Just as she had been taught in her Streatham Hill mothers' group's self-defence classes, what seemed like a lifetime ago. Who would have thought that her most dangerous would-be assailant would end up being a quaintly bespectacled elderly neighbour, rather than a hooded rogue on a dark south London street? His grip loosened and he fell to his knees, staring up at her with confused eyes. He looked down at the syringe sticking into his arm before falling onto his side on the gravel in front of his house.

Daphne used the moment to turn and run down past the five-bar gate where she had so recently enjoyed chatting to her neighbour, gravel spinning in all directions as she skidded along towards Cranberry Farmhouse, now just yards away.

Tears of relief began to roll as she registered James's car still in the drive. *He hasn't left yet – thank God!*

Aware that her door keys were still in her handbag back at the doctor's house, she ran without stopping straight to the back door of her house, knowing it would be open for the dog to come and go at leisure. She threw herself into the kitchen, where James was sat at the table, staring at his laptop with headphones over his ears, the dog snoring contentedly in a basket at his feet.

James looked up, surprised, and then concerned when he saw her face. 'Oh dear – did I miss pick up?'

'James, JAMES, call the police. CALL THE BLOODY POLICE!'

Epilogue

Daphne stood staring at the fields that lay opposite her gate, a mug of tea in hand and one foot propped up against the bottom rung of her five-bar 'Suffolk' gate. Not for the first time, she marvelled at how the scene in front of her resembled a Constable painting, with its freshness of light and endless romantic sky filled with the fluffiest of rolling clouds. Real enough to smell the ever-present scent of manure that lingered in the air, yet almost too perfect to the eye, to the point of feeling surreal – as though she had stepped into a painting herself. *Surely the real world shouldn't look this good?* she thought as she quietly sipped her tea and took it all in.

Beneath the sky, the landscape had taken on an almost golden sheen, with fields and distant woodland resplendent in their pre-autumnal beauty, hints of gold, red and brown just starting to appear in the trees and hedgerows that bordered the lanes as far as the eye could see. Beautiful, whimsical Norfolk with its big, open skies and endless horizon. She loved it here – despite everything that had happened. She'd been told on many an occasion that September was probably the most abundant month for the farmers' growing season, and it pleased her that she could not only identify but predict the seasonal changes occurring around her. Autumn was approaching swiftly, and with that the start of a new ploughing season was just beginning. Full circle, she thought.

To her left, an estate agent's van was about to pull off, having just completed the erection of a 'For Sale' sign on her neighbour's fence. Her absent neighbour, she corrected herself mentally. A neighbour who was now awaiting sentencing for one count of murder and one of false imprisonment. She shuddered momentarily at the thought of how close it may have come to two counts of murder as she waved the driver off, opening her gate a fraction to allow herself though and walking towards the old coach house to collect the mug that the estate agent had left on the low flint wall that curved up towards the drive.

She stood, staring up the drive and then at the sign for a few minutes, remembering the events of the previous year. The events that had led to the house being put on the market. In fact, the old Oates residence was for sale for the first time in over eighty years, the sales brochure had excitedly stated. 'Ripe for conversion, subject to planning approval' and ready for someone to 'put their own stamp on it', it gushed.

Daphne wasn't normally one for changing the integrity of a period property too much, but for once she was all behind someone sweeping in and 'putting their stamp' on the coach house – whatever that meant. It needed its old ghosts and bottled-up emotions to be swept away, in her opinion, and what better way than to be modernised in some shape or form? A fresher, newer and more positive energy was needed to flush out the spirits of regret that still lingered in the wallpaper that hadn't been changed for seven decades. The wallpaper that she once thought 'charming'.

She wondered who her new neighbours would be. A family, she imagined – hoped . . .

How wonderful it would have been to have Minerva and Silvanus move next door, but they were getting used to their new life as landlords of Wellingborough House, having declined to give up their cottage in the woods in favour of having tenants in Wellingborough until Silvanus was old enough to decide whether he wished to live there himself.

Augusta had given up the grand old residence to Charles's grandchild with surprising willingness, almost eager to be rid of her own past demons. She was now ensconced on a luxury cruise somewhere in the Mediterranean until further notice, and with no fixed abode. Something that she had long wanted to do, but for which Charles had never been ready or willing. It seemed that, despite the sadness of losing her husband still being fresh in her mind, the unfortunate circumstances had offered up at least one positive outcome: that of forcing her to take stock of her half-lived life and embarking on the adventurous pursuits that she had denied herself during her marriage. She may not quite have been a merry widow, but she was at least a widow of means, and that was surely the next best thing.

Marianne, on the other hand, was coming to terms with

being a woman without means – or at least without the means to send her son to the private school of her choice – much to the secret delight of said child. He had desperately wanted to attend the local high school with his friends anyway – so, as results went, at least he was happy, and in Daphne's opinion, the child's happiness was paramount. To the surprise of some, his mother had been reluctant to make any more waves in the community ever since it had been rumoured that someone had been seen driving a car erratically through Pepperbridge Village the night of Charles Papplewick's death, as well as stopping to hike up her skirt and urinate publicly in the middle of the street before being unceremoniously collected by her husband and cajoled home after an expletive-laden shouting match. This person was no longer wanted in connection with the murder inquiry, but the community had been placing bets as to who it might have been ever since the rumours had started, and with the still-circulating and anonymously written rogue issues of the *Village Pump* occasionally hinting at who it might have been . . . Marianne wasn't taking any chances of ruffling any feathers.

Anyway, as far Daphne was concerned, regardless of who her new neighbours might turn out to be, she was under a self-imposed strict embargo when it came to talking to strangers – and especially the seemingly innocent ones who might turn out to be wolves in sheep's clothing. She would stick to a London-style quick and non-committal wave to other villagers from now on . . .

She took one look back up the drive towards the doctor's house, before turning and walking quickly back towards her own gate.

Doctor Oates hadn't resisted arrest when a blustering and bewildered Inspector Hargreaves had eventually pulled up, sirens blaring, along with two other cars filled with two police officers, a community officer and a special constable for back-up.

Contrary to Daphne's fears, Ptolemy Oates had not managed to run off or escape during the time it had taken her to run and alert the police, but had remained in the same collapsed state that she had left him in. At first, standing at a safe distance after they had arrived to apprehend him, she had worried that perhaps she had poisoned him with his own syringe – oh, the irony of catching the murderer and then inadvertently killing him herself ... However, it was soon revealed that when the doctor had fallen onto his side, he had crushed the contents of his own pocket, a pocket where he had been concealing a glass bottle filled with chloroform, wrapped in a terry cloth. The same bottle that Daphne had seen him toying with agitatedly in the kitchen earlier. Thankfully for everyone concerned, the doctor's predilection for using chemicals and poisons rather than more basic tactics had been his downfall, and the subsequent crushing of his pocket had resulted in him unintentionally inhaling his own sinister method of restraint.

Daphne hadn't wanted to imagine what the doctor was planning to do had he succeeded in dragging her back into the house that day. She wondered if he had even known what he intended to do with her himself. He had seemed so undecided, standing in the kitchen before she had asked to see the books. At that point, the relief at having a purpose had been palpable; he had been so pleased to be given a short respite from plotting yet another murder. If that was indeed what he was contemplating. She would never know. How had she turned from history companion to potential second victim? It had all escalated so fast.

If there was one thing that she had learned, it was to never again 'assume' anything. Her mother had always warned her, 'Never assume, Daphne. To assume makes an ASS out of U and ME!', and she was right. Nancy Warburton had assumed that Patsy was in love with Charles; Charles had assumed that Clover had not continued with her pregnancy – which produced Minerva; Minerva had assumed that her father didn't love her, and the rest was history.

Daphne's mind lingered on Nancy and Patsy for a moment longer. Patsy had finally told an astounded Nancy that she had not only never been in love with Charles, but that she had known that she was a lesbian for as long as she could remember, and Nancy – filled with love for her sister – had cried at the thought that Patsy had thought it best not to tell her. Years of regret and unspoken truths. Again, a reminder to never assume, and yet they had all done it.

In fact, if there was one glaringly large mistake that Daphne herself had made, it was the soft bigotry of her own assumptions when it came to the people of the parish of Pepperbridge. She had assumed that life in the countryside would be passive and the people passive too. She had left the grit of south London assuming that an established country doctor would be as solid and trustworthy as they appeared to be in vintage novels. Weren't they always the reliable types who came along to save the day? How wrong she was – life in the country wasn't a James Herriot novel. People were rarely what they seemed, and the complexity of the darker side of human emotions and relationships was the same, whether one was in the city or the country.

She sighed thoughtfully as she closed the gate and walked slowly back towards her own house to be greeted by a perky-tailed Byron who had been waiting patiently for her. Her beautiful, welcoming Cranberry Farmhouse, which had been witness to the intricacies and madness of human behaviour for three hundred years or more. Tomorrow would mark the start of another new autumn term at Pepperbridge Primary School and the house was abuzz with the children's excitement. The past year or so's had not fazed them at all, and she was glad of it – she had no desire to return to the big city, even if there may be the occasional death among the dahlias.

Death, murder, secrets and betrayals were all wrapped up in the bucolic beauty of a village nestled within fields and country air – who would have thought it? They had managed to survive their big move to the country – *just*. And despite it sometimes feeling as though they had been living here for many years already, she sensed that the adventure was only just beginning ...

Acknowledgements

Acknowledgements

I'd like to say thank you to the following people who all played a part in helping the *Potting Shed* seed to grow!

Christina Demosthenous at Renegade Books – for your unquestioning faith and enthusiasm in the world of Pudding Corner.

Oscar Janson-Smith at Gleam Titles – for believing that I can do more than set a pretty table!

Robyn Tyrer at Gleam Futures – cheerleader and manager extraordinaire

Millie Seaward and Emily Moran at Dialogue – for seeing, understanding and bringing to life the world that exists in my imagination.

Bringing a book from manuscript to what you are reading is a team effort.

Renegade Books would like to thank everyone who helped to publish *The Potting Shed Murder* in the UK.

Editorial
Christina Demosthenous
Eleanor Gaffney

Contracts
Megan Phillips
Bryony Hall
Amy Patrick
Sasha Duszynska Lewis
Anne Goddard

Sales
Caitriona Row
Dominic Smith
Frances Doyle
Hannah Methuen
Lucy Hine
Toluwalope Ayo-Ajala

Design
Ellen Rockwell

Production
Narges Nojoumi

Publicity
Millie Seaward

Marketing
Emily Moran

Operations
Kellie Barnfield
Millie Gibson
Sameera Patel
Sanjeev Braich

Finance
Andrew Smith
Ellie Barry

Copy-Editor
David Bamford

Proofreader
Saxon Bullock